A WORLD OF DECEIT

ALSO BY KATE FLORA

The Thea Kozak Mystery Series

Chosen for Death

Death in a Funhouse Mirror

Death at the Wheel

An Educated Death

Death in Paradise

Liberty or Death

Stalking Death

Death Warmed Over

Schooled in Death

Death Comes Knocking

———

The Joe Burgess Mystery Series

Playing God

The Angel of Knowlton Park

Redemption

And Grant You Peace

Led Astray

A Child Shall Lead Them

A World of Deceit

Such a Good Man

A WORLD OF DECEIT

A JOE BURGESS MYSTERY, BOOK 7

KATE FLORA

Book and cover design by eBook Prep
www.ebookprep.com

May, 2021
ISBN: 978-1-64457-091-3

ePublishing Works!
644 Shrewsbury Commons Ave
Ste 249
Shrewsbury PA 17361
United States of America

www.epublishingworks.com
Phone: 866-846-5123

ONE

Burgess was in a hammock under the pines, in a tee shirt and shorts, barefoot, his eyes closed. The summer breeze, warm and gentle, slid over his skin like a caress. Nearby, lake water lapped against the shore. Farther out, there was the muted roar of boat motors. Cedar waxwings bustled busily through the tree overhead. The book he'd been reading lay on his chest, ignored. Chris, the fiancée who wouldn't marry him, had taken the kids to the other side of the lake to rent paddle boats so he could have a quiet morning. He was on vacation. Absolutely alone. His phone was inside and turned off. No matter what emergency the city of Portland might have, for these two weeks that would have to be someone else's problem.

His latest homicide put to bed, he was hoping this vacation might restore his energy. Lately, he'd been feeling too old and tired for the job—the word "dinosaur" was cropping up too often in his thoughts—and retirement had been on his mind. Then he'd gotten a call from his favorite ER doc, Sarita Cohen, who had patched up his crime victims, and himself, many times. Her soft voice was tentative as she said, "Joe, I've taken a liberty here. I hope you won't be angry with me. But I was concerned that you were feeling so tired…" She'd given one of her gentle laughs. "Though with your job, it's no surprise. Anyway. I checked your thyroid function and I think, with medication, you can be more yourself again."

There was another laugh when he said, "The meanest, grouchiest cop in Portland?"

"That's the one. Anyway, stop by when you get a chance and I'll give you your prescription." A hesitation, because people who knew him didn't generally tell Detective Sergeant Joe Burgess what to do. "Do this. Get the script. Take the medication. It's going to help."

So he'd swung by the ER, gotten the prescription, and filled it. Now, while he waited for the miraculous return of his energy, he was practicing the mysterious art of being on vacation. Two days in, he was beginning to like it. He felt like his life had slowed down. There was no urgency. None of the daily pressure to track someone down, ask the right questions, and get results. He could walk across the yard and feel the softness of grass under his feet. Go down to the water and feel sand between his toes. Slide his body into the lake and feel refreshed as he floated on his back and watched the clouds.

It wouldn't last. Soon peace and quiet and squabbling birds would be a thing of memory. Day after tomorrow his sisters and their kids would be here and family chaos would reign. Chris had insisted that he invite his team members, Stan Perry, with his partner Lily and baby Autumn, and Terry Kyle, with Michelle and Anna and Lexie, so they would be coming, too. But today he was going to lie here and vegetate and someone else could attend to the world of bad guys and the world of family and friends.

His only companion was a dog. An obedient, well-trained dog named Fideau. Part Lab, part who knew what? His crime scene dog. That was often how cops got pets. The bad guys got arrested and sent to jail and a sad cat or dog was left behind, destined for the shelter unless it was adopted. Fideau loved kids. Loved swimming in the lake. And for some inexplicable reason, the silly animal loved Joe Burgess. Today, while Burgess napped in the hammock, Fideau was curled up in a patch of sun a few feet away, on guard lest anyone approach his new master. The beast had already protected him from two squirrels and a curious chipmunk.

He was just drifting off to sleep when Fideau started barking and he felt a hand on his shoulder, gently shaking him. He said, "Fideau, quiet," and the dog obeyed. He opened his eyes and for a moment he thought he was seeing a ghost. A small apparition stood beside the hammock. A small, skinny apparition with white blonde braids, pale skin, white shirt, white shorts, and clean white sneakers. A small girl, one his mother would have called a "fairy child." He figured she was eight or nine.

"Excuse me, sir," she said in a small voice. "I didn't want to disturb you, but I can't find our phone and I need to call for help."

"My phone is inside," he said, tipping himself out of the hammock and standing. "What is your emergency?"

Damn. He sounded just like one of those operators in dispatch who sat in a darkened room and dealt with emergencies all day long, not like a father talking to a small, frightened child.

He tried again. "What do you need help with?"

"It's Papa," she said. "He won't wake up."

"What's your father's name, and where are you staying?" he asked, adding, "I'm Joe Burgess. I'm a policeman."

"We're over there." She pointed toward the next cottage. "I'm afraid I don't know our address. Papa's name is Theodore. Ted. Ted Gabbro."

"You don't have a phone?" he asked.

"Papa has a cell phone, but I can't find it." The girl was on the verge of tears.

"Wait here," he said, "I'll get my phone, and then I'll come back to the cottage with you."

So much for a quiet day. He hurried up the steps and crossed the deck to the cottage. Inside, he quickly put on shoes, grabbed his phone, and rejoined the girl. "Let's go," he said. "What's your name?"

"Arielle," she said. "Ari. I'm nine."

Accompanied by the ever vigilant Fideau, they covered the distance between the two cottages quickly and he followed her inside. Fideau slipped in before he could shut the door. She led him to a bedroom at the back where a man lay in bed. Probably in his fifties, Burgess thought, examining him quickly. Burgess established that the man was still breathing, though possibly in a coma, and made the call to summon

EMTs and an ambulance, giving them the number of the fire road and which turn to take when they got close to the lake.

Although this was probably only a medical emergency, he'd walked into too many crime scenes not to take note of the room. Perfectly neat. Nothing but a closed suitcase. There was nothing on the nightstand. Not a phone, pills, no watch or water. He wondered why the man's window was open, when it didn't have a screen. They were beside a lake, and in Maine, mosquitoes were often called the state bird. Things didn't feel right.

It was ten-thirty. Late in the morning for the father of a young child to still be sleeping, even on vacation. He led the girl back into the main room and settled her in a chair. "How long did you try to wake him before you came and found me?" he asked.

"Not long. Maybe ten or fifteen minutes," she said. "But he didn't look right and I got scared."

"Does he often sleep so late?"

"Not usually. Just when we're on vacation," she said. "He's tired. He works very hard, so when he didn't get up this morning, I thought I should let him sleep. But then I remembered that he's supposed to meet with Mr. Fenton at eleven, so I tried to wake him." She stared at Burgess with frightened eyes. "And then he wouldn't wake up. Is he okay? Will he be okay? Will the doctors be able to wake him up?"

"I hope so. You were very smart to come and find me."

Burgess hated to be asking her questions an adult should be answering. She was only a child. This should not have to be her problem. But he had no one else to ask.

"Does your father have any medical conditions the doctors should be aware of?"

She nodded. "He's diabetic. He takes shots. But he knows that and he is never careless about his medicine or what he eats." She shook her head solemnly. "Never. But I thought he might need a shot this morning and I couldn't find his medicine bag." She looked bewildered. "Not his medicine bag or his phone. I don't know where they could have gone."

Burgess looked around. The cottage was almost obsessively neat. There were some art materials on the coffee table and two pairs of shoes, one large, one small, by the door. Otherwise, there were no signs of human habitation. He couldn't remember seeing any medical paraphernalia in the bedroom. Maybe it was in the bathroom? Or still in that suitcase?

"What about your mother? Is she here with you?" In his brief walk through the cottage, he hadn't seen any signs of an adult female presence.

The girl shook her head. "They're separated. I mean divorced. This was my time to be with my papa."

"So it's just the two of you?"

She nodded.

They should call her mother, he thought. *Get her here to care for her daughter until her father was better. If* he got better. What he'd seen in the bedroom didn't look good.

————

The girl looked so small and fragile. Such a pale child shouldn't be dressed in white, but in bright colors. Pinks or orange or green. Or Fourth of July's red, white, and blue.

"Did you have your breakfast yet?" he asked.

She shook her head. "We don't have food yet. We only got here last night and we brought a pizza with us. We were going to go shopping this morning, when Papa went to meet Mr. Fenton. But it's okay. I'm not really hungry."

Burgess checked the refrigerator. The girl was right. Nothing there except a few slices of pizza. Not even milk or juice. So much for her papa being careful about what he ate, never mind taking care of a child. Once the ambulance had come and gotten her father, he would take her back to the cottage and give her breakfast, then drive her to the hospital.

"You said you couldn't find your father's phone. Is that unusual?"

She nodded. "Very. Every night, when he tucks me in—when I'm with him and not my mom, I mean—he reminds me that in case I ever need it, his phone will be right beside his bed." Tears welled up. "He's never careless about that. But when I couldn't wake him, I looked for it, and it wasn't there. It wasn't anywhere in the room. It's not anywhere in the house."

Burgess found it odd that a man with a potentially serious medical condition would isolate himself and a small child in a cottage on a Maine lake, and not even provide some basic food or a way to call for help if there was an emergency. Ari said there was a phone but if so, where was it that she couldn't find it? He needed more information, but he didn't want to frighten the child more than she already was.

Sirens signaled the arrival of the ambulance, and Burgess told Fideau to stay with Ari while he led the EMTs into the bedroom. He waited while they evaluated the man, told them their patient's name and that he was an insulin-dependent diabetic, and learned where they were taking him. When he followed the stretcher into the other room, Ari was cowering in a corner of the couch, stroking Fideau's head which was in her lap. The dog looked at him and lifted one ear in an inquisitive gesture Burgess read as, "Am I doing the right thing, Boss?"

Burgess said, "Good dog." Then, to Ari, he said, "We'll go over to my cottage, get you breakfast, and then I'll take you to the hospital to see your father."

She nodded. She didn't speak, but she took his hand when he offered it, and he started to lead her out of the cottage. Then he hesitated. Too many things here didn't seem quite right. "Is there a key to the cottage somewhere? I don't like to leave it wide open."

She pointed to a key hanging on a hook just inside the door, then watched him as he checked the windows, closed and locked the open ones, and locked the doors.

"You are very careful," she said. "Is that how policemen are?"

"Sometimes." Burgess wanted to search the cottage, inside and out. Look in the man's suitcase. Ask Ari a bunch of questions that an adult should answer. But all of that could wait. She was a small, frightened, hungry child. He held out his hand again. She took it and followed him through the woods to his cottage.

"What does your father do?" he asked.

"He's a scientist."

There were many types of scientists, of course. "What kind of a scientist?"

She grinned, like she was very proud of this answer. "He's a geologist, Mr. Burgess. He's been up here in Maine looking for gold. That's why he is supposed to meet Mr. Fenton. Because he's found something. He says Mr. Fenton will be very excited about it. Papa says people think there isn't any gold left in Maine and that boy are they going to be surprised."

TWO

Back at his camp, he parked Ari at the table, left her patting Fideau, and went to the kitchen to see what he could offer her. Even in the small camp kitchen, there was plenty of food. His partner Chris was far better at figuring out what kids on vacation needed than Burgess would ever be. There were Honey Nut Cheerios, a tooth-breaking granola blend, and the bran cereal she insisted was good for him. Also healthy bread and English muffins.

"You want cereal and toast?" he asked.

"Yes, please."

God. Her voice was so small and timid.

"Cheerios?" he offered. That would be Neddy's choice, for sure, and Neddy was nine.

"Yes, please."

"Wheat toast or cinnamon raisin?"

A little spark when she said, "You have cinnamon raisin? I love that and my mom never gets it for me."

"Coming right up," he said, putting some in the toaster. "You want butter on it?"

His one day of rest and instead he's a short order cook for a frightened child. Did life have it in for him or what? He gave himself a mental kick. Serve and protect was what he did. And how would he have had it play out? No one home and the child's father dies? Which started his speculations running: where was the father's phone and what really happened in that cottage last night? Speculations that would have to wait.

"Yes. Butter. Please. Do you have orange juice? We're supposed to have some in the refrigerator, we got it last night, but I didn't see any when I looked. I was going to bring some to my father."

Something was very wrong with this picture.

The toast popped. He buttered it, poured cereal in a bowl, and took it to the table. Then he poured orange juice and brought her the milk and a spoon. He thought nine-year-olds liked to pour their own milk.

Burgess wished Chris was here. Then he could leave Ari in her capable hands and go back and search the cottage properly. But she was off enjoying her vacation and trying to let him have some peace and quiet.

The girl carefully poured milk on her cereal and then said, "Mr. Burgess. I've been patting the dog. I should wash my hands before I eat," so he directed her to the bathroom. When she came back, she said, "It's a very nice dog. What's its name?"

"Fideau." He spelled out his poor dog's silly name for her.

She giggled. "I thought that was only in comic books."

He put a finger to his lips. "Shh. Don't tell him that. He likes his name and he's very sensitive."

She polished off her second piece of toast and gave her empty plate a disappointed look. "I like my name, too," she said. "It's not from the Disney movie. It's my grandmother's name. My father's mother. My mom's mother is called Joan. I'm glad I wasn't named Joan. It's boring."

His little waif was perking right up, wasn't she? He knew that about children. Food could make such a difference in their energy and attitude. "Would you like more toast?" he asked.

"Yes. Please." A decisive nod. "Mr. Burgess, do you have children?"

It felt funny to be called 'Mr. Burgess.' People rarely did that. "Three."

"Boys or girls?"

"Two boys. Neddy. He's nine, like you, and Dylan, who is sixteen. And a daughter, Nina, who is fifteen."

She sighed. "I wish I had a brother or a sister. But maybe it's better this way. My father is always so busy and my mother doesn't really like having a child. When she thinks I'm not listening, she refers to me as 'the big mistake.' Which is why I'd rather live with my father, who is kind of absent-minded but who loves me very much. She won't let me, though. She says he'd wander off and forget me."

Whew! And he'd thought she was a quiet child.

Big mistake or not, if Ted Gabbro had to stay in the hospital, the mom was going to have to come and pick up her daughter. "Do you know your mother's phone number, Ari? We probably should call and let her know what's happened."

He gave the child her toast.

"Thank you, Mr. Burgess. I guess we have to hope my father is okay, because there's no way my mother will come and get me." She hesitated while she devoured the toast. Tiny and ethereal as she appeared, the child ate like a wolf. She said, "My mom and the man she's going to marry are in Scotland. On some walking trip, I think. She can't be reached, or more exactly, she told my father that whatever came up, he was just going to have to cope, because she was turning her phone off and no one was going to be able to reach her."

She shook her head, the little blond braids flapping. "She gets annoyed with him because, with his job, he's often in a place where the phones don't work. I think she planned this trip so that this time she can't be reached."

She got up and carried her dishes to the sink. "Thank you for breakfast, Mr. Burgess. Can we go to the hospital now? I need to know if my father is all right."

The nearest hospital was in Bridgton, and that's where they'd taken Ari's father. Burgess put on long pants, got his keys, and left a note for Chris. Then he told Fideau, who loved to ride along, to stay in the house, and he and Ari got in the Explorer. He didn't have to tell her to sit in the back. She automatically buckled herself into Neddy's usual spot. He put the address in his phone, started directions, and they were off.

During the ride, she asked him a lot of questions about where they were, what they were passing, and even about why he'd decided to become a police officer. He recognized the precocity of an only child, particularly one who spent most of her time in an adult world. He answered them until she wore him out, then said, "Ari. Enough."

That brought an unexpected giggle. She said, "You sound just like my father. Sometimes he says he's going to set the timer on his watch, and when it beeps, I have to stop talking. My mother's solution is that she doesn't listen to me, no matter what I'm saying. Which makes me sad. If it's important, like for school or something, I write her a note. Once I had to write her a note that said I thought I was going to throw up. She didn't read that one in time."

It should make her sad. At least she was healthy and cared for. He'd seen plenty of mistreated kids. His line of work led to those situations far too often. Heck, he had two of them in his own house. Seeing your father kill your mother wasn't conducive to a happy childhood. Nina and Neddy seemed to be thriving, but things could still trigger them. He and Chris worked hard to keep things on an even keel for them.

After dropping this depressing story on him, Ari fell silent.

The summer landscape rolled by. The western lakes and mountains were a lesser-known part of the state, at least in the minds of those who had only a superficial knowledge of Maine, but the traffic suggested plenty of people had discovered it and were busily recreating.

He turned off 302 and followed signs to the hospital, parking in the lot of a busy, modern-looking complex. He waited for Ari to slide down from the high seat and they headed into the Emergency Room and up to the information desk.

A pleasant, if somewhat harried, middle-aged woman greeted them.

"Theodore Gabbro," Burgess said. "Brought in by ambulance a little while ago?"

She tapped some keys and squinted at her screen. "Admitted. He's in the ICU." She looked at Ari. "Children aren't allowed."

"Detective Sergeant Burgess, Portland police," he said. "I'm the one who called the ambulance. Would it be possible to speak with the doctor who treated him?"

"You're a long way from Portland, Detective," she said, "and Dr.

Phillips is busy as a one-armed juggler today." Another glance at Ari. "Is this his daughter?"

Burgess nodded.

"I'll see what I can do. Why don't you take a seat…" She studied the busy room, then pointed to a pair of chairs along the wall. "There. And I'll talk to the doctor."

After the runaround Burgess sometimes got from the medical establishment, her attitude was refreshing.

He and Ari sat. Despite her busy chatter in the car, she was silent now and looked so small and lost.

Burgess hated ERs. They were such anxiety-producing places. He'd spent far too much time in them over the years. Cops saw so much damage, so much ugly stuff already, cast in the role of inadequate human bandages for the world's wounds.

He didn't like to have to sit among other people's pain and distress. All around there were people clutching towels to wounds, holding wailing, coughing babies or consoling sick children. There were the stoic elderly, pale or gray, gripping the places that hurt and not making a sound. There was usually someone off their meds, pacing in agitation and muttering while a friend or family member tried to calm them.

Not a good place for a young child already anxious about her father. As Burgess kept a close eye on a young man whose pacing was growing increasingly manic, he tried to distract her. "Do you know this Mr. Fenton, the man your father was supposed to meet this morning?"

Ari shook her head. "I don't think my father knows him, either. I mean, I think all of their arrangements were made by phone and on the computer. Mr. Fenton owns a piece of land. Owns it or has an option to buy it. He thought there might be gold there and he hired my father to investigate."

Which reminded Burgess that he hadn't seen a computer in the house. "Does your father have a computer with him?" he asked.

"He does. And he has an iPad. We both do. Mine is in my room. I tucked it under the bed when I went to sleep last night."

"I didn't see a computer in his room," Burgess said. His search had been cursory but a computer was hard to miss.

"It's probably still in the car," she said. "He left his briefcase and some other work stuff in the trunk. It was late and we were tired so he said he didn't need it 'til this morning. I mean he wouldn't have needed it until his meeting with Mr. Fenton. He said it was our first night together and in the camp and he wanted all of his attention for me."

She stopped and looked up at Burgess. "See, he knows he's absent-minded and tends to get caught up in his work, so he tries not to do that during our time together. He was even sorry about having to meet with Mr. Fenton, only he said that Mr. Fenton was impatient."

She sighed and shrugged her small shoulders. "My mother says he doesn't need to do this field work. She says he's a goddamned tenured professor and he's already rich, so why doesn't he stop wandering around looking for minerals and gold. She says normal people don't get excited about rocks. But that's just the way he is. He says you can't be a geologist sitting in an office."

Normally, Burgess was a very patient man. He had to be. It was a big part of the job. But wasting a precious vacation day in a place he hated, while the urge to examine the Gabbro's cottage as a potential crime scene was on him like an unscratchable itch, was excruciating.

He was trying to think of another question that would keep Ari talking when a door opened and thin, stork-like doctor, too young to look so worn, came out. The receptionist must have briefed him, because he looked around and immediately headed their way. He offered a hand to Burgess, and then to Ari. "Dr. Phillips," he said. "I'm sorry to be meeting you under these circumstances."

He gestured toward the door he'd just come through. "If you'll come with me."

He rushed away and Burgess followed, taking Ari's hand in his. Dr. Phillips led them into a small office and closed the door. Then he hesitated, looking from Ari to Burgess as though he didn't know which of them he should address. Finally he said, "Detective. Miss Gabbro. I'm afraid that Dr. Gabbro is...his condition is serious." He slid behind a cluttered desk, grabbed a pen, and looked at Burgess. "Are you a friend of Dr. Gabbro's?"

Ari answered. "Mr. Burgess is our neighbor," she said.

With an absent-minded father and an indifferent mother, Burgess figured she'd become experienced at saying the right things to adults who needed to be handled or reassured.

Apparently it did reassure Dr. Phillips. "So, Miss Gabbro…"

"Ari, please," she said.

"Ari. Is your father conscientious about managing his condition?"

"Very. He's a geologist, often out in the field. He has to be careful because he's usually alone. He can't risk getting sick."

The doctor looked at Burgess, as though for confirmation. Burgess shrugged. "She's pretty well-informed."

"Right. Yet it appears that he hasn't…that uh…he's in a coma, is the thing. We wouldn't expect to see this in a compliant patient."

Ari looked at Burgess. "Is he saying he doesn't think my father was properly managing his diabetes?" Her voice was a little snippy. She didn't like to hear her father criticized. Her poise was making the doctor miss a critical factor here. She was a child of nine, alone in Maine without a parent, and scared to death.

"He's careful," Ari insisted, jumping out of her chair and glaring up at the tall doctor, her hands on her hips. "Maybe he got a bad batch of insulin. That happened to him once."

Then she deflated. "Was it the pizza? He wouldn't usually have pizza. It's not healthy. But it was the first night of our vacation together and he wanted me to be happy. What I don't know…" She turned her focus on Burgess. "…is what happened to the orange juice we bought. It was there last night and not there this morning."

Burgess and the doctor exchanged looks. A bad batch of insulin? It sounded suspicious, like someone was manipulating Dr. Gabbro's life. Could they be entirely certain that it wasn't his precocious daughter?

"You're sure that you got orange juice?" Burgess said.

She nodded. "And milk."

"And put it in the refrigerator? You didn't leave it out in the car because you were both tired?"

Her chin lifted. "I may be only nine but I'm not stupid, Mr. Burgess, and neither is my father."

Then, because her father was in intensive care, her mother in Scotland, and she was being questioned by two strange men, Ari began to cry.

Burgess pulled her back onto her chair, gave her a handkerchief, and said, "Excuse us a minute." He motioned the doctor out into the hall.

"I have no idea what's going on here," he said. "Is it possible somebody tampered with his insulin? Is that something someone could do?"

The doctor glanced toward the closed door. "Not a child like her," he said.

"I'm not thinking about Arielle. It's just a hypothetical. I'm just wondering if we should contact the sheriff and have him look into it. That's all."

"But you're a detective."

"In Portland. I have no jurisdiction here."

The doc looked skeptical. "Plenty of diabetics get careless with their medication. Noncompliant. How well do you know Mr. Gabbro? Is there any reason to suspect someone might have tampered with his medication?"

"I've never met Gabbro," Burgess said. "Conscious. Ari came over this morning and asked for my help. They're renting the cottage next door. I went back with her, found him unconscious, and called the ambulance."

The doctor didn't blink. Probably dealt with all sorts of odd family and friend situations in his line of work, just as Burgess did. "This is intriguing," he said. "Wish I could talk further, but you saw the waiting room. I'm not sure what to tell you, beyond 'trust your instincts.' I'll get someone to examine Mr. Gabbro, see if anything seems untoward."

Untoward was an interesting choice of words, but Burgess didn't expect many doctors would say 'hinky' and 'suspicious' was more in his own line of work.

"Can Ari see him? What should I tell her? For that matter, do you have any sort of prognosis? I need to figure out what to do with her. It's a divorce situation. She says her mother's in Scotland and can't be reached."

"You really only met her this morning? Because she seems pretty comfortable with you."

Burgess sighed. He knew where this was going. He'd probably known since Ari told him her mother was in Scotland. Maybe there was an aunt or grandparent, but that would take some time. For now, his happy family vacation was about to acquire a plus one.

"The prognosis?" Dr. Phillips looked regretful. "Not good. But that could change. And no, unfortunately, she can't see him. Not now. They're still trying to get him stable and assess treatment options." He plucked a card from his pocket. "Not my department, but call me later and maybe I'll know more. I'm divorced. And I've got a daughter. I know what this is like for her."

Burgess thanked him, retrieved Ari, and headed out to the parking lot. "We can call later and they'll have more news," he said. "In the meantime, we need to figure out what to do with you. I'll need the names of relatives you can stay with."

The little girl sighed. "Don't know what to tell you, Mr. Burgess. My father has no relatives that I'd want to stay with. Aunt Annabella doesn't understand kids and Uncle Daniel would lose me on a street corner. My mother doesn't have family, except her parents who agree that I am a big mistake. I guess for now, until we can figure something out, I'll have to stay with you."

THREE

Chris's car was there when he got back, and the small kitchen was a happy chaos of wet, sunburned people making lunch, asking for things to be passed, and getting in each other's way. Neddy, clutching his plate, escaped from the fray and pushed past Burgess and Ari, heading for the picnic table on the wide deck. He set down his plate and came back, studying Ari with a big grin. "Oh boy, My Joe," he said, "did you bring me another sister?"

That brought Chris's head from the refrigerator, where she was digging for something. She looked at Burgess, tilted her head, and said, "Joe? What's going on?"

"This is Ari," he said, as the girl strode up to Chris and held out her hand. "She and her father are renting the cottage next door."

"I thought we left you alone so you could have some peace and quiet."

Burgess shrugged. "I don't go looking for trouble, Chris."

"You're like a magnet," she said, taking Ari's hand. "I'm Chris," she said. "We're making lunch. Are you hungry?"

"Yes, please," Ari said. "Are you Mrs. Burgess?"

Chris looked over at him and winked. "Sort of," she said.

Evidently the girl was used to undefined relationships, because she said, "Pleased to meet you. Mr. Burgess has been helping me. And my father. He's a diabetic and he's in the hospital. I'm very worried about him."

Chris said, "Dylan. Nina. Can you help Ari get some lunch, please." Then she grabbed Burgess's arm and dragged him down toward the lake. Amidst the sounds of lapping water, happy shouts, and boat motors, her glare seemed out of place.

When they were away from the kids, she said, "Explain." Then, "This is my vacation, too, you know."

"I'm sorry," he said. "I didn't know what else to do."

She waited, her arms folded.

Chris was the nicest and most understanding woman he'd ever met. But as she said, this was her vacation, too. And the whole family badly needed some quiet time, and fun, away from the demands of his job and hers.

"I was in the hammock," he began. "Snoozing. Fideau was chasing squirrels and suddenly he started barking. I felt a hand on my shoulder and there was Ari. She said they were renting the cottage next door, she couldn't wake her father up, and she couldn't find his phone anywhere. She asked if she could use our phone to call an ambulance. I got my phone and went back with her, determined that her father did need an ambulance, and called one. Then I brought her back here, gave her breakfast, then drove her to the hospital."

Chris was still glaring. "Why couldn't her mother do all that? Why did it have to be you?"

This wasn't about what he'd done. This was about a disruption, any disruption, in their long-awaited vacation. She just wanted some time when they could be together as a family without a police emergency and a phone call summoning him back to work. And she wanted him to have some genuine down time to see if the new medicine would work to revive him.

"Divorce. Mother's in Scotland. With her phone off. She doesn't want to be disturbed."

Chris's posture softened. She was a nurse who loved kids, and vacation or not, she wouldn't have him ignore a small child with an emergency. "And how is her father?"

"In the ICU. Diabetic coma. Doctor says it doesn't look good."

She said, "Oh," and put her arms around him. "Damn," she whispered. "Even on vacation, in a hammock, the world won't leave you alone."

"I know," he said, nuzzling her head with his chin. She smelled of sunscreen and shampoo. Her hair was soft. "What would have happened if I hadn't been here?"

Sometimes she would remind him that he wasn't the only competent detective in Portland. But this wasn't Portland. There was no team to call on. And he was competent.

Burgess looked over at the small girl sitting beside Neddy at the picnic table, the two of them chattering away like old friends. Ari had been swept into the family like she'd always belonged. "We've got nice kids, Mrs. sort of Burgess," he said.

"Despite all that's happened, I feel lucky." She paused. "But I really don't need a fourth."

"Me, neither. I'll be lucky if I can get these three through their teens without disaster. Dylan behind the wheel still gives me heart failure."

"I always wanted this," she said. "Never thought I'd have it."

Their family had come in two surprise packages. First a pair of foster children Chris wanted to adopt, children who'd been exposed to two major traumas. Then a son he never knew he had. It had been a wild few years, taking Burgess from a monkish bachelor to an amazing relationship to the bemused father of three.

They stood in shade of a big oak, feeling the summer breeze. Burgess wanted to stay right where they were. Freeze this moment and never move on. Summer. This lovely woman. Three happy children. But out of the corner of his eye, he saw a car roll past and stop at the Gabbro's cottage.

Hell and damn.

"Someone's over at Ari's cottage," he said. "I'd better check it out."

Chris sighed. "I suppose you'd better. Maybe it's a friend or relative who could..." She stopped but her eyes slid to Ari. "Check it out. But don't be long. We arranged for a man over at the marina to take us all on a ride around the lake this afternoon. And all means all."

Burgess walked around the cottage, out to the road, and the short distance to the next cottage. There was a dusty white Lincoln SUV parked beside Gabbro's car, and a stout, overdressed man was knocking on the cottage door. When the man heard Burgess's feet crunching on the gravel he turned, came down the steps, and thrust out a plump, sweaty hand to Burgess. "Orville Fenton," he said. "Are you Dr. Gabbro?"

"Neighbor," Burgess said, nodding toward the next cottage. "We're renting here for two weeks."

"Oh," Fenton said. He looked at the cottage where he'd been knocking. "I was supposed to meet with Dr. Gabbro this morning and he didn't show. Thought I'd track him down, in case he forgot. People on vacation, you know. They can get pretty absent-minded."

He wiped his damp hands on a pair of crisply creased khaki pants. "I don't suppose you know where he is?"

Burgess knew exactly where Gabbro was, but sharing information wasn't his style. "Sorry," he said. "Just wondering what you're doing here when Gabbro isn't home."

"Well, this is disappointing. He was all excited when we spoke two days ago. Said he had some interesting news for me." Fenton fished in an inner jacket pocket of his navy sports coat and got out a business card. Then took out a fancy pen and wrote something on the back. "If you see him, please give him this."

"Just a neighbor," Burgess said. "I don't know the man."

"Well…" Fenton flapped the card practically in Burgess's face. "Just take it, okay. Maybe you'll see him before I do."

It was easier to take it than stay here and discuss it, so Burgess put the card in his pocket.

Fenton turned and looked at the car in the driveway. "Odd, you know. His car is here. And he came highly recommended as a man who could be relied upon."

He looked back at Burgess, his broad red face creased with worry. "You don't suppose something has happened to him, do you? There are certain people who would be very eager to get their hands on his findings. That's why meeting so soon was important. I can't believe he forgot."

Burgess shrugged.

"I mean," Fenton said, giving Burgess a suspicious look, "why are you checking up on me if you don't even know the man? And if you don't know him, how do you know he's not home when his car is here?"

"Sorry," Burgess said.

"What the hell?" Fenton said. "You're not working with…"

He abruptly broke off. "I don't think you're being straight with me." With a shake of his head, Fenton stepped around Burgess, got in the Lincoln, and rolled away.

FOUR

C hris wouldn't like it, but while he was here, Burgess decided to do a quick search of the cottage to confirm some of the things he'd observed—and not observed—earlier. As soon as the Lincoln was out of sight, he unlocked the door and went inside.

Using his handkerchief since he didn't have search gloves with him, he opened the refrigerator and checked. Milk but no orange juice. Otherwise just the one lonely pizza box. Nothing in the trash under the sink.

He checked Gabbro's room. Pants and shirt neatly folded on a chair. The man's wallet and car keys in a pants pocket. Shoes with socks tucked in under the chair. A suitcase, unzipped but closed, beside the chair. He opened the case and looked through the contents. No insulin or medical supplies of any sort inside.

No phone on the bedside table or in the drawer. No medical supplies. Nothing but a pair of glasses.

He checked the rest of the room. Nothing.

Then he checked Ari's room. She seemed poised and competent but she was only nine. He found the iPad under the bed, a book beside the bed, and an open suitcase with a nightgown, a pair of jeans and a sweatshirt tossed on top.

Nothing in the living room except a small stack of board games and some books in a brown paper grocery bag. Nothing in the bathroom but Gabbro's kit with shaving equipment, two toothbrushes and some toothpaste, and two hairbrushes. He figured the purple one with clinging blond hair was Ari's.

He took the keys from Gabbro's pocket and checked the car. A stuffed briefcase in the trunk with a laptop and an iPad inside. Nothing in the car except some napkins and the remnants of snacks Ari had eaten.

He returned the keys to the pants pocket. Tucked Ari's clothes in her suitcase and got her toothbrush and hairbrush from the bathroom and locked the cottage. One last thing to search—the outside trashcan. Inside the otherwise empty can was an empty orange juice box.

All the signs of a deliberate attempt to harm Ted Gabbro.

He needed to get the county sheriff involved in this. Probably sooner rather than later. Whoever orchestrated this might come back. Remove that orange juice box. Get Gabbro's keys and take his briefcase. He was torn. Getting local law enforcement involved would take time, and an explanation of his suspicions, and maybe a territorial pissing contest.

He needed to go back to his cottage. Eat some lunch. Go on that family boat ride.

Sighing, he unlocked the cottage again, got Gabbro's keys, and put them in his pocket. Then he relocked the cottage. He put a plastic trash bag over the top of the trash can, put on the lid, and used a bungee cord lying on the ground nearby to fasten the lid down. Not much of a strategy but it might deter someone from removing the juice container and at least provide some opportunities to collect fingerprints.

He headed back down the road with Ari's suitcase and her father's briefcase, feeling burdened and irritated. It was the best he could do for now. He wanted to do so much more but this was not his case. His jurisdiction. If the shoe were on the other foot, he'd take the head off anyone who did a half-assed job like this and possibly mucked up a crime scene. Too bad. The by-the-rules Burgess was on vacation and anyway, he'd always believed that in exigent circumstances, rules could be broken. The exigent circumstances right now being not further upsetting an angry sort of Mrs. Burgess and a small girl.

As he crunched down the road, feeling burdened as a camel, he was wondering what a geologist could possibly have done that made someone want to kill him. What Fenton's urgency was that made an immediate meeting so important. Whether it was still possible, these days, to have the likely discovery of gold be enough to inspire a killer.

Maybe what had happened to Ted Gabbro stemmed from some other part of his life. His ex-wife, for example. Safely away in Scotland where she couldn't be tied to the crime. Was there a way she would profit from Gabbro's death? What mother would do such a thing when her child was involved? When a child would be left to find the body and deal with the aftermath? Maybe a mother who regarded her only child as a big mistake?

He supposed it could also stem from some sort of academic rivalry. As someone had once said about that—the fights are so bitter because the stakes are so small. But bitter enough to try and kill someone? And how would someone pull it off? Who knew where Gabbro was heading and when he would be there? Who was cold-hearted enough to do this with a vulnerable child in the house, leaving her to find the body?

Still, there was no denying that Gabbro's phone and his essential medications were missing and someone had poured out that orange juice.

He took a moment to stick the briefcase in his car before going inside. The sight of it would trigger far too many questions from a girl who had already demonstrated a precocious curiosity.

If all went well, Dr. Theodore Gabbro would soon emerge from his coma and be able to answer the many questions posed by his mysterious situation and Burgess would never have to look inside that briefcase. Burgess sincerely hoped for all going well, but what Dr. Phillips had hinted at, though left unsaid, was that recovery was unlikely.

Dammit. He was on vacation. Rest. Recuperate. Revive. He was supposed to be doing these things while he waited for Dr. Cohen's magic pills to kick in. Burgess was a cynical detective with a head full of ugly. It was hard for him to believe in magic.

FIVE

The man who showed up to take them on their boat tour around the lake was a perfect blend of Maine and boat captain. In his sixties, Burgess thought, with wild, untamed white hair and beard. A faded blue chambray shirt. Baggy cargo shorts. And a neat navy blue captain's hat perched on his head. His boat was vintage, with lots of dark wood decking that was carefully tended, and some shiny brass fittings that were recently polished. A man who appreciated things and took care of them.

As they clambered aboard, he handed out life jackets, taking the time to be sure that Neddy and Ari knew how to put theirs on properly. Burgess liked the man's caution.

When they were settled, the man took a moment to describe the route they'd take, then slid the control forward and the boat roared out into the lake. It was exhilarating to speed through the sunny afternoon, cooled by wind and spray, and watch the succession of houses on the shore shoot past. Everything from traditional, rustic Maine cottages like the one they were renting to houses better described as mansions, complete with powerboats and sailboats and stacks of kayaks on their docks.

They slowed to pass kayakers paddling sedately along, and watched jet skiers buzzing about like angry bees. As one buzzed too close to a kayak, almost overturning it, and came back, the operator laughing as he did it again, Chris grabbed his arm and muttered, "I hate those things," in his ear. "What if it was one of our kids in that kayak?"

Given that they had a teenage son, Burgess thought it more likely it would be one of their kids on the jet ski. But Dylan wasn't mean. Like his father, he was a caretaker.

Their captain didn't mumble, he shouted and the kid on the jet ski gave him the finger.

The captain stopped the boat and called to the kayaker, "Betty, you okay?"

"Fine," she said. "But someone's got to stop him."

"I'll take care of it," the man said and turned to Burgess, "You want to steer for a minute. I've got to make a call."

Burgess steered while the man made a quick call to someone, said, "That prick kid is at it again. One of these days, he's going to kill someone." He gave a few particulars and hung up. Burgess relinquished the wheel and their pleasant tour went on. He wasn't surprised to see, a few minutes later, a warden service boat heading down the pond toward where they'd seen the rude kid on a jet ski. Maine lakes became a community to the people on their shores, and for the most part, that community was not very tolerant of bad actors who made the summer unpleasant for everyone.

They sailed on, Nina and Dylan in the back, heads together, laughing about something, while Neddy and Ari sat in the middle, holding hands. Another of his kids who was kind.

As long as they were on the lake, Burgess could push concern about Ari's father and the mysteries surrounding his condition out of his mind and enjoy the day. Eventually, he'd have to make a call and get the local sheriff involved. For now, imitating Neddy, he took Chris's hand.

"This was a great idea," he said.

"I'm glad you like it."

A few years ago, an angry bull chasing the solution to a nasty homicide, he'd pressed the deceased doctor's staff for answers, and one of those staffers was Chris. He still got angry. Still latched onto the search for truth and answers like a pit bull, but thanks to her, he was different. He could pick his head up from doggedly following a trail of clues or lies, and see good things as well. Back then, his transit through the world was determined and colder. She had put him back in touch with things his mother had taught him about seeing the beauty of the world. About slowing down. His mother had made him caring and observant. His father's legacy was anger and isolation. Fear of the damage he might do. Looking at his kids, he wondered what his legacy to them would be.

Chris squeezed his hand. "You're drifting," she said. "Stay with us."

Stay with us. That unfortunate choice of words brought back too many times when he'd held someone's hand and said that. Stay with me. Trying to hold people in this world when the next one was calling.

Another squeeze. "Joe. Stop it," she said. "It can wait until we're back."

He sometimes thought she knew him better than he knew himself.

The captain pulled into a small, quiet cove and idled the boat. No houses or docks, just green trees on the bank and reeds waving in the breeze. The lake's surface decked with round, green pond lily pads and scattered, lotus-like blossoms.

"I've got a treat for everyone," he said, opening a cooler.

Burgess wondered what was coming. What had the man chosen that might please a diverse audience?

"Hope you like whoopee pies," the man said.

Neddy let out a whoop of joy, but Burgess knew even the more restrained teens loved this particular treat. Sometimes, when his work took him along Maine's backroads, he'd stop at a farm stand and get these for everyone, including Chris. He didn't have a sweet tooth. He had a meat tooth. He was a growly old carnivore. Still, he enjoyed watching his family enjoy treats.

"Oops," the captain said. "I was expecting five of you." He looked into the empty cooler and shook his head.

"Not my thing," Burgess said. "I'd rather have steak."

The captain grinned. "Know what you mean. But look how happy they are."

Burgess looked at his family, and Ari, deep into chocolate cake and white filling. He used his handkerchief to wipe a bit of frosting from Chris's lip. Then got out his phone and snapped a picture. The phone said he'd missed two calls and had a voice message.

While the others enjoyed their treat in the peaceful cove, he pressed some buttons and listened to a dire message from Dr. Phillips.

SIX

W hen they were back at the cottage and the kids had gone to change into bathing suits, Burgess told Chris about the phone call, then stepped out onto the deck to make some calls of his own. First, to Dr. Phillips, who confirmed that Dr. Gabbro's condition was worsening and Burgess might consider whether his daughter should be given the opportunity to say goodbye. Second, to the county sheriff's department and a detective he knew, picking the person least likely to give him a ration of shit for sitting on the matter and walking through the crime scene.

He hadn't disturbed the scene, except for taking the keys from Gabbro's pocket and removing Ari's suitcase. But someone who was a tight-ass about procedure might disagree. Joe Burgess, a stickler for rules and the preservation of evidence, might disagree as well, if one of his people did what he'd done. He was giving himself a pass for Ari's sake. And his family's. Because—and perhaps this was hubris on his part—most people encountering the situation wouldn't have suspected a crime, even if Ari had reported the mystery of the missing phone and missing medicine.

He'd hoped Gabbro would rally and could become an essential witness to the facts. Without him, what was going on was a genuine mystery. Solving mysteries. That's what the cops were for. But not Joe Burgess. Not this time. In this case, he had no jurisdiction and no right to summon his team. He didn't even know whether the detective he was calling would let him into the investigation. She might not. Which meant sitting on his hands, something Burgess was going to be bad at. Patient and watchful? Sure. A passive observer? Not so much.

When Detective Nicole Ryder answered, she said, "What's up, Burgess? Calling to invite me to your retirement party?"

"Next year, Nikki. Got a few bad guys to catch first."

"Seriously? You're retiring?"

"Nope."

"Didn't think so. To what do I owe the pleasure?"

Burgess stepped aside as four kids in bathing suits went past, heading for the dock. Ari trailing behind like the last little duckling in the duck family. He had no idea whether she could swim. Fideau brought up the end of the parade, tail wagging.

He turned his back on the happy parade.

"We're renting a cottage for two weeks on Sowego Lake," he said. "And I think someone's tried to kill the man who is renting next door."

"You *think* there's been an attempted murder, Burgess?"

Burgess sighed. He needed to start from the beginning. Then she could ask her questions.

"Let me back up," he said. Then, "You got time for this?"

"Always have time for you," she said.

He'd helped her out a few times of the years. Stuff they all did for each other. He'd picked her because she was a good and careful detective who didn't cut corners. Because she could be trusted.

"So here's what happened." He described Ari coming to ask for help. What he'd found when he went with her to the cottage. And, just as important, what he hadn't found. No phone. No medical supplies. The empty orange juice container. He told her where Ted Gabbro was. What the doctor had to say about his condition. What Ari had said about finding gold. The missed appointment with Mr. Fenton followed by Fenton's appearance at the cottage. The fact that right now, Gabbro's daughter was with him.

"I closed and locked the windows, and I have the key to the

cottage." He debated telling her that he had Gabbro's briefcase, decided that he'd tell her that in person, when she was up to speed on the situation. And when she would have to yell at him personally and not over the phone. A strategic move.

"Really, Burgess," she said. "I'm surprised you haven't bagged and tagged everything and have a cuffed suspect waiting for me."

"I'm on vacation," he said.

Ryder laughed. No one who knew him would believe "Burgess" and "vacation" in the same sentence. "You around right now?" she said.

"I am. But here's the thing. I spoke Dr. Phillips maybe half an hour ago—he's the ER doc who admitted Gabbro and offered to be my contact person—and he says Gabbro isn't doing well. That maybe I should bring his daughter back there. Give her a chance to say goodbye."

"I don't get it. Why is the child with you? Why isn't she with her mother? Why isn't the mother handling this?"

"There's no mother in the picture. Parents are divorced. The child says her mother's on a hiking trip in Scotland with her soon-to-be next husband. Ari, the little girl, she's nine, says her mother has her phone turned off and doesn't want to hear about any problems. I've asked about other relatives. Nothing promising has come up yet. I'm hoping maybe, if we can find Dr. Gabbro's phone, we might locate someone."

"Yeah," she said, a sympathetic tone in her voice, "I hear you've become kind of a magnet for stray kids."

"Nikki. I do not need a fourth."

"So, you called social services yet?"

When he didn't answer, she said, "Thinking about the little girl, aren't you, Joe?" She sighed. "None of us have much faith in them, do we? Only when there's no alternative."

"Nikki, we're also social services," he said. Which was true. Cops spent their careers slapping bandages on society's wounds.

Burgess's primary reputation was as the meanest cop in Portland, earned from how hard he was on officers who failed to do the job well or carefully. He liked to think he'd mellowed over the years, but the label stuck.

He had another reputation he disliked just as much—as a cop with a soft spot for kids. If he believed in God, and goodness knows this job would test anyone's faith, he'd believe that God really wanted to test his limits. Why else did the universe keep sending him horrific cases involving children? This vacation was supposed to be a break from that, a chance to rest and recuperate after the most awful child abuse case he'd ever handled. A case that had left him flattened.

"You get a chance to speak with Mr. Gabbro?"

"Dr. Gabbro. He's a geology professor. I didn't. He was in a coma when I went back to the cottage with Ari. Arielle. And at the hospital, he was in the ICU and still unconscious."

"Hold on," she said. "I've got to put you on speaker so I can make some notes."

While she was getting set up, Burgess turned so he could watch the kids. Dylan and Nina, on paddle boards, were having a race out to the buoy that marked off the swimming area from boats, while Neddy was doing cannonballs off the float and Ari was paddling a few yards off the dock, watching him. She was smiling, and the two of them were calling back and forth, so he figured she wasn't just a passive observer. Chris was sitting at the end of the dock, her feet in the water, Fideau by her side, looking up at the creamy late afternoon clouds.

While his feelings about acquiring a ready-made family bounced around like crazy, she was genuinely happy.

"Okay," Ryder said, her voice sounding too loud and slightly off from the speaker's distortion. "Let's run through it again."

They ran through it again, and he could hear the faint sound of her pen as she took notes.

"So, here's what I'm going to do," she said. "First, I'll call the hospital and speak with Dr. Gabbro's doctors. If he's able, I'll head over there and interview him. Then I'll bring my team to the cottage, you can meet us there, and we'll do a proper search. Then I'm going to have to interview Arielle. Sound like a plan?"

She hesitated. "I sure hope we find that damned phone."

"It's a plan," he said. "Call me when you're heading to the cottage and I'll meet you there."

"Will do."

A silence. Then, "You know my boss may want to be there."

All she had to say. Ryder's boss was no one's favorite person. He was territorial, self-aggrandizing and far enough out of touch with on-the-ground details that whichever detective got the case had to ride herd on him to keep him from messing things up. Kind of like Burgess's captain back in Portland. What she was really saying was that she was happy to let Burgess in on the action but she couldn't say the same for Timothy O'Reilly. Or, as he was generally known in public safety world, Oh Really?, for the surprise he expressed whenever someone corrected him on a matter of crime scene procedure.

They took a moment to share mutual sighs.

"Let me know when you need me there," he said.

He watched the scene out in the lake thinking *Oh, crap! When was he going to take Ari to see her father? And go through that briefcase?*

The briefcase would have to be right now. He wanted to get it back into the trunk before Ryder and her team showed up, which made things far easier than trying to explain why he took it, and he wasn't putting it back until he'd vetted the contents. Hard to do in a small cottage with four kids around, including one who would recognize the briefcase and want to know what he was doing.

He walked out to the end of the dock and crouched down beside Chris. "I'm going to scoot down to the store and get some beer and pretzels and chips. Do you need anything?"

She smiled up at him. "I'm not going to ask what you're really doing. But in case you *are* going to the store, we could use more milk and maybe some lemonade? A loaf of cinnamon raisin bread, too. Someone seems to have eaten most of ours." She rested her head against his knee for a moment, then lifted it and made shooing motions. "Go on, then. It's going to be dinnertime soon and someone has to be here to man the grill."

Not the time to tell her he was likely to be next door, searching the cottage. There were limits to her tolerance. If Ryder came while he was cooking, he'd be staying at the grill.

Something of a sheepdog by nature, and still uneasily new to this parenting thing, he took one last look around. Neddy still jumping off the dock. Dylan and Nina on paddle boards. But where was Ari?

He looked around, increasingly frantic. He didn't want to be the guy who benevolently takes the child in only to carelessly let her drown. Finally, he saw her small head almost out to the buoy. Beyond that, she could find herself in the path of a motorboat and there were several of them on the lake. Despite Dylan's presence, a boatload of teenage boys had been by a few times to check Nina out.

He yelled, "Ari! Stop! Come back."

She didn't hear or didn't care and swam on.

Good old Joe Burgess. Got a soft spot for kids. Tries to help one and ends up letting her get mowed down by a boat? Burgess could swim, but he'd never reach her before she passed that marker.

"Dylan!" he roared.

When his son turned, he gestured toward the small swimmer. "Go get her."

Chris said, "What?" and jumped up.

He pointed to the small head close to the buoy. "Ari. There."

"Oh no." She grabbed his arm, clinging to him as they watched Dylan paddling his board toward the girl.

Dylan had spent the summer as a lifeguard at a Portland pool and Burgess had enjoyed watching his son grow into the role. He'd also watched, with a mixture of envy and nostalgia, as his handsome son— the boy who reminded him so much of his younger self—became a magnet both for teenage girls and the moms who lounged around the pool. Dylan had expressed confusion about the moms strutting their stuff. Now he watched his son in action as he paddled alongside Ari and cajoled her onto the board.

Burgess and Chris clung together as Dylan, strong and brown, wearing a smile of pleasure and triumph, brought the little girl back to the dock and helped her up the ladder.

"Here you go, Dad," he said. "Safe and sound." In his best authoritative lifeguard's voice, he said, "Ari, don't do that again, okay? You want to swim, you stay near the dock." He got a small, embarrassed nod.

By the time they had Ari wrapped in a towel, Dylan was paddling calmly away, back to racing with Nina.

Chris held Ari tight, saying, "Oh, Ari. You gave us such a fright. You can't swim out that far. You might get hit by a boat."

The girl, flustered by all the attention, started crying. Neddy, who hated to see anyone cry, wormed his way into Chris's arms and put his own arms around Ari. "It's okay," he said. "It's okay, Ari. They're not mad at you. They just want you to be safe."

We just want you to be safe. Burgess could have put that on a tee shirt and given one to every cop he knew.

SEVEN

When Neddy had cajoled Ari to join him in doing cannonballs, and Burgess and Chris's breathing had returned to normal, he said, "Got to run that errand."

"Right," she said. "And leave me behind to have heart failure."

"I'm leaving you reluctantly," he said. "And with an extremely competent lifeguard."

"Thank goodness for that." She kissed him. "You'd better bring me some chocolate. I need some propping up after this."

He snagged his keys, drove the Explorer down the road to a turnout, and parked. Fideau, unwilling to be left behind, had jumped in the truck with him. From the passenger seat, he nudged Burgess with his nose, those devoted doggy eyes fixed on him. "Yes, Fideau," Burgess said. "You're a good boy." Satisfied, the dog curled up and went to sleep.

Three kids and a dog? How on earth had this happened to him? All he needed now was a minivan.

He pulled on gloves, grabbed Gabbro's briefcase from the back, and went to work. Without passwords, whatever information was on the laptop and iPad was inaccessible, so he concentrated on the papers. There were maps and charts and handwritten notes, but nothing that Burgess could understand without a geologist in his pocket. There was some correspondence with Fenton that was bit more helpful, with references to geological survey maps and available pieces of land for sale, and some historical information about old mines in the area and where hobbyists had successfully searched for gold.

It appeared that Fenton had options to purchase several parcels of land, including at least one with an abandoned mine. He was waiting for Dr. Gabbro's findings before deciding whether to go ahead. There was an article from a 2003 Prospecting and Mining Journal and some articles by various Maine geologists. Burgess snapped photos of Fenton's letters. For the rest, and an understanding of Ammonoosuc volcanics, he would need an expert.

Nothing in the worn leather briefcase suggested a reason why someone would want to kill Dr. Gabbro. Nor did it illuminate any issues in Gabbros's personal or professional life that might have incited someone to crime. If this were Burgess's case, he or his team would be talking to people in Gabbro's department, as well as immediately on the phone to the state geologist—he was sure Maine had one—as well as some experts at the state's universities. They'd have asked people who knew Gabbro about relatives, close friends, possible romantic relationships, and about anyone with a grudge. They'd have scheduled a sit down with the imperious Mr. Fenton.

He had to keep reminding himself that this was *not* his case, and that any involvement he might have was a courtesy.

He finished with the briefcase and drove to a nearby convenience store, getting the things Chris wanted along with some beer and a lot of the kinds of junk food his kids loved. He also got another box of cereal along with the loaf of cinnamon raisin bread. If Ari kept eating the way she had at breakfast and lunch, they'd need it. He was almost at the register when he remember the chocolate. He snagged a couple bags of Dove milk chocolate and dark chocolate, and checked out, grabbing a bone for Fideau from the jar they kept on the counter.

He made a quick stop at Gabbro's cottage. Nothing seemed to have been disturbed. The cottage was secure and quiet. He returned the briefcase, put the car keys back in Gabbro's pants, locked the cottage, and headed home.

As he parked, his phone rang. Dr. Phillips again. Ari's visit could wait for the morning. Gabbro had stabilized. Relieved, Burgess got out of the truck, gave the treat to Fideau, and snagged his grocery bags. His phone rang again. Nikki Ryder. A delay in assembling her team. They'd be out in a few hours.

He was grateful for the reprieve. The grill was calling, along with four hungry kids and a woman who'd put up with far too much from him already.

He carried the groceries inside, tossing a bag of root vegetable chips to Nina, who was on her way to becoming a vegetarian food Nazi. He tossed the salt and vinegar chips to Dylan, and the bag of what he and his sister used to call "cheese worms" to Neddy and Ari, who were curled up like puppies on the couch looking at a book about unusual animals.

Burgess put away the milk, the lemonade, the bread and cereal, and turned to find Chris watching him. Her expression was part expectation and part someone expecting to be disappointed. When he held out the two bags of chocolates, she started to giggle.

"I really didn't think…" she began.

"That I'd remember?"

"Uh. Yes?"

"I try, Chris. I really do."

From the couch, Ari said, "Mr. Burgess? Do you know how my father is doing? Is there any news?"

Burgess studied the child, wishing he knew more about her. She was poised and curious. Quiet and a chatterbox. Tiny as a fairy child and ate like a horse. She was open about her mother's disinterest—if that was true and not just a lonely child's interpretation. Apparently frank about having no other interested relatives. But he was sure there was more to be learned. Much more. Things that might get uncovered when he gave her over to the tender questioning of Detective Nikki Ryder. He could ask questions himself but for now he wanted to preserve the temporary peace of this day, these hours.

He was a professional deliverer of bad news. A professional liar when necessary. He wasn't sure what he was being when he said, "Dr. Phillips called. He said your father is stable and that you should go and see him in the morning."

She sighed. "Will you be driving me again, Mr. Burgess?"

Neddy giggled. "It's not Mr. Burgess. It's Detective Burgess. Or Sergeant Burgess. But I call him 'my Joe.' I'll bet you can call him that, too. My Joe, is it okay if Ari calls you My Joe, too?"

Chris gave Burgess a light punch in the arm. "Soon everyone in Portland will be doing it. I can just imagine the chief calling down and asking if 'My Joe' has a moment to spare to update him."

"Don't start," he said.

"Can't help myself," she said. "My Joe brought me chocolate. Now, if he'll go and start the grill, we can feed this hungry lot. If you haven't ruined their appetites with all this junk food."

Her Joe went and started the grill, then stood on the deck, listening to the sounds around him. Birds doing their late afternoon thing. The busy hum of boats replaced by the splash of kayak paddles and quiet voices. He and his late mother used to be night owls together, quietly observing the world while everyone else slept. He'd brought those patient observation skills to his police work. Now he was getting reacquainted with them in the rest of his life.

He felt a twinge of sadness that she hadn't had a chance to know his children. She would have loved them so. That chance had been stolen from her by a careless doctor.

He shook off the memories and scraped down the grill, getting it ready for a new onslaught of burgers and dogs. Unless it was chicken. When it came to grilling, he just did what he was told.

The wind carrying the smells of grilling food from other cottages around the lake made him realize he was hungry.

Overhead, a plane climbed into the sky, a bright bit of silver with a long white trail behind it. Somewhere a woodpecker hammered away at a tree.

A car's tires crunched on the road.

This cottage and the one the Gabbros were renting were the last two places on this fire road. It was too early for Ryder and her crew. He stepped around the cottage to see who it was. A dusty red Jeep wrangler, traveling fast for the road, jerked to a stop at the next cottage. A man got out—strong, athletic, shaggy haired, in shorts and a tee shirt—and hurried to the cottage door. He banged on it, calling loudly enough for

Burgess to hear, "Gabbro? Gabbro? Dammit, Gabbro, answer the fucking door!"

EIGHT

Someone who knew Gabbro? Clearly someone who knew where Gabbro was staying. He had to check it out. Burgess untied his apron and draped it over the porch railing, then headed out to the road. Fideau, not wanting to be left out, came with him.

Burgess met the man back at the door as the newcomer completed his uninformative circuit of the cottage. He was maybe in his early thirties, strong-looking, with the beginning of a beer gut. Unshaven. Rusty-haired. Maybe six one? Scuffed work boots. Sunburned hands. A strip of white at his hairline like he'd been out in the sun a lot wearing a hat. And evidently a pleasant individual with finely honed social skills, as his first words to Burgess were, "Who the hell are you? Where the fuck's Gabbro?"

"You first," Burgess said. "Who are you and why are you looking for Dr. Gabbro?"

He watched the man consider. Assess. The assessment of someone used to be the Alpha dog, or at least a strong beta. Maybe someone whose work involved a lot of conflict or suspicion and didn't demand social graces.

As if to help with the assessment, Burgess's sidekick, Fideau, gave a low growl. Okay with Burgess if the man didn't know Fideau was just a big marshmallow.

Burgess was bigger. Hard-faced and scarred. And used to winning these contests. His work involved a lot of that. He waited and the other man folded. Stuck out a hand. "Sorry about that. Pete Sherman. I'm Dr. Gabbro's colleague. I've been consulting with him on his…uh…on a project. We were supposed to . . uh…meet today and he didn't call. Didn't show. That's not like Ted. He's a super orderly guy."

"Detective Sergeant Joe Burgess," Burgess said, taking the man's hand. "What's the project?"

"Uh…I'm not at liberty…" Sherman began. Stopped, his body going rigid. "Detective? Is something wrong? Has something happened to Ted?"

Burgess considered. He knew nothing about this man beyond outdoorsy, brash, and seemingly lacking social skills. He needed more before he revealed anything about Gabbro's situation.

"When were the two of you supposed to meet?"

"This afternoon. Around three. After he'd met with Fenton. That was supposed to determine whether we'd have future work…assignments." Sherman shifted nervously, as though even that had given too much away.

"About finding the gold, you mean? And whether Fenton should exercise his options?"

Sherman rocked back on his heels, shaking his head. "He told you about the…" Another shake, physical, like a dog shaking off water. "No. Ted would never. He's the most secretive damned man I've ever met. Barely even gives up his name, never mind a good morning." He kept shaking his head like a bobble-head doll, clearly upset by what he was hearing. "No. He wouldn't. Something's going on here. Something's wrong."

He patted his pocket, making sure he had his keys, then turned and started for the Jeep.

"Hold on," Burgess said. "You know Gabbro well?"

Sherman stopped, his "Why?" suspicious.

"He's in the hospital. Complications of his diabetes. We are renting the cottage next door." He pointed. "This morning his daughter came over, concerned because she couldn't wake Dr. Gabbro up. She's with us right now. The daughter. We're looking for someone who can take care of her. You know anything about his domestic situation? Family connections?"

"Ted's in the hospital?"

"Yes."

"From complications of his diabetes? That doesn't sound right. Ted takes care of himself. He knows the risks."

Burgess shrugged.

"Ari's with you?" Sherman said, switching from obstinate denial to concern. "Is she okay?"

So he knew her well enough to call her by her nickname? And care about her?

"Family connections?" Burgess repeated.

"Well, there's the bitch ex-wife. But she's away on some trip, Ted said. Ted's got a girlfriend. Well, lady friend down in Massachusetts. But I can't see her stepping in. She doesn't like Ari very much. Says the kid is spooky."

Burgess waited for more.

"Ted's got a sister. Annabella. Bella. She'd probably take Ari." Sherman scratched his head. "But I think she's off on some Outward Bound thing this week. I don't remember. Ted's not a great one for confiding. He's just kind of in love with rocks, you know?"

Burgess didn't know.

He did know he needed to get back and cook dinner for some hungry people.

"I've got to go," he said. "Family's waiting for dinner and I'm the cook. Feel free to come along. We've got beer."

No idea why he was saying this, except he needed both of them to relax and then maybe the guy would answer more questions. He didn't want to let the guy get away before Ryder came.

Sherman said, "Sure."

Then, "This isn't a trick, right?"

"I save my tricks for the bad guys."

Sherman's reactions told him this man wasn't a threat to Gabbro or his daughter, and might prove to be useful. The reaction Burgess was concerned about was Chris's. She wanted a family vacation, and now he was adding another stranger to the mix. He hoped there was enough food. Enough patience in this kind woman to allow another stray.

He led Sherman back to the cottage, said, "Give me a minute," tied on his apron, and checked the grill. It was definitely hot. He said, "Wait here," to Sherman and went inside, where Chris handed him a huge platter of chicken slathered with barbeque sauce, and a beer.

He carried them outside, where he found Fideau planted between Sherman and the cottage, guarding the family.

"It's okay, Fideau," Burgess said. He gave the beer to Sherman and put the chicken on the grill.

Sherman thanked him and said, "Where's Ari? Is she here with you? Is she okay? She and Ted are tight. Really tight. This must …she must be awfully upset. She finally gets her special time with her father and now this?"

"Ari's inside. I'll get her," Burgess said. He eyed the empty bottle in Sherman's hand. "You want another?"

"Yeah. I mean, please. This is…uh…a shock, you know. Ted's kind of like my mentor."

Burgess knew about all kinds of shocks. Sherman would have to tell him more about this one. He wasn't sure whether to ask for information now, or wait until Nikki Ryder could be there, too, so Sherman could tell the story to both of them instead of telling it twice. If Burgess let Ryder ask the questions, he could observe Sherman's demeanor. Observe or ask? The control freak in him wanted to ask. He said a mental "down, boy" to his control freak.

He went inside, got two more beers from the fridge, and said to Chris. "We've got another guest for dinner. I hope that's okay."

"It's not."

It looked like whatever points he'd scored with chocolate had expired.

He knew "All I was doing was sleeping in the hammock," wouldn't cut it. One reason they were perpetually engaged but not married was because of the hold the job had on him. The demands it made even when he wasn't on duty, and the risks involved.

"A friend of Gabbro's. And Ari's. I found him pounding on the door of their cottage."

Ari, like the children in this household, had the ears of a watchdog. She bounced off the couch saying, "Who is it, Mr…. uh…My Joe? Is it Uncle Pete?"

Burgess nodded and Ari flew out the door. Some comfort, Burgess supposed, to have found an adult who knew the child and could potentially supply some information about family and friends as well as about Gabbro and his work situation. This whole business sounded like a cop's version of a shaggy dog story, the kind that begins, "A worn-out cop goes on a family vacation…"

Burgess went back to tending his chicken. He slapped more barbeque sauce on and flipped the pieces. Turned down the heat a little so he wouldn't end up with food that was charred outside and raw inside. Somewhere there must be a book that declared outdoor grilling was the province of the American male. He didn't know why. Maybe because women wanted to get the guys out of their kitchens? Or because since guys at gatherings would grab beer and circle up to talk about sports—or in his case, the job—the women in their lives figured they might as well work while they talked.

Beside him, Ari had unwrapped from her propulsive hug around Pete Sherman's waist and the two of them had seated themselves on the edge of the deck, her short legs swinging, Sherman's big arm around her shoulders. In what Burgess was learning was her habit, she was filling him in at top speed about what had happened that morning in their cottage. Her version pretty much comported with the facts, right down to the mystery of the missing items.

Burgess watched Sherman take it in, observing the man's growing uneasiness as he tried not to let the child see how concerning her story was. Bad social manners but good with children. Or at least this child. Burgess's opinion of him rose.

Just as Ari was segueing directly into questions, Chris appeared to see how the chicken was doing. Burgess introduced them, and Sherman stood and almost shyly took her hand.

"Sorry to intrude on your dinner, ma'am," he said. "Your husband invited me along because I was concerned about Arielle here. She's a pretty good friend of mine."

Far better manners than he'd showed with Burgess, which was a good thing, since Chris had a soft spot for men who liked kids.

"It's fine, Mr. Sherman," she said. "We've got plenty and we're glad Ari has a friend."

She looked down at the girl. "Ari, could you pop inside and ask Nina to set another place at the table, please."

Ari scrambled up and went inside and Chris came over to check on Burgess's project. "Wow," she said. "It's not burned."

"Yet," Burgess said. "There's still time."

She cocked her head. "How long?"

"Ten minutes." He said it with certainty though in truth, he didn't know. But he had a secret weapon: an instant thermometer. A good cop always had some tricks up his sleeve. This was his grilling trick. Unfold the little thing, plunge that sharp prong into the chicken, and get an instant readout telling him whether the chicken was done.

He couldn't claim credit for the discovery. It had been a gift from one of his team members, and his best friend, Terry Kyle, after a conversation about men and grilling. Burgess confessed his general incompetence at the process and a few days later, a small, wrapped present had appeared on his desk. The card had read: Your Secret Weapon. So far, it had served him well.

Cops needed lots of secret weapons.

"You don't have to invite me to dinner," Sherman said.

"I think Ari would like it. So, tell me more about your relationship with Gabbro. Are you partners in some venture?"

Sherman looked uncomfortable. "I'm really not supposed to talk about it."

"Well, it's early days now. We don't have a good read on Gabbro or his life. But it's possible that his condition was deliberately induced, in which case, it is critical that you talk about what you and he were working on, and why it needs to be kept secret. If it turns out that someone wanted him disabled or dead, we...the investigators...will need to understand why."

Sherman didn't respond. He stood there looked around like he didn't quite understand where he was or why he was there. Burgess wished this weren't his problem. Indeed, if Sherman stalled long enough, they'd have dinner and then Nikki Ryder and her team would arrive and Burgess could turn the guy over to her. Ryder was an attractive woman, disarmingly so, but those who underestimated her did so at their peril. Ryder wasn't soft. She wasn't sweet. She had a chip on her shoulder the size of Katahdin and a whole lot to prove.

The reality was that of course Burgess would be turning this guy over to Ryder and her untender ministrations. But he still wanted answers himself. He deserved some compensation for having his perfect day in the hammock wrecked.

He let Sherman stew while he turned the chicken again. It was looking good, and his magic device said he was coming into the end zone.

Sherman had cleared his throat and said, "Look…" when Neddy came racing out of the cottage.

"My Joe," he said, "Chris says to ask do you want one corn or two?"

"Two," Burgess said.

"What about that guy?"

That guy also said two. And didn't continue with whatever it was he'd been going to say.

"You were saying?" Burgess prompted.

"I can't," Sherman said. "I have an obligation to Ted."

"To protect the person who tried to kill him?"

"I'm not protecting—"

"Sure you are. Without knowledge of Dr. Gabbro's current project, the police can't determine whether it had anything to do with the events at his rental cottage last night. Events that have left his daughter, Ari, alone and vulnerable. How is that a good thing? How does your silence help Dr. Gabbro now?"

"I can't discuss it without Dr. Gabbro's permission. Or Mr. Fenton's."

"You have Fenton's number?"

Sherman nodded.

"He knows you? Knows you've been working on his project?"

Another nod.

"So call him. Ask if it's okay to talk to the police about your geological research."

Sherman folded his arms and turned away. Tired. Sunburned. Dirty. Uncooperative. Burgess didn't know if the man lacked the ability to understand the gravity of the situation or whether he was just a stubborn son of a bitch who, once his mind was made up, was totally inflexible. He'd met both types.

Burgess gave up. Not his case, not his problem, while seeing that his family had a good vacation *was* his problem. Seeing that Chris, who'd been through such a lot with him lately, had a fun and restful vacation. For that matter, trying to have a vacation himself, giving Dr. Cohen's magic pills time to do their restorative work.

Those who knew him would say Burgess was like a dog with a bone, too tenacious to give up. He was trying to change that, but his tenacity had brought justice, and closure, to a lot of victims and their families. By now it had become as instinctive as choosing the seat in a restaurant where he could watch the room.

He checked his chicken. His gorgeous, crisp chicken that wasn't burned. It was done. He piled it on the platter Chris had given him and headed for the big picnic table on the deck. Out on the lake, the boats had gone silent for the night. He could hear the gentle sloshing of waves against the dock and somewhere the distant, demented cry of a loon.

They sat down at the table. Four kids. Three adults. The chicken. A platter of corn and a butter to roll it in. A tossed salad and a bowl of Chris's excellent homemade coleslaw. Even though the kids had all had whoopee pies, Burgess knew that in the kitchen there was blueberry pie.

Forget about Pete Sherman, which was hard to do, and Ari, also hard to do, and this would have been a perfect evening.

"So, Dad," Dylan said, "there's one of those drive-in movie theaters somewhere around here. Could we go sometime?"

He immediately thought of a half-dozen reasons to say no. Instead he said, "Sure. Well, it depends on what's playing. Whether it's suitable for Neddy." He didn't include Ari. She might be spending the night with them, until Detective Nikki Ryder could locate a suitable family member or contact social services, but she wasn't becoming part of his family vacation.

"Hey!" Neddy said. "I'm almost ten, you know. I'm not some baby."

"When is your birthday?" Chris asked, like she couldn't remember.

"Next Friday."

"Oh gosh," Dylan said. "Then you'll be in double digits, little bro."

Neddy looked at him anxiously. "Is that a good thing or a bad thing?"

"He's teasing," Nina said. "It just means that ten has a one and a zero, or two numbers, instead of nine which has only one."

Neddy said, "Oh. That's okay then," and settled down to eat.

Sherman didn't say a word until he'd demolished a big piece of chicken and two ears of corn. Then he said, "Thank you. This is delicious. Last two weeks, it's mostly been ham and cheese and peanut butter and jelly. Out in the field, you know."

"Where do you live, Pete?" Chris asked.

"Nowhere, really. That is, I have a small apartment in Augusta, a place to keep my stuff, but I move around a lot, wherever the work takes me, especially in the summer. I've got a…" He hesitated, looking at Neddy and Ari, then said, "I have an old, retired hearse that I use as kind of a…uh…mobile bedroom."

Neddy's eyes were wide. "You live in a hearse? Isn't that scary? And where do you go to the bathroom?"

Chris shook her head. "Let him finish his dinner, please."

Burgess was happily into his second piece of slippery, buttery corn when his phone rang.

Chris gave him a warning look as he wiped his fingers and checked it. Then answered.

Nikki Ryder said, "We're next door at the cottage. Care to join us?"

NINE

Despite Chris's glare, and the kids curious looks, Burgess excused himself and went next door. Nikki and her crew were standing by the door, looking impatient. When he appeared, she held out her hand for the key. He gave it to her and stepped back, knowing it was going to feel strange to be an onlooker after being the lead detective at so many scenes.

In a quiet aside so her team wouldn't hear, Nikki said, "Lucky for us, the boss has a family barbecue tonight and couldn't get away."

Like Burgess. Only he *had* gotten away. Did that make him a bad person? He figured it made him the same person he'd always been, the person he'd been when he met Chris and while he acquired this family. A man with divided loyalties, who'd been in love with the job long before he'd been in love with them. Chris would say he was being a jerk. That when you acquired a family, your first loyalty was to them, especially on a family vacation. She might be right. He tried. But he was also a creature of habit. A creature who couldn't sit on his hands next door knowing what was happening here.

He stood back while Nikki instructed her team. Then she turned to him. "Did you take anything out of the cottage? Anything at all?"

"I did. I took the little girl's suitcase back to my cottage."

"You check it first?"

"I did."

"Anything of interest?"

"Just her clothes and her books. Her iPad was under the bed. I also took that. She said her father had an iPad and a laptop with him, but they were probably still in the car. In the trunk in his briefcase."

"Right." She looked at him suspiciously. "You know where the car keys are?"

"I didn't see them in the bedroom. Maybe still in his pants pocket?"

"Right," she said again. "And you didn't take them, check the brief-case, and then put them back in his pocket?"

"Would you really want to know if I did?"

"I guess not. So here's the drill. You're here to watch. As a courtesy. Not your scene. Not your team. Got that?"

"Got it."

"Gonna be hard for you." She almost smiled. She said, "So what are we looking for?"

Burgess shrugged. Her case. Her team. Her search.

"Any sign of Gabbro's cell phone and his medicine. Here or anywhere around the cottage. Whoever took it might not have wanted it in their vehicle. Might have dumped it. When I came back with Ari this morning and found Gabbro unconscious, there was no sign of the phone or any diabetic's medication in the room. Or anywhere. She said he always left it beside the bed so she'd know where to find it."

"We'll need to talk to her," Nikki said.

"Of course."

"Soon. Go on."

"The bedroom window was wide open, which seemed odd because it has no screen when all the other windows have screens. So you might be looking for a screen. I didn't look closely to see if a screen might have been cut out. If there's still a frame there."

She nodded.

"You'll definitely be collecting the empty orange juice container in the trash can. Ari says they bought it last night before they arrived and it was gone the next morning when she went to get her father a glass of juice."

"Did he want juice?" Nikki asked.

"He was unconscious. She was trying to be a caretaker. She knew when he wasn't well, a glass of juice would help."

"Sounds like you've developed quite a relationship with the child in the course of a single day."

"It's been quite a day. She seems quiet and shy but she can be quite a chatterbox. She talked a lot on the way to the hospital."

A mosquito landed on his arm. "You mind if we talk inside? I'd rather not feed the mosquitoes."

She slapped at one on her face and said, "Good idea."

Burgess followed her into the cottage, stopping just inside the door and looking around. The room had seemed spacious this morning, when only he and Ari were there. Now, after Ryder instructed them, it became a small hive of activity as her team started their search.

He thought—probably all long-time detectives thought—that he'd know he was at a crime scene even if he was blindfolded. The soft voices, the small thuds of books, pillows, furniture being moved, drawers opened and closed, the creak of belts as the searchers bent and straightened. The sotto voce crackle of radios beneath it all.

He figured he should tell her about Peter Sherman. Not much to tell. Sherman hadn't been forthcoming. But he was a valuable witness and this was Ryder's case. For now. What was hanging over them was what would happen if Gabbro didn't recover. If he died and there was the possibility of foul play involved, which is what the missing items and the poured out juice suggested, the case would become the province of the Maine state police.

Before he could speak, Ryder said, "So if the car with the Mass plates is Gabbro's, who does the red Jeep belong to?"

"Guy named Peter Sherman. He works with Gabbro. Showed up this afternoon when Gabbro didn't appear for a scheduled meeting. I found him banging on the cottage door."

She cocked her head. "And where might he be now?"

Burgess, thinking it sounded like he was collecting her witnesses for her—unless it was that he was hiding them—said, "Over at my cottage."

"I think it's time I paid a visit to your cottage, Burgess, don't you?"

He swept a hand toward the door. "If you wish."

She had a quiet conversation with the man who seemed to be her senior guy and headed for the door.

He followed her out. Once they were away from her team, she turned on him. "Dammit, Burgess. What are you up to?"

He did not need two tough women mad at him. "Not up to anything except keeping him around until you showed up. Why wouldn't I? You think I *want* to spend my vacation up to my ears in witnesses? We don't even know there's been a crime, Nikki. Just some very suspicious circumstances."

"You think maybe it's the kid, just messing with things and then it all went wrong?"

"So far, I don't, though she's an odd little thing. But you should form your own conclusions."

A troubling possibility. What if she was right? What if this was Ari's way of trying to get her parents back together? Or to show her father he needed to have her with him? What if the only prints on that discarded juice container were Ari's?

Burgess was a good judge of character. Lot of cops were—until they weren't. He'd taken the child at face value, trusted her distress was genuine. But he hadn't pressed her, not when she was all alone and her father was in a hospital in critical condition. He thought he'd read her right, but what if he'd just introduced a little monster into his happy family vacation?

It was getting late. Chris would be settling the younger ones, getting them calm before bed. Dylan and Nina were likely playing some competitive game or watching one of the videos they brought.

What would Peter Sherman be doing? He must still be there, since his car was here. Burgess started walking faster. Suddenly he didn't like the idea of a strange child and a recalcitrant young man at the cottage with Chris when he wasn't there. As if she'd read his mind, Ryder sped up, too.

Burgess's heart was pounding by the time they stepped up onto the deck. Through the windows, he saw Nina and Dylan glued to the TV screen. Chris and Peter Sherman were finishing the dishes. No sign of Ari and Neddy.

TEN

W hen he and Ryder stepped into the room, everyone turned to watch them. Nina and Dylan a bit curious, Chris apprehensive, Sherman poised to run. Sherman's position made Burgess wonder if he and Nikki should have separated and covered two doors. He took a breath, made himself calm down, and said, "This is Detective Nicola Ryder, from the Cumberland County Sheriff's Department."

He introduced his family, and Peter Sherman, then let Ryder take the lead. As she stepped up to ask Sherman some questions, Burgess took Chris aside. "Are Neddy and Ari in bed?"

"They were exhausted," she said. "Nothing like an afternoon of cannonballs to wear kids out. I just checked them. They're both asleep."

"Where?"

She gave him a quizzical look, like the answer was obvious. "Neddy is in with Dylan and Ari is in Nina's room. Of course. And by the way, he says he doesn't want to be called Neddy anymore. He says it's a baby name and he's not a baby."

Almost double digits. He wasn't a baby. Burgess would miss the affectionate sound of "Neddy" though. Ned sounded like some grownup old duffer.

Chris paused, shot a glance at Ryder, and said, "And I don't think we should wake Ari up, even if Detective Ryder is anxious to speak with her. She's had a very hard day. I don't think it will be a productive conversation."

Ah. Add another duckling to her flock, and she immediately became protective.

"I know that look, Burgess," she said. "Don't you go putting me in some box like I'm an overprotective civilian getting in the way of whatever the cops want to do, okay? You introduce a scared child whose father is in critical condition into my house and of course I'm going to mother her."

"Yes, ma'am," he said.

Humor danced in her eyes as she said, "Don't 'yes, ma'am' me, Joe Burgess, like I'm someone who needs to be humored. You know I'm right."

"I know you're right."

She stepped closer and he put an arm around her waist.

"You look tired, Joe. This day did not do what it was supposed to do. Are you taking Dr. Cohen's pills?"

"I am. She said it would take a while."

"Right. She also said to take it easy."

"Am taking it easy."

"No. You're not."

Nikki Ryder was in the kitchen—basically just a corner of the big open room—talking to Peter Sherman. Now they heard raised voices.

Chris was there in a moment, her finger held to her lips. "You've got to lower your voices," she said. "There are children sleeping."

Sherman said, "Sorry."

Ryder said, "This is important."

But Chris lived with a cop. She wasn't taking any inconsiderate crap from some county detective.

Burgess tried not to smile when Ryder said, "Is Ari asleep? Because I also need to talk to her."

Chris, a long-time nurse used to dealing with pushy and obstinate people, folded her arms. "I'm sorry, but that's not happening. The child has been through enough today. Whatever it is, it can wait 'til morning."

"Ma'am," Ryder said again, "this is important."

"As is rest to a troubled child."

Ryder looked at him, about to ask for his help, then gave in. "Tomorrow. You'll call me as soon as she's awake?"

"We'll call you. Joe has your number?"

"He does." Ryder turned back to Peter Sherman. "Let's leave these people in peace. We can continue our talk next door."

Burgess felt a stab of something. Regret or feeling left out. Foolish when he didn't want this case.

Ryder herded Sherman before her like she was a sheepdog. At the door she paused. "Burgess. You *will* call me, right?"

"I will call you."

She left, letting the screen door slam shut behind her. An unmistakable 'fuck you' to Burgess and Chris. Still, she could have pushed it. Made them wake Ari up. She could have called social services and gotten them involved. So if she needed to slam a door to assert her authority, Burgess was fine with that.

Chris was not so fine, he could see, but she shrugged. "Cops," she said. "They can be so charming."

Through it all, Dylan and Nina had remained glued to the TV.

Burgess got a bottle of wine from the fridge, and two glasses, and looked at Chris. "Care for a nightcap?"

"I thought you'd never ask."

They sat at the end of the dock, feet dangling over the water, drinking wine and listening to the loons.

"Nikki. Detective Ryder. She asked me if I thought it was possible Ari did this herself," he said. "Hid the phone and his medicine and poured out the orange juice. Maybe as an attempt to bring her parents together. Or to show she needed to be with her father. I supposed it's possible. We really don't know anything about her. What do you think?"

She was silent as she considered. Sipped her wine. Said, "It's possible, I suppose. I've been fooled before. Kids can be pretty devious in divorce situations, we both know that. But she seems genuinely upset. I mean, she played with Neddy...uh...Ned. But there was an edginess about it. And she did take off swimming like that. I don't know if that was because she wasn't thinking or was all wound up or if it was deliberate. Something defiant or to make us pay attention to her. What was she like this morning when she came to ask you for help?"

"Scared. Very quiet and subdued. When she appeared, pale and timid and all dressed in white, she seemed like a frightened and needy child. After I'd given her breakfast and was driving her to the hospital, she was different. A total chatterbox. That's when she told me her mother was in Scotland, had her phone turned off, and didn't want to be disturbed. She also said that her mother refers to her as 'the big mistake.' From what she said, she's much happier with her father than with her mother, but her father is too busy to have much time for her. And, according to her, somewhat absent-minded."

Chris made a thoughtful sound. "A ploy for more of her father's attention that went badly wrong?"

"Could be. But I can't see her putting her father at risk like that," Burgess said, "if she's truly aware of his condition, as she seems to be. And why lose the phone when she might need it?"

"If she lost it."

"Yes. *If* she lost it. But if it was all a cry for attention, she could have retrieved the lost items and revived him. Or worst case scenario, she could have called for help herself. She wouldn't need to come to me for help. What if I hadn't been home?"

"She's only nine, Joe. Pretty young to do a complex analysis of the risks. Can't you imagine Neddy, I mean Ned, doing something foolish for attention and getting it all wrong?"

Chris held out her glass for more wine.

He poured.

"So where does Pete Sherman come into it?" she said. "Just a guy who works with Gabbro who turned up when Gabbro didn't show for their meeting?"

"That's what he says. He's a puzzle, for sure," Burgess said. "He seems to care for the girl. But he's so damned evasive it's hard to get a read."

Chris drank her wine and they listened to the sounds of the lake. "Is this what you do with Terry and Stan?" she asked.

"Kind of. Yes."

"I'm glad you're doing it with me. So tell me about Sherman. He's not exactly a social creature, is he?"

"He's not. I don't think someone becomes a field geologist because he likes to be around people. I think maybe he's okay one-on-one. I also think whatever he was working on with Gabbro, they wanted to keep it secret. That other people want their knowledge and if it gets out it puts Fenton's land deals at risk."

"But would someone go to such elaborate lengths for the possibility of a little gold? I thought there wasn't gold in Maine except what people sometimes find in streams. Hobbyists. And if this was a deliberate attack on Gabbro, they'd have to know about the cottage. And Gabbro's diabetes. And getting in and out can't have been easy. I didn't hear a car last night. Did you?"

"I didn't even hear Gabbro and Ari arrive," he said, surprised that he'd slept so soundly. "But thinking about gold. What if it's not a little, but a lot?" He put his arm around her. She was warm in the cooling evening air. "You'd make a good detective, you know," he said.

"Nurses often have to be detectives. We're good at getting people to give up their secrets."

"Did you learn any secrets from Sherman while you were doing dishes?"

"Not secrets, exactly, Joe. But I think he's scared. I think that's part of why he was so abrupt. He's got a deal or a contract or something with Dr. Gabbro, and someone else is putting pressure on him to share his—or their—discoveries. I think Gabbro is kind of a father figure to him, but he lives kind of hand-to-mouth and giving in to that pressure is tempting."

She took his hand and threaded her fingers through his. "Why can't we just have a peaceful vacation, Joe? It's so nice here and everyone needs rest and fun before school starts and you go back to work."

Then they lay back and watched the stars. One brilliant shooting star was so bright and green it left them breathless.

"Hey," she whispered, "want to go skinny dipping?"

Burgess imagined their two bodies colliding in the cool water. He hadn't been skinny dipping since he was around Dylan's age. "I do."

He stood up. He was unfastening his belt and she was about to pull her tee shirt over her head when Nina came running out of the cottage. "Mom. Dad. You've got to come quick," she said. "Ari is missing."

ELEVEN

They hurried inside after her and peered in through the bedroom door. It was a small, rustic room with bunkbeds along one wall. Chris had put Ari to sleep in the bottom bunk. Now it was empty, the covers tossed back. Small pink pajamas lay on the floor. The girl's white sneakers were gone.

"She got dressed," Chris said. "When I left her, her white shorts and tee shirt were folded up on top of her suitcase."

Harder to hide in the dark when you're wearing white, Burgess thought. *It was something.*

"I'm sorry," Nina said. "Dylan and I were so into our movie that we didn't see her go."

"Did you check Ned's room?" Burgess asked, thinking maybe Ari had gone in there to sleep since she was so comfortable with Ned.

"Of course we did. We even looked in your room and the bathroom. She's not here," Dylan said.

"Dammit," Burgess said. "I'll have to let Ryder know. Then we'll all look for her."

"Someone has to stay here," Chris reminded him. "In case Neddy... Ned...wakes up."

"I'll stay," Nina said.

Burgess got out his phone and stepped outside to make the call. Ryder was going to yell at him and he'd rather not have that conversation in front of his family. He preferred to maintain his status as the one who got to do the yelling as much as possible.

He stepped off the deck into the dark and dialed. What was the child thinking? They were miles from anywhere and she didn't know anyone. Maybe she was a sleep walker? Or maybe she was in the habit of running away when life got stressful. He didn't know. He hoped that Sherman did, or that at least Sherman knew who they might contact and ask.

She answered with a crisp "Ryder" Burgess read as her suspecting he wasn't going to leave her alone to conduct her investigation without him. Probably his own fault, and his reputation, that made people believe he couldn't leave an investigation alone.

He gave her back an equally crisp, "It's Burgess. Arielle Gabbro has run away. Is Sherman still there?"

"What's Sherman got to…what the fuck, Burgess? You can't keep track of one small girl?"

He heard her grab a breath, ready to tear into him, and cut her off. "Is Sherman still there? What he's got to do with this is that he's the only person we know of who has any knowledge of the child. Maybe he has some insights that would be helpful."

From the cottage door, he heard Chris say, "Darn it, Joe. She's taken my phone."

"He's here," Ryder said. "Hold on."

Out on the dock, a breeze had kept the bugs away. Here, the cottage blocked the breeze and mosquitoes seemed to be pouring out of the woods, sensing a perfect opportunity for a meal.

He gave up on privacy and went inside. Got the bug spray and took it back outside where he doused himself. He hated the smell but valued his blood. Over the years, he'd shed plenty of it.

When Sherman came on the phone, his, "This is Peter Sherman," sounded both ridiculously professional and shaky as hell.

"Burgess," Burgess said. "Ari's run away. Anything you can tell us about that? Does she sleepwalk? Does she often run away?"

Sherman cleared his throat. "Uh. Yeah. Yes. Ari does sometimes run away. When she's with her mother, I mean. Not when she's with Ted. She and her mother don't exactly get along, which is weird because Elyse. Elyse Gabbro, her mother, fought relentlessly for custody even though she really doesn't like Ari very much."

Burgess wanted to get back to the running away, but this information was too important to skip. Sherman was talking now because he was nervous and shaken. Better to get the info now, before he'd had time to reflect. He figured Ryder was listening on Sherman's end and making the same calculation.

"You know why Gabbro's ex was so determined to get custody of Ari?"

"Sure. Because Ted has money, and if Elyse got custody, she could wring more out of him. Ted will do anything for Ari."

"Ted Gabbro is wealthy?"

"Oh. Yeah. He's rolling in it."

This was certainly news. News that made Burgess wonder who else might be interested in that money. And whether Elyse Gabbro really *was* in Scotland.

"Getting back to Ari and her habit of running away. Tell us about that? Does she do it often? Is there someone particular she would run to?"

Another throat clearing. It couldn't be easy for someone as awkward and taciturn as Sherman to talk with one cop on the phone and another right beside him. He said, "Oh, she'll go to Bridget," like they knew what he meant. "Yeah. That's what she'll do. Except I don't know how she'll get in touch."

"I think she'll try to get in touch," Burgess said, well growled. He didn't like being scammed by a nine-year-old child. "Because she's stolen my wife...uh...Chris's phone." Not that Chris's phone would be useful, since Ari would need the password. Or Chris's thumb. "Who is Bridget?"

In the background, he heard Ryder cursing, then heard her asking the same question.

Sherman said, "Look. Could we all just sit down together and talk about this? It's...uh...I'm not too comfortable with the two of you... uh...leaning on me like this. Okay?"

"We don't care about your comfort."

Burgess and Ryder said it together, like a well-rehearsed team. Followed immediately by slightly different versions of "Who is Bridget?" and "How do we get in touch with her?"

Burgess couldn't see Sherman, but he could tell, from the stumbles and pauses, that together they'd reduced the man to a stammering wreck.

"Just take it slow and easy, Pete," he said. "One question at a time. Who is Bridget?"

"She's …uh…Gabbro's housekeeper. Uh, down in Massachusetts. She's been with…uh…the Gabbros. Since the divorce, I mean. With Ted."

"You think she'll come if Ari calls her?" Burgess heard Ryder ask.

"Oh. Yeah. Um. Yes. She's taken care of Ari since Ari was a baby. I mean, that's what I've heard. Been told, I mean, I wasn't around…uh, working with Ted…when Ari was a baby."

Damn the man. He could have told them about Bridget hours ago. Burgess figured Sherman had been so focused on protecting Gabbro's secrets that he hadn't considered telling them about someone who could take care of Ari while her father was in the hospital. A mind that ran to rocks, not people, despite his evident fondness for the girl.

"Do you know how to get in touch with her?" Burgess asked.

"Sure."

"Then would you call her, please, or give her number to Detective Ryder, so we can see if Ari has been in touch."

"Okay."

"Let me talk to Ryder," Burgess said.

She said, "Ryder."

He said, "You got all that? You want to make the call?"

"I did. I do. I'll call you when I know what's up."

"Great. Thanks. We're going to walk out the road, see if we can find the girl."

"If you *do* find her, tie her to something, will you please, so this doesn't happen again."

"You bet I will."

"I don't like this," she said.

Burgess didn't like it either, but what was he going to say? He was the one who'd kept Ari with him, thinking he was keeping her safe. Now she was out wandering in the night. A child who might be at risk. Who might have some value to a person interested in gold. Or Gabbro's money.

TWELVE

They left Nina in the cottage with her sleeping brother while the rest of them put on long pants and long sleeves, sprayed themselves liberally with bug repellent, armed themselves with flashlights and headed out. Even on vacation, Burgess made sure there were plenty of flashlights available and they all worked. Get caught once without a working flashlight in a dangerous situation and you won't let it happen again.

Chris drove her car out to the road to search for Ari along the roadside. She would drive two miles in one direction, then do two miles the other way. That was how far they speculated the girl could have gone in the time she'd been missing. Burgess and Dylan would search the woods along the dirt road that led to the cottage. Shortly after it left the tarred road, it branched.

When they reached that spot, they'd separate and check the side roads. In the dark, it would have been hard for Ari to tell which way led out to the main road. There weren't any signs other than last names or cottage names written on boards nailed to trees.

Burgess's stomach was in a knot. He hoped they'd find the girl and not come up empty handed. She couldn't have used Chris's phone to call the person named Bridget since the phone was password protected. That meant if they didn't find Ari, he and Ryder would have to consider the possibility that the girl had been taken by someone else.

He wondered why she hadn't told him about Bridget when he'd asked about relatives. Even if Bridget wasn't related, she was presumably someone Ari was close to. Someone who would have come if Ari had needed her. But Sherman hadn't mentioned Bridget initially, either. What was up with that? The most likely person to take charge of the child until her father recovered—if he recovered—and no one mentions her? What had initially appeared to be simply a father-daughter vacation with a non-custodial parent was looking a lot more complicated.

What was Ari up to? To sneak off at night like this, such a precise child must have had a plan. But what plan? Where was she going and why now? Why by herself in an unfamiliar place? If she was running to someone, if she *had* made a call to someone, it meant she'd been lying about her father's missing phone, which gave rise to a different set of questions.

Not his case. Not his problem.

Yeah, sure.

Burgess and Dylan reached the spot where the road forked without any sign of the girl. "This is just weird, Dad," his son said. "Why would she do this?"

"That is the central question," Burgess agreed. "If we find her, we'll ask. You've got your phone with you, right?"

"Right. Chris has Nina's phone."

With so much strange shit going on tonight, Burgess didn't like Nina being alone in the cottage without a phone, but the rest of them needed to stay in touch. It gave him an uneasy feeling, though.

They separated and headed off into the darkness, their powerful flashlights making eerie tunnels of light in the otherwise dark woods. He listened until the crunch of Dylan's footsteps faded away, then started walking

His phone rang. Ryder. "You find her yet?"

"Still out looking."

"Two things." She sounded brisk and impatient and something else. Annoyed. He didn't think it was with him.

"Go ahead."

"First, we…I…reached Gabbro's housekeeper. Bridget O'Toole. She's going to drive up in the morning. She'll take charge of Ari and will take the girl to the hospital to see her father. She…sometimes it's hard to get a read over the phone, as you know, but she didn't sound like a warm and fuzzy person. It was more like a 'what's that girl gone and done now' kind of thing. So that's one. Hope you can keep the girl safe until morning. Assuming you find her."

"Right," Burgess said. "I assume that's the good news?"

"Yes. The bad is it seems someone on my team isn't a team player. At least, someone's trying to climb up the ladder using me as a step and ratted you out to Oh Really, who kindly took the time to call and say no way did he want you involved in this case. I'm sorry. I know you've got a lot to offer. I think Oh Really is worried you might steal some of his glory."

She hesitated. "Like what we do is about glory."

"Guess I'll get back to looking for Ari," he said. "Thanks for the update, Nikki. And you know I'm here if you need me."

"Thanks. Maybe we can meet secretly in a dark parking lot and share updates."

He laughed. "It won't be my first time."

"It would be mine. Keep me posted, okay?"

"Will do."

Burgess put his phone away and started down the road again, kicking a stone in front of him. Police territorialism made him sick. They were on the same side, but sometimes you wouldn't know that from the way information was hidden, like it was a secret treasure, like police departments were secret club houses where you couldn't get in without the right password or handshake. He understood keeping information away from the public that could damage a case, but what justified keeping it from a fellow officer? It wasn't like he was someone who'd nosed under the tent just because he was curious.

His phone rang again. Chris. "I've gone two miles in each direction. There's "no sign of her." She sounded anxious and discouraged.

"Might as well come back," he said. "I'll feel safer if you're there with Nina and Ned."

She sighed. "I hate to stop calling him Neddy, you know. It's silly but it seems to fit him so well. And Ned. Well. It sounds like some old duffer. Or Nancy Drew's boyfriend. I suppose I always knew this was coming. I'm still not ready for it."

Funny how they'd both thought Ned sounded like an old duffer. "There are going to be an awful lot of things coming at us we're not ready for," he said.

"I know."

No sign of her?"

"Not yet. Dylan and I are walking the two roads that go out from the split. I haven't gotten very far. My phone keeps ringing."

"I'm sorry. I thought I should..."

"Chris. Come on. It wasn't a criticism." Something bumped his leg. He'd left Fideau in the cottage. Somehow, the dog had gotten out. Probably stared at Nina with sad eyes until she gave him what he wanted. "Hold on...Fideau's loose."

"Ask him to find Ari. Maybe he's secretly trained as a search dog and not just a dog who searches out Joe Burgess."

"I'll give it a try."

He put his phone away and patted the dog's head. "You want to help me find Ari?"

The dog cocked its head and stared up at him with clever eyes.

"Okay," Burgess said. "Go find her."

Like they'd been working together for years, the dog obediently set off down the road, trotting in a determined fashion until it was just a light blur in the dark. Burgess had always wanted a dog. The circumstances of his childhood had been so tenuous a dog was out of the question. Odd that fate should hand him one now.

He started walking the way Fideau had gone, scanning the roadsides and the road ahead, the bright beam piercing the darkness with blue-white light. A lot of people were scared of the dark, even cops. In their world, the monster in the closet or under the bed wasn't a childhood fear or a bad dream, it was reality. Bad guys did hide under beds and jump out of closets, crouch on top of furniture or at the tops of stairs and jump, thrust, punch or shoot. Cops did, and didn't, get used to it.

Even if you'd been in that dark house a hundred times, you couldn't let down your guard. A challenge since "I've seen it all before" created a false sense of security.

Up ahead, Fideau began to bark. Burgess didn't know the dog well enough yet to know whether this meant a raccoon or a fox or deer, or whether the dog was trying to tell him something. He stepped up his pace until he was almost jogging, and around a bend in the road he found Ari sitting on the ground, her back against a tree, Fideau standing guard.

When she spotted Burgess she said, "My Joe, will he bite me?"

"No, Ari, he won't bite you. He's just telling me that he's found you and I should hurry up. Right, Fideau?" He gave the dog a pat, then knelt down beside the girl. She looked small and cold in only a tee shirt and shorts, her face streaked with dirty tears, the red welts of mosquito bites on her bare arms and legs.

"Are you all right?" he asked.

A sob and a nod.

"Can you walk or do you want me to carry you?"

She stood, small and defiant. "I can walk."

"Good, then let's go before the mosquitoes get what's left of you."

He held out his hand and she took it. Burgess on one side and Fideau on the other, they started back.

"Got to make some calls," Burgess said. He dropped her hand and got out his phone. He called Dylan and said, "I found her." Then called Chris with the same message, and then Nikki Ryder.

"I'm coming over," she said. "No more of this wait until morning stuff." She disconnected before he could reply.

"Is everyone mad at me?" Ari asked.

"Well, Chris isn't happy that you stole her phone."

"Borrowed. I was going to give it back."

"You have to ask if you want to borrow something, Ari. If you take it without asking, that's stealing."

"Is not," she said.

Burgess was not parsing the rules with a defiant nine-year-old. "Where were you going?" he asked.

"To the hospital. To see my dad."

"In the middle of the night? When it's twenty miles away?"

"I didn't know that."

"Ari. We drove there this morning."

She didn't reply.

"Where were you really going?"

"Not telling you. It's none of your business."

"Were you planning to meet someone?"

"Not telling."

Ah. Kids. They required more patience than defiant adults and it was hard to repress the urge to give some of them a smart swat on the ass. Burgess was a dinosaur. He didn't believe in beating children but sometimes—usually with a smart-mouthed teenager—he itched to apply a little physical discipline. But not with a nine-year-old. He had one of those of his own. He knew better.

He decided that he'd let Ryder be the tough guy. He walked on in silence. If she had something to share, the ball was in her court. If she didn't? He could enjoy the quiet night, the softness of wind in the tall pines. The steady rhythm of big feet and small ones crunching on the gravel road. He could hear the distant lapping of the lake and smell the lake water. Despite the stubborn little person walking with him, forcing him to slow his pace, he could appreciate the sense of being alone, on vacation, attuned to the natural world in a way his usual day-to-day didn't let him.

At the fork, they found Dylan waiting for them.

"Hey, pipsqueak," he said to Ari, "I saved you from those power-boats so you could do this? That wasn't very nice."

"Sorry," Ari said. "I didn't mean to upset anyone."

"Yeah. Right. You give Chris and my dad heart attacks but you didn't mean anything by it? Like we're supposed to believe that."

"Believe what you want," the little brat said.

Dylan, who'd spent his summer dealing with bratty kids, walked off.

"Is he mad at me?" Ari asked.

"What do you think? You aren't being very nice."

"I run away all the time," Ari said. "It's no big deal."

Burgess kind of wished he could walk off, too.

They walked on, Ari's steps getting slower and slower, like a kid dawdling on her way to school.

Instead of cajoling, Burgess picked her up and walked faster. "Bridget is coming in the morning to get you," he said.

He felt her stiffen. "Oh hell," she said. "Why did you have to go and do that? She is not good news."

THIRTEEN

When they got back, Dylan and Nina had gone to their rooms, no doubt to avoid any adult fireworks that might be happening. Burgess wished he could follow their example. Instead, he had Chris and Nikki Ryder waiting at the table, both in the middle of eating blueberry pie.

"Pie?" Chris said, holding out her hand for her phone.

"Please," he said. "Do we have ice cream?"

Chris looked at Ryder. "Four kids in the house. It's summer. And he wonders if there's ice cream."

"Don't pile on or anything," he said.

Chris said, "Ari, go wash your face. The pink washcloth, remember? Then Detective Ryder needs to speak with you." She got up to get his pie.

He sat down across from Ryder. Before he opened his mouth, she said, "Don't tell me to go easy on the kid, okay, Burgess?"

"I wasn't going to." Her case. Her problem.

"Good." She gestured at the pie with her fork. "Your wife make this?"

"I don't have a wife."

Gad. He sounded almost as sullen as Ari had on their walk back.

Not his fault Chris wouldn't marry him. Except, of course, it was absolutely his fault that he didn't want to take a desk job.

"Sorry," he said.

Ryder nodded. Didn't say anything.

Chris delivered the pie and sat down. Then got up again. "Oh. I made coffee. Do you want some?"

He was so tired he didn't think it would keep him awake, and pie and coffee were good together. Besides, he was still sort of hoping that once Ryder had dealt with Ari and the child had gone to bed, he and Chris might pick up where they were when Nina had come running out with the news about Ari.

Beside him, Chris put a hand on his leg under the table. Looked like they were on the same wavelength.

They waited. They ate pie. Ari didn't appear.

"I'll get her," Chris said. She knocked on the bathroom door and spoke sharply. "No. You can't stay in there. There's only one bathroom and other people need to use it, too."

The bathroom window was small, but so was Ari. While Chris gave way to Ryder trying to induce the girl to come out, Burgess went outside and stationed himself outside the window. He could hear Ryder's voice as the window opened and two white legs wiggled out. He let her get most of her torso out before he grabbed her and carried her inside.

Every moment with this child strengthened his wish that he'd never opened his eyes in the hammock this morning and responded to her request for help. More than thirty years on the job reminded him that when someone, particularly a child, needs help, you don't say no just because you'd rather snooze or because they might be difficult. He'd never be the cop—the person—who just said no.

As if the night couldn't get any crazier, they'd just settled down, Ari and Ryder in the living area, he and Chris at the table while he finished his pie, when someone knocked on the door. Knocked being a polite euphemism for banged and yelled.

"Next year we are taking our vacation somewhere totally remote. Alaska, maybe. Or on an island. Or a houseboat," Chris muttered, making no move to go and answer it. The look she gave him was perfectly clear: you brought this mess down on us, now deal with it.

He pushed back from the table and lumbered toward the rear of the cottage, snapping on the outside light and jerking open the door with a glare. The fastidious Mr. Fenton was on the doorstep.

"Quiet down, dammit, the kids are sleeping."

"Look, I need to—"

Burgess went out, closing the door behind him, pushing Fenton away from the cottage with not quite gentle hands. When they were far enough from the door, he said, "You can start by apologizing for disturbing us."

"Yes, but—"

"There *is* no but."

Fenton's expression was a mix of irritation and confusion. Was it possible no one had ever asked him to apologize before, even for a late-night visit to someone's house? Were rude intrusions his M.O.?

"Look, okay, I'm sorry, but—"

Burgess already had a sleeping family, a lovely woman who needed his attention, a difficult child, and an annoyed cop on his hands. He had no patience for this. "What the hell do you want that justifies disturbing us at this hour?"

"I need to know what's going on with Dr. Gabbro. And how to locate Peter Sherman. I know you said you didn't know Gabbro, but I've talked with the hospital, and you're the one who called it in, so you *must* know him. I've got a deadline coming up, and—"

Burgess heard the door open and shut, quiet footsteps on the grass, and Ryder appeared beside him.

"Detective Nicola Ryder, Cumberland County Sheriff's Department," she said. "And you are?"

"Orville Fenton. What the hell is going on? Why are two cops involved? What's the story with Gabbro? The hospital wouldn't tell me a damned thing. I got the info about this guy—" A finger jabbed at Burgess. "From one of the EMTs. And where's Sherman? He's working with Gabbro. Supposed to be in touch and I haven't heard from him either."

"And we are what?" Ryder asked quietly. "Their answering service?"

"Look, lady, this is important." Fenton gestured at Burgess. "I told this guy, earlier, that it was important that I speak with Gabbro or his assistant and he says he doesn't know Gabbro. I'm up against a deadline and I need their information. Then I find he's the one who called the ambulance. I can't find—"

"Detective Ryder," she interrupted. "Not lady. And Detective Sergeant Burgess, not this guy. Got it?"

Burgess, having put in his time being the tough one, was happy to cede the field to Ryder, who seemed to be enjoying herself.

Fenton looked confused, and obviously insufficiently chastened, as he immediately repeated his demands for information.

"Dr. Gabbro's in the hospital," Ryder said. "And why are two detectives here? Because his condition may not be an accident. Would you know anything about that, Mr. Fenton? Know any reason why someone might have wanted to harm Dr. Gabbro?"

Fenton shook his head, not indicating that he didn't know but more of a thought-clearing gesture that reminded Burgess of something bovine shaking off flies.

Ryder looked at Burgess. "Would you mind if we came inside and asked Mr. Fenton a few questions?"

"You done with Ari?"

She shook her head.

"It's your call, but I think you should take them one at a time."

She considered. Nodded. "Right. Kid's enough of a challenge without another distraction." She pointed at the Lincoln SUV that was parked behind Chris's car. "That your vehicle?"

Fenton nodded. He still looked like he wasn't following the conversation.

"Great," Ryder said. "Why don't you go back and sit in it, and I'll come get you when I'm ready for you."

"Look," he said, "I'm a busy man."

"And I'm a busy woman." She pointed at his car. "Go. Wait. Now."

Fenton hesitated.

"Now," Ryder said.

He shambled off, shaking his head.

"That was kind of fun," she said as they turned to go back inside. "You think he knows anything?"

"He knows what Gabbro and Sherman were working on, because

he hired Gabbro. That's something. And if this land deal is so time sensitive, and if there are genuine reasons for Sherman to be so secretive, that might give you a clue about who might have had an interest in putting Gabbro out of commission."

"Righteo," she said. "Back to the tough little babe."

"She is that."

They both grinned.

Ari was sitting on the couch, her arms folded over her chest, looking stubborn and sullen.

Chris was still at the table, sipping her coffee. He sat down beside her, picked up his fork, and attacked his pie.

"Is this how our whole vacation is going to be?" she asked. "Detective Burgess instead of My Joe? Cops in our living room and strangers banging on the door?"

"Not if I can help it."

"You're not going to get sucked in?"

"I'm not planning to." Moving along, and meaning to distract her, he said, "What's our schedule for the rest of the week?"

"Tomorrow is a hang around and do nothing day. Maybe you can try the hammock again. The next day Stan and Terry and their families are coming out, so you'll be cooking steak and burgers and dogs. Then I think Dylan and Nina are having some friends out for the afternoon the next day."

"What about Sandy and Moira and the kids?"

Burgess didn't always get along with his sisters, especially Sandy, but he was making an effort and Chris thought it was good for the kids to know their cousins.

Burgess hadn't seen his niece Cherry since she'd led Dylan on an escapade that had nearly gotten them—and him—killed, so seeing her again would be awkward. But they were family. He sighed.

"Oh. Right," she said. "They're coming with Terry and Stan. I figured once we had a few people, the more the merrier. And Doro, of course."

Doro. Dorothy. Her mother. The kids' grandmother. She was so happy to have this passel of children to love and they were lucky to have her. He and Chris were, too. Doro picked up the slack when their jobs kept them away from home.

The last time they'd all been together, for a Fourth of July picnic, all hell had broken loose. Not with the family, but in his professional life. The case he was still trying to recover from. He shivered.

"That day? I'm locking your phone in the trunk of my car," she said. "Yours. Stan's. Terry's. No one is going to call any of you out to a crime scene."

He liked that idea. Sat on his instinctive need to argue or to say that at least Stan Perry and Terry Kyle, the rest of his team, needed to be available and on call. They could try and tell Chris that themselves. He'd promised her a vacation. He needed to do as little as possible to screw that up more than he already had.

The bottle of wine and their two glasses were still sitting on the counter. Despite having just had coffee and pie, he picked them up and said, "Let's go back to what we were doing before we were interrupted."

Chris looked at Nikki Ryder, still sitting in their living room.

"Nikki," Burgess said. "We're going to go sit on the dock."

"Have fun," Ryder said.

Chris picked up two towels and the bug spray and followed him out. They sat down again at the end of the dock, feet dangling over the water. He poured the wine. They sat shoulder to shoulder and listened to the night.

After a while, Chris said, "Do you think Ari is disturbed? Is there something wrong with her?"

"Not my department," he said. "She's definitely willful and it doesn't sound like her home situation is very good. She wasn't happy when I told her Bridget, the housekeeper, was coming to get her, either, so there's probably not some warm and nurturing relationship there. Maybe acting out is a grab for attention. Or a way of having some control over her life. She's in a very scary situation right now and doesn't know how to navigate it."

He put an arm around her shoulders. "Know what? I don't want to think about troubled little girls right now. I just want to be. Right here. Right now."

"Still up for that swim?" she whispered.

"Sure. You?"

It was a new moon night. Very dark and private. They shed their clothes and climbed down the ladder into the lake. It made Burgess feel like a teenager again. A horny teenager undeterred by cool water and excited by the possibility of being discovered. Which they were, by Ryder appearing at the top of the ladder, but not before they'd had their fun.

"Anyone ever tell you it's time to grow up, Joe?"

"Often. I'm working on it."

"Well, I'm out of here. Gonna go see what I can wring out of Fenton. One of you want to put that child to bed. Or tie her to the bed? Nail the windows shut. Whatever will keep her safe for the night?"

Chris laughed. "Sure you don't want to take her with you?"

"Very sure."

"Then give us a minute. Keep an eye on her 'till we get inside."

Ryder sighed. "I can't believe you two."

"Right," Burgess said. "And you have never gone skinny dipping, have you, Nikki? You've always been a model of rectitude?"

"Not answering that question."

She walked away.

Not wanting to have to do another nocturnal search for Ari, they quickly dried off and scrambled into their clothes.

Ryder was drumming softly on the table with her fingernails.

Ari was curled up on the couch, sound asleep.

Burgess, in the doorway, held his breath, hoping nothing more would happen before morning, even though he knew wishing and hoping and dreaming and even planning were not the stuff of a cop's world.

Nikki left. Burgess carried Ari into the bedroom and tucked her in. Then he and Chris went to bed. She fell asleep. He lay there in the dark, waiting for another shoe to drop.

FOURTEEN

He finally allowed himself to fall into an uneasy asleep. No shoes dropped until the next morning, when Chris woke him to say that Bridget had arrived to collect Ari.

"Did Nikki Ryder want to talk with Bridget?" she asked.

He was still clearing cobwebs from his brain. He held up a hand, signaling for her to wait. It wasn't like him to be so slow waking up. He had years of experience in being instantly awake and ready to go. Maybe Dr. Cohen's pills were taking him in the opposite direction— toward slowing down? A secret plot between her and Chris? The time they met, they'd gotten along famously.

"Take your time," Chris said, sliding a cup of coffee onto the night-stand. "She can wait."

She left, closing the door behind her.

He found his phone and called Ryder. "Bridget is here to get Ari," he said. "Did you want to talk with her?"

"It's okay," she said. "I think. She says she's going to stay at the cottage for now, until Dr. Gabbro's condition…uh…resolves."

"One way or the other," he said.

"Right."

"You know how that's looking?"

83

"I'm not supposed to talk to you," she said. "Oh Really's been kind of adamant about that."

"We're talking."

"Same as yesterday," she said. "But it doesn't look good." She sighed. "He'd better survive. I hate getting invested and putting in the time, only to have it snatched by the Staties."

"I know. We still do what we do."

"Gotta go," she said. "All right?"

Meaning she wasn't alone.

"Just a couple of yes or no question?'"

"Yes."

"You get anything useful from Fenton last night?"

"Uh…no."

"Sherman?'"

"Yes."

"Did…"

"Gotta go," she said. "See you later."

Which he took to mean if he wanted to know more it would involve one of those meetings in a dark parking lot they'd joked about. Cops joked about dark things. It helped them on their journey to the light.

It seemed like a thousand years since he'd been snoozing in the hammock. He wanted to go back to bed. Sleep the day away, untroubled by phone calls or people showing up with urgent problems. But it was Chris's vacation, too. She needed some time in the hammock without the demands of the family, too.

He got up and pulled on yesterday's slightly damp clothes, the reason they were damp making him smile. He carried his coffee cup into the living room.

Ari was sitting in a chair, arms folded, glaring at a woman seated across from her on the couch. The woman was absolutely nondescript. Middle aged. Middle sized. Plainish but not plain. Her hair was short but not cropped, a graying brown that could accurately be called mouse-colored. Her face was pleasant, but firm. She was a woman who could disappear in any crowd. She was holding a coffee cup and talking with Chris, very comfortable with ignoring Ari's glare.

"Here's Joe," Chris told her. "He can give you more details."

Burgess shook her hand. Got her full name: Bridget O'Toole. Asked how her drive had been. Fine. No problems. Why she'd come up early.

"Where are the kids?" he asked Chris.

"Sleeping," she said.

It was nine-thirty, so that seemed right. He was learning that teenagers would sleep as much as anyone would let them, a luxury he'd rarely been afforded. Neddy, now Ned, still asleep was a bigger surprise. He was more of a pop up and explore each new day type. He must have worn himself out yesterday.

"Let's talk outside," he suggested.

"You want some breakfast?" Chris asked.

"Soon. After I finish waking up."

They left Ari in her chair—nobody needed a mad at the world child around them—and settled at the picnic table.

After Burgess had filled the woman in on what had happened with Dr. Gabbro, he said, "Do you mind answering a few questions?"

"I don't mind at all," she said, with a faint trace of an Irish accent. "Though I think I probably answered them already for your colleague last night."

Torn between telling the truth—that Ryder wasn't his colleague—and getting some answers he badly wanted, Burgess went for a slight evasion. "Just confirming a few things," he said. "It's a puzzling situation."

"I'm sure it is." She nodded a vigorous affirmative "Dr. Gabbro can be a bit puzzling at the best of times, and I've been with him for years. He's the genuine article, an absent-minded professor. Mrs. Gabbro that was, before the divorce, she always despaired of him. Said he couldn't be relied on about anything unless it involved rocks. Don't see the attraction, myself. But the professor lives and breathes them. A kind and generous man, Dr. Gabbro, despite his eccentricities. So what was it you needed to know?"

"For starters, Ari told us that her mother is in Scotland and can't be reached. Is that the case?"

Another vigorous nod. "Oh. Mrs. Gabbro, she can be a fierce one, you know. Not very maternal, if you get my drift. Always happy to leave caring for Arielle to me. She and Arielle, you know, they were never easy with each other. So when she said she wanted a vacation where she couldn't be disturbed, Dr. Gabbro and I took her at her word. But how she could leave her only child like that, with no way of getting in touch, knowing about Dr. Gabbro's condition, I do not know. See, Mrs. Gabbro, her Christian name is Elyse, she's always been one put herself first."

She paused the flow of words for a moment, looking at Burgess. "I hope you don't get me wrong. I'm not speaking badly of her, Detective. She'd say the same thing about herself. She's always been a bit on the selfish side, see, and now she's moving on. She said she's lived enough of her life for others, which I took to mean the professor and Arielle, and it's her turn now."

She cast a quick glance toward the cottage and lowered her voice. "Though that man she intends to marry? He'll be no kind of father to the child. He's quite open about the fact that he doesn't like children. Has none of his own, see. And Arielle? Well, I love her, of course. I've been caring for her since she was born, but she's never been the easiest child. So how's that supposed to work out, see, with Arielle having to live with her mother and all and a man not used to children. Not interested, he says."

She huffed indignantly. "And her...Mrs. Gabbro...being the one insisted on custody."

To be on the safe side—and know all the players—Burgess got the intended's name. Anthony "Tony" Leblanc.

O'Toole cast another glance at the cottage. "The custody? It's not like she wanted Arielle. Did it for the money, see. She knew she'd get a lot more from the courts if she had the child. Not what Dr. Gabbro wanted. He and Arielle, they're closer as two peas, now, aren't they? But Elyse...Mrs. Gabbro...she got him all twisted around about how he'd have to give up his field work if he wanted to keep the child. Which certainly wasn't the case, him having me and all. As if I hadn't always looked after the child."

She sighed. "Such a mess. Of course, I stayed out of it. Not my place, see, to get mixed up in that, though of course if they'd had me into court and asked me, I would have told the judge that the child belonged to her father."

Burgess wondered if he'd ever have to ask a question or if this outpouring would answer everything he needed to know. But now Bridget O'Toole, her piece said, had fallen silent. Informative yet it felt false somehow. Almost theatrical. But some people were theatrical.

His turn. He said, "What can you tell me about Dr. Gabbro's health. His diabetes?"

"Ah. That. It's a puzzling situation, it is. I've been with him, the doctor and Mrs., since they were married. She never was one interested in keeping house, see. With Arielle since she was born. He's had the diabetes all along and always so very careful about managing it, see, because of his being out in the field and needing to be sure he could take care of himself. Your colleague, last night, she said that his works, which he uses to take care of himself, that they were gone and Arielle couldn't find them anywhere. That now, like I told her, it don't make sense. Not with someone as careful as him."

Chris said, happy to get away from this onslaught of words, said, "Can I get either of you more coffee?"

Burgess said, "Please?"

Bridget O'Toole said she was full up, thanks, having stopped on the road at one of those Dunking places.

"So, as far you know, Dr. Gabbro was never careless about his insulin?"

"Never. He even carried a whole extra set of the works, or whatever they're called, in his car or in his pack, if he was in the field. He told me once he never wanted to chance little Arielle having to spend all of her life with her mother. Which…" A long pause, while she stared at Burgess to be sure he got her meaning, "which might be the case if he doesn't recover."

A pause for breath, as though all this talking exhausted her. Burgess's impression was that the woman loved to talk. He also wasn't sure how much of what she was saying was the truth. Despite the apparently spontaneous quality of her speech, it felt almost rehearsed. Shaded, at least. By whom, and why, he had no idea. Or whether it was simply a role she played—that of the faithful, if gossipy servant. Loved the child, knew she was trouble. Yadda yadda.

"I'm sorry to be asking so many questions," he said, "but we really don't have anyone else to ask. Yet. Is Dr. Gabbro wealthy?"

"Oh, yes. He's quite wealthy. At least, that's what I've been led to believe. He certainly never worries about paying for anything. And when they were in the divorce, see, he was glad to give her, Mrs. Gabbro, whatever she wanted. I think, though it might be unkind to say it, that he just wanted her—the woman, the yelling, the scenes—gone. He likes a quiet life, Dr. Gabbro does. She was all 'let's have some people in' or 'we should take a trip, Bridget can watch Ari' or 'let's go out to dinner.' Never mind that I'd already fixed something."

"What about relatives? Does he have family members he is close to?"

Bridget considered.

Burgess waited, wondering whether there were too many or too few or whether she was pondering on her own particular definition of "close to."

After a bit, she said, "There's his sister Annabella. Bella. She's a Gabbro as well, as she kept her name when she was married. Divorced now. And he's got a younger brother, Daniel. They aren't so close though. He's…uh…kind of the black sheep of the family. Blew through his share of the family money pretty quick. He's more likely to come around for hand-outs than for company, but he's fond of Arielle. She's the only child among the three of them, see."

"Is Bella also close to Arielle?"

Bridget shook her head. "Not so much. I imagine she'd like to be, seeing as she's not got a child of her own, but she's not so good at how she goes about it. She seems to think the child should pay attention to her, and not the other way 'round, and Arielle's not going to fawn over someone just because that's what they want. Quite the opposite, really. She can be quite stubborn about how she is with people. Being nice to 'em and all."

"Is the sister also wealthy?"

Bridget considered this. She might be willing to talk his ear off, but she wanted to be precise about it. Finally she said, "She's got enough. Had a husband for a while who went through some of it, but she got smart and sent him packing. Plus, she's an attorney, so she has a good living."

"What about close friends?"

"Of the professor? There's not so many. He's kind of solitary, see. Likes his own company. There's that young fellow he has working for him. Peter Sherman. They're close. Sherman is like Gabbro when he was young. Loves nothing better than being out in the field."

"There's no new woman in Gabbro's life?" he asked.

Bridget sat up straighter and gave him a look that was a lot like Ari's glare. "Oh, her? The one that thinks he's going to marry her? Fat chance of that. I know what she's all about. It's marrying him for his money. She's not interested in him nor the child. He's at that age, see, where a man can get his head turned."

In his experience, men could get their heads turned at any age, often with disastrous results. "What can you tell me about her? Her name? Where she lives? The state of their relationship? Are they engaged?"

Another huff. This Bridget was a regular steam engine. "Her name is Delores Something Something Lopez. She lives in Cambridge, as do we. She's his assistant at the college. As for the state of their relationship, he thinks she's someone fun to spend time with when he's lonely, which she's got him thinking is a lot of the time, and she thinks they're engaged, although I've heard him say to her, 'Now, Delores, let's not rush things. We barely know each other and you don't have a relation-ship with Ari.' Of course, she doesn't want a relationship with Arielle. She wants the girl to be full-time with her mother."

Not someone likely to have harmed Dr. Gabbro, Burgess thought. By this time, he was feeling pretty sorry for Ari. Except for her father, no one seemed to want her very much, except as a pawn in their schemes. "What about enemies?" he said. "Do you know of anyone with a grudge against the professor who might want to harm him?"

"Now, how could anyone..." she began. Then stopped. Huffed. Sighed. "I wish I didn't have to be doing this. Talking bad about people."

He waited.

"But you know, the missus, Mrs. Gabbro that was, she's always after more, always thinking she didn't get a fair share, despite how generous he was. I can't speak for the new boyfriend, but likely he'd be with her on that, except for their being across the pond in Scotland and all. There a man, used to be Dr. Gabbro's assistant before he got Peter Sherman. His name's Alan Prescott. He resented being replaced by Sherman. But people don't try to kill each other over the likes of that."

Burgess had seen people kill each other for myriad reasons, some of them as shockingly trivial as a fight over a TV remote or who got the last beer.

"Anyone else? Relatives? Co-workers? Clients?"

She looked puzzled. "Clients?"

"People who contracted with Dr. Gabbro for his services. Like Orville Fenton."

"Why would one of his clients try to kill him?"

Burgess countered with another question. "Do you know whether Dr. Gabbro has someone who helps with scheduling, with billing, with writing his reports? A secretary, assistant, or office manager? Is that Delores Lopez?"

She hissed again. "That would be her. The woman that thinks he'll marry her."

Burgess wondered whether Bridget O'Toole had designs on Gabbro herself. Had she stuck faithfully by, waiting to be noticed as the woman he could trust and rely on?

One more question, or line of questions, and he was done. He was hungry and any unnecessary time in this woman's company was not how he wanted to spend his day. "Does Dr. Gabbro have an attorney? And someone who manages his finances?"

"With that, alas, I'm afraid I can't help you. I'm about keeping the house and the child. He and I never discussed his legal or financial matters. It'll all be in his files, should it come to that. Let us both pray that it doesn't."

With that he heartily agreed. He had one more question. "Is Ari in the habit of running away?"

Again she considered before answering. "Not in the usual sense," she said, finally. "Just, see, that her mother lives about three blocks from us, and sometimes Ari takes it into her head to come to us. And does. Even if it's not her time to be with her father. She's not very happy with her mother."

"Thank you. You've been very helpful. We'll be here if you and Ari need anything. Did you discuss how you'll get a key with Detective Ryder?"

Bridget O'Toole consulted her watch, a delicate gold one that didn't seem to suit her sturdy wrist. Burgess reminded himself that everyone had their vanities and predilections and it wasn't up to him to judge.

Of course, he was quite given to quick judgments. It went with the job. He also struggled to keep an open mind.

"I'm supposed to meet her at a quarter past ten. Which is now. I'll just pop in and get Arielle," she said.

She more lumbered than popped, which Burgess could relate to, being a lumberer himself.

Before he was on his feet, though, she was back out, holding Ari's little pink suitcase, a foot-dragging, head-bent Ari trailing behind.

"Bye, Ari," he said.

By way of farewell, she turned and glared. Yesterday's pale, scared fairy child had morphed into a sullen brat. Maybe being fought over but not wanted would do that. Burgess went inside to look for breakfast.

FIFTEEN

"That woman could talk anyone's ear off," Chris said when he came inside. "I could never do your job."

"And I could never be as patient and kind as you are. I suffer fools badly and I was born impatient."

"Tell me something I don't know," she said. "Actually, you know, you are patient and kind when the situation calls for it. Though impatient? Absolutely."

She put some bread in the toaster. "You want eggs?"

He sighed. "I want my day in the hammock back." He looked out the window, where the hammock beckoned. "But I think it's your turn."

"Eggs?"

"Two. Please. You know you don't have to wait on me, Chris." He was about to say he'd survived on his own for many years before he met her. Figured it wasn't the right thing to say. "Not that I don't like being waited on."

She broke two eggs into a pan. "If I really cared about you, it would be bran cereal with blue milk and maybe a small bowl of berries." She put his toast on a plate. "Only then you'd stop somewhere on your way in to work and grab something bad for you anyway. Wouldn't you?"

"I've got cop habits," he said. "Eat when you can is ingrained. You can't eat a salad while driving. And bran cereal would not be good for my disposition."

"Why I don't bother," she said.

She changed the subject. "So today, I think I'm going to sit on the deck and read a book. You can ride herd on the troops. Hey. Are you listening to me?"

He was watching two guys on a jet ski swoop on the inside of the buoy that marked the swimming area. Probably looking for Nina. He still remembered being a teenage boy. He knew the impact a girl like Nina—small but curvy with her marvelous red-gold hair—could have. But he was kind of a stickler for rules. His kids or someone else's could be swimming out there. He had the number of the warden who patrolled the lake. He could make a call if he needed to.

"Sorry. Watching that jet ski."

"Right. So you can scare away bad guys. I'm sure the patented Burgess glare will do the trick." She picked up her book. "I'm going outside to read in the hammock. And if some lost waif in trouble happens along, I'll send the creature on to you. You're the trouble magnet."

She got a pillow, her book, and a sun hat and went out.

Burgess finished his breakfast in peace. Enjoy peace when you can ought to be another cop motto, because those moments were few and far between. It was peaceful sitting at the breakfast bar, Chris outside reading. All three kids asleep. Sometimes he wished he could capture moments like this, like in a photograph. Or slow down time.

Wishing was a fairytale thing. Or a civilian thing. He'd barely finished washing his dishes when there was a knock at the door, the back door, and Fideau started barking. He said, "Fideau, quiet," and hurried to answer it before whoever was there woke the kids up. It was selfish, but he wanted a little more quiet time before the day exploded.

Nikki Ryder, all bright-eyed and ready to take on the day, was on the doorstep. "We need to talk," she said.

He put a finger to his lips and stepped outside. "Kids are still asleep," he said.

They stepped away from the cottage into the shade of a tall oak. "It's ten-thirty," she said.

"Teenagers."

She nodded. "So I guess you spoke with Bridget O'Toole?"

"If you can call listening and nodding speaking with someone. Actually, I did ask some questions. Same ones you asked, probably. Sounds like there are a number of potential suspects who might want Gabbro out of the picture. Ex-wife. Her boyfriend. His former assistant. Maybe some of Gabbro's siblings. Whoever is interested in the land Gabbro was exploring. Did I miss anybody?"

Ryder shook her head.

"So, what's up?"

"O'Reilly. He really wants you out of the picture. I'm pretty much forbidden to share anything with you. What did you do to piss him off so much?"

"Truth?"

"What else?"

"We had a joint operation a while back. I shared some info. He blabbed it to the wrong people, nearly blew the whole opp. I called him on it."

Ryder turned and looked toward the lake. "Do I want to know the whole story?"

"Probably better to preserve your innocence."

"Right." She smiled. "Innocent is always the first thing people assume about me. Sure you don't mean ignorance?"

He joined her in looking at the lake. It was a perfect August morning. "Being underestimated isn't always a bad thing. It can give you real advantage sometimes."

She shrugged. "I think I'm chronically underestimated and it pisses me off."

"I get it," Burgess said. "For various reasons, I've spent most of my career being pissed off."

"Unless you're chasing bad guys."

"Even then. People...bosses...command staff...have a way of interfering. Like doing the job isn't hard enough without rocks in the path."

"So here's the thing," Ryder said. "Neither of us was completely joking when we talked about meeting in a dark parking lot." She shrugged. "Territorialism often infuriates me. Probably because I'm female, and you know, we're pretty good at collaboration. And because it's just plain stupid to refuse anything helpful. The case came to you. And you're a great sounding board. But I am just a worker bee. I can talk to you now, because I'm already here. But going forward? I think Oh Really is gonna give me a partner to keep tabs on me."

"And?"

"You always were one to get right to the point. And so from now on, I'll try to keep you in the loop, but it may be at odd hours. And maybe in that parking lot. Or more particularly, in the lot of that convenience store down the road."

"If I can get away," he said. "I've got a partner watching me, too. One with some ideas about what it means to be on vacation." He watched the jet ski swooping back. Something was going to have to be done about that. "So where are we? Is Gabbro hanging on? Did you get everything you need from Bridget O'Toole?"

"Gabbro's unchanged. O'Toole talked my ear off. And I couldn't really get anything useful out of Fenton. What a pompous ass. It doesn't seem to have registered with him that keeping secrets might be the reason Gabbro is in the condition he's in. I don't know enough about his options on property. I don't know who else is interested. I don't know what Gabbro found that could possibly make someone want to kill him. That's what I'm looking into today. I'll nose around, talk to local people and the deputy who patrols this area, see what I can learn. The state geologist is away talking rocks with a room full of other geologists on the other side of the country, so I'll have wait on his insights."

"Sounds like Gabbro's domestic arrangements are complicated."

"If people didn't have complicated domestic arrangements, we wouldn't have jobs, Burgess."

"I'm on vacation," he said. "I have handed off complications to others."

"And I will try to respect that. I hope you'll be a sounding board, though. From time to time?"

"Absolutely," he said. "You being so innocent and all."

She punched his arm like he was her big brother. He figured that was kind of the role he was playing here. He'd been a pretty good big brother, though if you asked his sister Sandy she'd probably disagree.

"Keep me up on things when you can," he said. "If you can."

"Will do."

"What about searching for those missing items. His medication. His phone. You have a plan about those?"

"Why yes, Detective Burgess, I do. When my new partner arrives, we'll do a more thorough search of the property and then along the roadside out to the main road. We don't find anything there, we'll expand the search to out along the main road. Though a sensible bad guy—or gal—probably carried them away. Dumped in a trash can or a dumpster somewhere."

Burgess had an idea. "You might fingerprint the refrigerator."

"Why?"

"Because insulin needs to be refrigerated."

"Right." She nodded.

It was so easy to overlook things like that. Like checking Gabbro's car to see if someone had tried the locks. But he wasn't her boss or even her colleague. He was just a guy that trouble found whenever it went looking. And a guy who didn't want to offend her by making too many suggestions. Then he immediately made another. "You going to check his phone records?"

"Burgess. This is not my first rodeo."

"Right. Sorry. Not so innocent," he said.

"Exactly."

She walked off. Then turned with a smile and said, "Stay out of trouble."

He'd try. But that would be hard to do if trouble kept finding him.

Fideau nosed his hand, which was the animal's signal that Burgess needed to give him some attention. Burgess got the soggy tennis ball he kept for such occasions and they played for a while. He thought Fideau was an excellent addition to the family. Patient, well-trained, and fun.

The day passed uneventfully. True to her word, Chris stayed in the hammock, reading. Nina and Dylan seemed content to spend the time on their paddle boards. Balancing. Racing. Falling off. Laughing. Lying in the sun on their towels to warm up and then starting again.

Neddy floated around for a while in an oversized inner tube, then switched to his mask and snorkel and went searching for what might be on the floor of the lake. He popped up from time to time to report his findings. Fish. A turtle. Oh, ugh, an eel. He reported several beer cans and some bottles, which he collected in a little pile on the dock. The convenience store took returnables and had a nice stash of what, in Burgess's day, had been penny candy. Now it was nickel candy. Still something to get excited about. The boy was happily counting his riches.

Burgess was inside, fixing lunch for the troops, when Ned came bursting through the door, very excited, and handed Burgess a dripping insulated lunch bag. The bag was green with small cartoon animals on it.

"Look, My Joe. This is so cool. Do you think maybe we could clean it up and I could use it for my snack for school? I'll bet it fell off somebody's boat. But I found it so I can keep it, right?"

Burgess's investigative brain immediately said insulin. Need to keep it cold. What if? He said, "Put it in the sink and go back outside, Ned. You're dripping wet."

"But I found it, My Joe. It's mine. I want to see what's inside."

"Outside. Towel. Now. We'll look at it when you're dry."

Actually, they wouldn't. He would put on gloves, check the contents, and if it was what he suspected it might be, he'd set it aside to dry and no one would touch it, just in case it was still possible to raise fingerprints.

Ned would hate him. Nikki Ryder might feel like he was stepping on her toes, and he was feeling like some cartoon character who kept saying "not my fault' despite being present every time something happened.

He was putting on gloves when a still dripping Ned came racing back in. "I'm dry," he said.

"And I'm the man in the moon."

Ned, who could be pretty literal, studied him. "Nope," he said. "You're not."

"And you're not dry. Go back outside and finished drying off."

Instead, the boy who didn't miss much said, "Why are you putting on gloves?"

People were often wrong when they thought they could fool kids. He opted for the truth.

"Because it might be Ari's father's missing medicine. I want to check. And if someone bad threw it in the lake, there might be fingerprints."

"You mean like someone tried to hurt Ari's dad on purpose?"

Burgess realized he hadn't told the kids anything about Gabbro's situation. Too late now. Then he had an idea.

"Hold on while I look inside." He carefully unzipped the bag and opened it. Definitely not someone's lost lunch. He had to call Ryder.

"Ned, I have to call the detective who is investigating whether something bad happened to Ari's father. Now, thanks to you, we know his insulin bag ended up in the water. That's important evidence you found. Now, we suspect there may also be a missing phone," he said. "Maybe someone threw that in the lake, too. Think you might be able to find it?"

"I'll look," Ned said eagerly, excited to be part of an investigation. "Is there a reward?"

Burgess didn't believe in rewarding people for doing their civic duty, but Ned was just a kid. "Sure," he said. "Five dollars to spend down at the store?"

"Oh yeah. That'd be great!"

Ned was out the door before Burgess could say more. The phone might not be down there, or was buried. But Neddy—Ned—was a tenacious child. If it was down there, there was as good a chance that he'd find it as if they brought in a team of divers.

Burgess set the lunch bag on a stack of paper towels and called Ryder.

SIXTEEN

Ryder said, "I guess you've missed me, huh? Jeez, Burgess, it's only been a few hours. I've got nothing new to share."

Right. Like he was some overeager rookie? "Too busy to miss you," he said. "I'm making lunch."

"Oh. And you wanted to know if I'd like a sandwich?"

"More like I wanted to know if you'd like to come a pick up the lunch cooler filled with insulin that my kid just dragged up from the bottom of the lake."

Her response was somewhere between a sigh and a growl. "I don't believe this. We've been out here pawing through the bushes for hours. And you what? Just somehow find it?"

What the hell was that 'somehow' about? Like he could help it if Ned found some evidence? He repressed his instinctive, "You want me to throw it back?" She was probably tired and sweaty and bug-bitten. That could make a person less than charming. Instead he said, "It's here waiting for you when you want to collect it. Who knows? Maybe the lab can raise some fingerprints?"

"On my way," she said. "I don't suppose you've got the missing phone, too?"

"I've got my diver out looking for it now."

"And your diver is how old?"

"Nine. Well, almost ten, as he'll be quick to tell you."

"You're not worried he might muck things up?"

"Give me a break, Nikki. How does a little kid muck up the bottom of a lake?"

"With his feet."

Burgess considered hanging up. He went for silence instead. Silence could work wonders.

"Sorry. It's hot and buggy and I'd rather be swimming in the lake and Oh Really has saddled me with a newbie who seems to have no concept of personal hygiene. The stink seems to keep the bugs off him but drives them all to me. Crap. Listen to me. I'm not usually such a baby."

"Not so innocent," he said.

"You got that right. Okay. I'm on my way."

Burgess finished making sandwiches, piled them on a platter, and poured a bag of chips into a bowl. He put carrot sticks and sugar pod peas in another bowl. Put it all on a big tray with a stack of paper plates and napkins, and carried it all out to the picnic table. He went back inside for paper cups and a big pitcher of lemonade. He set that on the table and called Chris and the kids.

Ned put down his mask and snorkel, wrapped himself in a towel, and announced, "I found important evidence in one of My Joe's cases and now I'm looking for more," to his big brother and sister.

"Way to go, Little Bro," Dylan said.

Nina said, "Really, Neddy? What did you find?"

Chris gave him a "what are you getting the kids into" look, so Burgess explained the mystery that surrounded Dr. Gabbro's health situation. He told them that it was not his case but he knew the detectives who were working on it were looking for some items which were missing from the cottage and would be glad to have Ned's find.

He was reaching for a sandwich when Ryder appeared, looking hot and disheveled. "Sorry to disturb you all. If I could just have a moment with Burgess?"

"I found it!" Ned said, leaping up. "You need a moment with me."

This was what you got, Burgess thought, catching Chris's attempt to hide her smile, *when you put so much effort into bringing a traumatized child out of his shell.*

"This is Ned," he said. "And Ned, this is Detective Nikki Ryder. She works for the Cumberland County Sheriff's Department."

After they shook hands, Ned said, "Does that mean you don't work with My Joe?"

"Only when our cases overlap, which sometimes happens." Ryder turned toward the lake. "Is it possible for you to show me where you found the bag?"

The boy looked out at the lake, shook his head, and said, "Did you bring your bathing suit?"

"I'm afraid not. Maybe after I collect the bag from your dad and you finish lunch, you could swim out and show me?"

"I can try," Ned said, hesitating. "It's right near where I saw that eel. Only the eel swam away, so that won't help much, I guess." He considered. "There was a bottle down there, too. It was broken, though, so I wouldn't be able to return it. So I left it there. I might be able to find it again."

"That would be great if you could," Ryder said.

"Okay. I'll try. Now can I show you the bag I found?"

When Ryder hesitated, looking at Burgess, Ned said, "I won't touch it."

"A detective's child," Ryder said.

Burgess nodded. He knew Chris wasn't pleased about having family lunch interrupted, nor about one of the kids getting involved in a case. Once again Burgess felt like a defensive little kid saying, "Not my fault." It was only his fault in that he'd responded to the summons to the Gabbro's cottage not only like a neighbor but like a detective. He'd noticed things. Wondered about things. He couldn't help it. If a child had shown up bleeding, Chris would have responded like a nurse. It was who they were.

He knew better than to say anything.

"Let's show the detective that bag, Ned," he said.

As the boy turned to lead them into the cottage, Ryder's phone rang. She looked down, made a face, and answered. The face was all Burgess need to know it was Oh Really? calling.

She didn't step away to take the call, which he understood was because she wanted him to overheard. Oh Really? was loud enough to be heard across the lake. His "What the fuck, Ryder?" blasted out of the phone.

Chris frowned.

Nina and Dylan exchanged looks and smothered giggles.

Burgess knew Ryder was showing, rather than telling, that the partner Oh Really? had assigned was the classic suck-up who'd spied on her and called the boss as soon as she took the call about the bag and headed over to the cottage.

"What the fuck?" was followed by "Why the hell are you hanging around with Burgess when I told you to keep him out of this?"

Ryder's voice was flat and neutral as she said, "Burgess's son found what may be Dr. Gabbro's insulin bag at the bottom of the lake."

There was a moment of silence as Oh Really? tried to twist this against Burgess in some way, came up short, and snapped, "Well, get the goddamned bag and get back to work."

Still in a neutral voice, though the tension in her body told a different story, Ryder said, "If the bag is there, the phone may be, too. You want to get some divers out?"

That pretty much shut him up. Along with being as dense as a piece of granite, O'Reilly was also known for being a bully. He liked to yell at his people. Ryder's calm questions were taking that away from him.

"Do it," he said, and disconnected.

Ryder smiled at Ned. "Sorry you had to hear that. My boss sometimes has terrible manners."

Ned waved an airy hand. "It's okay, Detective Ryder. My Joe doesn't swear at home, but I know other people do."

My Joe followed Ryder and Ned into the cottage, still feeling Chris's disapproval through the closed door, and feeling regret about his uneaten sandwich. The cop's life. His life. Right now suck was the word. One Chris didn't like the kids—or him—to use.

Ned hung back, watching Ryder put on gloves and carefully check the bag he'd found.

She nodded and looked at Burgess. "Got a paper bag I could use?"

He produced the bag. She carefully lifted the lunch bag and put it inside. Nodded at Burgess. Said, "Ned, thank you for finding this. It's a valuable part of our investigation."

"As soon as I've finished lunch, and waited, like Chris makes me do before I swim, I'll go back and see if I can find the phone." He hesitated, probably remembering her comment about sending out divers, "Unless you don't want me to?"

"I do want you to," she said.

Carefully holding the paper bag, she looked at Burgess. "I'm off then. Sorry to disrupt your lunch." An apologetic smile. "Your vacation. Your life."

He nodded. "Trouble finds me. Watch your back."

"Looks like I'll have to."

She left through the other door and he and Ned went back to finish lunch.

Nina and Dylan were still eating. Chris was staring at her empty plate like something was supposed to be there. Ned, ignoring the undercurrents and flushed with excitement at getting to be part of an investigation, started gobbling his sandwich. The sooner he was done, the sooner he could get back to looking for that phone.

Burgess ate more slowly, trying to figure out how to fix things with Chris. He knew "But I didn't do anything" wouldn't fly. This wasn't about logic. This was about dreams and expectations. Her vision of a summer vacation with the family she'd wanted for so long.

He looked over at the two bright orange kayaks that came with the cottage. Then at his son.

"Dylan, can you keep an eye on Ned for an hour? Chris and I want to go kayaking."

Dylan, who seemed to enjoy the role of big brother, nodded. "Sure, Dad." Then, with a wicked grin, added, "Don't you and Chris want to try out the paddle boards?"

"We do. Just not right now. Maybe after dark, when you kids are asleep and no one can see us wobbling until we fall off."

Nina was looking out at the lake, where the two boys on jet skis were heading their way. "Dad, is there anything we can do about those jerks? Those jetski waves make it hard to use our paddle boards and they're coming into the swimming area. Someone could get hurt, like Neddy or Ari."

The big sister, who'd had to be a caretaker for her little brother since their mother died. Was killed by their father. She shouldn't have to be worrying about things like that on this perfect summer day.

"I'll take care of it," he said.

Chris had stopped staring at her plate and switched her gaze to him. "We're going kayaking?"

"Why not? Unless you don't want to?"

"Of course I want to. I just didn't think…" She quit while she was ahead.

Burgess wasn't the kayaking type. Not because he didn't enjoy outdoor activities or water sports, though. Because he was always working. Kayaking was the perfect solution to her bad mood. No one would bother him with crime-related problems while he was out on the water.

Burgess figured her gloom was lifting. His clues were the way she bounced out of her seat and started quickly clearing the table. While she did that, he called the warden who patrolled the lake and told him about the boys on jet skis. Got the assurance that things would be taken care of.

He went inside for a bathing suit and a hat. Gave Ned the necessary warning to obey his brother. Put on a life jacket. Remembered his phone was still in his pocket. He took it inside and left it on the counter.

To hell with the problems of the world. He was on vacation.

SEVENTEEN

It was an almost perfect trip. They paddled along the shore of the lake, enjoying the cries of children and the laughs of vacationing adults. It was one of those amazingly clear blue August days with clouds just beginning to mass on the horizon. As they piled up, they looked like mountains of whipped cream on top of an ice cream sundae. Chris's smile, as she paddled along, was the cherry on top.

Burgess tried to let himself be, to enjoy the moment and not let his thoughts drift to questions about Gabbro and how his essential medicine had ended up in the lake. A lifetime of assessing criminal activity was hard to shake off, so he concentrated on Chris's pleasure, her smile at being together on a lovely day. It almost worked. For minutes at a time he was just a guy paddling along a peaceful summer lake. Chris had no idea how hard for him that was and he didn't need her to.

They were almost back to the cottage when he saw the boys on jet skis again. They were swooping far inside the buoy marking the no boats zone, zipping close to the dock where Nina and Dylan were lying in the sun. He didn't see Ned, which worried him. He started paddling faster.

Beside him, Chris said, "What?" as Burgess yelled, "Hey! Stop that! Get out of here!"

The boys, obviously believing they were untouchable, zoomed close to the kayaks, almost overturning them, then zipped off, laughing. Burgess memorized their registration numbers. It didn't look like his call to the warden had done any good, but these kids hadn't seen the last of him.

He and Chris reached the shore and Burgess helped her haul up her kayak. They raced onto the dock where two apparently oblivious teenagers lounged in the sun. There was no sign of Ned.

"Where is Ned?" Burgess demanded.

Dylan jumped up, anxiously searching the water beside the dock. "He's right…" The pointing arm froze in mid-air. He looked around. "He was right there a minute ago…honestly, Dad, I've been watching him. He was right there."

As though in response to their anxiety and that sudden stab of dread, a cloud drifted over the sun, darkening the bright afternoon.

A heart-stopping moment. Burgess was about to say something scathing about Dylan being not much of a lifeguard when Ned popped up, waving something in his hand, a look of absolute joy on his face. "Look, My Joe! Look, Chris! Look, guys. I found it! I found the phone."

Dylan's frozen arm dropped. Burgess choked back his remark. Chris gave an audible sigh of relief.

"Good job, Ned," Burgess said. "Let's see what you've got."

Beside him, Chris gave Dylan a hug.

They all watched Ned swim one handed over to the dock. He shot up the ladder, dropped his mask and snorkel, and handed Burgess the phone.

Burgess held it gingerly between two fingers. He was proud of Ned for finding it, it was important, but he didn't want to deal with it right now. They were having such a nice family afternoon. He hated to bring Ryder or her partner back here, resented even a small additional interference in their peaceful day.

Figuring sooner was better than later, he headed inside, a grinning, capering Ned trailing behind.

Chris said, "Ned. Towel."

Dylan said, "Way to go, Little Bro."

Dylan's words reminded Burgess that his son had been raised with two younger siblings by a mother who loved them all and a father who favored his own kids over the one he'd inherited through the marriage. Dylan never mentioned them, but Burgess wondered if he missed them. Burgess had only learned of his son's existence when the mother, an old girlfriend who'd never disclosed her pregnancy, died, and her widower was only too happy to send Dylan to the father he'd never known.

"Oh, Dad," Dylan said, "Ari came over a little while ago. She wanted to know if she could swim with us. I felt like a rat telling her no, but without you and Chris here, it didn't feel right. She's a funny kid, you know, she can be so pitiful and needy that you want to take care of her, and then it's like a switch's been flipped. I said no and she turned into this sullen, angry brat and stomped away."

Just what Burgess had observed. "Yeah. She's a mystery, that one," he agreed. He took the phone inside.

Ned, wrapped in a towel but still dripping, followed him inside, asking questions as fast as he could talk. Burgess answered what he could. The boy's last question was the most predictable: when would he get his five dollars and when would Burgess take him to the store to spend it?

"Depends on how the day goes. Probably tomorrow morning. Think you can wait that long?"

Ned gave him a squint-eyed look. "Of course I can wait. I'm not a baby. I'm almost ten." He watched as Burgess tore off a pile of paper towels and set the dripping phone on them. Burgess's mind was running the questions he'd ask if it was his own case. Could the phone be revived or data retrieved? What might be on it that was useful and could they get it from Gabbro's service provider? What about fingerprints on the phone? Where had Ned found it? Closer to their cottage or to Gabbro's, and how far out? If they'd waited for Ryder's divers, the spot would have been marked and they'd know these things. But if Ned hadn't found the lunch bag, they might never have looked in the lake, when they had only the word of a rather unstable child that things were missing at all.

Still, Ryder had been looking.

It was time to call her. Again. As he dialed, he wondered what he'd get this time. Another impatient snap? Would she come herself or send her partner, the miserable little snitch?

He got an exasperated "What now, Burgess?" that made him so glad he'd bothered to call. He knew the case—and concern for victims—trumped personality conflicts, but he was on vacation.

"Ned found the phone," he said, and because he was feeling perverse, he added, "it's in the kitchen if you want it," and hung up. So much for rest and relaxation restoring him.

He went back outside, Ned trailing behind him, and looked out at the lake. It was getting to be the time of day when things quieted down, but those annoying jet skis, like wasps in the fall, were still swarming around and coming too close.

Did the world *want* to try his temper? He called the warden again. Earlier, he'd just left a voicemail message, knowing, from their boat captain, that these boys were notorious and already on the warden service's radar. Were they so well connected they were untouchable?

This time, someone answered, so he identified himself as Detective Sergeant Burgess from Portland, explained they were renting a cottage on the lake, and said they were being harassed by two young men on jet skis who were violating the safe shore area, threatening his children's safety, and had nearly swamped their kayaks a little earlier. He gave the registration numbers for the jet skis, then asked, "Do they have some kind of special privilege on this lake or can you shut them down?"

A gruff voice with a hint of amusement said, "They *think* they have privilege, for sure. This is our fifth call today and I've cited them twice. Six citations this week, which puts them into Class E category. Guess it's time to speak with their parents. Let me know if they bother you again."

Parents like that—the ones who had to know their kids were breaking the law repeatedly—thought they were protecting their kids from evil law enforcement but were actually creating monsters. He could write a book, "How to Create Monsters," and parents who reflexively cleared the way for their misbehaving kids would be among stars of the show. He still remembered being a teenager. Was reminded of it more frequently when he looked at his son and saw himself. But while he understood being reckless and making a mistake, he wasn't sympathetic to repeatedly putting other people at risk and thinking that was fun.

Chris interrupted his reverie with a warm hand on his arm. "Do you mind driving the kids down to the store? There's a consensus that we need ice cream sundaes after dinner, which means we need more ice cream and some chocolate sauce. And someone is eager to collect five dollars and go on a candy spree." She gave him the smile that had caught him in the first place. One he couldn't say no to.

"Sure. Just let me change. I am not going to the store in my bathing suit."

"No problem. Take your time. Fideau and I are going to sit here and read."

He thought it pretty likely the dog could read. It certainly read minds, and probably hearts. At least when it wasn't distracted by a squirrel or needed to protect the family from strangers.

"You need anything?"

"If they have gin and tonic, I see my afternoon getting even better."

He had one chore to do before that errand. He asked Ned if he could find the spot where the phone had been. When he got a "yes," he rooted around in the storage shed, found a float, some rope, and a brick, and gave them to Ned to mark the spot. He wanted to see if it was possible that Ari had tossed the phone. After he and Ned had experimented by throwing a few rocks, Ned's marker said that wasn't likely. Ned's throws were far short of the mark, and he was taller and stronger than Ari.

When that was done, Chris said, "Guys, Dad will take you to the store if you get dressed pronto."

A file of children in bathing suits rushed past them, heading inside.

"I'll see about that gin. Oh. I called Nikki Ryder about the phone Ned found. It's on the kitchen counter. Someone will be along to collect it. I don't need to be here for that. And Fideau will definitely let you when they arrive."

"I never thought about having a dog," she said, "but I like it. He's good company and he's as protective as you are."

"Replaced by a dog." He sighed.

"Did I say replaced? And if they have limes, get one or two. I'm envisioning a lovely summer evening."

The trip to the store was a trip. Burgess was learning that an expedition with all three kids was never uncomplicated. Nina wanted special low calorie frozen yogurt, Dylan thought that was stupid, and while they argued and Ned took forever to choose his candy, Burgess snagged chocolate sauce, a can of whipped cream, and bottle of gin, two bottles of tonic, two limes, more junk food, and a six-pack of beer. He told Ned to hurry up and told Dylan and Nina they could each choose an ice cream, and he got a salami, a baguette of crisp French bread, some brie, and a bottle of white wine. He figured he'd better get out before he broke the bank. They paid and were on their way to Burgess's truck when a green warden service truck pulled in beside them.

The green-clad warden who got out looked at Burgess's car and at Burgess and said, "Detective?"

Burgess nodded.

"I've spoken to those boys. And their parents. Gave them more tickets and told them they'll be getting a summons to court." He shook his head. "Entitlement goes right through the roof around here, come summer. Just a head's up—those are bad, bad kids. You might keep an eye out, the next few days."

"Thanks for the warning."

Burgess told the kids to get in the car. As they scrambled in, he said, in a low voice, "You mean the next few nights?"

"Afraid I do."

Burgess thanked him again and headed home. Even though it meant a potential interference with his quiet vacation, he felt a little elated. Bad guys—young or old—were something he understood, and now he even had a watchdog.

EIGHTEEN

Back home, they shoved their ice cream into an already stuffed refrigerator and put the rest of their purchases away. The cell phone was gone.

While the kids settled down with books and devices, Burgess fixed two gin and tonics—heavy on the gin—and carried them outside. Chris was curled up in an Adirondack chair, reading. She looked up when came out, smiled, and held out her hand. "For me?"

"This is what you ordered, right?"

"Right. Guess I'm still getting used to being with someone who listens to what I say and genuinely wants to make me happy."

That was nice to hear. "Sure you don't want to marry me?" he said. "Almost Mrs. Burgess?"

She looked down at the diamond on her finger. "I'm certainly tempted." She moved on, as he knew she would. "So some guy came to get that phone. Young. Abrupt. No manners at all." She shrugged. "Maybe he was just scared. Fideau didn't take to him and let him know it. I'm learning that our dog is a good judge of character."

"Haven't met him, but O'Reilly, Nikki Ryder's boss, assigned him to watch her. In part because he doesn't want Ryder talking to me."

"That's just stupid."

He sat in the chair beside her. "When I was a kid, I wanted a dog so badly. I used to beg my mother, couldn't we please have a dog. She always said no, and never explained why. When I was older, I realized there were two very good reasons. First, because we could barely feed ourselves. There wasn't anything left over for dog food. But the bigger reason was that my father was such a bully, such a violent and manipulative man, he would have used hurting the dog as a way to control her. Another way to control her. Control all of us. She didn't want her children exposed to that."

Chris set down her drink and put her hand over his. "Well, you've got one now."

"Seems more like he has me."

"With all the looking out you do, it's only fair you get a little looking after."

They sipped their drinks and listened to late afternoon bird calls. It was a peaceful time of day. He tried not to think about Gabbro and Ari and what might be going on next door. About the warden's warning and whether he should take it seriously. He liked being a detective. Well, he just *was* a detective. Like it or not, it was deeply ingrained. At moments like this, though, he wondered what it would be like to have taken some different path, one that didn't have him sitting beside a peaceful Maine lake next to a lovely woman wondering what might go wrong.

He let the silence wash over him, being as present as he could. Then the silence was disturbed by his stomach's rumble.

Chris laughed. "That the old cop gut wondering what's for dinner?"

"I guess it is."

"Almost Mrs. Burgess thinks we're having pizza, and believe it or not, that little store delivers."

He couldn't believe it. But it was true that many Maine businesses made most of their money from June to October, so offering services to people on the lakes made a lot of sense.

"Pizza sounds good. Not having to drive to pick it up sounds even better. Who is in charge of dinner tonight?"

"Dylan and Nina. He's calling in the order and she's going to make a salad."

"Great. So the old folks just get to sit here and watch the lake?"

"Exactly." She laughed. "You know I'm not old, Joe, don't you?"

Chris was forty-two. Burgess was old. Or felt old. Especially lately. Waiting for Dr. Cohen's magic was frustrating.

"I know. I meant older than—"

"I know what you meant."

They settled into a companionable silence. On vacation. The kids organizing dinner. It was great.

"We all set for tomorrow?" he asked.

"When the hordes arrive?"

"Yes."

"I've got tons of burgers and dogs and buns. I've got coleslaw. Lemonade. Those cute little bottles of Coke. Sandy is making a potato salad. Terry and Michelle are bringing watermelon, whoopee pies, and squirt guns. She wasn't sure, because of the baby and all, but I think Stan and Lily are bringing chocolate chip cookies. And beer. And your sister Moira is bringing wine. Chips and dip. And a veggie platter for people who don't eat chips. Oh, and Doro is making her special bean salad. I promise you, there will be enough to eat."

"Gonna be a madhouse."

"I know," she said happily. "I'm going to like it."

After a long silence, she said, "And this time, you are not going to get called out to some awful crime. Maybe Terry and Stan, Joe, but not you. Promise me."

Burgess was good at reading voices and this one was full of menace. "I'm on vacation," he said, hoping that would be answer enough. He didn't like to make promises he might have to break. Despite the peace, despite how restful this felt, with the lake lapping and loons beginning their evening concert, his cop gut was telling him there was trouble on the horizon.

He told it to settle down, and like a well-trained dog, it did. But its shadow still lurked there.

Chris set her empty glass on the wide arm of the chair and stood. "I'll go tell the kids it's time to start planning dinner. Could take a while to get that pizza delivered and someone who will remain unnamed is hungry."

She picked up the glass, and said, through a yawn, "I'm going to make another. You want one?"

"Sure. Go light on the gin, though."

"You got it."

She went inside. He stayed in his chair, thinking. Could they have a big party right next door and not invite Ari and her caretaker? It would please Ned to have someone his own age. It would not please Chris, who wanted to keep the Gabbro situation at an arm's length. He decided he'd let her make the call. And not tonight. Tonight things were peaceful and going so well, why inject controversy into the equation?

She came back, gave him his drink, and curled up in her chair again.

"We should get some chairs like this for our back deck. They're comfortable."

"Kind of big." He was imagining hauling them up the stairs.

"Or for the yard. And you know, I've been thinking that maybe it's time to get rid of your tenants and take over the whole house."

Fine with him. When he'd lived there alone, it had been financially sensible to have tenants in the downstairs apartment. But if he was honest, he was tired of the smell of other people's cooking drifting up the stairs. Tired of reminding the kids to not wear shoes in the house and walk quietly. Tired of those periodic complaints about things that needed to be repaired. "Their lease is up soon," he said. "How were you thinking of using the space?"

"Just maybe as a place for Dylan to have his own room. And maybe space for the kids to gather with their friends so we could have some peace and quiet. Like, I don't know, a rec room? With a kitchen and an extra bathroom. Do you know that I've never seen it?"

He hadn't realized that.

"Mostly I want the driveway and the garage and the back yard just for us. No one watching our comings and goings or being disturbed by them. I want to start a garden next spring. Gardening is getting very popular, you know. You might even get into it."

Burgess thought it was enough to keep the lawn mowed, the bushes trimmed, and the house repaired so they didn't live in a hovel. But he was no homemaker. The changes Chris had wrought in his life were all positives except her dislike of the way his job owned him and made her scared.

Dylan stuck his head out. "Pizza's coming in twenty-five minutes. You want to eat inside or out?"

Burgess slapped at a mosquito on his arm. There was no breeze tonight. "In," he said.

"Out," Chris said. "I've got bug spray and citronella candles."

"Better get them," he said. "I'm donating a lot of blood to the mosquito red cross."

She went inside to get them.

Despite the bugs, he stayed in the chair. Something family vacation didn't afford was time alone and he craved it.

Time alone. Time to think. Then again, maybe time to think wasn't such a good idea right now. His thoughts would go immediately to Gabbro and who might want to harm him. He turned sideways to look over at the next door cottage. It seemed too dark and quiet. Maybe Bridget O'Toole had taken Ari back to Massachusetts.

But Dylan said she'd been over in the afternoon, wanting to swim with Ned. Maybe they went out for dinner.

"I will not worry about it," he muttered, as he continued to stare at the cottage, looking for a light.

NINETEEN

The effect of sun and swimming made everyone so sleepy they were all in bed before ten. Burgess was tired but not sleepy, so he lay in the bed beside Chris trying to stay still and not wake her. Eventually he decided that two generous gin and tonics were likely to keep her asleep for a while and he got up quietly, pulled on pants and shirt, and went to sit in the living room.

It was a very dark night with beautiful stars, a soft breeze, and the kind of hush that falls on the world when most people are asleep. It was his favorite time. He sat without turning on a light and listened to the night sounds, content until he heard a sound that wasn't right.

He stood, crossed to the door, and wiggled his feet into his shoes. Then, recalling the warden's cryptic warning, he got his gun and his flashlight and let himself out the door, closing it slowly so it wouldn't do what he'd always thought of as the "cottage slam."

On the deck he paused, utterly still, listening. He heard feet crunching on gravel and the faint whisper of voices. He stepped down from the deck and went around the side of the cottage, pausing at the corner to listen again. Fideau came with him, somehow knowing to be quiet.

The voices were close now, and some rustling sounds told him his nocturnal visitors were crouched down near the back door.

He heard one voice say, "Go ahead. Do it!"

Whatever it was, it wasn't good. He stepped around the corner, absolutely quiet, walking the way he'd learned to walk years ago in a dangerous foreign country, a quiet walk that had served him well over the years. He was less than four feet away when he snapped on the light.

Two teenage boys that he figured were the ones from the jet skis were bent down, shoving balls of crumpled up newspapers under the wooden steps. A pile of sticks were nearby. One of them was holding a box of wooden kitchen matches. It didn't take a detective to know what they were up to.

Cops spent their lives exercising control in the face of awful human behavior, and Burgess was no exception. Where the safety of his family was involved, though, Burgess allowed himself to feel his rage.

He said, "Police. Drop the matches. Stand up, face me, and put your hands on your heads." Not so loud it would wake those sleeping inside but loud enough to make the need for cooperation clear.

One them stood, the other shifted in his crouch until his back was to the cottage, getting ready to run.

Burgess said, "Don't even think about it. You run, you'll be sorry. I'm an armed police officer."

The boy rose, stood beside his companion, and put his hands on his head. They looked surprised. Sullen. Shifty.

Burgess walked them over to his truck. Said, "Face the truck. Put your hands on the roof and keep them there."

He got handcuffs from his bag and cuffed them together with the cuffs running through the door handle. He was about to search them when one of the boys said, "Look, mister, do you know who I am?"

Burgess had five dollars for each time he'd heard that, he'd be rich and could retire.

"I don't care," he said.

"Well, you should care, because——"

"Lower your voice. My family is sleeping." He snapped it out in gruff, angry tones. They're trying to set a cottage full of sleeping people on fire and they don't get that it's serious?

117

"Because you're going to be in a lot of trouble if I get arrested," the kid continued.

Burgess said, "And so are you. Now be quiet. Don't talk. You've got nothing to say that I want to hear."

"Look, mister…"

"Detective. Or Sergeant. Not mister."

"Look, Detective . ." Little pissant couldn't keep the sneer from his voice. "We were just fooling around, you know. It's no big deal. No reason to call the police."

"Really? You've got crumpled newspaper and kindling stuffed under a wooden step attached to a cottage where people are sleeping. You've got matches in your hand. And it's no big deal? Wrong. It's a very big deal. An aggravated criminal mischief kind of a deal. A class C crime kind of a deal."

"We didn't start the fire." The other boy, in a shaky voice. He, at least, seemed to understand the seriousness of this.

"Come on, Mister. We didn't mean anything. We weren't going to hurt anybody."

"Detective," Burgess said. "And just how did you plan to keep that from happening? You bring a fire extinguisher with you? You planned to hang around to be sure the fire didn't get out of control?"

"It was just…you know…kind of a prank," the scared boy said.

Some prank. Maybe burn down a cottage and kill some people? Burgess understood adolescent brains were still developing but this was something a seven-year-old knew was dangerous and wrong.

"Be quiet," he said. "You're annoying me."

He searched them, took their wallets and their phones, and checked their ages—both seventeen—and their names. One of them was the son of the president of the state senate. Big whoop. He left them there and stepped away to call the sheriff's department. He told the dispatcher where he was, who he was, and that he'd just found two teenagers attempting to set fire to the cottage where he and his family were sleeping. He said he was holding them until deputies could arrive. He asked that they approach without lights or sirens since people in other cottages were also sleeping.

He figured mentioning attempted arson would get him help in a hurry and he was not wrong.

He didn't share their names. They could pull the "do you know who I am?" card when the deputies arrived. Given their attitudes, their behavior on the jet skis today, and what the warden had said, local police might already be quite familiar with the lads.

Before the sheriff's department arrived, he used his flashlight and his phone to snap pictures of the scene. Then he took pictures of the two boys.

He didn't speak to them. There was nothing to say and he wasn't interested in hearing any more threatening or self-serving bullshit. One of them, Mr. Do-You-Know-Who-I-Am, kept trying to speak. After Burgess told him a few times to be quiet, Burgess got his taser out, showed it to him, and asked if he needed to use it. The kid finally shut up.

They were good-looking kids. Tanned and well-nourished, with shaggy sun-blonded hair, and looked enough alike to be brothers. Burgess figured them for cousins, with the mouthy one the instigator and the quiet one the follower. The quiet one had the good sense to look scared. Trying to burn down a house full of sleeping people wasn't just a big joke.

Burgess shivered. His cop gut had come through once again. But what if he'd been sleeping?

Before the deputies arrived, his phone rang. Nikki Ryder. She skipped hello, went straight to, "I just heard. Is everyone okay?"

"Everyone's okay because I was awake, Nikki. Otherwise, very likely everyone would maybe be dead. Speaking of sleeping, why aren't you in bed?"

She countered with a question of her own. "Who are they?"

He gave her the names.

"Crap," she said. "Them again. Danny Sterling-Jones will be the leader. Sean Jones is his cousin. Follows Danny around and lets himself get talked into trouble. The two of them are like a juvenile crime wave. We've been scooping them up all summer for small stuff. Lawyers do their mumbo jumbo or our soft-hearted judge doesn't want to ruin promising young lives, and they walk. As a result, Sterling-Jones believes he's untouchable."

"So he told me. Many times. Not this time, though. If they get away with this, Nikki, they're going to kill someone before the season's over."

"You don't have to tell me that."

"I *do* have to tell you." Burgess was stunned by the anger he felt. Professional distancing be damned. This was his family.

"I hear you," she said. A shrinky, throw away phrase he'd usually dismiss. But she meant she heard his anger. His fear. His so-far repressed desire to beat those to kids to a bloody pulp and dump them somewhere far from help. His shaky grip on self-control.

"Thank you," he said. "So why are you still up? It's one in the morning."

"Trying to track down Peter Sherman. He called and left a message for me. He sounded scared. Or upset. Said it was urgent. But I can't find him."

"You check Gabbro's cottage?"

"Not yet. I just got in from something else. Got the message and started looking for him."

Burgess thought she sounded defensive. Likely because she wasn't supposed to be talking to him, though at this time of night, he'd bet Oh Really's ill-mannered little spy was tucked up in bed.

"He told me where he was staying. He's not there," Ryder said. "I had the Augusta police check his apartment. He's not there. I was heading out your way to see if his vehicle might be at the cottage when your call came in. You mind stepping next door and see if his red Jeep is there?"

Burgess looked at his captives. "Cops are on their way," he said. "Be good."

He liked to tell bad guys to be good. Such irony. Before he left, he got a mini voice-activated recorder from his bag, set it to record, and left it sitting on the roof of his truck. If they chose to speak to each other about the crime, who knew? He might get a pretty detailed confession.

He walked down the drive to the road and turned right, his light bouncing off trees and bushes that appeared an eerie silver in the flashlight's glow. Fideau was at his side, silent except for toenails clicking and the soft clink of tags on his collar.

As he got closer to the Gabbro cottage, he could see three vehicles parked there—Gabbro's car, a small, dark sedan with a Massachusetts plate, and Peter Sherman's sporty red Jeep. What was it doing there at this hour?

He would leave answering that question to Ryder. Before he headed back, he called her.

"Sherman's Jeep is at Gabbro's cottage," he said.

"Thank you. I guess I'll see you soon."

He guessed she would. But her concern about Sherman's message, urgent enough to have her awake and looking in the middle of the night, and the mystery of why Sherman's Jeep was there, bothered him.

He was here. He was awake and had to stay awake until he could hand off those two idiots to the local cops. He might as well check it out.

He kept walking toward the Jeep and the cottage, staying to the side of the road where pine needles softened his footsteps, until he got to the Jeep. He used his flashlight to check inside. Empty. He checked Bridget O'Toole's car. Empty. He walked around the cottage, looking not for something in particular, but for anything out of the ordinary. The place was dark and quiet.

Something urged him to go farther, to check out by the dock. He checked the dock. Under the two kayaks pulled up on the bank. Was ready to call it a night when Fideau alerted and his flashlight beam caught a bit of white at the edge of the water.

He really didn't want to check it out, despite already being here and sensing something wrong. He could hear Chris's voice as clearly as if she was standing beside him. "There are other officers who can handle things, Joe. It doesn't have to be you." Her very firm, "When we go on this vacation, I want you to be on vacation, not pretending to be with us when your mind is somewhere else. Can you do that? Please?"

He'd said yes and now look at him. Sneaking around someone else's yard in the middle of the night, looking for trouble that wasn't his to look for.

But he was a cop. Maybe stupid to have put himself here, but here he was. And his flashlight said there was something to look at.

He focused on the spot where he'd seen that flash of white.

It was a hand. A human hand. The hand of a large man who was floating face down in the lake, bobbing in the gentle waves.

He turned the body over. It was Peter Sherman. Still warm. Maybe it was not too late for measures to save his life.

TWENTY

Taking lifesaving measures with a large, wet body was never any fun. As Burgess labored, he wished, as he had many times before, that he could communicate by thought. Tell his phone to call Ryder. Tell the phone to call an ambulance. Telepathically tell his son, who'd recently had lifesaving classes for his summer job, to get up and get the hell over here and help. None of those things could happen while he was working on Sherman. He needed his attention and his breath for the job at hand. Tilt the head back. Breathing and chest compressions. Breathing and chest compressions.

It was strangely exhausting, trying to breathe life into someone. He was on the cusp of giving up when Sherman choked. Coughed up some water. Gasped and coughed some more. "It's okay. You're okay. Help is on the way," Burgess said, turning him on his side. Sherman had a nasty head wound.

Burgess grabbed his phone and called for an ambulance. Then he called Ryder.

"Where are you?" he asked.

"Just turning down the road to your…"

"I'm at Gabbro's," he said. "Found Peter Sherman floating in the lake."

"Dead?"

"Supposed to be. I think I've brought him back. I've called for an ambulance. I'm on the grass in front of the cottage. Your guys are probably at my cottage by now. Can you stop and give them a head's up about what's happening. Why I'm not there? Tell 'em I'll be there soon."

"Roger that," she said.

He hung up. Looked toward his cottage, where he could see two patrol cars arriving. Lights flashing but mercifully without sirens blasting.

It really didn't matter. By the time this was over, between the voices and the squawking radios, everyone would be awake, Chris would have killed him, and his family would be in a state. He wasn't entirely joking when he thought of himself as a man with his own personal dark cloud. Or a too-sensitive cop's gut, honed by years of experience, something he wished he could bequeath to some up and coming cop so he could simply be on vacation and get a good night's sleep.

Right behind the patrol cars came Ryder. He saw her vehicle pause as she updated them about the situation, then zip past them. She disappeared from view but he heard her door slam and then running footsteps.

"Can you deal with this, Nikki? I've got to—"

"Deal with those two hooligans. I've got it. Go."

Hooligan. A word he hadn't heard in a long time. He gave her a quick summary of what he'd found. Then, leaving Nikki to deal with Sherman and Bridget O'Toole, if she woke, he went.

He found two officers listening in a bored manner to the complaints of his would-be arsonists.

"Detective Sergeant Joe Burgess, Portland police," he said. "I found these two attempting to set fire to the cottage we're renting."

He motioned for them to join him away from the suspect's ears and grabbed the recorder from the truck roof.

"Randy Davenport," the older, salt-and-pepper officer said, "and this is Sam Ryder. No relation to Nikki."

In a quiet voice, Burgess described what he'd found when rustling noises woke him and he came outside to see what was going on. He showed them the photos on his phone of the newspaper and kindling under the steps and the box of wooden matches. "We had a problem with them earlier in the day," he said, "when they were racing their jet skis inside the swimming area. When I yelled at them, they tried to swamp our kayaks. I spoke with the warden about it. He said it had been an on-going problem and he'd talk to them. He said he's given them multiple tickets for their behavior. Sterling-Jones, he's the taller one, seems to think he's untouchable."

"These two," Davenport jerked his chin toward the boys, "are pretty much a two-man, or two-boy, crime wave. All petty stuff. Judge keeps letting them off. Dunno if it's who his daddy is or just misplaced kindness. Anyway, lucky for you that they got stopped this time."

He rocked back on his heels and looked at the cottage. "These old wooden cottages catch fire, they're gone in a flash."

Burgess felt a chill at the words. From Davenport's face, he knew the man felt it, too.

"I hope he'll take this seriously. Those two could have killed my whole family."

"We know." Davenport got out a notebook and wrote down the details of Burgess's statement and Burgess's contact information. "Can you send me those photos you took?"

"Sure." Burgess got the man's information and sent them. He said, "I left a recorder on the roof while I went next door to check something for Ryder. Shall we see if it caught anything?"

Davenport grinned. "Smart," he said.

Burgess pressed play and they got an earful, starting with Jones saying, "Setting the fire was your goddamned stupid idea, Danny. Did you not think maybe we'd burn down the cottage and kill people?"

"The fuck you complaining about? You're here, aren't you? You brought the matches, didn't you? It doesn't matter anyway. Like you think the judge is going take this seriously, when nothing happened? She likes us, Cousin. She thinks we're nice young men who get into a little mischief. Just a boys will be boys kind of thing." Sterling-Jones laughed like it was all a big joke.

His cousin wasn't so sanguine. "Jeez, Danny. Jeez. What if we'd lit the thing and they hadn't woken up?"

Danny, with a sneer, "What do you mean what if? We *were* gonna light the thing. Look, don't be a baby. Nothing happened and nothing's gonna happen to us."

It went on, but they'd all heard enough.

"Better send me that, too," Davenport said.

"You can take the recorder. I've got another. And here are their wallets and phones."

They took the recorder. And Danny Sterling-Jones and Sean Jones. Replaced Burgess's handcuffs with some of their own. Told Burgess to stop in tomorrow and file a report. And they left.

Through some miracle, his family managed to sleep through it all.

Burgess put his gun and handcuffs back in the car and went next door to see if Ryder needed help. As he approached, he heard Bridget O'Toole's voice from the cottage door, asking Ryder questions.

"What the hell is going on here?"

"It's Peter Sherman," he said. "Someone attacked him and left him to drown."

That should have told the woman all she needed to know and also told her the cops needed to focus on Sherman. Instead, she said, "Well, you need to take him away from here right now. It won't be good for the child, for Arielle, to see something like this after what's already happened with her father."

Like Peter Sherman, dragged back from death, was an annoying bit of flotsam they should take away so as to leave her undisturbed. Like she wasn't the one speaking so loudly she was likely to wake the child.

"Dammit, Joe," Ryder said softly. "I've already told her to back off and be quiet three times. Can you?"

He was happy to help manage Bridget O'Toole, who seemed to be unable get beyond her outrage that they were saving a dying man on her lawn. He heard the words "my own lawn" at least three times before he reached the cottage door where she was standing and figured that anyone around the lake who was close by had also heard her.

When he reached Bridget O'Toole, he snapped, "Lower your voice. You're going to wake up all your neighbors."

She said, "And why should that be any concern of mine?"

He'd been on the fence about her before. Now she tipped him

firmly in the direction of dislike. He abandoned politeness. Walked right up to her where she stood in the doorway, dwarfing her with his size and invading her personal space. He said, "Just shut the fuck up. We're trying to save this man's life and your damned noise isn't helping. Go back inside. Close the door behind you. And stop being a bother."

"What right have you…"

"Enough! You want me to arrest you for interfering with a crime scene?" She could take her attitude and entitlement back to Massachusetts and leave them the heck alone. He put his hands on her shoulders, turned her around, and pushed her firmly back inside. "And stay there," he ordered.

As he closed the door he heard Ari, awakened by her caretaker's commotion, wanting to know what was happening. He understood now why Ari hadn't expressed joy when she learned O'Toole was coming.

It made Burgess grateful his family hadn't woken. They'd still have to be told what had happened. At some point. Then everyone would be upset and Chris would give him those "you've ruined our vacation" looks like he'd conjured juvenile delinquents up just to annoy her. And he wouldn't be able to suggest the alternative would have been to let them burn the cottage.

Christ! Why couldn't anything ever be simple?

He rejoined Ryder next to the shivering Peter Sherman. "How can I help?"

"Stay with him while I get a blanket and my camera from the car." She rose to her feet with a sigh. "Thanks for dealing with the dragon. Why people can't use common sense at a time like this always escapes me."

"It's a self-centered world," he said. "And we get to see people at their worst."

"Wish I knew what Sherman was doing here."

"When things calm down, you can ask. Ask her. Ask him."

"Right. We'll secure the scene. Do a search in the morning. Maybe find some answers."

Burgess rarely waited for the morning when he wanted to search a scene. One of the reasons for his reputation as a hardass. He was like the freaking post office—neither snow, nor rain, nor heat nor gloom of night and all that.

Ryder returned with the blanket and wrapped it around Sherman, who was shivering so badly his teeth were knocking.

"They'd better get here soon or we'll lose him again," Burgess whispered.

"If we can get him to my car, we can turn on the heat," she said.

So that's what they did. Burgess did the heavy lifting because he was taller and Sherman wasn't a small man. They tucked him into the front seat of Ryder's car and turned on the heat full blast.

She ducked into her trunk and came out with some bug spray. She sprayed herself then handed it to him.

"Bet you were a girl scout," he said.

"Scouts aren't the only ones who believe in being prepared. I was an outdoorsy girl. Hunting. Fishing with my dad."

"Right."

They leaned against the running car. Except for the engine's rumble, the night was very quiet.

"The night is so peaceful it's hard to believe we're dealing with an arson attempt and an attempted homicide," he said.

"We could tape off the scene while we wait," she said.

"Except we don't know where the scene is, do we?"

"Check the Jeep?"

"That we can do," he said, "but Nikki, you aren't supposed to have anything to do with me."

"If it weren't for you, Joe, Sherman would be dead. What made you decided to look down by the water?"

"In the water," he corrected. "Wondering why Sherman's Jeep would be there. What he would be doing. The most likely thing, it seemed to me, was that he was worried about Ari's safety and appointed himself her guardian. That he was out there looking after her. It would have been...still would be a big help if he'd let us know what this was about. People never get it that keeping secrets can lead to bad results."

In the distance, they could hear approaching sirens.

His tangle with those two idiot kids hadn't woken his family but Burgess was pretty sure this would.

"I'd better get back," he said. "This is sure to wake everyone and if they find me gone, they'll panic." He paused. "Or someone is going to be seriously pissed off that I'm over here instead of home with them."

"Go on, then." Ryder made almost invisible shooing motions. "I'll wake up that idiot Oh Really has assigned to me. Maybe have him spend the rest of the night guarding the scene. Except he'll think that's beneath him. Patrol's job." She sighed. "Kids these days. Think everything's beneath them."

Burgess laughed. Ryder was single and not that old. "Keep me in the loop," he said.

Ryder's phone announced a text. She checked it and looked at Burgess. "As if I didn't have enough trouble. It's Oh Really. He's on his way here."

"And I'm out of here," he said. "Leaving you to explain how I was the one who pulled Sherman out of the lake."

"Thanks a lot, Burgess."

"Serve and protect," he said.

As he started back, Ryder said, "Dark parking lots, Joe. Because we have to stop meeting like this."

He crunched away down the gravel road.

His foot hit the deck just as flashing lights became visible on the road. He stepped into the living room as Chris emerged from the bedroom. She was wearing the blue nightgown that he loved and her long hair was free from her usual braid.

"What's going on?" she said.

"Something happening next door. Cops and ambulance are there."

"Then I'm glad you're here." She hugged him, and didn't say anything about his wet clothes.

TWENTY-ONE

When Chris woke him hours later with a cup of coffee, Burgess tried to be cheerful, though he felt like he could have slept all day. There was no sleeping all day, though. Not when hordes of company were due in a few hours for an afternoon of swimming and hanging out followed by a cook-out. The wet clothes he'd left on a chair were gone.

She kindly let him finish his coffee and get dressed before she sat down across from him and said, "Now tell me what really happened last night."

He might pretend to slip things past her, and she might pretend to let him, but Chris didn't miss much. "A lot."

"I know that, Detective Sergeant Burgess. I'm looking for the details."

"The kids?"

"Have gone out. Dylan drove them to the store to pick up some things for me."

Burgess hadn't heard a thing.

He debated how to begin. "How about I saved us all from a terrible death?"

Hell of a way to start the conversation. He tried to protect his family

130

from the dark side of his life, a task made harder when the dark side turned up on his doorstep.

"Go on," she said. "Wait. Let me get some coffee. I imagine this story isn't going to be short."

She got herself coffee and poured more for him.

"You want to go outside?" he asked. "It looks nice out there."

"As long as this isn't a ploy to distract me."

"You think I could?"

She shook her head, picked up her cup, and led the way outside. Not looking at him, she said, "This is supposed to be our vacation."

He didn't know what to say, so he stayed silent.

"So what was going on last night? Why did you come back soaking wet?"

"I'd better start from the beginning," he said.

She folded her arms and leaned away from him. "Yes. You'd better."

"I couldn't sleep," he said. "I just had this feeling…"

"Your cop's gut?"

"You can call it whatever you want, but it's the instinct that tells me when something isn't right. We learn to listen to it, Chris, because it's honed by experience."

She still looked skeptical, though he would bet, if he pressed her, that nurses could tell when a patient was lying. Or worried. Or hiding something. Or had a condition the doctors missed.

He hated to play the "us vs. them" game, but the truth was that there were things in his life that were hard to explain to someone outside the job. He skipped trying to explain an instinct for danger and dove into the facts.

"I was awake and I heard some noises outside. I got my flashlight and went around the cottage. I found two boys—the teenagers who'd been harassing us earlier with those jet skis—stuffing newspaper and kindling under the steps by the back door. They had a box of wooden kitchen matches and as I came around the corner one of them was saying to the other, 'Come on. Just do it.' I stopped them before they could light the match."

He watched her face as she processed that.

"My God. Joe. What if they'd—"

"Luckily, they didn't. I secured them and called the sheriff's patrol who came and arrested them."

She still looked shocked. "But why would anyone do something like that? We could have all been killed."

"They're young. They're stupid. They don't think things through. And they've been bailed out so many times they think they're untouchable." He put a hand over hers. "I know. It's scary. It's awful. I'm just glad I was awake."

"But what if you hadn't been? I didn't even look to see if this place has smoke detectors. Or a fire extinguisher."

"I did. It does." That was instinct, too. Come into a room, look around, check things out. What's there. What's there that shouldn't be. What's not that should be.

She left her chair and curled up in his lap. "Why can't we just have a peaceful vacation?"

If Chris and the kids were renting this cottage without him, would things have gone more smoothly? Those boys would still have invaded the swimming area to stare at Nina. Their carelessness would still have put the kids in danger but Chris might not have called the wardens. More live and let live than he was.

"I know what you're thinking," she said.

"What?"

"That we might be better off without you. But we wouldn't. And if you weren't here, that man next door, Dr. Gabbro, would be dead."

"Unless you were here. You're a nurse. You would have known what to do."

"We might both have been gone."

She was silent for a long time. Thinking. "I probably wouldn't have wondered why his phone and his medicine were missing." Then she said, "Do I dare ask how your clothes got wet last night?"

Because the woman he loved didn't miss much, and knew when to ask and when to let things go. Last night she'd let it go because she knew he was exhausted. He was such a great companion. Gone too much of the time and exhausted the rest.

"Nikki Ryder was trying to reach Peter Sherman," he said. "Sherman had called her, left a message, sounding upset, and asked for a call back as soon as possible. She couldn't reach him and she asked me to check next door and see if his Jeep was there."

He stopped, unwilling to bring another almost death into the conversation.

But nurses were just as used to prodding for essential information as cops. She said, "And?"

"And I...uh...went next door. Found the Jeep. It seemed odd that he'd be there, so I checked around the cottage, thinking maybe he was playing night watchman or something. That there was a threat to Ari he wouldn't share with us."

"No," she interrupted. "Just no. Please tell me you didn't find a body."

"Almost," he said, knowing that sounded ridiculous. "He was floating in the lake. He'd been hit on the head and left to drown."

Telling the story, he realized the attack on Sherman must have happened shortly before he arrived. But he'd seen no one and hadn't heard a vehicle. Had he heard something else? A boat motor? The splash of oars? Something being distracted by the two would-be arsonists had kept him from noticing? He'd have to think about that.

But Chris was waiting for the rest of the story. She said, "And?"

"And I pulled him out. Gave him CPR. Called an ambulance. Then I called Ryder and handed the whole mess over to her."

"How can I say I wish you hadn't gone over there when it would have meant someone died? But I wish you hadn't, Joe. I wish we lived ordinary lives like other people."

"Me, too." Meaning he wished she could live an ordinary life. He might long for more energy. To protect her and the kids. But he liked the life he'd chosen. Or the life that had chosen him. It was hard and took a toll, but he and his team did good work.

He tried to keep off his face that he knew what was coming. The sore spot in their relationship. She'd met him as a cop. Said she respected that he was a cop and understood that it was his calling. But lately, there had been this refrain, as though she couldn't stop herself. They'd both been single and childless when they met. Now they had this family and being maternal had made her wish for different things.

"Why do you keep doing it, Joe? You could retire anytime. You've got savings and you'd get a pension and I'm still working."

She wasn't going to like his answer. She never liked this answer, but he tried to tell her the truth as much as he could. "Because it's who I am," he said. "It's what I do."

"Other cops aren't like this," she said. "They're not danger junkies. They don't go on vacation and get mixed up in all sorts of conflicts and mysteries."

No sense in pointing out that these recent issues had come to him. That didn't help. He went for a generalization instead. "The good ones are. Cops are cops whether we're at work or on vacation. Ask Terry, or even Stan, if they see the world differently. If they spot trouble and have to stop and sort it out. Ask Michelle what Terry is like. Whether he can drive by trouble without stopping."

"I think I will," she said, climbing out of his lap.

Was this vacation's true purpose to show their relationship in a new light? Reveal to both them that despite their love for each other, going forward was impossible? Burgess knew that she needed to talk about things. That was her way of processing. But if it was the same conversation, over and over, where did it get them? Maybe they needed couples counseling? To sit in a room with someone else who could act as a neutral referee? He was skeptical. What if the person they found also suggested that he consider changing his job to save the relationship? Was he just being a stubborn old fool if he refused to consider it?

Great way to start the day. He was suddenly so exhausted he wanted to go back to bed. But company was expected.

"What do we need to do to get ready for the onslaught?" he asked.

She smiled at the change of subject, but it was a weary smile. She, too, saw this conversation as leading somewhere they didn't want to go.

"I forgot to ask the kids to buy some ice and I think we might need more beer. If you don't mind?"

He got it. She was giving him a chance to get away. Make phone calls if he needed to and give her a chance to push discouragement and anxiety away and put on her party face.

What did you do on your summer vacation? Saved two lives. Or saved seven lives. Caught two bad guys. Went skinny dipping and kayaking and ruined a wonderful relationship by doing what he was trained to do. How did other cops handle the conflict between relationships and the job? He knew part of the answer was that they didn't. That's why lots of other cops were divorced. But he wasn't even married and at this rate, never would be.

As if someone knew he needed a distraction, his phone rang. A reminder that he needed to file a police report about last night's incident. Burgess said he'd do that now.

He put on shoes. Got his keys and his wallet. Went to the kitchen, where Chris was mixing something in a big bowl.

"I love you," he said. "I love our family. I'm sorry this keeps happening."

She hugged him. "I know, Joe. I know. I just...I don't know if I can go on living like this."

Apology accepted and filed away. Life went on.

Burgess went forth like a hunter-gatherer in search of ice and peace of mind.

TWENTY-TWO

He filed the police report. His next stop should have been the convenience store but he wasn't ready to go home. He drove aimlessly. Or thought it was aimless until he found himself turning into the hospital parking lot.

Gabbro was still in the ICU and only family could visit. Burgess didn't feel like pulling the "I'm the one who got him here" card. He didn't feel heroic. He just felt generally pissed off and out of sorts with the world. Then he asked about Peter Sherman. He couldn't visit Sherman, either. The police were with him. Couldn't ask the questions pressing on him like lead weights.

He send Ryder a text, saying he was here and asking for an update on Sherman's condition.

He got back a terse, "He's okay. Will recover. Won't talk to us. Where are you?"

He texted back: "In the parking lot. Oh Really or his stooge with you?"

"Stooge. Super pissed he missed the fun last night."

"Think Sherman would talk to me?"

"He's too scare to talk to anyone. We've got guards on the door."

He should talk to me. I saved his fucking life, Burgess thought. People clammed up at the most ridiculous times. Didn't get it that sometimes sharing information protected them. He texted: "You search next door this morning?"

"What? You slept right through it?" A bit of Ryder irony.

"Saving people is exhausting."

"Don't I know it. I'll send Stoogie for coffee. Want me to step out so we can talk?"

"Is there anything to talk about? Anything new? You got weapon? Suspects?"

"Nah. I figure you'll find 'em for me."

"Not if I want to stay alive myself."

"Right. You're on vacation. Threat from a different direction."

"Got that right."

"Catch you later."

"Dark parking lot?"

"You bet."

A total waste of time. Burgess got in the truck and started to drive again. He needed to get home. Wanted to be anywhere but. He didn't see the landscape or the perfect August day. He saw his father, red-faced and tipsy, raising a fist to strike his mother. He heard her quiet voice explaining the violence. "Your father is not a happy man. He feels he's failed at his work and is overwhelmed by his responsibilities."

Overwhelmed by an undemanding blue collar job? By a family that bent over backward not to provoke him? By a wife who worked harder than he did, cleaning demanding people's houses, then did all the work at home? She'd never said a word yet Burgess lived his whole life with the fear that he'd inherited his father's nature, that he'd become a violent man himself. He'd resolved to do good, make the world a better, a safer place. Trusted that it was his calling.

Burgess had spent much of his life avoiding relationships, fearing he'd be bad at it and fail his partner just as his father had. Despite the route he'd chosen, was he failing still? If he'd made a mistake letting Chris, and then Nina and Ned into his life, it was a hell of a big mistake.

He pounded the steering wheel. Dammit! What was he supposed to do? He couldn't retire. Going from a hundred miles per hour to zero would kill him. As for driving a desk like Chris wanted? A nice, safe job? That would kill him, too.

He was going far too fast for these narrow roads. He slowed his truck. His breathing. Tried to put his temper away. Just in time, too. As he rounded the next curve, there was a toddler on a plastic bike right in the middle of the road. No parent in sight.

He stopped in the road, put on his flashers, and carefully steered the child to the side.

"Stay right there," he ordered.

He pulled the truck to the side, parked, and got out.

The child looked at him warily.

"Where's your mommy?" Burgess asked.

All he got was a stare. He looked at the house. Quiet. No signs of life. He held out his hand to the child. "Let's go find your mommy or daddy."

After a moment of consideration, the child—a small boy in shorts and tee shirt Burgess took to be between two and three—rose from the vehicle and cautiously took his hand. Together they walked up the driveway and up the steps.

Burgess had found a number of wandering children over the years. Usually when he'd gone looking for the parents he'd found filth, neglect, drugs, or alcohol or all of that. This was a neat house with a well-tended yard and bright geraniums in pots. A fairly new Subaru parked in front of the garage. He knocked on the door with his free hand, called, "Is anybody home?" When he got no response, he opened the door and stepped inside. A neat living room. Toys in a corner. A basket of folded laundry beside the couch. The house smelled like someone had recently baked cookies.

"Where shall we look for your mommy?" he asked the boy.

"In her bedroom?" the child said. "She was feeling icky." He scooped a hand in front of his tiny belly. "She's pregant."

Crap, Burgess thought. *So many things could go wrong with a pregnancy.* He hoped she was just resting and the child had sneaked out. "Show me where," Burgess said, releasing the boy's hand. The child set off down a hallway, leading Burgess into a pretty bedroom where a woman lay on the bed. She turned toward them as they entered. Sat up, full of anxiety. Said, "Caleb?" to the boy and "Who are you?" to Burgess.

"I found him in the road, ma'am," Burgess said.

She went from sleepy confusion to full-on panic in a second. "Caleb! What were you doing out of the house?"

The boy gave his frightened mother such an innocent smile. "I was riding my bike."

"Come here," she said, opening her arms. She scooped the boy up and held him tight.

"I don't know what to say. He's never…Caleb is a good boy. I…oh my God! What if he'd been…" She burst into tears. "That door is supposed to be locked."

The child and his mother made such a picture. Both small and fair with floating gold curls. She looked too young to be a mother at all, never mind a mother expecting her second child. But that was his age. Everyone looked too young to him these days.

"I unlock it, Mommy," the boy said.

"Well, he's okay. He's safe. You might want to put a hook higher on that door, though," Burgess said. "Now that he's tall enough to let himself out."

"I'm so humiliated," she said, following him as he headed for the door. When she saw the Explorer, she stopped, her face flushing red. "You're a police officer, aren't you?" she said.

"Yes, ma'am."

"So is my husband. If this gets back to him…oh, dear. Please say you won't tell him."

"Ma'am," Burgess said, knowing the shame she'd heap on herself would be more than punishment enough, "I don't know who your husband is, so there's no way I could tell him, is there? I'm leaving now. Will leave if you can assure me that you and Caleb will be okay."

She looked at the child in her arms. "Caleb, can you tell the nice man that you are all right?"

The boy gave Burgess a big smile. "I'm okay," he said, "and I'll take care of Mama and my baby sister, so they will be okay, too."

Burgess held up a palm. "Give me five," he said. The small hand smacked his, and he left.

He didn't start shaking until he was back in the Explorer. What if he'd still been driving like a maniac? It took him at least five miles before he was calm again.

When he pulled in at the store, the warden's truck was there. The man greeted him with a concerned look. "Your family okay, Burgess? I heard about last night."

"Fine. Everyone's fine. I was awake so nothing happened. I appreciate the head's up, though."

"Hate to think what might have happened if you weren't." The man gestured toward the truck. "On my way to confiscate those jet skis. Maybe bring some peace and quiet to the lake. Lotta people will be glad to see them go."

"Sterling-Jones and his cousin been bailed out yet?"

The warden shook his head. Smiled. "I heard someone recorded a conversation where Danny said nothing would happen because the judge liked them and thought they were just mischievous boys. Buncha BS like that. I heard someone played that for the judge and she decided maybe they needed to learn a lesson. Plus, attempting to burn down a cottage occupied by a cop and his family? Guess that didn't sit well, either."

The smile didn't last. "They'll get out soon enough and then we'll all be in trouble."

"Makes it hard to enjoy vacation."

"I'll keep an eye out."

He studied Burgess's face, which was probably set and angry, since that's what he was feeling inside and he wasn't making an effort to look neutral. "You're not the only one, you know. The pranks those boys have pulled have done a lot of harm. Comes down to it, they get out and something happens to 'em, you won't be near the top of the list."

"Such a waste," Burgess said.

"See it all the time. Do public safety long enough, you can get kinda cynical."

Burgess nodded. "Roger that."

The warden got in his truck and drove off.

Burgess headed inside. His phone rang.

Chris said, "Did you get lost?"

"In my thoughts."

She was silent. Anger? Wondering? Regret? He didn't know. He decided he wouldn't tell her he'd stopped to rescue a small child playing in the road. It would only reinforce her certainty that he attracted trouble.

"I'll be there soon. Is there anything else you need?"

"I need you," she said, and hung up.

TWENTY-THREE

He bought the things she asked for, loaded the groceries and two bags of ice in the truck, and headed back to the cottage. For the next several hours, he expected the onslaught of guests would keep him too busy to think, which was fine.

Even without guests, things were pretty crazy. Dylan was out on the deck, on the phone, and from his posture—back to everyone and crouched over the phone—Burgess deduced that he was talking to a girl. Inside, Nina was watching something on her tablet and taking notes on a pad she'd perched on the arm of the couch. She'd recently announced she wanted to be a fashion designer and was now addicted to TV programs, websites, and YouTube videos about fashion design. Her dearest wish was to own a sewing machine, and she was saving her babysitting money to buy one.

Dylan had given his brother a couple dollars and Ned couldn't wait to show off all the candy he'd picked. He was prancing around clutching a brown paper bag like it was the pot of gold at the end of the rainbow.

Chris gave Burgess a cool look and started putting the groceries away.

He figured he'd let her have her pique. He picked up his book, meaning to head for the hammock, not to read but to look like he was reading while he processed how to handle the situation here, and his frustration with two attempted homicides next door that he'd been deeply involved in yet locked out of. The drive was supposed to have allowed him to do that, but it hadn't. It had only provided more evidence that trouble found him not matter what he did to avoid it.

He didn't get far.

Before he could escape, Chris said, "Joe…that little girl was over here again. Wanted to know if she could swim with Ned. I said it wasn't a good time as we were having a party. She went away in tears and now I feel awful. I just wish you'd never brought her here because I really don't like her and I don't want her hanging around. There's something not quite right about her. About that whole situation. She's so weirdly precocious."

Her vehement dislike of the child surprised him. This was not the Chris he knew. Ordinarily she was generous and compassionate. More so than he. He wanted to ask was what was the harm in including another child when there would be so many of them here already. He could tell from her face it wasn't the right response.

Ned, who'd been listening, said, "What does not quite right mean? I like Ari. I'd like her to come and swim with me."

"Maybe another day, Ned," he said. "Today you've got your cousins coming, and Terry is bringing Lexi and Anna. Jared is coming, and Cherry and Maddie."

"But they're all older than me, except for Stan and Lily's baby."

"Anna and Jared are almost your age."

"But Ari is my friend."

Chris was still watching, and it was clear she didn't want Ari included. He said, "Well, Ned, with so many people around, it would be hard to keep track of her. Remember when she swam too far out and Dylan had to rescue her?"

"Is that why Mom doesn't like her?"

He wanted to give the classic parental response, "I don't know. You'll have to ask her." He was fumbling for something else when he was saved by the bell, or at least by a knock on the door. Terry and Michelle with Anna and Lexi. The girls were wearing bright summer dresses over their bathing suits and Michelle had denim cut-offs and a red tee shirt, her blond hair in a ponytail. She looked pretty and happy and Terry didn't look worn down, as he often did.

They greeted Chris and Ned, handed over food and beer, and Burgess led them outside to the deck. On the way, he grabbed a beer, nudged Nina off her device and then Dylan off the phone. The game was afoot.

He tried not to think about the last time they were all together. A Fourth of July cook-out that had been spoiled by a call about a body. Today, no one would be calling him—he'd buried his phone at the bottom of his suitcase—but Terry and Stan were still on the roster.

Terry Kyle, who was pretty good at reading his mind, said, "I left my phone in the car. Michelle said if I got called out to a case today, it was over."

Burgess looked over at Michelle, who was talking to Nina about something. He was startled to see how grownup Nina was. She could have been Michelle's sister.

"She won't leave you, Ter," he said.

"If I don't propose soon, she will. She's made that very clear."

Kyle was gun shy about marriage after a nasty divorce from the woman they all called "the pms queen." The woman had been the bitch from hell, making Kyle's life miserable for so long he still didn't trust his luck now that he'd found Michelle.

"You going to propose?"

"I'll get to it."

There was a sullen note in Kyle's voice, so Burgess dropped it.

A moment later, Stan Perry joined them, his baby daughter Autumn tucked in the crook of his arm, asleep.

"Cute," Burgess said.

"Not sure I'm going to survive this," Perry said. "She looks adorable now, but she's totally nocturnal and she won't stop crying unless she's held."

As if the prove her daddy right, the baby began to fuss. With a grin, he offered the baby to Burgess.

Burgess put her on his shoulder and patted her back. Autumn settled right down.

Kyle looked at Perry. "And you thought he couldn't."

"Yeah. He never ceases to amaze me," Perry said. "So Joe, I hear you've had some seriously bad business going on next door."

"If you consider what may be two attempted murders seriously bad business."

"I do," Kyle said. "I consider one attempted murder bad business. Oh Really giving you a hard time?"

O'Reilly's reputation was well known in the law enforcement community. "Not my problem," Burgess said. "He's giving Ryder a hard time."

"And you're just sitting on your hands and letting her handle it? Doesn't sound like you, Joe," Stan Perry said.

"Oh, I just save 'em, then I hand it over to Nikki." He shot a glance at Chris. "Oh Really's not the only one pressuring me to stay out of it."

Kyle put a hand on his shoulder. "Must be hard."

"Harder than I thought, that's for sure." He turned so Chris couldn't see his face. "She wants me to retire. Or at least take a desk job. Every time I think we've reached an understanding, it seems like something happens that sends us right back to square one."

"Well…" Kyle turned away from Michelle, and Perry followed suit. They must have looked pretty suspicious, three big men with their heads together and their backs to the group. "Well," Kyle said, "that last one was enough to send any cop running."

"We saved some lives," Burgess said. "We caught some bad guys. You know what would have happened if we'd run. If we'd left it to the B team." The B team was their inside joke. There *was* no B team.

"It tore some pretty big holes in our souls," Kyle said. "You know it did, Joe. You're not alone, either. Michelle's on my case, too. She wants me doing something safer. Which, I'm sorry, because I love her and love having her in my life, but I can't do."

The baby stirred and Burgess rubbed her back. She was only a few weeks old and so amazingly small. "What about you, Stan? Lily want you tucked up in a nice safe berth, too?"

Stan Perry was a wild-man. Burgess constantly had to keep an eye on him or he'd get himself in trouble, but he was settling down, and always a valuable member of the team. Usually, just at the moment when he'd tried Burgess's patience to the point of explosion, he'd have a sudden insight, or lark off on an investigation of his own and come back, like a hunting dog, with something useful clamped between his teeth.

"What were we supposed to do?" Burgess asked. "A call comes in for a body on a running path and we all say 'sorry, we're at a picnic, send someone else?' I thought Chris and I were on the same page. I was doing this when she met me."

He stopped. These guys would understand. When you've stood shoulder-to-shoulder at a gruesome scene, you bonded. But he didn't like to be a complainer. "Sorry. Just kind of wound up today."

Like he was Burgess's therapy dog, Fideau appeared, nosing his knee and giving him devoted doggy looks.

Perry and Kyle patted him and told him he was a good dog.

"Too damned good a dog for someone like that monster McCann," Kyle said. "You taking good care of him, Joe?"

"More like he takes good care of me," Burgess said. They'd arrested Fideau's former owner for a trafficking scheme and the dog had somehow ended up with Burgess.

"I would have taken him," Stan said, "but our landlord doesn't allow dogs. He barely allows babies."

Michelle came over to join them, grinning broadly at the sight of Burgess with a tiny infant on his shoulder. "Looks good on you," she said.

"I think I've got enough kids," he said. "The girls okay about summer ending and going back to school?"

"Well, Lexi can't wait. She's starting high school and plans to be the star of the soccer team and run cross country. I worry about boys, but unlike a lot of girls her age, she doesn't seem to care about them, while they definitely care about her."

She looked over to where the kids were gathered on the dock. Kyle's older daughter was tall and lean, like him, with his dark hair and piercing blue eyes.

Ned was holding court and Burgess figured he was telling the tale of finding the missing medical equipment and searching for the cell phone.

"Anna's not so keen," Michelle said. "Middle school girls can be such bitches and she's kind of behind on development. It's a shame kids get pushed to grow up so fast. She's still such a happy kid. Wish she could stay that way."

She started to walk away. "You guys be good, okay?"

The three of them looked at each other, took a collective decision not to say, "We try," and nodded.

Looking the other way, Burgess could see Ari in her white shorts and shirt, folded into a glum ball on the neighboring dock. He felt mean for not including her but it wasn't worth a fight with Chris.

Staring at the dock made him think of last night. Peter Sherman's injuries had been recent or he wouldn't have been alive when Burgess went over there, unless he had stumbled around for a while before falling into the lake, and the wound had looked fresh. But Burgess was sure no one had come down the road. He'd been awake, sitting on the deck, and then out there by the road dealing with his nocturnal pyromaniacs. He would have seen. Or heard. And there hadn't been a fourth vehicle at the cottage. So either Sherman's attacker had come from inside the cottage, which meant Ari or Bridget O'Toole or someone they were hiding, or the attacker had come from the lake.

Had he heard a boat? The quiet hum of a motor or the soft splash of oars?

"You okay, Joe?" Kyle asked.

Burgess pulled himself back. "Fine. Just thinking about last night." He described the events to Kyle and Perry, then shoved wondering about whether someone had come by water into a locker in his head. If he didn't find a way to keep himself present at this picnic, Chris would be even more irritated with him.

"We need more beer," he said. "Stan? You want to grab some?"

Stan Perry grinned and hurried off, leaving Burgess with a small baby and his best friend.

"I'd say it used to be simple," Kyle said, "but it's never simple. It's better. Michelle takes care of me and she genuinely loves the girls."

"I could say the same about Chris. She's really happy about having kids and puts up with me most of the time. It's the pressure to quit or drive a desk that gets to me. I'm not going to work forever. I'm an old war horse soon to be put out to pasture. I just wish she wouldn't rush me. The damnedest thing is that she thinks I go looking for trouble--"

"When trouble finds you," Kyle finished. "Yeah. I know. Sometimes I feel like an idiot when I think 'what does she want me to do, ignore this stuff?' I try to keep my mouth shut, though. Couple days ago, I stopped a break-in across the street. I was home. I saw the guy. I called dispatch, then got my gun and went over there. She thinks I should have stayed home. She said, 'what if the guy had a gun?' I mean, if we didn't go into situations where someone might have a gun, we couldn't do the job."

They never did this. Never sat around and bitched about their relationships. Well, Kyle had talked a lot about his when his ex was trying to turn the kids against him and then wanted to take them out of state, and yes, Stan had felt trapped when Lily got pregnant, but the usual bitching? They didn't do it. They were happy with the women in their lives. So what was going on today?

Burgess didn't have an answer. He said, "Chris thinks I'm going to spoil this vacation. Or that I already have."

Then Kyle, his conscience, the friend who kept him balanced, made a radical suggestion, "Maybe it isn't about you. Maybe something's going on with her."

Burgess, who was supposed to be observant, was surprised. It was definitely something to think about.

Stan came back with the beer.

Burgess shifted Autumn to the crook of his arm so he had a hand free for his beer. She looked so tiny and vulnerable. So utterly dependent on people to take care of her. "This," he said, dipping his chin toward the baby, "is why we do what we do. Why we see trouble and respond to it."

"Roger that. Now we'd better join the ladies," Kyle said. "Someone's going to get annoyed if she's left to watch the kids while we circle up with beer and talk shop. Especially since they aren't her kids."

"We're watching one," Burgess said. He liked the small, warm weight of the baby.

They were strolling back to the group when Nina appeared at his side. "Can I hold her?" she asked. "Lily says it's okay."

148

"Just don't get any ideas," he teased.

"Maybe in a decade or so," she said. "I just like babies and Autumn is such a sweetie. I wish you and mom would have a baby."

"I'm too old," he said. "And though I love you all dearly, I think I have enough kids."

"You better seal the chimney against storks," she said, and wandered away.

Chris probably wouldn't have told Nina that she couldn't have kids. She was a pretty private person, despite being delighted to have a daughter. As she'd told Burgess, "Now we'll have someone to look after us in our old age."

He politely refrained from noting that he was practically in old age. If she hadn't noticed, that was fine.

His sister Sandy, her husband, and their girls Cherry and Maddie arrived, then his other sister, Moira, and her husband Patrick and son Jared. Everyone carrying food and drink and ready to enjoy a perfect summer afternoon. Burgess didn't miss the fact that Cherry slunk past him, head down, refusing to look at him. Sandy said, "She's still feeling embarrassed about the thing with Dylan."

The "thing" being Cherry convincing Dylan, who didn't have a license, to take Chris's car without permission and drive her to a remote place to confront a murder suspect. The thing that had almost gotten Burgess and his son killed.

He and Terry and Stan, plus the other two husbands, sat in chairs at the edge of the water and watched the hilarious antics of all the kids trying to stand up on paddle boards. The afternoon was blissfully free of wild teens on jet skis zooming into the swimming zone. Gradually, enjoying beer, snacks, and good company, paired with warm sun, Burgess felt himself relaxing. Only then was he aware of how tense and edgy he'd been. He shifted his chair so he couldn't see Ari, sitting by herself on the dock.

Nina had returned the baby to Lily, and the women were grouped around her, admiring the baby and talking kids and family. He assumed they were talking kids and family. For all Burgess knew, they were plotting the overthrow of the government by force and violence.

Eventually, the afternoon heat drove everyone into the water, even

Burgess, though he didn't like his kids, and his sisters—or anyone, really—to see his scars. They were too vivid proof of the dangers of the job.

He was wrapped in a towel, enjoying a post-swim beer, when Chris poked him and said, "It's time to start the grill."

He pulled on a tee shirt and went to work. As he turned on the gas and scraped the cast iron surface, he was jerked back to the Fourth of July, to that moment when, with everyone fed, he finally got to enjoy a hot, juicy burger. He'd been one bite in when the phone rang. That was why today his phone was inside the cottage. If anyone's phone rang, it would be Kyle's or Perry's.

Chris brought him a tray of burgers and dogs and another of buns and he went to work. Kyle and Perry came to watch and lend moral support while the women carried bowls and platters of food, plastic plates and silverware, and cartons of lemonade and ice tea to the picnic table. To ward off bad luck, he ate a burger while he was still cooking. Finished it down to the last bite and no one's phone rang.

"You're waiting for it, aren't you?" Kyle said.

"What's he waiting for?" Perry asked. "Something to eat? He already had a burger. And he wouldn't give me one, either."

Stan Perry liked to call him "Dad" and rather often acted like Burgess's careless or bratty kid. Today he was just joking, which he made clear when he said, "Well, I turned my phone off. If I didn't, Lily would have a fit. She hasn't forgotten the Fourth."

"As if any of us could ever forget that," Perry said.

They couldn't. A call out to a mutilated young girl's body had led them to a trafficking ring and horrific abuse.

Burgess concentrated on cooking. The same cop gut that had had him up in the night was sending out signals again. Sometimes they were specific. More often, it was an anxious sense of something going wrong. But he could never fool Kyle.

"What is it, Joe? Something wrong?"

Burgess flipped the burgers and slid a batch of hot dogs into rolls. Chris liked them delicately browned. He and the kids liked them black. "Something's going wrong," he said. "I just don't know what."

"Like last night wasn't enough?" Kyle said.

"I'm trying to be on vacation, as you can see," Burgess said, waving his spatula like scepter over the grill.

"And life just won't let you," Kyle intoned.

Burgess had once compared the cop's gut to dowsing. Dowsers searched for water and trusted their rods to find it. A cop's gut dowsed for bad guys and bad acts. Found them pretty often, too. That and danger. He'd learned to trust it.

Trailed by the rest of his team, he carried the second heaping platter of burgers and dogs to the table. He might have worried about all those kids descending like locusts, but there was still plenty to eat. He piled his plate with food—a burger and a dog and potato salad and coleslaw and bean and corn salad. He carried it out to the dock where he sat down beside Chris.

"Starving," he said.

"Not for long."

Her smile and the teasing note in her voice told him that for now the strain between them was gone.

"Kids are having a good time," he said, digging in. "You want to try paddle boarding in a while?"

"I think I'm watching the baby while Stan and Lily give it a try. She's an adorable baby and Stan does seem to be taking to the daddy role surprisingly well."

"He does," Burgess agreed. "I admit I had my doubts."

Chris kissed him and got up. "Just going to check and see if anyone needs anything."

His sister Sandy took her place. "Cherry's scared to talk to you," she said.

He waited. Almost everything Sandy said was a criticism of him in some form, but this wasn't his fault.

"So maybe you could…uh…say something to her?" she said. "Let her know that you don't hate her?"

He could be as stubborn as anyone, but that wasn't the case here. The only way his niece would get beyond what she'd done was to talk to him. Say she was sorry and get forgiven. It wouldn't work if he went to her and offered forgiveness. "She knows I don't hate her but she's got to make the first move, Sandy."

There were days when Burgess felt like a tired old priest, spending his days hearing confessions and offering absolution where it could be given. He was working on the tired part with Dr. Cohen's pills. He wouldn't mind handing off the rest of the job to someone else, too.

Of course his sister wasn't done. "For some reason, since the thing happened, she's been really mean to Maddie. Can you think why?"

"I don't know, Sandy. Maybe because Maddie gave us the password which helped us figure out her plan? Sometimes when people feel guilty they project that guilt onto someone else. It makes it easier for them."

She sighed and rested her head on his shoulder. "Maybe you're right. I don't know how our mom did it, you know? Trying to deal with Dad and working and taking care of us. You know how I used to say you didn't understand, because you didn't have kids? Well. That was dumb and I'm sorry."

His sister apologizing was like the whipped cream and cherry on a sundae.

He was enjoying it, and their unusual closeness, when Bridget O'Toole came running into the yard, waving her arms and yelling like a character from a bad movie. "Help me!" she yelled. "I need help! Arielle has disappeared."

TWENTY-FOUR

No one spoke and no decision was taken. Burgess and Kyle and Perry simply automatically headed toward O'Toole. Even as he and his team moved toward her, Burgess was trying to remember when he'd last see the girl. Before he went swimming. Later, he'd looked over and seen that the guilt-inducing white presence was gone. Had she gone inside to eat or for some project? Had she gone swimming under O'Toole's watchful eye and he hadn't noticed?

Not his case. Not their case. If the child was genuinely missing, it was a matter for the county sheriff. Still, Burgess started asking questions as soon as they reached the distraught woman.

"How long has she been gone?" he asked.

O'Toole shrugged. Despite the cry for help, she looked more peeved than concerned. "Can't say for certain. I was reading. She was reading. Reading and sulking because she couldn't come to your party. I was inside, away from the heat, see, and she was outside on the porch on that sofa thing. It had been a while since I'd seen her so I decided to check and she was gone."

"Give us an estimate," Burgess said. "Ten minutes? Half an hour? What?"

"Can't say for certain. Maybe it was forty minutes? Or a bit longer. I confess I was quite deeply into my book."

Burgess restrained himself from shaking her and reminding her that her job was to look after the child.

"When you saw that she was missing, what did you do?"

"I looked around the cottage. I walked out on the dock and looked around the water, see, in case she'd gone swimming again without telling me. You know yourself she can be a willful child. I checked around the cottage and in the cars and Mr. Sherman's Jeep. Then I came over here."

"You haven't called the sheriff? The police?" Burgess asked.

"But you are the police," she said. Her tone annoyed him, there was an air of 'I'm going to drop this in your lap. It's really not my problem,' that didn't fit her caretaker's role. As if she sensed his disapproval, she said, "This is supposed to be my vacation, see, when Arielle is with Dr. Gabbro and they're both away from the house. I had plans."

Burgess said, "We'll take a look around, but you need to call the sheriff. Start with Detective Ryder. She'll want to know and she will know what to do."

Kyle said, "Is the child in the habit of running away?"

O'Toole nodded. "Not so much when she's with her father, see. They're close as two peas. But when she's with her mother, she often comes to us. The mother, Mrs. Gabbro that was before the divorce, says Arielle is tiresome. Yet she won't let the girl live with her father. It's for the money, see."

Kyle looked at him and Burgess nodded. "The father's in the hospital, complications of diabetes," he explained, "maybe complications caused by someone throwing his medication in the lake, and the mother is in Scotland on a walking trip. Ms. O'Toole is the father's housekeeper."

Kyle asked, "Ms. O'Toole, do you think the child was planning to go to the hospital to see her father?"

"Why would she, when she was just there this morning? Not that it was much of a visit, him still being in intensive care and all. Though I wouldn't be that surprised if she wanted to go back, thinking she knew better than the doctors. Very possessive about her father, the girl is."

"Can you think of anyplace else she might have gone?"

She looked around, at the lake and the shore and the woods, then shrugged. "There is no place. Likely she's just done it to annoy me. She does that."

"When she does that," Kyle said, "does she normally come back or does she make it your job to find her?"

Burgess was content to let Kyle take the lead. He'd gotten enough grief from his attention to the case.

"She comes back. But she doesn't know the area around here," O'Toole said. "There's no place for her to go, see, like no parks or that." She looked at the three of them. "I don't know what more to tell you. She's gone and all and I have no idea how to find her."

"How long is she usually gone for?"

"Oh, an hour or so."

"And it's been around an hour since you last saw her?" Kyle said, maybe knowing her forty minutes was fudged.

Burgess's focus had been on Bridget O'Toole and on wondering if they should organize a search. Now he realized that Ned and Fideau had joined them. He wondered if Fideau had some ideas about where to look. The dog had done a good job finding Ari the last time she ran away. But it was Ned, his sunburned, wild-haired son, draped in a soaking wet towel, who had useful information.

"My Joe," he said, leaning his cold, wet self against Burgess's leg and looking up at the gathered adults, "are you all talking about Ari?"

"We are. Ms. O'Toole says she's run away."

"No she hasn't," Ned said with a decisive nod of his head. "She's gone in a boat. Or been taken. While you were swimming. I was on the dock feeling sad that she couldn't come over when we were all having fun and she was alone. She was out on her dock, so we waved to each other. And then I saw a boat come in and a person in the boat motioned her to come closer, then kind of leaned toward her and pulled her into the boat."

"And you didn't tell anyone?" Burgess said, trying to keep accusation from his tone.

The boy shrugged. "I tried to tell Mom. But she just hushed me.

Said she didn't want Ari here and didn't want me to nag her about it. She told me to leave it alone and just be quiet."

Ned shrugged his bony shoulders. "So I did what I was told."

"How long ago was this?"

"I don't know. I'm not so good at time." He held out a skinny arm. "And I've got no watch. Maybe half an hour or so?"

Burgess knelt down so he wasn't towering over the boy, and Kyle and Perry followed his lead. "What can you tell us about the people in the boat? Male? Female? How many?"

Slow down, he reminded himself. Take the questions one at a time. He looked up at Bridget O'Toole, who was standing there uselessly. "Call Detective Ryder," he reminded her. "Now."

She said, "But…"

"No buts. Do it. Now."

Burgess turned his attention back to Ned, breaking his questions down into short answer.

"Ned. How many people were in the boat?"

"Two."

"Male or female?"

His son hesitated. "I'm not sure."

"It's okay, Neddy," Kyle said. "We're not looking for the right answer. We're looking for information."

The boy, who'd fallen into a discouraged slump, straightened. "I think one was a man and the other was a woman, but they were both wearing life jackets, and it was on the far side of the dock, away from us, so I didn't get a good look. I just saw the boat come in and then those arms reaching up for her."

"You're doing great," Kyle said. "Did it look more like she jumped or like she was pulled into the boat?"

"Pulled."

"Can you tell us anything about the boat?"

"It was big. Uh. Biggish. I really don't know much about boats, Uncle Terry. But it was mostly black and had a big motor on the back."

"Did it have numbers on the side? Black numbers?"

Ned nodded. "White letters. But I couldn't read them because they were so far away."

"So mostly black boat. Any other colors?"

"White. And the person I think was a man was sitting in the back and the other person was in front of him on a seat. And the engine was mostly quiet and made a rumbling sound."

"You're doing great," Kyle said again. "I guess that's about it."

Burgess had one more question. "Was the person who pulled Ari into the boat the one you think was a woman or a man?"

"The woman. Oh. And she had blonde hair, really light. Like Ari's."

Ari's mother, Burgess wondered. The woman who was supposed to be in Scotland? But why would she need to kidnap her child when she could just show up? "Did Ari seem to struggle? Did she look scared?"

"I'm sorry," Ned said. "I really couldn't tell. She didn't yell or scream or anything. I'm not sure she was struggling but like I said, I couldn't see very well. It all happened really fast."

Better than a lot of the witnesses Burgess dealt with. "Thank you, Ned," he said. "You have been a great witness. Now you'd better get back. I think it's almost time for those whoopee pies and watermelon."

"And another beer," Kyle said. After Ned scampered off, he added, "So much for being on vacation."

"Trying," Burgess said. "How do I say no when it's right on my doorstep?"

He looked over at Bridget O'Toole. She was standing just as before, in a passive waiting posture, like once she'd told them about the problem, it was their job to fix it. Stolid. Silent. Unconcerned. He was sure she hadn't made the call. He had an irrational desire to see if he could tip her over. Maybe together he and Kyle and Perry could toss her in the lake.

"Did you call Detective Ryder?" he asked.

"Oh. No. Not yet. I was waiting until you were done with that boy, see. I wasn't sure what to tell her."

"Well, stop waiting and call her. You just heard everything we heard, so that's what you tell her. That it looks like Ari was pulled off the dock by two people, maybe a man and a woman, in a large black boat with a large outboard motor. Maybe an hour, forty-five minutes ago? She can work with that."

He walked away, Kyle and Perry coming with him. They were all about helping the weak, vulnerable, and helpless, but had little patience for people who wouldn't help themselves. Or wouldn't help the people they were responsible for.

As they got cold beers from the cooler, Perry said, "What do you think that's about?"

Burgess shrugged. "I honestly have no idea. It could be something to do with her father's work as a geologist, he's been looking into the possibility of gold on some properties that an investor he works for has options on, and may have found gold. Peter Sherman, the geologist who was working with Dr. Gabbro, Ari's father, is very closed-mouthed about their findings. He's the guy I pulled out of the lake last night after he was knocked on the head and left to drown. Or it could be a family thing. The situation with the little girl and her family is a real mess. There was an unpleasant divorce and some custody issues. Maybe some greedy relatives. Whether it's about Dr. Gabbro's work or his family, it's serious enough to have people trying to kill. The only thing I know for sure is that according to Chris and Oh Really, it is not my problem and I'd better not make it one."

He stared over at the empty dock, then out at the lake. "I have a different problem—Chris is not acting like herself."

"Because she doesn't want you involved in finding a missing child?" Kyle said. "That doesn't sound like her."

"It's more than that. She doesn't want me involved in any of this, never mind that two people might have died if I hadn't gotten involved. Two people plus me and my family—though that's another story. She's edgy and irritable and sees everything as a threat to our vacation. And she wants me to retire."

Stan Perry said, "There's a message from the universe here, you know."

"And what would that be?"

Perry shook his head. "You already know."

Burgess did know—that a detective couldn't turn his back when people were in danger. He thought there was another message too, the one Kyle had suggested—that something might be going on with Chris unrelated to the mess next door. Something he needed to investigate.

"Leave the man alone, Stan," Kyle said. "He's trying to recover from trauma."

"Aren't we all?"

Burgess couldn't argue with that. It had been an intense and wrenching summer. He still got so tired it felt like vampires must be sucking his blood while he slept.

They stood by the edge of the lake, enjoying the cool breeze that had come up, thinking of the hard things they'd done together, giving themselves a few minute of peace before joining their families.

Burgess didn't care about whoopee pies but there were some delicious brownies. He snagged one, then went to join Chris, who was sitting on the dock with his sister Sandy.

"You ladies enjoying yourselves?" he asked.

"I ate too much," Sandy said. "I always do. Food at picnics is always so delicious I can't help myself."

"I'm staying away from the brownies," Chris said. "I had one and it only made me want to eat two more."

He sat down beside her, finishing his brownie and forcing himself not to ask her about her response to what Ned had seen, nor to pry into what else might be bothering her. He didn't want to have a fight or to spoil her day.

"Think we should rent this place again next summer?" he asked.

She was silent for a long time, leaving him wondering whether she disliked the cottage for some reason or whether she felt that it was tainted by all the trouble around them. Finally, she sighed and said, "If I'm still around."

That gave rise to a new kind of speculation—was she saying she wasn't sure they'd be together? Was she planning to leave him if he didn't quit his job or transfer to something safer? Or was this a hint about something else, the something bothering her that wasn't about him?

Like a cloud over the sun, her words pulled a dark curtain over a lovely summer afternoon. Whatever was going on, it was not something that they would be discussing with a houseful of family and friends.

Sitting beside her, when she was so uncharacteristically distant, made him uncomfortable. He could wait out a bad guy forever. A good woman? Not so much. He was about to get up and go back to talking with Stan and Terry, people he did understand, when the scream of sirens and flashing lights announced that the police were arriving next door.

He stayed put. If he got up now, Chris would be angry with him. Ned, who had been swimming again, came and sat beside him, his body cold and slippery as he nestled against Burgess for some warmth.

"Do you think Ari is okay, My Joe?" he asked.

"I hope so. She seems pretty capable," Burgess said. "And I'm sure the police know what to do."

"But you're the police. So why aren't you helping?"

Again, a moment when "ask your mother" was the appropriate, and forbidden, response. Instead, he gave Ned a quick description of jurisdiction and how he wasn't the police around here, only in Portland.

Ned said, "But it was you who went looking for Ari when she ran away and you're the one who went to the cottage when her father wouldn't wake up and you're the one who saved that man who almost drowned last night."

Perfectly logical. "Because I was here, Ned, when someone needed help, before the local police could get here."

"And you're here now, and you're a good detective, so why don't you—"

"Ned. Stop," Chris said. "This isn't his job. It's not his problem, okay? We're supposed to be on vacation. So just drop it."

"You just don't want him to help because you don't like Ari, when she might be in real trouble. That's not very nice," Ned said. He got to his feet and walked away.

TWENTY-FIVE

W atching the police cars next door and sitting on his hands was hard, but Burgess stayed put, deliberately keeping his focus on his family and friends. The kids took turns on the paddle boards and using some of the outdoor games he and Chris had brought. After a while, Chris's depressed silence drove him back to Perry and Kyle, and they passed the time catching him up on new cases and department gossip. He never missed the politics, but there were always plenty of funny stories. A bunch of cops gathered around could make their jobs sound like an endless series of funny adventures.

Recounting the dark stuff was saved for when they were alone together, away from family and friends who weren't on the job. Today they kept it light. They were all recovering and happy to keep bad memories at an arm's length.

At some point, Lily had handed Autumn over to Stan again, who had, in turn, passed her to Burgess. He seemed to have the magic touch to calm a fussy baby. Holding her, though, dredged up memories of other fussy babies. Sometimes he thought that the only way to escape a lifetime of people's bad acts was to become a hermit. When he was single and monastic, that might have been a possibility. Now he had children to raise.

"Here comes trouble," Kyle said.

Trouble in the form of Nikki Ryder was heading toward them. No way for Burgess to hide or pretend he was busy. He knew what she wanted. What he'd want if their positions were reversed. She wanted to talk to Ned, who was the best witness she had to what had happened to Arielle Gabbro. And Ryder coming into the midst of their summer picnic would make Chris even more irritated than she already was.

Well. He loved Chris and would go to great lengths to protect her from the dark world he inhabited, but a missing child trumped her anger.

Ryder said, "Afternoon, gentlemen."

They responded in kind.

She said, "I'm looking for a witness. Little red-haired boy. About ten. Name of Ned. You know where I could find him?"

Burgess sighed. "You're going to get me divorced, Nikki, and I haven't even managed to get married yet."

"I know, Joe. And I'm sorry. But that woman who's supposed to be looking after the girl? She is worse than useless. Doesn't know. Doesn't think. Can't say. I get that the girl is difficult, but maybe it's because of what she has to deal with." She paused. "Where did you get that baby?"

"Borrowed her from Stan."

Ryder smiled. "Wish I had a picture. No one would believe it."

Stan Perry said, "Haven't you heard? Burgess is the baby whisperer."

Kyle said, "What did she tell you? That woman next door."

Ryder rolled her eyes. "Said she was reading. The girl was on the dock. When she looked up, the girl was gone."

"That's all?"

Ryder shrugged. "Why? Did you guys tell her what she needed to say and she forgot her lines?"

"Pretty much," Kyle said. "She was there when we spoke with Ned. She heard what he had to say and then we summarized it for her, what to say when she called you."

"All I got was that the child was missing."

Burgess said, "I'll get Ned. He can tell you what he saw."

Ned and Jared were playing something involved bouncing a ball back and forth between their paddles. Doing a good job, too. Jared was bigger and older but Ned was holding his own.

"Ned, we need you for a minute. Detective Ryder wants to ask you about Ari and what you saw."

"I already told everything I know, My Joe."

"But not to Detective Ryder. So come along, okay."

When Ned seemed to be ignoring him, he raised his voice. "Now, Ned. She's waiting."

Reluctantly, the boy put down his paddle. "Now Mom is going to be mad at me, and it's all your fault," he muttered as he followed Burgess over to where Ryder was waiting.

"She can't be mad at you for doing your civic duty, Ned. You're just doing what every responsible citizen is supposed to do—giving useful information to the police."

"I already did. I told you. And Uncle Terry. And Stan. You're all police. And that woman with the funny accent who's supposed to be taking care of Ari was there. She can tell the police."

She could. Of course. But Ryder was a detective. She'd want to hear it first hand from a witness anyway.

He said, "You're an important witness to what looks like a kidnapping, Ned. When a detective is investigating a serious crime like that, she will want to hear the story directly from the witness himself. That's you. It's how we work. Often, talking to the witness produces important information that even the witness didn't know he knew."

Now Ned was intrigued. Also hesitant. He said, "So Mom can't be mad at me, because I'm doing what I'm supposed to be doing?"

"Exactly."

"That's okay, then."

Burgess thought Chris would still be mad, but not at Ned. At him. For getting one of their kids messed up in this. As though he could police what they saw. Or as though if Burgess knew one of the kids possessed important information, he wasn't supposed to act on it.

He wasn't being unfair in imagining her take on things. This was the Chris he was seeing even if it wasn't the Chris he knew.

Tonight, when everyone was settled, he would talk to her. Learn what this was really about. He'd rather go into a bar full of armed motorcycle outlaws than face this, but life didn't always come with the choices he wanted to make. Analyzed honestly, it rarely gave him desirable choices. If he'd wanted a fun career, he would have joined the circus.

He realized he was still holding the baby, a tiny bundle sleeping peacefully on his arm. He was a tough guy, scarred inside and out, holding a baby and giving a civics lesson to a nine-year-old boy. Detective Sergeant Joe Burgess, civics teacher and baby whisperer. The idea made him smile.

He introduced Ryder and Ned. "Detective Nikki Ryder, this is Ned Mallett."

Ned very politely put out a hand and Ryder shook it. "Pleased to meet you," she said. "I understand that you were a witness to Arielle Gabbro's abduction?"

"I saw someone pull her into a boat," Ned said.

Somehow, Burgess, Kyle, and Perry had arranged themselves around Ned like a trio of bodyguards. Ryder looked at them. "Honestly, guys, stand down, okay? I'm just asking Ned some questions."

She made a face at them and switched her attention back to Ned. "Let's start at the beginning. Where were you when this happened?"

Ned pointed at their dock. "I was sitting there. Getting warm so I could go swimming again."

"Good. And where was Arielle?"

"Ari was over there on her dock. She was being sad because my mom wouldn't let her come to our picnic."

"At some point, you saw a boat?"

Ned nodded. "Black and white boat with a black motor. There were two people in the boat. I think it was a man and a woman but I'm not sure because they came in on the far side of the dock and they were wearing hats and life jackets."

"What kind of hats were they wearing?"

"Baseball hats."

"What did the people in the boat do?"

"They came over on the other side of the dock, going very slowly, and they turned and came right alongside the dock. Ari was watching them. I don't know if they said anything to her or she said anything to them because I was too far away, but then I saw Ari jump to her feet and she yelled something that I couldn't hear and then one of the people in the boat, the one toward the front not the person back by the motor, stood up and grabbed Ari by the leg. Ari tried to get away. She was kicking at the person but then she kind of fell and the person pulled her down into the boat. It...the boat, I mean...turned then, and the engine got very loud and it went away really fast."

"That's great, Ned," Ryder said. "Did you notice which way the boat went?"

Ned turned toward the lake and pointed north. "That way."

"Can you tell me anything about the people in the boat?"

"It was pretty far away. One of them, the one I think is a woman, the one who grabbed Ari, had hair like Ari's. Blond that's almost white."

Ryder nodded. "What about the woman who looks after Ari. What did she do?"

Ned looked at her, puzzled. Then he said, "She didn't do anything. I don't think she noticed that Ari was gone. Ari doesn't like her very much. She says that O'Toole—that's what she calls her, I'm not being rude, Detective—doesn't really like her but pretends to like her because she wants Ari's father to think she's a good caretaker. Ari says what Bridget really wants is to marry her father and become rich and not have to keep house anymore, which is why she doesn't like the woman Ari's father *is* going to marry."

He stopped to catch his breath and looked at Burgess. "My Joe, am I doing this right? Am I being a good citizen like I'm sposed to?"

"You're a total winner, Neddy," Burgess said. "I mean Ned."

"It's okay. You can call me Neddy if you want."

Burgess caught the boy with the arm that wasn't holding the baby and gave him a hug. Then he looked at Ryder. "Is there anything else?"

She shook her head. "No. Ned has been very helpful. Oh. One last question. Ned, on the front of the boat, on the side, there would be some big numbers and letters. Did you notice them?"

Ned nodded.

"Do you remember any of them?"

"I'm sorry, Detective Ryder," Ned said, "it all happened too fast. But sometimes when I can't remember I wait a while and then it comes back to me."

"Let's hope that happens this time. Now you should go back to your picnic. I'm sure Joe will call me if you remember anything else."

Ned scampered off before she could ask anything else.

"He's a nice boy," Ryder said.

"No credit to me," Burgess said. "I try to be kind and keep him on an even keel. He's had a couple of horrific traumas in his life, so Chris and I are trying to smooth out the bumps where we can."

"I heard." She looked out at the lake, so big and blue. "Better start asking around, see if we can locate that boat. The girl doesn't have a cell phone, does she?"

"She doesn't. That's how I met her," Burgess said. "Her father was unconscious and his phone was missing. The one we found in the lake. Ned found in the lake. Oh Really gonna be pissed because I, or at least one of my kids, is involved again?"

"You know he is."

"Because he's an idiot," Perry said.

Ryder smiled. "I'm not allowed to agree with you."

"Take care, Nikki," Kyle said. "Hope you find the girl. Let us know if we can help. Send smoke signals or something so no one can trace the contact."

"I'll leave a message in the hollow oak," she said. "Though I guess you guys probably didn't read Nancy Drew, did you?"

"I had little sisters," Burgess said.

"And I have two daughters," Kyle added.

"Autumn is too young to read," Perry said.

"Later, guys." With a salute, Ryder left them.

They had kept it light-hearted for Ned's sake, but all three of them felt the weight Ryder was carrying. A child was missing. Two of the three people close to the child were in the hospital and the third was useless. Her mother was supposed to be in another country. And the day was drawing to a close.

TWENTY-SIX

They put on their party faces and rejoined the group. Chris and Sandy were putting food away. Moira and Patrick were off in a corner having a fight, which was how they communicated. It wouldn't be a family event if they didn't have a fight. Chris's mother, Doro, was out on the water, trying out a paddleboard while Dylan coached her and Nina swam alongside. That Chris came with Doro was an extra bonus for the kids. Burgess was reminded that he and Chris were supposed to try those boards. Probably now was not the right time, though. Not when she was in such a bad mood.

Stan went to speak with Lily, probably about whether it was time to go home. By some kind of miracle, they'd gotten through the whole afternoon without a call from dispatch. He could see how relaxed Kyle and Perry were. They all needed some time off.

He realized that he was still holding Autumn and that she was badly in need of a change. Time to return her to mom and dad. Not that he hadn't changed plenty of babies and toddlers. Right up there with crime scene dogs and cats were crime scene kids, found in the midst of chaos and trauma. Recently, he'd scooped a small toddler off the middle of a street while he was driving Dylan to school. And today there had been that little boy in the middle of the road.

He returned the wet, fretful infant to Lily and turned, almost bumping into his niece, Cherry.

"Hey, Uncle Joe," she said, her face going red. "Are you still mad at me?"

"For getting me shot and almost getting Dylan killed? Why would I be mad?"

"Oh, crap," she said, and burst into tears.

Burgess put an arm around her shoulders and led her away from the crowd. "I was mad, kiddo. With good reason. I don't stay mad." He gave her a squeeze. "Aren't you my first ever niece? Didn't I used to babysit you when you were little so your parents could go out?"

He thought about what a small, sweet creature she'd been, how mesmerized he'd been by her perfect eyebrows, tiny finger and toes. "I hope you learned something from the experience."

"You bet I did. And don't ask me what I've learned, okay? Mom is on my case all the time now. She barely lets me out of her sight. I'm like grounded forever."

At her age, a few weeks was forever. Especially in the summer. He skipped "grounded is better than dead." Instead he said, "You'll have to earn back their trust, Cherry. You know that." He changed the subject. "I hear you've been being mean to Maddie. Is that true?"

She looked away. Then down at the ground. Finally said, "I guess so."

"Why?"

"Because she told. Because she gave you and Mom my password."

"So it would have been better if she'd kept out of it, and we hadn't found you? If Dylan got killed and you ended up being trafficked for sex?"

"God. You're as bad as she is."

"She? Your mother, you mean?"

"Yeah."

"You haven't answered my question, Cherry. Do you think it would have been better if Maddie hadn't helped us so we could rescue you?"

She pulled away from him. "Oh. I don't know. I just don't like that she knew so much about my business."

"She's your sister. She looks up to you. And she helped save your life.

You might be a little more grateful. Look, what happened to you and Dylan was traumatic. I get that. You need time to process. To recover. Maybe even to talk to someone about it. But you also should try to be nicer to Maddie. Don't spoil what's left of her summer because you made some bad decisions. And by the way, if you haven't already done so, you should thank your mother for caring enough to call me."

She stepped away, said, "Oh to hell with you, Uncle Joe. I make one mistake because I'm trying to be like you and you won't let me forget it. No one will." She flounced away.

Won't let her forget it? He wasn't the one who brought it up.

No wonder Sandy looked so worn down these days. What had happened with Cherry was terrifying and now she had her two girls fighting when everyone should have been being deeply grateful that things had turned out okay. People weren't very good at being grateful.

He was glad to be spending time with Kyle and Perry when there wasn't a body in the room, but otherwise this wasn't turning out to be a very pleasant day.

He wandered over to the picnic table, hoping there might be a brownie left. There was and he snagged it. He was watching Doro on the paddleboard as he ate it when Chris came out with his phone.

"Burying it in your suitcase doesn't work. It keeps ringing," she said. "If you don't want calls, turn the damned thing off."

"I thought I did turn it off."

He took it from her, planning to turn it off now, but did a quick check for messages first. It was a habit too ingrained to break.

Several calls from a number he didn't recognize, and two voicemails. When he checked, they were from Peter Sherman.

Sherman sounded anxious in the first one, thanking Burgess for saving him and asking for Burgess to call him back, please. It was important, he had information that would be useful to the investigation. The second voicemail, from about an hour ago, was more frantic. Sherman needed to share what he knew before they got to him. Could Burgess please call him back. It was urgent.

Burgess had to call him back. He stepped away from everyone, around the side of the cottage, and called the number Sherman had left.

"I was afraid you'd never call," Sherman said. "Can you come here? To the hospital? Please? I'm sure they're going to try again. To kill me. I need to talk to you."

What Burgess got for returning the call. Burgess hated putting Sherman off. The man was clearly terrified. But this was Ryder's case. "I can call Detective Ryder and have her come by. If you have something to say, tell it to her. It's her case. As for your life being in danger? She says you have a guard on your door."

"Look…" Sherman's voice was getting weaker. "You know someone tried to kill me. Of course they're going to try again."

"Ryder will…"

"Okay. Listen. In case you can't come. In my Jeep. Inside the covering on the spare tire. That's where you'll find my notes. About the gold. What we found and where we found it. If that's what this is about. But I'm not sure that it is. Gabbro's ex. She's supposed to be in Scotland. But she's not. I saw…"

A woman's voice interrupted him. Burgess hoped it was a nurse and not an assassin. "Burgess. I've got to go. They want to do some scans of my head. The injury. To see…"

"Let me talk to the nurse," Burgess said.

A woman came on and said, "Hello?" in an unwelcoming voice.

"Detective Sergeant Burgess, Portland police," Burgess said. "I'm the one who found Mr. Sherman last night. Has hospital security put a guard on Mr. Sherman?"

"Sir. Detective. That's not my—"

That's not my job. He had five dollars for every time someone had said that? "Is there someone guarding the patient?"

All he got was silence. "Never mind," he said. "Please tell Mr. Sherman to call me when he's done with his tests."

He disconnected and called Ryder.

"What's the matter, Joe," she said. "Still haven't seen enough of me?"

He skipped "too much" and told her what Sherman had said, that the man had information he wanted to share and was afraid someone would make another attempt on his life before he could.

She sighed. "It never ends, does it?"

"Do you have someone watching him?"

"I do. Sorry this keeps coming back to you. I can tell Chris isn't pleased."

Of course Ryder hadn't missed that. She was a good cop. Much as he resented the anxiety it caused, he skipped telling her she needed to do better than try. He wasn't her sergeant. This wasn't his case.

As though their conversation had summoned her, Chris appeared at the corner of the cottage. "Get off the phone," she snapped. "Our guests are leaving."

In his ear, Ryder said, "Uh oh. You'd better go. I'll take care of Sherman."

Before someone else did, he hoped. Burgess put his phone away. "Trying to save someone's life," he said.

"I don't care."

She did care. He knew that. Chris was one of the most generous and compassionate people he knew. Whatever was bothering her was big and he would find out what it was as soon as the day quieted down and he could get her alone.

In the meantime, he had company and kids to attend to. He started around to the other side, where people were gathering to say their good-byes. Before he got there, his sister Sandy snagged him.

"Thank you," she said.

"For what? Pissing off your daughter?"

She smiled. "That's not hard to do. All anyone has to do is breathe and she has a fit. No. For telling her to be kind to her sister. I doubt that it will work, but at least you said it. And however she's acting right now, Cherry looks up to you, so maybe it will do some good."

She hugged him. Middle child. Not the only boy or the only girl. She'd had a lot to cope with. A lot of chips on her shoulders.

"She's a good kid, Sandy. It's natural to want to blame someone else for your mistakes but she'll get over it. Hopefully, with some lessons learned."

His sister sighed. "I hope so. I'm about ready to put her out on the curb with the trash. Luckily, Roger has more patience with her. I can't imagine two more years of this before she's done with high school."

"It doesn't sound true now, but they'll pass in a blur and you'll wonder where they went."

His sister smiled. "Long as it's not a blur of flashing blue lights and heart-stopping phone calls."

"You can always call me."

She rested her head briefly against his shoulder. "And you know I will."

She gathered her family, her picnic basket, and other assorted items, and they left.

His other sister, Moira, left, and then Terry and Michelle and Anna and Lexi. Chris had the kids going around with trash bags, collecting plates and cups. Stan Perry was loading the car with assorted baby gear when Lily handed Burgess the baby. "Do your magic, will you, Joe? She won't stop fussing."

Burgess put the baby on his shoulder and rubbed her back, murmuring quiet advice about being kind to her parents. She settled down and fell asleep. As he handed her back to her grateful parents, he wished he could put Chris on his shoulder and calm her the same way. He had some skills in that department, but today he didn't think they'd work.

He stood in his rented yard, surrounded by his family, as a perfect summer day faded, looking next door toward the Gabbro cottage, and wondering when—and how—he was going to get over there to retrieve Peter Sherman's papers before the wrong person got to them first.

TWENTY-SEVEN

Burgess knew the necessity of securing those papers would be like an unscratchable itch until he retrieved them. With all the mysterious activities involving the Gabbros, and people visible and invisible coming and going, it was too risky to leave them there. He got his chance when Chris poured herself a glass of wine and sat at the table to play a game of Yahtzee with the kids. He wasn't invited to join them.

He slipped out the back door and loped out to the road and next door to the Gabbro cottage. Expecting at any moment that Bridget O'Toole would appear and demand to know what he was doing, he quietly slipped the tire cover off. Taped firmly to the inside with silver duct tape he found a manila envelope. He unstuck it, replaced the cover, and headed home. Resisting the temptation to examine it at once, he locked it in his truck under a pile of gear. Before going inside, he sent Ryder a text that he had Sherman's papers and asked her not to come for them until the morning.

He needed some quiet time with his family—with Chris—without any police interference.

The rest of the evening passed uneventfully. The game was a huge success, if the noise level was an indication, and after he provided a snack of left-over burgers and dogs which vanished like they were all starving, the kids went to bed, leaving him alone with Chris.

He poured himself some wine and invited her to join him outside.

"There are bugs," she said. "And I'm tired. Dealing with so many people was a lot of work."

"People had fun, though."

"Except for a kidnapping next door that Ned witnessed. Cherry being stupid. Moira and Patrick fighting. Oh, and Ned getting mad at me because I wouldn't let him invite Ari. Otherwise I guess it was a good day. Doro had fun with the paddle board. I wouldn't be surprised if she decides to get herself one."

"We have to try them. Maybe tomorrow, if the weather is good."

"If you don't have to go off with Nikki Ryder and save someone's life."

"What's really going on, Chris? I've always been a cop. That hasn't changed, and we both believe saving lives is important."

"Nothing is going on," she said.

When she didn't want to be pushed, she could shut down. Shut him out. But sometimes things had to be pushed.

"Chris. Please. I read people for a living. You're upset about something and it's making you angry and bitter and spoiling your vacation. What's going on? Is something wrong with you? Are you sick? Is that what you don't want to tell me?"

"Dammit, Joe. Can't I just have some privacy?"

"If that's what you want. What you believe you need. But if it's turning you into someone you're not, someone so unhappy, maybe it would be good to talk about it."

She didn't say anything but he knew she was considering telling him what it was.

He waited, patience one of his virtues most of the time.

After a silence that felt monumental, she said, in a rush, "I had a mammogram, Joe, and they found something and now they want to do a biopsy and I'm afraid it will be cancer and I'll die and then the kids will only have you and you keep taking chances and getting into dangerous situations and what if something happens to you and then they've got no one? You want Dylan and Nina, at their age, trying to raise Ned?"

That was a big burden for her to be carrying alone. He took her hand and led her over to the couch, then sat beside her and put his arm around her. "It's not going to be cancer. Even if it is, the treatments are much better and the survival rates are high."

"And what if I have to…" She stopped, unable to say it.

This was harder than talking to the monsters his job dished up. Or assault victims. Or abused children. It was so close and personal.

"Chris…we'll deal with it. It will be okay. I won't love you less. You won't be less of the person I love. You know me better than that."

This whole conversation was shorthand for a much longer conversation, for all the things they might say to each other, but somehow, it was enough. She wriggled her head between his arm and his chest and stayed there. She didn't say anything but he knew she was crying. He could feel her tears on his chest.

She lashed out because she was scared for their kids. He might wish she could have just told him, but he understood. He wasn't the only one here who was awkward at relationships. She was way better than he was, but she had her own baggage. Her scars might be emotional, her experience not with solitude but with a bad marriage, but they were real.

"Did you seriously think my feelings for you might change, Chris?" he whispered, resting his chin on her soft hair. "You've beaten down the wall and captured the castle. You've conquered me. I'm yours. Stuck to you like a remora."

"But if I…"

"Need surgery? Then I'll be with you every step of the way. Die? You won't. You wouldn't leave me sad and alone with a houseful of kids and a dog."

"He's your dog," she said.

"I thought you told me Ned needed a dog? That's why I brought him home."

"Nobody told Fideau that. He thinks Joe Burgess needed a dog."

Fideau, who appeared to be sleeping peacefully on his bed, got up at the sound of his name and nosed his way into Burgess's lap, looking soulfully up at Chris.

"He reads minds, you know," Burgess said.

"I think he does."

They stayed that way, man, woman, and dog, for a long time. Finally, Chris pulled away. "I'm an idiot," she said, "thinking I couldn't tell you about this."

"Maybe I'm an idiot for not pressing you sooner. I wonder, do two idiots make one smart person?"

"They make something good," she said. "Let's go to bed."

They got up, policed the room a bit, locked the doors, and turned off the lights. Burgess turned off his phone. Then they stood together in the dark, looking out at the lake. "It's so peaceful, Joe. And the kids love it here. I think we should rent it again next summer. I like planning that far ahead."

They checked the kids—all three asleep—and went to bed. He hoped he could sleep. He was exhausted and needed a night with no fire-setters and no assault victims to disturb him.

Miraculously, he did sleep, and they got through the whole night without an interruption. He woke early, made coffee, and brought a cup to Chris. That made her smile and her smile was always a good start to the day.

When Dylan got up, he asked if it was okay to take Chris's car and for the three of them to go a little way down the road to a place where they could play mini-golf and get lunch. Burgess didn't know if this was his sometimes insightful son figuring that he and Chris needed some alone time, or whether he genuinely wanted to play mini-golf. And he didn't care. It was a great idea.

After the kids had had breakfast and Burgess had given his son a handful of twenties, they left and he and Chris were alone to enjoy some peace and quiet. They were changed into swimsuits with tee-shirts over them and putting on their life jackets, intending to do their paddle board trial without an audience, when Nikki Ryder knocked on the door.

"Got time for coffee?" Chris asked.

Burgess thought that was a good sign.

"It's your vacation," Ryder said. "I just stopped in to pick something up."

"It's in my truck," Burgess said. "I'll get it."

As he snagged his keys and headed out, he heard Chris say, "Any word on the little girl? On Ari?"

He lingered in the doorway to listen.

"We're still looking," Ryder said. "I may have found someone who can identify that boat. I'm heading there as soon as I check in with O'Toole, see if she's heard anything."

"I wonder how Bridget O'Toole's doing? Her caretaker? Is she in a state?" Chris asked.

"Honestly? If her behavior yesterday is any clue, she's suspiciously unconcerned."

So much, Burgess thought, *for O'Toole's claim to love the child and have practically raised her. No wonder the girl kept running away.*

But O'Toole claimed Ari was running *to* her. Or at least to her father. Every new twist and turn in this business made him more grateful that it wasn't his case.

He hurried out to the truck and grabbed the envelope, curious about the implications of what it held but knowing if he looked it would raise questions that weren't his to answer. He got back in time to hear Ryder say, "I wonder at choosing a person like her to care for a young child. There's no warmth in her."

He handed her the envelope. "You get a chance to speak with Sherman last night?"

She shook her head. "He was asleep when I got there and the dragon of a nurse on his floor wouldn't let me wake him. At least they had security in place. I just hope they didn't forget when the shift changed."

Burgess knew all about hospitalized victims and witnesses and carelessness. He'd seen it way too often. If this were his case, he'd have been knocking on Ryder's door to get Sherman's papers at six in the morning on his way to the hospital. He never trusted the world to keep people safe and he didn't like time to pass when a witness might have vital information. On reflection, he thought he would have visited Sherman yesterday and let no nurse, dragon or otherwise, keep him from hearing what the man had to say.

Not his case. Not his case. He was on vacation. About to go play in the lake. Was it arrogance or just experience that made him keep wanting to stick his oar into the investigation instead of the water? He'd heard there was a Chinese proverb that if you save someone's life, you're responsible for them. In that case, he should be responsible for a lot of people, but a cop couldn't do that. There were too many new lives to protect.

It wasn't his fault that the investigation kept coming to him, but at least he could stay out of it when it didn't. Unless Ryder asked for his advice, he should just leave it alone.

She finished her coffee and left.

They put on their life jackets and headed down to the water. He was going to be bad at this, he was sure. The only splash he'd make was the enormous one when he fell off the board. Chris would be balanced and graceful.

They got on the boards, slowly stood up, and began carefully paddling out into the lake. He'd about reached the end of the dock when Ryder reappeared.

They stopped paddling and waited. This better not take long. Balancing was harder when the board wasn't moving.

"Burgess," Ryder yelled. "O'Toole and her car are gone. Did you hear her leave?"

Crap. He finally gets a good night's sleep and misses something important.

"Sorry," he called. "Her car was there last night when I got the papers. I didn't hear her leave."

Ryder wasn't done. "Chris? Did you hear anything?"

"Only Joe snoring," Chris said.

"I don't snore!"

"Last night you did, so I poked you with an elbow and you turned over and the snoring stopped."

Ryder left without saying thanks. Hard to watch people having fun when your own situation has just gotten more complicated.

He and Chris paddled along on the still morning lake. Going out a little past the dock, then in again. Not ready to tackle the wider lake. It was lovely and peaceful and he was having fun. No motor boats making wakes. No noisy jet skis. Just a few kayakers, the splash of paddles and quiet conversation.

"I was sure I'd fall right over," Chris said.

"Me, too. No wonder Doro liked it so much."

"Wish I could be more like her. She's so willing to throw herself at fun and adventure."

"You don't think acquiring three troubled kids is enough of an adventure, even if it isn't always fun?"

"I think it's pretty wonderful, Joe, and at the same time, kind of a 'be careful what you wish for' thing. I'm never sure I'm doing it right or doing enough."

"Well, ma'am, as an experienced police officer, I'd say if you're worried about that, you're probably doing fine."

It was then that they heard the chainsaw buzz of a jet ski, heading very fast in their direction, driven by a large man in a red shirt. As it zoomed closer, Burgess saw it was aiming right toward their boards.

He heard several people cry, "Watch out!" "Hey, be careful!" and "Stop!" from the shore.

"Head for the shore, Chris!" he said, putting his board between her and the on-coming menace.

It wasn't much of a weapon, but as the jet ski passed so close he could see the malicious gleam in the man's eyes—an older man, not a kid—Burgess swung his paddle, knocking the man off the machine just as he fell off his board into the water.

TWENTY-EIGHT

As the jet ski idled and rocked in the water, Burgess looked toward shore to be sure that Chris was safe. She was just pulling her board onto the beach. Then she ran out the dock calling, "Joe! Joe! Are you okay?" Fideau was right beside her, as though sharing her concern.

So much for their peaceful morning together. "I'm fine," he said. He looked around for the man he'd knocked off the jet ski. Didn't see him anywhere.

Towing his board, he swam to retrieve his paddle. He climbed back on the board, cautiously standing up again. To onlookers it must have seemed like a whale climbing onto the board. Not something he liked doing before an audience.

He heard the putt, putt of a small engine. Fideau barked as an older man in a boat nosed carefully around the end of the dock. "Hey, Mister," the man said. "Are you okay? I thought that fellow was going to kill you. You and the missus."

"We're fine, no thanks to him."

"Well, I seen you try to fend him off with that paddle. Looks like you knocked him clean off that damned thing. Be a better world if them things had never been invented."

Burgess, rocking unsteadily on his board, couldn't agree more.

"You see the operator around anywhere?" he asked. "The guy in the red shirt? I don't think he was wearing a life jacket."

He scanned the surface of the lake, joined by the man in the boat.

"Never mind that it's the law to wear a life jacket," the man said, "like having money or being important will keep you from drowning." He swiveled his head and looked around. "Nope. Don't see him. Guess we'd better get the wardens out." He pulled a phone from his pocket and started dialing.

Burgess dropped to his knees and floated on his board, listening. His bad knee reminded him that this was not a good position.

"Oh, yeah, Hank, it's Bob Larson, over to the other side of the lake. Caleb Sterling, the one whose kids you picked up a few days ago after they were harassing some people in one of the cottages with their jet skis? Well, seems Caleb took it upon himself to get him some revenge, came after the couple from that cottage who were out paddle boarding and tried to run 'em down. Guy fended him off with an oar and now that dang jet ski's bobbing around out here, still running, and we can't see no sign of Caleb. You'd maybe better get some people out."

The man who'd called himself Bob tucked the phone away. "Warden will be along. I'd better turn the damned thing off. You sure you and the missus are okay?"

"Pure luck," Burgess said. "I think I'd better go and see how my wife is doing. She looks pretty shaken up."

"You do that," said the man in the boat. "I'll cruise around a bit, see if there's any sign of Sterling. He's always been a hothead. Sure didn't take him long to get himself another one of those damned jet skis. Unless maybe the judge give it back. The law can be mighty stupid some times."

Burgess, despite being the law himself, couldn't argue with that. Liberal judges, or ones that were too friendly with prominent citizens, made his job much harder. He believed in one law for all, an attitude that sometimes got him in trouble with those higher up the food chain.

The guy in the boat was still talking. "Caleb never learned he can do himself as much harm as he does to others." He shook his head in regret. "Waste of energy. Man has talent if only he'd figure out how to use it." He paused to scan the lake again. "Kinda worryin' we don't see him anywhere."

"Joe Burgess," Burgess said, thinking down the road he might need some witnesses.

"Bob Larson," the man said, pointing at a neat yellow cottage with white shutters. As if he'd read Burgess's thoughts, he said, "You need me as a witness or anything, I live just over there. And I can put you in touch with the other people who was watching. Because you can bet that Caleb's gonna try and make out it was your fault."

Burgess had seen plenty of that—of the type of people who created bad situations and then said, "Not my fault," and tried to put the blame on others. He wondered if the man Larson had referred to as Caleb was the one of the boy's fathers who was in the legislature? He also wondered if he could see more from up on the dock. He was paddling the board ashore when Fideau started barking again. He saw where the dog was focused and spotted the man from the jet ski—that red tee shirt was hard to miss—pulling himself up the bank on the other side of the dock. The man didn't appear to be injured.

No way was he taking a chance on the man reaching Chris before he did. Or letting the big jerk get bitten by a faithful, protective dog. He didn't know whether Fideau would bite, but the dog didn't like anyone approaching his people. Paddling hard, he raced for the shore, beached the board, and hurried out onto the dock. He called, "Quiet. Come here," to the dog and planted himself in front of Chris as he watched the man stand up and head toward them.

She turned toward him and rushed into his arms. "Dammit, Joe. We were having so much fun."

Then she spotted the man in the red shirt. "Is that him? Oh, Joe, that's the guy from the jet ski isn't it?"

"It is."

Bob, the man in the boat, came around the dock and idled near them. "Don't guess we need the warden to get out a search party after all. I'll just call Hank and tell him to come pick Caleb up, that's okay with you."

"That's fine with us," Burgess said. "Appreciate your help."

"We mostly have a quiet summer and a good bunch of folks here. But there are exceptions, and he's one of them. I'll make that call." He sketched a salute and started motoring away.

The man in the red shirt was on the ramp to the dock now, rushing toward them. Fideau, trying to obey Burgess's command to be quiet, trembled beside his leg, wanting to charge. Burgess knew the feeling. He'd had to exercise the same restraint many times.

The approaching man was bigger than Burgess had realized, and steaming mad, like what had just happened was Burgess's fault and not his own. A cut over one eye was bleeding heavily but rage seemed to be making him indifferent to the pain.

"What the fuck were you trying to do?" he roared, storming toward them, fists up. "You coulda killed me."

"Likewise," Burgess said, which obviously confused the man. He put himself between the angry man and Chris.

Fideau gave a warning bark. "Quiet," Burgess said. The dog quieted but stayed beside him, trembling with eagerness to tell their visitor he wasn't wanted. Or who was boss.

Out on the water, he sensed that the man in the boat had stopped and was watching. Once again becoming Burgess's witness.

"You knocked me right off my fucking machine."

Despite the man's rage and murderous intent, Burgess found the situation vaguely amusing, his mind going to other fucking machines, to the way some people, men mostly, treated their machines as extensions of themselves, as symbols of their virility—the cars, trucks, motorcycles, and even power tools they wielded to show off. To the people who thought they *were* fucking machines, his friend Stan Perry among them. Before life, and Lily, had settled him down, Perry had let the little one-eyed guy lead him into a lot of trouble.

He kept his amusement off his face. Nothing further enrages a bully than being laughed at.

"Yes, I did," he said, "to keep you from riding right over the two of us. You saying you think we should have just stayed there and let you run us down? Not made an effort to defend ourselves? Is that what I'm hearing?" He kept his voice calm and low, deliberately unprovocative.

Behind him, he heard Chris's sharp intake of breath, worried that he was waving a red flag in front of this angry bull.

He didn't turn to reassure her. You never turned your back on an unstable character like this. There were rules most people played by that bullies routinely ignored.

"I am fucking going to kill you," the man said, coming closer. "Do you know who I am?"

"Does that matter? I mean, if you're going to kill me, is it important that I know who did it? After all, if I'm dead, I can't report you to the police anyway."

He pointed to the man watching from the boat. "But he can. And he *does* know who you are. And all those people watching from the shore. Even if you are God Himself, which your behavior seriously suggests you are not, deliberately causing harm to others in front of a bunch of witnesses isn't easy to walk away from, is it?"

The man hesitated, turning slightly to look at the man in the boat and the watchers on the shore. Then he uttered the phrase that was almost every criminal's mantra when he finds himself trapped: "What the Fuck?"

Burgess watched the man's thought process as he tried to figure out what to do next. Follow through on his threat to kill Burgess? Stopping short of that, push Burgess around, maybe deliver a few blows to intimidate and show who was boss? Burgess's bet was that this man often resorted to physical abuse to make his point. His location, on someone else's dock with an audience and no ready means of escape, made things more difficult. Burgess thought the man was probably a sneak, doing his intimidation and dirty work where witnesses couldn't see him. Except maybe an entourage of hangers on and suck-ups.

The fellow had another problem, too, that would arise after—if—he followed through on his threat. Having to swim out to his jet ski and clamber awkwardly onto the machine lacked the macho impact he wanted and probably was used to. A man doesn't suddenly become a bully one day in midlife. Most likely this guy had been one for a long time, maybe even since childhood and had gotten away with it so often he believed he was untouchable.

What Burgess could see, that his harasser couldn't because, facing

Burgess, his back was to the land, was that a warden service truck had stopped at his cottage and a man was getting out.

It seemed too soon for the warden to be responding to Bob's call. Maybe someone else had called after seeing the man use a jet ski as a weapon. They had quite an audience by now. Possibly others who shared Bob Larson's view that jet skis were unwelcome on this part of the lake.

"I think you should leave," Burgess said. "We don't want you here. You're spoiling our vacation."

"Yeah? And how am I supposed to do that? Fly out to my fucking jet ski?" The man practically shouted it, considerately giving his audience more entertainment.

"You can swim," Burgess said.

The bully was so deep into trying to decide what to do next, he didn't hear footsteps on the dock as the warden approached.

"I still need to teach you a goddamned lesson. You got my kid in trouble just for some boyish prank—"

"You can stop right there," Burgess said, letting some of his anger loose and raising his voice for the benefit of the approaching warden and their audience on the shore. "Trying to set fire to a cottage where a family is sleeping is not a prank. Would you think it was a prank if someone was attempting to set your place on fire? What if they succeeded?"

The man said, "Oh fuck you," which was the predictable response when someone found himself at a loss for words. He drew back his arm, readying himself to take a swing at Burgess. The warden standing behind him caught the arm in a quick maneuver that brought the man to his knees, and just like that, Mr. Do You Know Who I Am? was handcuffed and under arrest.

Burgess stepped back and put his arm around Chris. She turned toward him and buried her face in his shoulder. "I was so scared," she whispered. "And you seemed so calm."

"Am calm," he said. "This piece of crap is just like a hundred other two-bit bullies who think they're tough and important."

"But he's big. And younger than you are. And so mad."

"Well, I wasn't worried for me, and you didn't think I was going to let him get at you, did you? Even if he got past me, you think he'd get past Fideau?"

That made her smile. "My hero," she said. "Heroes." She patted the dog's head. "Hard to believe I thought we were going to have a quiet vacation on a lake. I think I'll go make us some lunch." She waved her hand languidly before her face. "All this macho posturing has made me very hungry. I'm thinking of giant sandwiches and cold beer. And some dog treats."

Giant sandwiches and cold beer sounded good to him. He'd skip the dog treats. Burgess walked her past the warden and his prisoner. The warden followed them, one hand firmly on their attacker's upper arm.

When Chris was inside, out of earshot, the warden told the man to "stay put" and pulled Burgess aside.

"You know who this is, right?"

"He didn't introduce himself, but I assume he's a politician and the father of one of those kids whose jet skis you confiscated."

"He is. Just want to give you a head's up that this might not be the end of it. He's got friends in low places."

Burgess smiled at the phrase. "We'll be careful."

"Wish you didn't have to be, Detective, but you and me, we're not naïve."

"Can't afford to be." Burgess point to where the jet ski was still bobbing the water. "What are you planning to do with that thing?"

"Bob will secure it so it doesn't float off, get in someone's way. I got a guy coming with a boat. He'll tow it back to our dock across the lake." He looked at the man he'd just arrested. The man's face was scarlet with humiliation and rage. Burgess wished he could have hit him. A few little reminders to make him think twice before bullying someone. The man was big, but Burgess was trained and experienced, which most bullies weren't. But he hadn't wanted to get into it in front of Chris. This was supposed to be their quiet morning together. That's why Dylan had organized the mini-golf expedition.

"That whole family thinks they're untouchable," the warden said. "Always doing stupid stuff. But attempted murder? Twice? That's really off the rails. Hate to say it, but if I was you, I'd think about going back home to Portland."

"It's our vacation," Burgess said. "The family needs this."

"Well, they don't need that." A chin jerk toward the bleeding man. "Or to get burned in their beds. You aren't gonna have much of a vacation if you gotta stand guard all night."

"Looks like all day, too." Burgess looked up at the sunny blue sky. "You're serious? You think he might try something else? Even after this?"

The warden shrugged. "You know what people are like. Sometimes they've just gotta win, show people who's boss, even when they're only making trouble for themselves. Pig-headed. Bull-headed. Wrong-headed. Choose your term. People get away with too much, they come to think they're untouchable."

This was not good news, nor how he wanted to spend his vacation. He wanted Chris and the kids happy and relaxed.

Chris would ask: "What about you, Joe? Don't you need to be happy and relaxed?" and it would be a fair question. Truth was if they were happy, he was happy, and as for relaxed? He'd tried that a few days ago and gotten a truckload of crap instead. Relax wasn't in his vocabulary— verbal or physical.

Burgess looked at the warden, a pleasant-faced, scrappy guy with a wary manner and observant eyes. Someone you'd want on your side in a fight. This guy wasn't making idle conversation. He was giving Burgess a warning he didn't want to give, from one man who lived in the real world of bad guys and bad acts to another.

"Right. So what do you need for your report?"

"I'll just put this guy in the truck and then I can get the story. 'Course, I already got an earful on the phone. Them folks on the shore were pretty worried about you two. Meaning if this should come to trial and you need witnesses, I've got a list of names and numbers. Not surprising. People are sick of Caleb Sterling acting like a five-hundred-pound canary, and his son Danny and his nephew Sean didn't fall far from that freakin' tree."

The warden walked Caleb Sterling to the truck. Came back with a notebook. He and Burgess sat at the picnic table while Burgess told his story. Chris came out to offer iced tea or beer, then she went back inside. Burgess didn't like how she looked. She looked scared and worried and like even if she hadn't heard the warden's advice, she thought maybe they should go back to Portland.

He wasn't ready yet. Not ready to let some puffed up piece of shit push him around and ruin his family's vacation. He'd keep an eye on things, and if Sterling got bail, he might have to call in some favors.

TWENTY-NINE

Chris was quiet as they ate their sandwiches. He wondered what she'd say when she finally spoke. Something casual? A comment about the morning's confrontation? A suggestion that they should go back to Portland? He was glad she didn't ask what he was thinking.

She wouldn't like his answer if she did. He was wondering, as he sometimes did when his job or his character seemed to be screwing things up, whether it might be better for everyone if he let her go. Freed her for a relationship with someone who didn't bring such a lot of drama into everyday life. She deserved so much more than he had to offer. She wanted openness, which ran contrary to the life he lived. She wanted stability for the kids, which his ability to attract bad guys into their orbit didn't provide. She wanted a man who would bring her peace of mind and security, which a cop's life, with its inherent danger, didn't have.

They both said, "I've been thinking..." at the same time. He was glad to let her go first.

"Do you think little Ari is okay?"

That wasn't what he was expecting at all. Yesterday she'd been so hostile toward the child he thought she was probably happy to have the child gone. Out of sight, out of mind and all that.

He had no answers for her. To please her, he was trying to stay out of the loop despite how frustrating that information void was. It had felt like a physical effort to give Ryder those papers from Sherman's car without reading them. He didn't much like having her bring concerns about the child back into their sphere, so he left it there and didn't start speculating about what might be going on.

"I really don't know, Chris. That situation is such a mess that I'm glad it's not my case, and I have no new information since yesterday. I don't know whether they've found her. Whether her father is recovering. What's the situation with Peter Sherman. Or why Ari's caretaker has gone, unless she's gone to find the girl. Nikki Ryder was puzzled that she was gone, so it doesn't look like they've been communicating."

She said, "Oh. I just thought you might—"

"You didn't want us involved with the child," he reminded her. "So we're not. I haven't asked any questions so I don't have any information."

"You sound angry. I only wanted to have a day with family and friends. That's not wrong."

"I sound frustrated," he corrected. "Trying to have a nice vacation. Trying to see that you have a nice vacation. People and their problems keep screwing it up and I'm trying not to get drawn in."

"I was scared out there, Joe, when we were paddle boarding. Really scared. I'm not sure we're safe here. It sounds silly, I know, but look at everything that's happened since we got here. None of that should be happening. It's just a rental cottage on a lake." She sighed. "Sorry. I don't know what to do."

Looking out at the lake, not at him, she added, "You're supposed to be resting. Recuperating. Waiting for your thyroid pills to start doing their job. All this drama isn't helping with that."

"Just so we're clear that I didn't invite this drama, Chris."

"I know you didn't. It's just…I don't know…things happen and you get drawn in. You can't help it sometimes. I know that. But it affects all of us."

Feeling defensive, he said, "I didn't having anything to do with those kids on jet skis, Chris. Except for trying to stop it. Would you rather that I sat passively and let people get away with dangerous behavior? Let

Ari's father die? Let those kids burn down the cottage and Peter Sherman die? Is that what you want? I am trying to please you. I am sitting on my hands about a child's kidnapping…possible kidnapping… because you don't want me involved. Do you know how hard that is?"

All the suppressed anger he'd felt at that bully on the dock was pouring out. Not anger at her, though she'd see it that way, but anger at their circumstances. Anger and frustration at being in the middle of some complicated crime he couldn't investigate. At his family being targeted by a bunch of bullies just because they'd dare to complain about someone's unlawful aggression. He said, "Maybe you're right that I'm a magnet. That if I were less confrontational we wouldn't have these problems. Maybe if I'm gone things will settle down and get more peaceful for you."

Referring only to their clashes with the jet skis. Nothing he'd done had caused the problems with the Gabbros.

He knew his anger was irrational. Chris was just trying to parse this by talking it out. Trying to come to an understanding about what bothered her and whether it would be better for the family to go back home where they were safe. To understand how much she could ask of him and what he was willing to do.

What she wouldn't see, maybe couldn't see, were the compromises he'd already made just by letting her into his life and then agreeing to her desire to adopt Ned and Nina. She'd made compromises too. Of course. Including taking in another child when Dylan come to live with them. If he did a cost/benefit analysis, the benefits far outweighed the costs. He liked having a family, loved Chris and being with her. He enjoyed having a lively and lovely home and all those delicious meals.

He was still frustrated, though, by the demands home and family made on his time and on his ability to totally immerse himself in his work. He no longer had the time, and his mind free, to ponder on what was happening in his cases—the habit of thinking he'd developed over many years to help him see the big picture. Sometimes he resorted to claiming he'd be late just so he could sit in the truck and think. Other times, he used the space between work and home to stow away the darkness so he didn't bring it home, trailing gloom and ugliness like he was tracking mud into the house.

He knew she understood what his work demanded just as he understood what she needed from their relationship—honesty, a willingness to confide, and steadiness. He'd tried to give her those things. Did give her those things. It wasn't unreasonable for her to want a peaceful, crime-free vacation. Nor for her to care enough about what he'd just gone through to be protective about his health and state-of-mind. Circumstances neither of them could have predicted had thrown crime, and criminals, in their laps. She was rightly frustrated about that just as he was reasonably unable to ignore a situation that called on his expertise.

Thus the dilemma they found themselves in. She wanted a peaceful vacation that required him to ignore everything he was trained to do. "I know it's a Popeye cliché to say this, Chris, but I am who I am. I'm a cop. Been a cop for a very long time. I can't close my eyes or my mind to what's going on just because we're on vacation. I'm not trying to spoil your fun. Yours or the kids. You know that. But attempted murder, arson and kidnapping—they're all part of my day-to-day. Just like caring for people is part of yours."

He spread his arms wide in a "what to do?" gesture. "If you think it will help, I can go back to Portland. You can stay here without someone whose presence constantly reminds you of the bad things going on, and I can hang out in the back yard in my hammock, far from the Gabbros or Nikki Ryder and that whole mess."

She looked so sad and he hated to make her sad.

If he expected her to say no, he should stay, it was because he sometimes forgot in the middle of their comfortable domesticity how independent she could be. How early in their relationship she'd brought him soup when he was injured. What had she said then? She'd bring him soup but wouldn't stay. That he was too cranky and set in his ways and she was too proud and independent?

That could be the motto over their door.

"Maybe you should go," she said. "I'd offer to but I want the kids to get to finish their vacation here."

"What will we tell them?" he asked, feeling like a jerk for being ridiculously relieved.

"The truth. That you were too distracted by what was happening next door to get the rest you need and so you went home for a few days."

Sort of the truth. Fine with him. He lived in a world where truths were often individual and not absolute. Where there was a Rashomon quality to so many events.

"What about Dylan?" he said.

"What about Dylan? You want to separate him from the others because he's yours biologically? Just when they've really bonded as siblings? When Dylan is so comfortable calling Ned 'Little Bro'? Don't be a jerk, Joe. It's not the kids' fault that we're conflicted right now. They've all been through enough. I am not going to worry them about this when it's likely that next week things will be fine again."

Chris was such an optimist.

"I hope so," he said. "Life without you would be like every day without sunshine."

Uh oh. She smiled at that, and he was a total fool for her smiles. "We're not over, Joe. We're just giving each other a little breathing space, right?"

"Right."

"You should go before the kids get home. Be less awkward that way, don't you think? And take your dog with you."

He did think. Didn't even argue that Fideau wasn't his dog. He went inside, changed from shorts to slacks, grabbed his stuff, and headed out to the truck, Fideau at his side. He tossed his stuff in the back seat, let the dog jump in, and came back to the cottage. He had to give her a goodbye hug. He didn't want to leave things on a bleak note.

Of course, holding her made it harder to leave. In the end he stopped smelling her soft hair and holding her soft body. Got in the truck. And headed back to Portland.

On the way, he called Nikki Ryder for an update on the case.

THIRTY

"Hear you had a run-in with Caleb Sterling," she said when she answered. "Aren't you supposed to be on vacation?"

"Wish he knew that. You know he came to me. Came at me. Guess he usually gets away with that?"

"He does. You should keep your eyes open."

"If he gets bail. I would think he presents a danger to others."

"But the law doesn't always agree."

"Sadly true," he said. "Anyway, I think I've given up on vacation. I'm just a great big trouble magnet. So what's the story on Arielle Gabbro? You find her yet?"

Instead of answering, she said, "I know we need the tourist dollars but I sure wish people would stay home instead of bringing their troubles to us. This Gabbro thing is like a three-ring circus with me trying to be ring-master while Oh Really looks over my shoulder and keeps scaring the animals."

"I've got one of those in Portland," he said.

"I've heard. Also heard you guys had a chance to get rid of your problem child and you saved his life instead."

"Serve and protect," he said. "We couldn't help ourselves."

"Not sure I'd be so noble, given the choice."

"Don't be. I've lived to regret it."

"Don't suppose you've got time for coffee?" she said.

"Actually, I do. Where?"

She named a coffee shop he knew. He said, "They allow dogs?"

She said, "You have a dog?"

"Actually, a dog has me."

"Well, bring the pup along."

They agreed to meet there in half an hour. Relaxing in the hammock didn't seem to have worked for him, but the anticipation of sitting down with Ryder and talking shop made him both easy and excited. He snapped on the radio and settled into driving. Not even the idiocy of summer drivers—the frequently used term was "Massholes" since that's where many of them came from —spoiled his mood.

He got iced coffee. Fideau got a bone. She got some iced vanilla chai concoction. Lots of sugar. He knew how sugar kept a tired detective going. They took a table in the corner, Fideau settled down at Burgess's feet, and Ryder started filling him in.

"We found the boat that snatched the girl. From a place that rents boats by the hour. Your boy's description was very helpful. Unfortunately, the person in charge of rentals is a pimply teenage boy who had his eye on a girl and can't tell us a damned thing about who rented the boat, beyond they paid cash and it was a man and a woman. Not age, size, hair color. Nothing. They went out. They came back. They drove off. He didn't notice whether they had a third person with them. I frankly don't think he would have noticed if Godzilla had tried to rent a boat. A classic case of hormones making someone stupid."

She sighed and sipped her drink. She looked tired. Chasing one crisis after another—some of them happening at night—would do that. "So I followed up with Sherman to see if he had anything useful to say about who attacked him, but he can't remember. It's the usual thing that happens with blow to the head, and nearly dying didn't help. But he did say that he thought he'd seen Ari's mother, Elyse—Gabbro's ex—even though she's supposed to be in Scotland, though he was quite fuzzy on the details, like where and when. It doesn't help that he's scared some-one's going to come after him again. I pressed him but between what he thinks he can't tell us, and his muddled memory, I can't get a clear picture of why someone would want to kill him. I hate to say this, Joe, but I think you might have better luck with him. I got the impression he trusts you."

Because he was a guy? Or because he'd saved Sherman's life? Burgess figured it was the latter. "I thought this thing revolved around gold."

"So did I. The business about Gabbro's medicine and his phone disappearing when he had an important meeting scheduled with Fenton suggests that. But the more I get into this, the more I think the land deals and the gold might all be a smoke-screen. Or a sideshow. That something else is going on."

"Did you get a chance to look at Sherman's papers?"

"I did. But they don't help. I'll need a geologist to make sense of them."

"Why do you think something else is going on?"

"Because the family situation is so screwed up, Joe. If this is about Gabbro's findings, why take Ari? Gabbro's in no shape to be influenced by that. And family is where all this began. For example, does it really make sense that Ari's mother would go to Scotland and not leave any way to contact her? Even if she isn't the world's best mother, from what we've learned, she still has an interest in the child for financial reasons. Something happens to Ari and maybe the money is gone. So she would want to look responsible, wouldn't she?"

Her straw slurped as she reached the bottom of her drink and Fideau lifted his head to look at her. She regarded the glass with regret, like she was having a debate with herself about being allowed a second, then shook her head. "And then that housekeeper, Joe! She's like something from a gothic novel or some English mystery where the house and housekeeper are dark and forbidding. I wouldn't leave a child with her for five minutes. That story about how Ari keeps running away? It's not to her, whatever BS she may spout about being attached to the child. The girl just wants to live with her father, who, by the way, isn't very impressive as a parent either."

Ryder paused to catch her breath. "Sorry. This thing's got me all wound up."

"When's the last time you slept, Nikki?"

"Besides a catnap? I can't remember."

"So I'll big-brother you and remind you that you can't function well if you don't get some sleep."

"Right." She smiled. "And does my big brother take his own advice?"

"He tries. And often fails. But being a big brother means looking after others whether they like it or not. What's your instinct about the possibility that there was no mysterious intruder and Ari tossed the medicine and phone in the lake herself?"

"She's an odd child, for sure, but I don't think she'd take a chance like that. I mean, if she wanted to prove that her father needed her, that's a pretty extreme way of showing it, nearly killing him. Which would have happened if you hadn't been home to help. She couldn't have counted on that."

"But would she think it through like that, Nikki? She's only nine."

"A pretty clever nine, Joe. And I felt like she was sincere in wanting this week with her father to herself. Why blow that up?"

"Unless she hid the phone and threw it away later, when she realized the awful mess she'd made?" Burgess said. He told her about setting out the float where Ned had found the phone. "I had Ned throw a test rock. He was off by twenty feet and he's stronger and fitter than Ari. But we can't know for sure."

"But if was Ari, what is the attack on Sherman about? And the girl didn't drag herself off that dock."

They both shrugged. Burgess was amused at how easily they worked together. Like he *was* her big brother. At least she didn't call him "Dad" like Stan Perry did. Being tired all the time already made him feel ancient. Probably Chris needed someone younger instead of a battered old hulk.

He dragged himself away from "poor me" speculations. "Was there anything in your conversations with Bridget O'Toole that sheds light on her sudden disappearance? She didn't mention leaving or tell you she planned to go somewhere?" he asked.

"Nothing. I stopped by there to check Sherman's Jeep and to ask her some further questions about Ari, and that family, and she was gone. She knew I was coming by this morning. We talked briefly last night and arranged to meet. She didn't call to say she was going out and I called when I got there and found her gone and she didn't answer."

"You think she's somehow involved in Ari's kidnapping?"

"All I can say is the situation is suspicious. She didn't answer when I knocked, so I tried the door, in case something had happened to her. After Gabbro and Sherman, that seemed possible. The cottage was unlocked but aside from some food in the refrigerator, everything was gone. Her things and Arielle's. No clothes. No books. No games. No electronics. The only sign anyone had been there other than the food was a child's bathing suit and a towel drying on the line, like she'd left in a hurry and forgotten it."

Ryder shrugged. "So was she involved? I don't know. Can't know. But unless she knows something, unless she's somehow involved, why would she take off, instead of staying and waiting for some news about the child? Instead of waiting for the child to be returned? If we find Ari now, there's no place to take her and no one to take her to. You know, Joe, I've met plenty of irresponsible people. That's who the job leads us to much of the time, but this woman supposedly drove up here from Massachusetts to look after the girl. Claims she's been with the child since birth. Why on earth would she leave without a word? Or a note?"

"It doesn't sound like another kidnapping," he said. "Kidnappers generally don't carefully pack up before leaving with the victim's car." Changing the subject, he asked, "Was anyone able to provide any solid information about Elyse Gabbro's trip to Scotland? Information you could use to verify that that's where she went?"

"I've got someone checking airlines. No joy there. But it's a slow process."

He switched subjects again. "Did you interview Fenton?"

"The guy who hired Gabbro? Sort of. Not the most forthcoming fellow. He's a pretentious asshole who's hiding something but I don't know if it is only the details of Gabbro's search for gold and rivals for the property he holds options on or if there's more."

"What more would there be?"

"Someone else's money involved? Like Fenton is the middle man for someone even more secretive than he is? Maybe somebody dangerous?

It would explain why Fenton is so uptight about getting his hands on this land."

"You know who the other buyer is? Or buyers who are putting pressure on the deal and making this time sensitive? And when this option expires?"

"No. I don't know about other buyers or why this is so time-sensitive. As I said, Fenton wasn't helpful. Both pompous and furtive, if you can imagine that. And the realtor who is handling those parcels has been dodging my calls."

"Yeah. Realtors. I've found them so helpful. You could pretend to be a buyer and make an appointment to meet him. Or her."

"Of course. I mean I have got the appointment. Earliest I could get was tomorrow. Summer, you know. Everyone wants to look at Maine real estate."

He nodded. "I don't mean to be pushy. I know it's your case. Just a habit. I'm used to talking things through."

"Not a problem," she said. "I'd love to be talking this through with my partner, my usual partner, but Oh Really's saddled me with this kid. I mean, this thing is complicated and I've got a partner who thinks his whole job is to spy on me. He's green. He's not smart. His work ethic is crappy. He's utterly useless as a sounding board."

"So how did you ditch him to talk to me?"

She grinned. "I've got him interviewing everyone who works or lives near the boat rental, seeing if anyone noticed the couple who rented that boat. I told him it didn't take two of us to do that and I had something else to follow up."

"Speaking of follow up, can the lab lift any prints from that lunch bag?"

"Maybe. Sometime before hell freezes over."

"And the phone? Dead?"

"Joe, this isn't my first rodeo. You know how slowly the lab works. I've got a request to his provider for his phone records."

"Sorry," he said. "Don't mean to step on your toes. What about Sherman's phone?"

"He didn't have it on him, so it didn't die in the lake. I've got his keys but I didn't find it in his Jeep."

"What about his other car?"

"What other car?" Ryder asked.

"He said he has a retired hearse he uses when he's out in the field. I guess he couldn't have both of them here, though, so maybe that's in Augusta."

"But wouldn't he have his phone with him?"

"You'll have to ask him that."

"Why don't *you* ask him that?"

This was the second time she'd suggested he might have better luck with Peter Sherman. "You serious about this? You'd let me talk to Sherman?"

"I can't ask for your help here, Joe. Department politics and all that. So this is only a casual suggestion, along the lines of 'If you happened to visit your friend Peter Sherman, and he happened to say something you thought might be interesting to me.' You get the picture?"

"I'll see what I can do, Nikki."

He realized he hadn't asked about Gabbro. "So, Ted Gabbro. How is he doing?"

"Improving. They still won't let me interview him, though. You know how hospitals are."

He did. "I sometimes find a way around that," he said.

"I've heard. Like mowing down anyone who gets in your way? I can't see myself doing that. Maybe I could dress up in scrubs?"

"That would be cute."

"What the hell, Burgess. Cute and I do not appear in the same sentence."

"Right. Sorry."

He felt frustration coming back. When he was out of the loop and fretting, he imagined that Ryder and those inside the investigation knew a whole lot more. Now, seeing her frustration, he was replacing his on-vacation frustration with a detective's frustration when nothing broke his way. At least that was a frustration he was familiar with. No wonder Ryder looked exhausted. Trying to move boulders from the path in order to get somewhere *was* exhausting, especially with a partner who wasn't helping, people disappearing, and witnesses and institutions refusing to cooperate.

"You really want me to go and see Sherman?" he asked.

She nodded. "It might help. I'd come with you but somehow Oh Really's little toady would find out and then…"

She didn't need to finish.

He nodded. "I'll do that now. Nothing else to do. I'll let you know if I learn anything."

"What happened to vacation? Chris throw you out?"

"Close. More like I threw me out. I seem to be a magnet for trouble wherever I go."

"That gonna happen to me?"

He shrugged. "I don't know about you. You're still young. I think there's hope for you."

He left her sitting at the table, looking too weary to stand up. He and Fideau went out to the truck.

"What do you think, Buddy?" he asked. "We gonna solve this thing?"

Fideau gave a very Lassie-like bark, and Burgess headed for the hospital, Fideau's head in his lap. Too bad the dog couldn't talk. He'd send Fideau into the hospital to get information. The dog was awfully good at charming people and reading minds.

THIRTY-ONE

He parked in the shade and left the windows part-way open so Fideau wouldn't get too hot, hoping no do-gooders decided it wasn't enough and called the cops. It wasn't likely that the dog would get a warm reception in the hospital. Maybe he should get the guy a service dog vest like everyone else did. Fideau had already done more service than most of the mutts who wore those things—like finding Ari, for instance. He had the potential to be a serious working dog. But not right now.

He poured water into the bowl he kept in the truck, patted the dog's head, and said, "Be back soon, Buddy. Behave yourself."

The dog did that spooky thing again, where he tipped his head slightly and looked right into Burgess's eyes, like he really understood. Like he would do more to help if he could.

Burgess went inside.

Despite all the time he spent in hospitals, he hated them. Far too often, his visits weren't to deliver some bad guy in need of repair but because he needed repair himself. Today, thank goodness, that wasn't the case. All the repair he needed was Dr. Cohen's pills, although in truth he felt more energized by having a crime victim to interview.

He found his way to Peter Sherman's room quite easily and found

Sherman in a chair by the window, staring gloomily out at the bright summer day.

"How you doing, Peter?" he asked.

Sherman turned slowly away from the window in a move Burgess recognized. It was the 'oh hell, not another cheery hospital functionary' look. Sherman brightened when he saw it was Burgess and not someone who'd come to take his vitals. Of course Burgess was there for a different set of vitals—vital information.

"Can you get me out of here?" Sherman said.

"What do the docs say?"

"That because of the concussion, they want to observe me for another day. Or something like that. All that doc speak, it's hard to figure out what they're saying."

"How are you feeling?"

"Restless. Pissed off. My head aches and these damned stitches itch."

Been there. "You remember anything about what happened to you?"

"It's pretty fuzzy. Maybe you can help." Sherman looked at him, like he was trying to read where Burgess was coming from. Like he was wondering if Burgess could be trusted. "Where did you find me? That night. At Gabbro's cottage. And how did you happen to be there?"

Sherman's question didn't sound suspicious. More like someone trying to get reoriented, so Burgess gave him a detailed answer.

"It was late, but I was awake because I was dealing with some trouble at my cottage. A couple of teenagers thought it would be fun to set the place on fire. I heard noises and went out to investigate. While I was dealing with them, Detective Ryder called. She said you had left her a message that you needed to speak to her and that it was important. She'd been trying to locate you but you weren't answering your phone and weren't home in Augusta or where you were staying here. She asked me if I could go next door to the Gabbro cottage and see if your Jeep was there."

"But I still don't understand," Sherman interrupted. "My Jeep was parked on the road and I was in the lake. How did you find me?"

"I was curious about what you were doing there. Whether there was trouble of some kind. You seem to be quite attached to Ari, so I wondered if you might be watching out for her. The cottage was dark and quiet. I walked around outside and didn't see anything amiss but I also didn't see you. Then I checked down by the water and I found you."

He gave Sherman time to absorb that, then asked, "What were you doing there?"

Sherman gave the answer Burgess expected. He said, "You're right. I was worried about Ari. What had happened with her father was... uh...odd and Bridget isn't the sharpest tool in the shed. I wasn't confident she could be trusted to...uh...be vigilant. So I decided I'd...I don't know...hang around outside. Make sure nothing happened."

"Why were you worried?" He left it open-ended.

Sherman's mouth pursed with concentration. "I...it's still hard for me to think, Detective. I...uh...what happened with Ted was strange. Suspicious. I know there's been speculation that maybe Ari did something. But that's not right. She's not like that. She would never do anything to risk hurting her father. They're too close for that. She depends on him. So I was concerned that someone else..."

"Why were you afraid something might happen to Ari? Did you think there was a threat beyond the matter of the gold and Orville Fenton's real estate options?"

Sherman touched the bandage on his head, looking troubled. "I can't...there was something..." He looked at Burgess. Sheepish. Ashamed. Frustrated by his absent memory.

"You've been very closed-mouthed about what you and Gabbro found on that property you were exploring. But now that there have been attacks on both of you, it's important that law enforcement knows what you've found, or at least whether it could be the reason for the attacks."

Again, he left it open-ended.

"You got the stuff...the papers from my...from the Jeep?"

"Detective Ryder has them, but she says she'll need your help... yours or someone's...to interpret them."

Sherman sat up straighter, tense and alarmed. "She can't show those papers to anyone else."

"Can she show them to you? Will you explain to her what they mean?" He hated to pass the chance to get information along to Ryder. He was too curious. But it was her case.

Sherman's reply was slow and reluctant. "Sure. If she wants to come by and bring them, I'll talk to her. I know I didn't...uh...I wanted you. I...uh...to thank you, you know."

"You can trust her," Burgess said. "But tell me, if you can, did you find gold, or the likely presence of gold, on that land?"

Sherman nodded.

"Enough to be worth killing for?" He wanted Sherman's opinion. In Burgess's opinion, people would kill for almost anything. But this involved real estate, and maybe big money.

"I really can't say."

"Can't say from a geology standpoint or from a reluctance to share information?"

"Geology," Sherman said. "It's...uh...complicated." They'd gone all around Robin Hood's barn and, back at the barn door, Burgess knew no more than when they started, except that Sherman's concern for Ari didn't seem to stem from geology. He tried a different question. "At some point, you said you didn't think Ari's mother, Elyse, was really in Scotland. That you had seen her here. Is that right?"

Sherman nodded.

"Do you remember when? And where?"

Sherman shrugged. "I don't...it's not..." He seemed to have moved past reluctance to talk, and was struggling to get this right. To be helpful. "I could be wrong," he said. "Thing is, I'm not a hundred percent sure. It wasn't a good sighting. She was in a car. I was going one way, she the other." He considered. "She was in the passenger seat of a small, shiny car. One of those boxy little things that comes in strange colors. A Kia, I think."

"What color?"

"Kind of a light metallic green?"

"Maine license plate?"

Sherman nodded.

"Where was this?"

Sherman named the main road that ran into a town at the bottom of the lake. "About three miles outside of town."

"Did you notice the driver?"

"Not really. Male. A big guy, or he seemed big, I mean tall, sitting down. I mean, compared to Elyse."

"And Elyse is how tall?"

Sherman considered. "Medium, I'd say. Maybe five five or six."

"What does she look like?"

Sherman grinned. "Uh, let's put it this way, if you see Elyse, you'll notice her. She's got that white blond hair, like Ari, and she's slender but curvy, kind of like Ted's new girlfriend. Uh, his office assistant who thinks she's his girlfriend. It's funny, kinda, that generally Ted's pretty oblivious about women, like I don't think he has any idea that Bridget has been hoping she'll be the next Mrs. Gabbro. He's got…Ted, I mean…very little sense when it comes to who he's attracted to. Unsuitable women, I mean. First Elyse, and now his assistant, who is kind of a dumb bunny." He hesitated. "I hope you're not offended by me saying that?"

"Not at all. I've had enough training on non-sexist behavior that I could teach it. But some women *are* dumb bunnies." He wondered what the male equivalent was. Numb nuts, maybe. Said, "Elyse was unsuitable?"

"For a scientist, yes. She's totally interested in fun and parties and her social standing. She craves stimulation and attention, while Ted, well, he'll start thinking about something, someplace he wants to explore, or some theory he has about rock formation, and he'll just drift away. Elyse probably has no idea what he does, just that he has money and doesn't…didn't care how she spent it."

Since Sherman seemed to be quite willing to discuss Gabbro and his family, Burgess figured he'd ask a blunt question. "Would there be any advantage to Elyse if Ted Gabbro were dead?"

Sherman considered. "I'm not sure, except that she'd have custody of Ari, and Ari would probably inherit. Ted might have it all in trusts or something, though. After going through their nasty divorce, I know he gave some thought to his assets. And Elyse. He may be fairly described as an absent-minded professor, but Ted's no dummy."

"But you don't know any details?"

"Afraid not."

"Anyone else besides the ex-wife who might benefit?"

"Like I said, I don't know what Ted has done to protect his money, but he's got two siblings who are as greedy as Elyse. At least his brother is. His sister might be more interested in getting her hands on Ari. From what I've seen, she's totally unsuited to raise a child, though I'm sure she doesn't know that."

"Any thoughts on who might have taken Ari? And why?"

Uh oh. Burgess had made the assumption that Sherman was up-to-date on the details of Gabbro's life. He figured Ryder had tried to question him about both his assault and Ari's disappearance. His reaction—practically jumping out of his chair—said that was not the case.

"Peter," Burgess said it firmly. "Calm down. Sit down and I'll fill you in." Thank goodness there wasn't a nurse here. He'd be tossed out on his ear for upsetting a patient.

Sometimes Burgess did that on purpose. Not this time. He made this mistake because he hadn't been kept in the loop.

Sherman sat but he didn't calm down. The questions started pouring out. "What are you saying? Ari's been taken? Have you found her? Is she okay?" Then, before Burgess could begin to answer, Sherman said, "I hope you don't think I had something to do with it?" He folded his arms and glared at Burgess. "What are you up to, anyway? I thought you weren't involved in this case, but here you are, asking me all these questions. Why?"

Burgess answered the last question first. "Detective Ryder asked me to come. She said you wanted to talk to me."

Sherman, a little embarrassed, looked away. "Okay. So whatever I tell you, you tell her?"

"That's right. So, to answer your question, yes, Ari is missing. The information is meager. All we know is two people, a man and a woman, rented a boat yesterday and came to the cottage and scooped Ari off the dock. She didn't appear to fight them, but the witness is another child, so we don't have much to go on. Circling back to the beginning of our conversation, the night you were attacked, you were at Gabbro's cottage because you were worried about something happening to Ari. Can you tell me what was worrying you?"

Sherman sighed. "True, Ari's an odd little duck who acts way too grown up for nine, but I like her. And her situation isn't good. She's been too much of a pawn between her parents. Much of the time, Ted's oblivious to what an automaton O'Toole is and leaves Ari in her company. He also isn't attuned to his brother and his sister. Their greed. Their interests. I shouldn't speak ill of my boss. Gabbro is brilliant. He's also indulged himself in being an absent-minded professor to the detriment of his child."

Sherman leaned forward as though he was inviting Burgess to share his distress. "It's not like there's an obvious threat. Let's say that there are too many people around Ted with questionable motives. Without him in the picture, I was concerned that she would be vulnerable."

"Vulnerable as in what happened? That someone might take her? What would be the point?"

Sherman struggled with his answer. He looked awful. Burgess had to end this soon and let the man rest.

"The point? Could be a number of things. Ransom? Leverage? Custody? I'm not sure, Detective. Just, you know, that I have . . . had such an uneasy feeling about Ari's safety."

"I should go. Let you get some rest," Burgess said. "Just two more questions. First, did you see or hear the person who attacked you?"

"I heard movement down by the water. Went to check it out. There was a man there, pulling up a boat. Then I heard footsteps behind me. I started to turn and that's when someone hit me on the head. I didn't see anyone, but I know there were two people and I know they came by boat. The strange thing is that I didn't hear a motor and then after I got hit, I didn't hear anything. I have no idea how long I was there in the water before you came along, but I'm damned glad you did."

"One last question and I'll go. Did you have a phone on you when you were attacked?"

"Sure. In my pocket."

"Neither the EMTs nor the police found a phone."

Sherman looked both puzzled and concerned. "You think they took my phone?"

"I really don't know. Is there anything on your phone that might be useful to someone? Concerning Gabbro's assignment to look for gold, I mean?"

Sherman shook his head. "They'd need my password anyway."

Burgess put his card down beside the bed. "In case you think of something else."

"You'll share this with Ryder so I don't have to go through it all again?" Sherman sounded wearily belligerent.

Burgess knew how that felt. "I will."

"Sure you can't get me out of here," Sherman said, since, "since you got me in?" He gave Burgess a lopsided smile. "I've got work to do."

"Sorry. I've got absolute no pull around here. You should give yourself some time to get well anyway. You don't want to be out in the field and get some post-concussion effects."

Sherman said, "Right," but he didn't sound convinced.

Burgess was leaving when a nurse appeared and gave him a dirty look before checking on her patient. "You cops are all alike," she said.

"Yeah," Burgess agreed. "Serve, protect, and harass. I suppose I should have just let him drown." He walked away before she could reply.

Chris was a nurse, and he knew plenty of other good ones, but ones like this, defensive and angry and always ready to complain? He had no use for them.

He checked on Gabbro, but they still wouldn't let Burgess see him. Besides, Fideau had waited long enough.

He went out to the truck where he found more trouble waiting.

THIRTY-TWO

A police car was parked behind his vehicle, and an officer and a
stocky, iron-haired woman were engaged in conversation. To put
it more correctly, the officer was engaged in conversation. The woman
was yelling.

Burgess stopped a safe six feet away. "Is there a problem, Officer?"

The cop turned, instantly recognized him as another cop, and said,
"Ms. Galloway here thinks you are abusing your dog."

Burgess feigned surprise. "Abuse Fideau? You've got to be kidding.
I'm parked in the shade, the windows are open, there's a nice breeze
today, and he has water." He opened the door and Fideau jumped out,
shook himself, and offered a paw to the officer.

"He hasn't even forgotten his manners," Burgess said. "Now, Fideau,
give your paw to the lady."

Fideau gave him a look, which Burgess understood to mean, "You
want me to shake hands with her, when she's been yelling and making a
scene?"

Burgess nodded. "Be nice, now."

It was funny how, even though he'd only had the dog for a month,
they seemed to have some kind of Vulcan mind-meld. The dog was
fuckin' brilliant.

Fideau approached the woman cautiously, paused to give her his head tilt questioning look, then stuck out his paw.

She just stared.

"If you don't shake his paw, he'll be deeply offended," Burgess said. "He's a very sensitive dog."

"He's an abused dog," she said, cautiously shaking Fideau's paw. When she dropped it, Fideau returned to Burgess and lay down at his feet.

Burgess turned to the officer. "Detective Sergeant Joe Burgess, Portland police," he said, offering his own paw.

"Officer Jared Burns."

"Oh, right," the woman snapped. "Now you'll let him go because he's another cop."

"No, ma'am. I'll let him go because the dog is fine and he did everything right to ensure that."

"He left that dog in a hot car for over an hour!"

Burgess checked his watch. "Thirty-five minutes," he said. At most. He was an efficient interviewer.

"An hour," she insisted. "Your vehicle was parked here when I arrived."

"Are you sure?" Burgess said, taking a step closer. He was a big man with a scarred face and cold cop's eyes and he wasn't averse to using that when he needed to. "What are you doing here in this parking lot? Besides standing beside my car and making trouble, I mean."

"Visiting my sister."

"And how long were you with your sister?"

"A long time."

Burgess knew she was lying, or perhaps to put it more kindly, exaggerating. "If Officer Burns checks with your sister and her nurse, they'll confirm that?"

She didn't answer.

"Which vehicle is yours?" he asked.

She pointed to a white sedan at the far end of the row. A short walk to the hospital entrance, a long walk to his truck.

"So you parked there, and your route to the door took you past my truck?" he said. "Or were you on your own self-authorized pet patrol?"

She didn't answer.

"If I were to check the records of the local police department, how many animal abuse complaints would I find that you've made?"

Burns turned away to hide a smile.

She got very red in the face but didn't answer.

"Ms. Galloway, I commend you for your interest in protecting animals left in hot cars, none of us want to see pets suffer, but perhaps you might use some judgment before you call the police? It's summer, a very busy time for local police. I'm sure Officer Burns here has more important things to do than harass people who've been responsible about their pets."

"I'm just trying to save the animals," she huffed, and stormed off toward her car.

"I never said this, Burgess," Burns said, "but thank you. If that buys us even a day or two without her nosy trouble-making, the department will be grateful. Great dog, by the way. Where'd you get him?"

"Belonged to a guy we arrested for trafficking young girls."

"Crime scene dog," Burns said. "I've got a crime scene cat. Well. Gotta run. There *are* real matters that need my attention."

"Anything new on that little girl who was kidnapped?"

"Sadly, no. But everyone's on the lookout. You know the family?"

Burgess shook his head. "Renting the cottage next door."

"So much for a quiet vacation, huh?"

Burns got in his cruiser and drove away.

Burgess and Fideau got in his truck. "You did good out there, Buddy," Burgess said. Having a dog was definitely growing on him.

Fideau, who preferred to sit in the front, nosed his arm, like he understood perfectly.

"Where shall we go next?"

He remembered he still had the card Fenton had left with him to give to Gabbro. He'd never had a chance to deliver it. Now, before he got on the road, he took out his wallet and extracted the card. There was an address and a phone number. He used his map program to look up the address. It wasn't far away. He skipped the phone number. Cops often liked to make their visits a surprise and he very much wanted to surprise Fenton. The man might not know anything, but it was important to check. After all, it was an impending visit with Fenton, and Gabbro's unresponsive state, that had dragged him into this in the first place. You might say he was owed.

He told the phone to give him directions and started driving.

Orville Fenton was clearly a man who valued his privacy. Despite the frequent warnings from town's police and fire to make addresses easy to find, his house number was subtle, black on a dark tree trunk. The drive to the house was long and wound through a dark, well-maintained forest. By the time he reached the place, Burgess was half-expecting a castle, complete with moat and guards. Instead, it was an impressive modern house, set at the back of a wide expanse of green lawn edged with large rhododendrons, lilac, and other carefully chosen, well-maintained shrubs. Quite the showplace.

Who was Orville Fenton, and what did he do that he could afford to live like this?

There was a guard of a sort—a big, menacing German Shepherd that came at him, barking up a storm. The kind of dog that said, "You'd better not get out of that vehicle or I'll eat you up."

Burgess looked at Fideau. "What do you think, Buddy? Is that dog really going to eat me?"

He could swear Fideau nodded, and gave him a look that seemed to say, "Animals like that give us all a bad name." Burgess wondered whether dogs did judge each other. Whether, like people, they mostly got along but had personalities and some those personalities were not friendly. Of course there was training. Burgess was trained to observe. Sense danger. Be in charge. Maybe this menacing creature was a lot like him. He'd learned to keep his growling out of sight.

So much for the surprise visit. If Fenton was home, his noisy sentry had definitely alerted him. Burgess grabbed his pepper spray and got out of the truck. The dog came closer, snarling, menacing. Burgess said, "Quiet," in a firm voice.

Magically, it worked. The dog went quiet, but stayed between him and the house as he approached. He and the dog got to the front door. Burgess rang the bell and waited. Nothing happened. He rang again. Still nothing.

"Nobody home?" he asked the dog.

All he got was an anxious and agitated look.

Maybe Fenton was out and had left the dog in charge. Maybe the man had an aversion to answering his door to strangers. Still, Burgess's instincts told him something wasn't right. He followed the walk back to the driveway and the garage. It was one of those garage doors with some narrow, horizontal windows mounted high on the door. High wasn't a problem for him. He peered in. There were two vehicles in the garage. The Lincoln SUV Fenton had been driving when he visited Gabbro's cottage, and a Range Rover. It was a three-car garage. The third space held a boat on a trailer.

Burgess looked at the dog. "Where's your master?" he asked.

The dog just stared back.

Burgess walked around the side of the garage and along the back of the house, peering in windows. The inside was nicely furnished, if a bit overdone, neat, and empty. He stepped up onto a deck, passing a large family room and kitchen. Neat. Empty. He moved to another set of windows and a glass slider opening to a second deck with lounge chairs and a hot tub. The curtains were open, showing these sliders opened to a large bedroom. Masculine furnishings. Neat. Empty.

Burgess reached the end of the house without seeing any signs of life. Cars home and no one in sight? It might merely be that Fenton had a third car and was using that. But his gut, his instinct for something wrong, was saying no. Farther into the lawn there was a landscaped area around a fenced swimming pool. Instead of finishing his circuit, checking the side and the front, something was drawing him toward the pool. If anyone was home on a warm summer day, that was where they'd be.

He crossed the lawn on a bluestone path set into the grass, opened the gate, and stepped inside. There were more lounge chairs. At the far end, a table with four chairs and an unopened umbrella outside a small pool house. The pool was clean and blue and inviting, except for the fully dressed male body floating face down in the shallow end. A heavy man with graying hair long enough to float away from his head. He was wearing khaki slacks with a belt. A blue shirt. Brown leather dress shoes. No one's usual swimming costume. He hadn't been caught by surprise during a swim.

Before he disturbed anything, Burgess got out his phone and took some pictures. Even when it wasn't his case or his problem—the lie he kept telling himself—he had a cop's routines. He quickly surveyed the area. Nothing of note. Nothing seemed disturbed. There were no items of interest.

He didn't want to jump in and haul the body out. He was pretty sure CPR would do no good this time. He used the pool net to pull the body toward him, close enough so he could kneel down and check for signs of life. He rolled up his sleeves and examined the man.

The body was limp and cold. He couldn't find a pulse. He could see no obvious signs of injury but didn't want to disturb the scene. He turned the body slightly to see the face. It was definitely Fenton. The beginnings of lividity suggested the man had been dead for a while.

He walked around the pool area, checking more closely. Tried to examine the pool house but the door was locked.

He pulled out his phone.

THIRTY-THREE

Ryder's brisk, "What now, Joe?" made him so glad he'd called her. Of course, once he delivered his news, she would be even less glad. He should be wearing a black shroud and carrying a damned scythe, the way things were going. Grim Reaper Burgess. Unfortunately, it fit.

"Did you talk with Sherman? Is there something I should know?" she said.

"I did talk with Sherman, but that's not why I'm calling."

"I think I'm going to hang up now."

"That wouldn't be a bad idea. I can go straight to the state police with this one, save you the trouble, but I thought you'd want to know," he said. "There's a man floating in Fenton's swimming pool. It's Orville Fenton. At least I believe it is. He's definitely dead."

"Jesus, Joe. How? What? What are you doing at Fenton's? Can't stay away from my case?"

"I guess that's right. Trying to figure out what's going on with this whole Gabbro business. I didn't get any answers here, unless the fact that someone wanted Fenton dead is a clue."

"I'm on my way," she said. Then, "You don't think this is an accident? Couldn't he have been swimming and gotten a cramp or had a heart attack of something?"

"Not unless he was in the habit of swimming fully dressed and wearing expensive leather shoes."

"Oh crap. Look, I'm going to have to call Oh Really on this one, and the staties. Do you want to wait around or just be an anonymous tip?"

"Can you hold off calling him until you get here?"

"I guess letting Mr. Fenton wait a few more minutes won't hurt. I was on my way to the hospital, but I can do that later. Be there in fifteen, okay?"

"Be warned. There is a big, scary German Shepherd standing guard. He's dying to eat someone."

"But not you?"

"He didn't even take a bite."

"What *are* you, Joe? The Grim Reaper and a dog whisperer?"

"Beats me, Nikki. See you soon."

Not his case, but he had fifteen minutes alone at Fenton's house and he was going to use them. He had to check. Make sure there weren't other injured people inside. He went back to the truck and got gloves. Fideau gave him a pleading look, so he let the dog out, watching warily as his dog met the menacing Shepherd. It didn't take long to discover that Fideau was as good at making friends with other dogs as with people. The two dogs dashed off across the grass, eager to play. Hoping Ryder's fifteen was more like twenty, Burgess went around the house to see if any of the doors or sliders were unlocked.

The bedroom slider was, so he slipped off his shoes and went in. The bedroom wasn't promising. It was a sterile, showplace room. Thick beige carpeting, shiny black furniture, a fancy black and beige comforter and a pile of pillows. A tall black armoire, black dresser. Black velvety armchair. No desk. And strangely, unless it was behind a hidden panel, no closet. No clothes or shoes or books. Nothing that suggested the room was occupied. A door led to a huge black and white bathroom. Acres of marble, intricate black and white tiled floor. A shower big enough for two.

He moved on. Checked two more empty bedrooms and bathrooms.

He passed a large, formal living room with windows looking onto the lawn, the kitchen, and a family room. Walked through a roomy foyer with a sturdy front door. At last he came to Fenton's study. All dark wood desk, bookcases, and built-in filing cabinets. Dark leather chairs.

There was a laptop on the desk. He gently tapped the spacebar and it came alive, asking for his password. He slid open the desk drawer and found, as was way too common, a yellow sticky note with the owner's most frequently used passwords. It was as though people saw no need for security. Or as though they thought no one would ever think to look in a desk drawer. Maybe Fenton didn't worry because he had the dog?

Burgess typed in the password, wondering where to start. He decided on Fenton's email.

Wishing he had one of his kids with him, so much more deft with computers than he, he began to sort. Fenton was meticulous. Communications were sorted into files. More useful if he had any idea what the file names meant. He took a photo of the file names. After clicking through a few of them, he found correspondence between Gabbro and Fenton. No time to read through all of it, so he just skimmed the basics. Pretty much what he'd seen in Gabbro's briefcase. He wrote the details identifying the relevant properties and went on searching. After that he skimmed. Photographed. Skimmed. He'd just reached a file of correspondence with a different Gabbro when the dog's explosive barking alerted him to Ryder's arrival. Damn! No time to read through it. He got out his phone and snapped pictures of the index of dates and subjects, then snapped quick photos of the most recent emails.

He closed the email and the computer, put his phone away, and retraced his steps. He'd just finished tying his shoes when Ryder came around the corner of the house, trailed by the two dogs.

She waved. "Haven't been eaten yet," she called.

The way the big dog trailed her, she must be the dog whisperer. He hurried to meet her. "The pool's this way."

She noticed his gloves, pulled out a pair of her own, and snapped them on. "You check the house? Make sure we don't have any more victims?"

"I did. It's empty."

"How'd you get in?"

"Slider was unlocked."

"Anything?"

"You'll see. It's a show house. Few signs that anyone lives there."

She followed him through the gate to the pool, immediately fixing on the body. "You checked for signs of life?" A question she probably wouldn't ask someone else who was on vacation and happened to find a body. That person would get concern, comfort, and sympathy. Or should.

"I did. I used the pool net to get him close enough. He's cold. I saw no signs of injury. Lividity has started."

She stared morosely at the man in the water. "Damn you anyway," she told him. "I had plans for later."

She sighed. "Instead I'm going to be here, the good little doobie, being sidelined while self-important state police come in and take over." She looked at Burgess. "I hate turning this over to the state police, Joe. We've put in so much time." She gave him a quick grin. "Strike that we. I've put in so much time and a guy who claims to be on vacation keeps showing up at my crime scenes."

"Hot date?" he asked. Ryder had married young, realized a guy who sat home and drank while she worked, and who got mad when no one fixed his dinner, wasn't a keeper. She had been gun shy ever since.

"I don't know yet. Friend set me up. Could be hot. Could be another loser. I've met plenty of those. I doubt if I'll get a second chance if I cancel now, so I'll probably never know."

"And you can't exactly invite him along."

"I didn't invite anyone along, Burgess. You just keep popping up like we're playing Whack-a-Mole."

"Not me who keeps popping up, Nikki, it's the bad guys. I'm just batting cleanup here."

She gave him a "yeah, right" look. "Okay. Walk me through it."

He walked her through it, updating her along the way with what he'd learned from Peter Sherman. "Sherman thinks Fenton's interest in the property, and in having Gabbro look for gold, might have been pretextual, that maybe he was acting for someone else, though Sherman has no idea who that might be. He did say that there are a number of people who might have an interest in Gabbro's demise, or in getting custody of Ari. And that Bridget O'Toole was angling to become the next Mrs. Gabbro while Gabbro is oblivious. He says Gabbro has a habit of getting involved with unsuitable women."

"Unsuitable?"

"Babes. Dumb bunnies. Women who won't be compatible companions for an obsessive scientist."

She frowned.. "I hear the phrase 'dumb bunny' too often. Sometimes even directed at me. You have a daughter, Joe. I think you should purge it from your vocabulary."

Nina definitely wasn't a dumb bunny. "I'll try," he said. "So what now? You want me leave so you can call Oh Really? How do we…uh, you explain how you found Mr. Fenton?"

It was hot in the sun and he was thinking about his hammock and a cold beer, or a swim in the lake. Wondering what the kids were up to and what Chris might be making for dinner. Then he remembered that he wasn't going back to the cottage. He and Chris were taking a break. The family vacation was going on without him. He was going back to Portland, where the place would be hot and stuffy until the air conditioning kicked in. No lake. No hammock. There might be beer.

Ryder said, "An anonymous call?"

"That'll just put you in the middle of another mess when someone wants to trace the call because the caller might be a suspect, Nikki. Just tell him, tell whoever the state sends, that I came to ask Fenton some questions."

"They'll want to know why you were asking questions."

"Then they can ask me, can't they? All you know is that I've been interested in the case because it happened next door. Because I was the one who found Gabbro. And Peter Sherman. Because my son became friends with Ari and he's the witness who saw her being abducted. Tell them that I'm too much of a cop not to be curious about what's going on, even when I am on vacation. Even if you did tell me, more than once, to stay out of it, because it's not my case."

Ryder looked skeptical. "I'm going to say all that?"

"Oh, you can let them pull it out of you. Just be reluctant. And puzzled. You can do that."

"You have more faith in me than I have in myself."

Burgess shrugged. "If Oh Really yells, he yells. Just lower your eyes and act chastened while chanting 'asshole, asshole, asshole' to yourself."

Ryder grinned.

He called Fideau over. "And don't forget to get animal control to pick up the dog. He may not have eaten you or me, but I'll bet he'll find one of those staties real tasty."

"Nice working with you, Joe. I mean not working with you," she said.

"You'll keep me posted?"

"Do what I can. If the state police detectives keep me posted."

They shared a moment of frustration at the prospect of another public safety agency coming in and taking over. Agencies could be so territorial, their own included. But that was how it was in Maine. Burgess could do his own investigations because he was in Portland, but in most of the rural state, it was the state's own detectives who investigated when there was a homicide.

"On the bright side," he said, "maybe they'll nudge you out and you'll be gone in time for that date."

"Goodbye, Joe," she said.

She turned away and started dialing.

Burgess, glad to leave the problem of the man in the pool to her, went back to his truck. He poured some water in Fideau's bowl. The dog slurped happily. Then they got in, cranked up the air, and headed for Portland.

THIRTY-FOUR

He wasn't sure if there was food in the house. They'd tried to empty the refrigerator before they went on vacation. He stopped at his favorite deli, where Melina, the owner, had a soft spot for cops and fed them a lot.

Her face fell when she saw him. "Oh dear, Sergeant Burgess. Oh dear. I only have a little bit of meatloaf left. I have other things very good, if you need to feed your team, but only that little bit of meatloaf. What will do?" She started listing options.

He held up his hands. "It's okay. It's fine, Melina. It's just for me today. But I wouldn't mind a few cookies."

"One meatloaf on whole grain bread, and some cookies. Cookies I've got. You want chocolate chip or oatmeal raisin?"

Feeling like a little kid, he said, "Could I have both?"

She put her hands on her hips and studied him. "Have you been good? Catching lots of bad guys?"

"I have. But right now I'm on vacation."

She shook her head in disbelief. "No. I do not believe what you are saying. You are not a man who takes vacations. I know this."

"But my family…" he began.

"Your family can go on vacation. You can try to go with them but something will happen. It is just the way you are made."

She should hang out a sign: Sandwich Maker and Therapist. She was good. "I'm trying," he said.

"Yes. You should do that." As she spoke, her hands were moving. If there were a Guiness record for sandwich-making speed, she would probably win. She finished his sandwich and wrapped it and said, "Now, for your second sandwich? I have some nice turkey. It's real. I cook that turkey myself. And I know in summer people think they want to eat light, but I have also some stuffing and cranberry sauce, and you will love it. Trust me. You will love it."

The hands kept moving. She smiled at Burgess. "So you are no feeding your friends, Terry and Stan? They won't be sad if you don't be bringing them food?"

"They'll just have to be sad, Melina. I'm not going to be seeing them tonight."

"Ah. Well. Just in case, I will make sandwiches for them, too. You don't see them, you can eat tomorrow. They will keep. I will put in cookies for them, too."

"I'm trying to lose some weight," he said.

"You have lost some weight. You look fine now. You don't want to get thin because then your skin will hang like bag and you will look like old man instead of big, handsome man with scary scar."

It seemed she had his whole life organized, so Burgess stayed quiet and let her make decisions for him. It was only after he'd paid and carried the sandwiches and a dog treat for Fideau to the truck that he realized he might be seeing Kyle and Perry later. For all that he'd said he was going back to Portland—and meant it—there was no way he would leave his family unprotected if Caleb Sterling wasn't locked up in jail. He'd find out what the situation with Sterling's arrest was as soon as he'd gone inside and cranked up the air.

He made the call, learned Sterling was being arraigned, and there was no news yet concerning his release. He got himself a beer and settled down to review the shots he'd taken of Orville Fenton's email.

Then he changed his mind and called Kyle. Got the usual brisk,

"Kyle, Investigations," followed by "What do you want, Joe? Getting bored on vacation?"

"You available if I need you tonight?"

"For what? We talking guys circle up or helping you stick your nose into some county business?"

"Guess news travels, huh?"

"Let's put it this way, I've been expecting your call."

"And we think we have private lives."

"You actually think that?"

"Just a naïve fellow, I guess. What did you hear?"

"You had a dust-up with a five-hundred-pound canary named Sterling and this time Sterling went to jail."

"That sounds about right. I sent myself home to Portland, figuring I've become such a trouble magnet Chris and the kids would have a better vacation without me."

"So you're at home?"

"I am."

"Got any food in the house? Michelle and the girls have gone off to have a 'women only' day. Spa stuff and shopping, then a chick flick. I was not invited."

"Melina made us sandwiches."

"Us?"

"Lately everyone can read my mind. She thought you and Stan would need to be fed, too."

"Well, she's at least one for two. Got beer?"

"I do."

"Be there in an hour."

Burgess didn't mind. Kyle had always been his sounding board. The fact that Kyle was expecting his call pleased and surprised him. He wasn't transparent. But they'd worked together a long time and the law enforcement community was tight, O'Reilly notwithstanding.

He looked at the bag of sandwiches and at the clock. Getting close to five. By now, Sterling's fate should have been decided, but no one had called. It might have been bureaucratic ineptitude. It might have been a reluctance on the part of those involved to let Burgess know the outcome because the justice system had failed again. He was betting on the latter.

He made a couple of calls and got no answer, which was answer enough. Truth was that he would have been content to stay here, drink beer with Kyle, and have a quiet evening. He wasn't keen on hanging out in mosquito-infested woods waiting for the bad guy to appear. But he'd spent more of his life in the equivalent of bug-infested woods than he had in the easy-going company of his friends.

While he waited for Kyle, he took a look at the photos he'd taken of correspondence on Fenton's computer. There were the ones between Fenton and Gabbro, as expected. But in the images from the group he'd photographed but not read, he found he was looking at correspondence between a D. Gabbro and Fenton. Pretty damning correspondence, too, in an oblique way. Burgess hadn't made his way through all of them, but one from a few days earlier, from a D. Gabbro to Fenton, was scarily cryptic: *Well, that didn't work. What do we do now? Do you think S will be a problem?*

Did it mean what he thought it meant? That D was Gabbro's brother, Daniel? And the cc to Belladona? Was that Gabbro's sister? Was this a family affair? And the reference to S? Did it mean Peter Sherman?

He assumed the state police had taken Gabbro's laptop and were looking at this, but who was there to tell them what the relationships were? Would they sensibly consult Ryder? He wondered if Bridget O'Toole was involved and that might be why she had taken off this morning. Had she left so she wouldn't be around to answer questions? Was this a plot among all of them, just Gabbro's siblings, or was he just letting his speculations run wild? For all he knew, D. Gabbro was a potential purchaser as well. Could even be no relation, though that seemed highly unlikely.

What about Ari's kidnapping? Had Gabbro's siblings taken her? Or if the woman on the boat with hair like Ari's was Elyse Gabbro, and Sherman was right that she was around, was she working with D. Gabbro? Ned had described the man on the boat as a hefty man. Might an internet or criminal records search turn up a photo of Daniel Gabbro?

He also wondered why she was taken? What purpose did it serve in their scheme, if such there was? Why not just let her stay with O'Toole? Because even if O'Toole didn't care much about the child, her loyalty would be to Ted Gabbro? An awful lot of questions he couldn't answer. Not about the Gabbros, or O'Toole or about Gabbro's ex, Elyse, and whether she was also involved. All he had on that score was Peter Sherman's uncertain belief that he'd seen her.

He could pull the vacation card and declare it was not his problem. Right. Like anyone who knew him would believe that. Burgess never checked "serve and protect" at the door. He was puzzling about why an evidently wealthy man like Fenton might get involved in something like this when Kyle arrived. Kyle was dressed in black right down to his shoes and socks.

The first thing Kyle said was, "You hear anything yet?"

"I think they're afraid to tell me."

"You got that right. Despite what could have been construed as attempted murder and was clearly reckless endangerment, my sources say Sterling was released on bail, and a pathetically small bail at that."

"I'm not surprised. Disappointed, though."

"Like I always say. We catch 'em, then the injustice system lets 'em go."

"Why justice wears a blindfold. She can't bear to see what the system is doing."

He gave Kyle a beer and a plate, pointed to the bag of sandwiches, and said, "The meatloaf is mine but Melina says the turkey is just as good. You want chips?"

Kyle nodded. "So what's up with this kidnapping? And all the other crap that's going on out there?"

"Still trying to figure it out."

There were footsteps on the stairs and a knock on the door. Fideau was instantly alert and gave a warning bark.

Burgess said, "Quiet, Fideau." He looked at Kyle. "Think it's Stan?"

"Seems likely."

"I thought he was on baby duty."

"Maybe he got the night off."

"To help me out?"

"All for one and one for all," Kyle said, grinning.

Burgess opened the door and Stan Perry came in. "Oh boy! It's been too long," he said. He spotted the bag on the table. "Don't tell me. Melina's?"

Burgess said, "Not meatloaf, if that makes any difference. They're turkey and stuffing and cranberry. She seemed to know you guys would show up and be hungry. I think she has 'the sight' or something."

Perry got himself a plate and a beer. "Do we get cookies?"

"What do you think?"

"I think that even though you hate it when we call you "Dad" no one else ever gives us cookies. So what's on for tonight."

Burgess saw that Perry was wearing dark jeans and a dark shirt over his dark tee shirt. Dressed for night duty like Kyle.

"Protecting my family. You're here, so I guess you've heard about Sterling?"

"I have. The old grapevine's definitely been buzzing."

"No one called me."

"Right," Kyle said, "because everyone knows that you'd take Sterling apart and give him to a lobsterman for bait."

"I'm not the violent type."

"And I am Shirley Temple."

Tall, lean, wiry Kyle, with his fierce blue eyes, cropped dark hair, and scarily calm demeanor, was about as far from Shirley Temple as a person could get. No dancing. No sunshine. But you wouldn't want Shirley Temple watching your back.

"Any word on that kidnapped girl?" Perry asked.

"Nothing I've heard," Burgess said. "Ryder says they're looking but they've got little to go on."

"Heard you found a body today," Perry said. "You really are no good at going on vacation. So much crazy stuff happens around you places ought to pay you to stay away. Unless they want to attract ghouls and blood maggots."

"I'm flattered," Burgess said. He sat down and started eating. Fideau instantly appeared at his side.

"Bet Melina didn't make a sandwich for the dog," Kyle said. "You know that my girls are totally in love with him. Now they want to know why we don't have a dog. Except for Michelle, of course. She wants a baby."

"Babies are nice," Stan Perry said. "At least Autumn is."

Perry had been such a player before he met Lily.

"So far," Kyle said. "Although she might keep on being good. Some babies just have naturally calm temperaments. My mother says I was hell on wheels from the moment I was born. She says I was never still, even when I was asleep. She says I ate like a horse and never gained enough weight and Michelle says I haven't changed a bit. Oh. Did I mention that I'm getting married?"

Burgess and Perry both said, "About time," together and Kyle grinned.

Burgess said, "When?"

"Soon. I expect she will tell me when she's ready."

"You going to have a wedding?" Perry asked. "A real wedding."

"That's what I hear. The girls are crazy excited."

"And you?" Burgess asked. "You doing okay with this?"

"I kind of bounce around. You know. My ex really did a job on me. I don't have to tell you that."

"Took all my self-control not to do something unlawful," Burgess said.

"Your mother really helped me stay on an even keel, that's for sure."

"She was a wise woman."

There was a moment of silence as three tough guys remembered a small, sweet woman.

Burgess liked Nikki Ryder and had been comfortable working with her, but his ingrained habit when a case was complicated was to touch base with his team and get their reactions. So now, as they ate, he told them everything he knew about Ted Gabbro's situation, the attack on Sherman, the body he'd found today, and what he'd seen on Fenton's computer.

"The housekeeper/nanny took off this morning without telling anyone, and the little girl is still missing. Thoughts?"

"Think we should drop back to 109 and see what we can learn about the players," Kyle said. "It may not be much, but it's worth a try."

Stan Perry seconded the idea, and so that became their plan.

"What about Caleb Sterling?" Kyle asked. "What are we doing about him?"

"That's for later. Stake out the house and make sure nothing happens. If you're up for that."

"You think we dressed like this because we're fashionable?" Kyle said.

Something was lurking in the back of Burgess's mind, but he couldn't get hold of it. Maybe, as was often the case, if he let it simmer and did something else, it would surface.

THIRTY-FIVE

They were at Portland police headquarters, 109 for short, going through records. So far, there was little to go on. They'd found some domestic stuff around Gabbro's divorce from Elyse. Neither party had behaved very well, but she was far and away the winner in the trouble-making sweeps. They'd all been to enough domestics to know divorce, or even the threat of divorce, could lead to all-out war and insanely bad behavior. Elyse Gabbro had been the make scenes, throw her husband's clothes on bushes all over town, sugar in the gas tank type. It was not much of a stretch to imagine her doing something as ugly as tinkering with her husband's essential medication.

They'd need to know more about the divorce agreement and Gabbro's wills or trusts to do an adequate analysis of her potential as a suspect. Would having full custody of Ari be enough for her to get her hands on Gabbro's money or would her hands be tied by trusts and trustees? Could she have some side deal with Gabbro's siblings? Were they also beneficiaries of his will?

Was any of this more than mere speculation? But those emails on Fenton's computer said something was going on. None of this answered the pressing question of why Ari had been kidnapped and whether she was in danger.

Burgess didn't have the authority to dig further. Not his case, just his curiosity. Except it was definitely more than that. Too much murder and attempted murder right next door that he'd been drawn into for him to pretend that he wasn't involved. That's why they were here, digging. He was walking an absurd tightrope but refused to step off.

They found nothing on Gabbro's sister of a criminal nature. She was an attorney at a large law firm and doing well. Unless the incentive was custody of Arielle, Burgess could see little reason for her to get involved in a homicide or a kidnapping scheme. But public records weren't always the best source of information about a person's character or propensities. They were just information. If it were his case, he'd be digging deeper. He and probably one of his team would be in Massachusetts asking questions.

The records concerning Gabbro's brother Daniel were another story. A bankruptcy, some arrests for minor infractions, a little financial fraud. A not uncommon profile for a well-to-do man fallen on hard times, and a profile that indicated a willingness to commit bad acts for financial gain.

On Bridget O'Toole, there was nothing. A suspicious nothing. No address, no phone, and most concerning, no driver's license and no vehicle registered in her name. At least none issued to her at Gabbro's address, where she claimed to live, and to have lived for many years. Given the Boston area's Irish heritage, women named Bridget O'Toole were as a common as cheese. Fewer in Cambridge and none of the photos resembled the woman he'd met. Yet she'd driven up from Cambridge in her own car, or so she said, and driven away again. She wasn't a stranger. Ari had definitely recognized her, even if it was a resentful recognition.

"I'm going to look at vehicles registered to Ted Gabbro," Burgess said. "Maybe he owns the car."

"And I'm looking at cars registered to Annabella Gabbro," Kyle said.

"Does that mean I get Daniel again?" Perry said.

"Why yes, I guess it does," Burgess said. "Is that a problem?"

"No problem, Boss." Perry bent over his computer.

When Burgess finished with Gabbro, finding just the one car he'd driven to Maine, he decided to look up Tony LeBlanc, Elyse Gabbro's intended. Strangely, for a man who lived in the city, LeBlanc owned two cars, an Audi SUV and a Toyota Corolla. Bridget O'Toole had been driving a Corolla.

She might have rented a car, of course, and used Gabbro's when they were at home. But it sounded like he was often away on field trips. And anyway, a man doing field work in rough terrain wasn't likely to be driving a Corolla. Maybe she didn't need a car in the city? Maybe Bridget O'Toole wasn't her real name. Burgess realized he'd never had a chance to check her story with Ari. The girl obviously knew O'Toole but whether it was a long acquaintance, as the woman claimed, or she'd only been with them since the divorce, Burgess didn't know.

The what ifs and maybes ran on in an endless string.

Which reminded Burgess of something he'd wondered about when she showed up at his cottage to collect Ari. How she'd gotten there from Cambridge so early in the day and whether she might not have been telling the truth about that drive. Had she actually stayed somewhere nearby the night before? He had too many questions to sit on his hands.

He called Nikki Ryder.

"I'm sorry, Joe," she said when she answered.

"About Sterling, you mean?" he said. "I'm not sorry, I'm furious. We cops are a small community in Maine, but no one had the decency to give me a call. I had to pick it up from cop-to-cop gossip. That's not good."

"There are plenty of assholes in our business, as you well know, and the justice system does its best to screw us at every turn. Is that what you're calling about?"

"Sterling? Or the justice system? Neither one, actually. Wondering whether you ever established that Bridget O'Toole actually drove up from Cambridge the morning after Gabbro's incident?"

"She said she did."

"Establish," Burgess said.

"No, Detective Sergeant, I didn't. What's up? Why are you asking?"

"You see any identification?"

"Joe." She sounded impatient. And very tired. "What are you getting at? This is not your case, remember? I am keeping you in the loop as a courtesy when I can. But I'm not comfortable with you starting to second guess me." She grabbed a breath, silent for bit, then said, "So why are you asking about Bridget O'Toole?"

"I can't find any record of our Bridget O'Toole holding a Massachusetts driver's license."

There was a long silence on her end. "I'm not going to ask how you know that, am I?"

"I don't think so, Nikki. I just wondered, is all. There's something about her that felt...feels off. How's it going with the Fenton thing?"

"About as expected. Not much to go on. Maybe the ME will find something. Or they'll find a full confession on his laptop? You were right about that house. It's so sterile I wonder if he really lived there."

"Things went okay with the state cops?"

"About as expected," she said again. "Once they'd taken over and gotten my story, I was fine to go if I wanted. A smooth hand-off, except, of course, that some state police detective wants to talk to you and is kind of pissed that you left before he arrived."

"I'm pretty easy to find," he said. "And absolutely the soul of cooperation."

Ryder laughed. "You really believe that?"

"I believe I can be a royal pain in the ass when I want to be, but no one involved in the case has made me want to. Yet."

"I told them where you are staying."

"Well, they won't have any joy there. I'm in Portland. Gave the family a break from all the trouble and turmoil I attract."

Ryder laughed again. "Oh, that'll piss them off. I don't imagine Chris will take kindly to being strong-armed about your whereabouts."

"She'll just tell them where I am and send them packing. Unless they get pushy or forget their manners."

"Both of which are entirely possible."

"Did your canvass of businesses around the boat rental turn up anything?" Burgess had a thought. "I should have asked. Are you alone? Can you talk or is your nosy sidekick there?"

"My nosy sidekick has the endurance and stamina of a consumptive, Joe. Long about five or so, he crashes and has to go home. I'm wondering if he still lives with mom and dad and is supposed to be home in time for dinner. Except I don't see how he got to be a detective when he's such a wimp. Unless it's an act and he's got me bugged or is hiding somewhere watching me. Maybe listening right now. I'm going to have to dig into who he's related to."

"This case," Burgess said. "It's all about relationships."

"So, to get back your question about the canvass? Actually, yes. Kid at the ice cream stand noticed them. I guess before she hid her figure under her life jacket, the woman was quite a looker."

"White blonde hair? Curvy? Real eye candy?"

"Sounds right."

"That could be Elyse Gabbro."

"How do you know?"

"Sounds like Peter Sherman's description of her." Burgess realized he hadn't looked for Elyse Gabbro's license. "You should do a license search. Show her picture to the guy at the ice cream stand. I'm kind of surprised the kid who rented them the boat didn't notice her."

"Too distracted by the girl *he* was watching. If that even was Elyse Gabbro. But isn't Elyse Gabbro in Scotland? And anyway, why would she want to kidnap her own child? Why would she need to? As the custodial parent, she could just show up and take the kid, right?"

"Not if there's joint custody and it's his time with the child. Though likely an exception might be made because of Gabbro's condition. I don't know where his housekeeper would fit in. Maybe as long as she's available, Gabbro still has custody. But isn't it more complicated than that? She tells everyone she's away and unreachable, so how would she even know that Gabbro is in the hospital? Who would have told her what was going on?"

"You certainly have a knack for complicating things."

"It's been said. I like to think I have a knack for clarifying things. For sorting and organizing."

"Well, maybe I could do that, too, if I had Stan and Terry instead of a feckless snoop."

"I am a lucky man," he agreed.

"They with you now? Even though it's not your case and not their case? Just sitting around the old Portland PD doing my work for me?"

"Do you really mind, as long as I keep you informed about what we find?"

She sighed. "I wish I were there."

"You're welcome to join us."

"Right. And the way gossip works, Oh Really would hear about it before morning. He already ripped me a new one when he learned that you were the one who found Fenton's body. I'm pretty much blistered from head to toe. And of course he had to do it in front of the state police detectives. Probably thinks that makes him look like a big man instead of a big jerk but it undermines the heck out of me."

"I think they already know his reputation, Nikki. And yours, which is that you are an excellent detective. Dark parking lot, then," he said.

"Can I ask you something?"

"Sure. What?"

"Are you guys planning on staking out the cottage tonight, just in case that asshat Sterling decides to do something stupid?"

As if the whole bunch hadn't already done several stupid things. "You mean *another* stupid thing. What do you think?"

"What I *know* is that you love your family and wouldn't let anything happen to them, even if you are supposed to be staying away. So you'll be there."

He made an affirmative noise.

"And I'll see you there," she said. "I've always preferred mosquito-infested woods to a dark parking lot."

"You don't have to be there," he said.

"Oh. I think I do."

"Fine. Just don't tell the staties where to find me."

He was pulling up Elyse Gabbro's license when Stan Perry appeared beside him. Blonde. Attractive. With a Cambridge address.

"Joe," Perry said, "you need to see this."

THIRTY-SIX

On Perry's screen was a photo from Fenton's local paper of two people admiring an antique teak motor boat. The caption was, "Local developer Orville Fenton and Swedish visitor Elyse Hensson at the boat show." Perry looked up. "Swedish visitor? Elyse Hensson? Did we know she was using that name?"

Burgess could see why the reporter had chosen to photograph them. Elyse Gabbro or Hensson, in a clinging summer dress, her hair blowing in the wind, was stunning and Fenton, smartly dressed despite his excess weight, looked prosperous and important. Probably was important locally.

"No one ever mentioned it to me and Ryder didn't say anything. I assume she knew Elyse's name so she could search whether or not the woman who was Gabbro's ex and Ari's mother actually went to Scotland. If in fact that is her name. Send me the picture, will you. And send it to Ryder, too."

He gave Perry Nikki Ryder's email. "And what's the date on that?"

Perry told him. Two days ago, the woman on Elyse Gabbro's license, calling herself Elyse Hensson, had been in the lakeside town where the Burgess family was vacationing and in Fenton's company. Not very subtle about being seen in public, in Maine, despite supposedly being in Scotland, was she? What was up with that?

If she and Fenton were the ones who snatched Ari, what was their reason for doing so? If she was here and knew about Gabbro's condition, why not simply show up and take custody of her daughter. What had Ari said? Her mother didn't like her much, didn't really want her around. And how did Elyse whatever her name was get involved with Fenton? Was she the secret investor behind Fenton that Peter Sherman had suspected? Was she somewhere in the correspondence Burgess hadn't had time to go through. He hadn't noticed any Henssons, but then, he hadn't been looking. Could he have missed an E. or Elyse Gabbro amidst all the other Gabbros? At that pace? Of course he could.

If she and Fenton were somehow involved in something, that still didn't explain the attack on Sherman, did it? Unless it was because he would recognize her? Somehow interfere with her scheme? Or had someone else attacked Sherman? Maybe Gabbro's siblings? Perhaps even Bridget O'Toole, who'd then covered herself by appearing in the doorway and complaining loudly about their attempts to save Sherman?

Was Fenton's hiring of Gabbro just a ploy to get him to Maine, isolated from neighbors, colleagues, and friends in order to stage his death? But hadn't Ari said that her father actually had found gold on the property Fenton was interested in? Was it possible Fenton knew about the gold already? Fenton or someone who hired him?

Burgess wasn't going to be able to get any answers from Fenton, that was for sure. And it looked like Peter Sherman wasn't part of any conspiracy. He was just the capable assistant providing his geological expertise, as interested in rocks as his boss. Burgess might have been more suspicious if Sherman hadn't been attacked, but few people allow themselves to be hit on the head and drowned to help hide a conspiracy.

Unless Burgess was simply inventing a conspiracy to fit the facts? Committing the sin he counseled other cops about of letting his theories get ahead of the facts? Then, how to explain a woman who was almost certainly Elyse Gabbro in Fenton's company? What was that about? Why had she lied about being in Scotland? Was she still around here or had she taken her daughter and gone back to Cambridge? That was something Ryder could check with a call to Cambridge police but he couldn't. Or was Elyse Gabbro still here, planning to make another run at Gabbro as soon as he was left unguarded? He wouldn't be in the hospital forever.

There had been no sign of a woman at Fenton's place. No sign of anyone but Fenton, at least from what Burgess had seen on his hasty walk-through.

That something he couldn't quite remember lurked there, waiting for his attention. It might come if he could sit quietly and wait, but right now, that option wasn't available.

He really needed that dark parking lot meeting with Ryder. If she was sincere about showing up tonight, it would be a dark woods or dark lakeside meeting, either of which was fine with him. He needed more information to sort whether the same people who wanted Gabbro dead were the ones who wanted Fenton dead. He knew too little about Fenton—his business, his lifestyle, his enemies.

His brain was awash with all the questions he wanted answered that were not his to ask. An exquisite torture life had designed for him.

It was getting late. Probably time for them to make a plan and head out to the lake. At least late in the evening the roads would be quieter, populated mostly by teenagers and drunks. Hopefully, by the time they got out there, Chris and the kids would be asleep. The point of this expedition was to protect them, not to worry them.

Before he rounded up the troops, he did a quick search for Elyse Hensson in Cambridge. He didn't find her.

Even though he'd said nothing to Kyle and hadn't even called Perry, they were both dressed for a night operation, right down to dark, rubber-soled shoes. They'd worked together long enough to become mutual mind-readers.

"Insect-repellent," Kyle said, fingering his shirt.

"Mine, too." Perry said.

Burgess, underdressed or underprepared, would have to rely on bug spray.

"You bringing the dog?" Kyle asked.

"I'm bringing the dog. He seems to be very well-behaved and he'll be upset if I leave him behind."

"He needs to get used to it," Perry said. "I can't see the brass being okay with you coming to work with a dog in tow."

"If I'm at 109 during the day, Fideau will stay home. Cote sometimes brings in that little rat dog we gave him, and Fideau is such a canine snob he'd eat it just for the honor of the thing." Captain Paul Cote was Burgess's nemesis. Like Nikki Ryder's O'Reilly, he was the kind of boss who inserted himself into investigations but was ignorant about procedure, forcing other cops to work around him as they struggled to protect their scenes from his "bull in the china shop" antics.

"He'd better be quiet or else we'll end up spending a night in the bug-filled woods for nothing."

"I'll speak to him firmly," Burgess said.

Laughing, they shut down their computers, grabbed their gear, and headed out. Stan Perry would be watching where the camp road turned off the main road. Burgess and Fideau would be down at the waterfront in case someone came by boat, which is what it appeared Peter Sherman's attackers had done as well as Ari's kidnappers. Kyle would be watching the rear of the cottage.

As soon as they turned off the road, Perry backed into a little turnout and parked. A little farther down the road, there was a track running into the woods that didn't lead to any cottage. Burgess and Kyle backed their vehicles in there far enough down to be hidden from sight. They doused themselves with bug spray, then moved silently down the road and into position. It was a deeply dark night with only a sliver of a moon. Out on the lake, loons were calling. A nice breeze was coming up to help keep the bugs down.

The cottage was quiet, the only visible light the one in the kitchen that they left on in case some kid needed water or a snack in the night. As they got into position, they heard Ryder's car, lights off, creep slowly past and stop at the Gabbro cottage. She would wait between Burgess's cottage and Gabbro's in case someone came that way.

Then they all settled in to watch.

A little after midnight, as the frustrated mosquitoes buzzed but didn't bite, Burgess heard a sound out on the water. His eyes were now adjusted to the dark, and he watched, poised and alert, as a boat quietly pulled along the dock, tied up to the ladder, and three men climbed out.

Beside him, Fideau stiffened but didn't bark. Burgess sent a silent text to the others.

THIRTY-SEVEN

Their identity was entirely predictable. Caleb Sterling, his son Danny, and his nephew Sean. Dressed like Burgess's team in black. Burgess watched from the shadows as they unloaded gas cans, then clambered onto the dock. They weren't very quiet about it. It seemed that having pending criminal cases wasn't acting as any sort of deterrent. The leniency of the legal system had let them believe they were untouchable.

He shivered, knowing what might have happened if he and the others weren't here, followed by anger at people who could consider torching an occupied cottage as acceptable behavior.

Beside him, Fideau almost growled. He was an amazing dog.

As they gathered their weapons of destruction and headed for the cottage, Burgess couldn't see them but he knew Kyle and Perry had joined him.

This time, he was not going to be subtle or make any pretense of politeness. He drew his gun, and waited. Hard as patience was, they wanted to catch them in the act: a delicate balance as things would have to happen so quickly.

He felt Kyle's hand on his arm. An unspoken reminder not to let his temper get away even if it was justified. So often, through the years, Kyle had helped him keep his balance. Often, like now, without words.

Despite the cool and the quiet, the peaceful lapping of the lake, the night felt charged. There was something electric in the air, singing between them as they waited, tense as wires, for the moment to spring into action.

The three arsonists crossed the lawn. As they reached the deck and stepped up onto it, bending down and opening their cans, Burgess stepped out to meet them.

Like they'd trained for this for years, the others joined him, so that the would-be killers, heady with glee as they prepared to incinerate a sleeping family, found themselves facing three armed men. Big, angry, implacable armed men.

Without speaking, the three turned back toward their boat, as though this was simply deterrence and Burgess's team would just let them walk away. Why not? Everyone else let them walk. Nikki Ryder was there, blocking the way, her gun pointed directly at Caleb Sterling.

Burgess admired her skill at managing to get behind them so quietly.

Like his team, she was all in black.

In the moment before she spoke, he half-expected Sterling to say, "Do you know who I am?"

They all knew who he was—a would-be murderer. A man with no values. No humanity. No sense that anyone other than himself and his family mattered. A criminal of the basest kind.

Burgess, who had investigated the deaths of someone he hated as well as someone he loved, could have told him: everyone matters. A death was not insignificant because the person wasn't important.

"Police," she said. "Put down those cans and put your hands on your heads. Now."

When they hesitated, she snapped, "I said do it now!"

The presence of four armed police must not have been a sufficient deterrent. The three of them rushed Ryder, knocking her off her feet.

Burgess yelled, "Stop!" and fired a warning shot.

Ryder flipped and put a single shot neatly in Caleb Sterling's leg. He went down screaming.

Burgess figured that would probably wake his family, but kept his concentration on the group in front of him.

Slowly, as though they were still considering whether to run, and chance getting shot, or comply, the two boys set down the gas cans they carried.

"You guys got some spare cuffs?" Ryder asked. "I've only got two sets."

Kyle stepped past her and flipped Caleb Sterling, who was screaming for an ambulance, over on his stomach. As he pulled Sterling's hands together, the man kept protesting, insisting they couldn't handcuff an injured man. Never mind that for safety reasons they did it all the time.

"Shut the fuck up before you wake everyone for miles," Kyle said. "You think I give a fuck about a little boo boo on your leg?"

"Boo boo? Jesus. I'm hurt! I'm shot. I need help now."

Ignoring his demands, Kyle searched him, finding matches and a lighter, a cell phone, and a flashlight. "You were planning to kill people," Kyle said. "And you want us to be sympathetic? How about some sympathy for that family you planned to roast?"

"Oh fuck you," Sterling said.

Ryder cuffed Danny and gave cuffs to Burgess to do Sean. They searched all three. Matches, lighters, flashlights, cell phones. Danny also had a hunting knife on his belt and a packet of pills in his pocket that might be drugs.

"You got a prescription for these?" Ryder asked. "'Cuz it's not hard to figure out what these are."

The boy didn't reply.

Before Ryder got on her radio to call for patrol officers to come pick up the boys, and an ambulance for Sterling, they lined the three up against the supports of the deck. She said, "Don't move," and they stepped away to talk.

But Burgess was puzzled that all the commotion and a gunshot hadn't brought his family out to see what was wrong. He realized he hadn't seen Chris's car. He'd been so focused on their mission he hadn't wondered about that. He said, "Be right back" and stepped inside to check on Chris and the kids.

The cottage was empty.

He found a note from Chris on the counter.

Dear Joe, I was worried that those troublemakers might come back, and uneasy about being here without you, so we're going back to Portland. Knowing you, I'm betting you stepped away to keep us safe and you'll be back tonight to keep watch. Hope the mosquitoes don't eat you alive, and I'll see you soon. Call me if it's not too late when you get this. P.S. The kids are worried about you, so if we don't talk tonight, call me in the morning. P.P.S. I don't think I'm going to like sleeping alone. You may be a big lug who doesn't always know how to do relationships, but I'll take awkward over lonely any day.

Chris.

It was late but he knew she wouldn't sleep if she was worrying about him, so he gave her a quick call.

"Sorry if I woke you," he said. "I was afraid you'd worry."

"I did worry. Am worried. You at the cottage?"

"I am."

"Still in one piece?"

"I am."

"You catch some bad guys?"

"I did. We did."

"Good job. Now I'm going back to sleep. We'll be out for breakfast. Be there."

"I will be here. You aren't the only one who doesn't like to sleep alone, you know."

"Oh, Joe." There was laughter in her voice. 'Believe me. I know."

Which, of course she did. Just like she'd predicted his actions tonight. Scary, but he thought it was okay.

He went back outside.

Sterling was moaning and swearing and carrying on like he was the first person in the world who'd ever gotten shot committing a crime. Burgess wasn't too sympathetic. He'd gotten shot committing good acts and hadn't moaned at all. He might have sworn, though. The two boys were looking a little scared. They should have been a lot scared. Fideau was planted in front of them, teeth bared, looking like he was ready to charge.

"Can you call off your dog?" Sean said in a quivering voice. "I think he's going to bite us."

Burgess said, "I wouldn't blame him" to the kid and "Good dog," to Fideau and patted the dog. Fideau gave him that knowing look, like he was saying, "I'm doing the right thing, Boss, aren't I?" Burgess stepped past the prisoners and the dog and joined the others.

"That was too fuckin' easy," Perry said.

"It ain't over yet," Burgess reminded him. "Catching these guys is like catching a mouse in your house and letting it go outside. It'll be right back. Already arrested these idiots once and yet here they are. All these idiots. I can't imagine what judge, faced with the facts of what they did, let them go again."

"So, here's what I think we should do," Kyle said, raising his voice so the bad guys could hear. "We take 'em somewhere far away, some-place real deserted, take away their shoes, and let 'em go to find their way home."

"Wish I'd done that the first time," Burgess said. "Then maybe we wouldn't be dealing with them again. What do you think, Nikki?"

"I think I'm humming my favorite tune and didn't hear any of that."

"Good call," Kyle said. "What do you think, Joe? And do we take the dad along, or just leave him here?"

"That is the problem, isn't it," Burgess said. "They need to be a lot more scared than they are right now. Be easier if Nikki hadn't shot one of 'em, but I don't see that she had a choice."

It was then—the brain worked in mysterious ways, he knew—that the thing that had been lurking in the back of his brain popped out. On the long driveway into Fenton's property, he'd seen a small track leading off into the woods and just caught a glimpse of a building mostly hidden by trees. It had interested him and at the time, he'd wondered what Fenton used it for. But after finding the body, dealing with that, and need to leave so Ryder could report the death, he'd forgotten about it.

"Nikki, when they searched Fenton's property, do you know whether they searched that building back in the woods about half-way down the drive?"

No one seemed surprised by his change of subject.

Ryder shook her head. "I don't think they looked at it. Why?"

"Just wondering. That picture of Fenton and Elyse Gabbro—or Hensson—together. I've been wondering where she's staying. Whether she's still around. Maybe it's just full of old tractor parts or something, but if it's livable, it could be the perfect place for someone to hide out, waiting for a second chance at Gabbro and maybe even Sherman. Just speculating, of course. Not my case. I just…"

"Can't stay out of it," Ryder, Perry and Kyle spoke at once.

Burgess wondered if he'd always been this predictable. Probably not. For years his specialty had been being the meanest cop in Portland. Keeping other cops on their toes. Except for Kyle and Perry, no one had gotten close enough to read him.

"We can go check it out," Ryder said. "Though if we find anything, I'll have to share it with the 'real detectives.' Because I absolutely don't need sleep, it's only old guys like you who do."

"And I'm on vacation." Burgess thought it was becoming his new refrain. "But what are we going to do with them?"

Kyle said, "We could put them back in the boat and set it adrift. Hate to lose a pair of good handcuffs, though. And if they happened to capsize, we'd be in a world of shit. Other ideas?"

Stan said, "Joe, do you have any rope in your truck?"

Cops carried a lot of interesting things in their vehicles just in case. Blankets. Teddy bears. Nonlethal weapons. Spare clothes. Traffic cones. Spike strips.

Burgess considered. "Probably not. Nikki?"

She shook her head. "Got duct tape, though."

"That'll work."

The deck was about four feet off the ground, supported by a series of wooden posts. It didn't take long for them to duct tape their three arsonists to the posts. They also duct taped three loudly complaining mouths. They'd examined Caleb Sterling's wound. It wasn't serious, it just hurt like hell. A hospital visit could wait.

"We'll be back for you in a little bit," Burgess said reassuringly. "Give you some time to meditate on your sins and consider whether you're ready to reform. And while you're doing that, consider that a less kind person wouldn't have taken your murderous caper so lightly. There's a big time shortage of lobster bait this summer."

He was so glad he didn't have to listen to their responses. A tiresome recital of their rights and no doubt something about police brutality. Something about suing Burgess. Wrecking Ryder's career. It was always all about rights and never about responsibility. What about *their* brutality?

A month ago, he'd been worried that he was too old and tired to go on. Times like this made him wonder if he was too cynical. If he'd lost his ability to step back and be dispassionate. A lot was asked of police officers—a lot of taking abuse without responding, a lot of seeing the worst things people could do and remaining calm and able to function, a lot of abused children who'd likely grow up to be abusers themselves. A lot of patiently following the rules when they wanted to beat the crap out of someone.

There were cops out there who were violent just for the fun of it. To let off steam. Because they could. In the face of that, duct taping three men who'd planned to commit multiple homicides to some posts for a few hours wasn't all that bad. Bad in the rule book. Not so bad in the real world. Bad cops would have tossed them into the boat, doused them with their own gasoline, tossed in some matches, and called it an accident.

Good cops just took it and went on doing their jobs..

"You want to check out that building?" Ryder asked, interrupting his reverie.

"I do."

"What do we do with the rest of your team?"

"They can go back to the bosom of their families. Or they can come along. Terry? Stan? What's your pleasure?"

"I am definitely up for another adventure," Kyle said. "It's been a while."

Totally untrue. It had been a ghastly summer. There was a kind of liberation here that came from choosing to deal with this instead of having it forced on them.

Stan reluctantly shook his head. "I would be, but I try to do one of the nightly feedings so Lily can get some sleep. I mean, she's nursing, but if I get Autumn up and changed, it helps. Sorry. I hate to pass up a good time." Even in the dark, they could see his grin. "Not that picking up that little mite and seeing her sweet face isn't also a good time."

"Oh ho!" Kyle said. "Wildman Stan is a thing of the past."

"I never thought..." Perry started to say. "Never mind. Just never mind."

And so the two musketeers headed off with Ryder, knowing Stan's Wildman days were only on hiatus, while the third went home to rock the baby.

THIRTY-EIGHT

hree cars driving together this late at night practically represented a traffic jam. Unless it was a parade. They drove quietly, the dark sky overhead brilliant with stars. Keeping a proper distance as they passed mostly dark, silent houses and a few where parties were going on, brightly lit, with a commotion that had spilled outside. Burgess instinctively slowed to be sure everything was okay. Ahead of him, he saw Ryder was doing the same.

You could take the cop out of the city. Send him on vacation, but unless you blinded him or put a bag over his head, he was going to be watching what he passed.

Ahead, Ryder put on her blinker. Burgess slowed and put his on so Kyle could see where they were going.

Ryder turned her lights off and they followed suit. The police should be done with the Fenton scene, but just in case, they didn't want to blow their chance to inspect the building. He felt a twinge of guilt for involving Ryder in this, given her boss's disapproval, but she'd been on the same page. Neither of them wanted to have to hand over their speculations before they'd finished their job. Fideau sat beside him, looking out curiously. Burgess wondered if his previous owner had any idea what a fine dog this was. Then he wondered why the man had wanted a dog at all. Maybe to intimidate people? More specifically, the young girls he was trafficking. The dog must have hated that.

"Did you used to scare people, Fideau?" he asked.

The dog gave him an "I'm not that kind of dog" look. Then ducked his head, as if he was saying, "They made me do it."

"Right. Sorry. I was just wondering."

Gad but this driveway was long. Abruptly, Ryder swung the wheel and turned onto an overgrown dirt track. He realized the building was visible from the driveway only when the metal roof caught the sun. Possibly by the time the state police detectives arrived, the reflection was gone and the building was invisible.

He wasn't right on her tail, which was a good thing because very abruptly she braked and swung into an opening in the trees. He passed her and tucked in beside her. No room for Kyle beside them, so he turned around so he was ready for a quick getaway and pulled to the side of the road.

They got out and stood in the darkness and silence, waiting and listening. Fideau was right at his side, leaning against his leg.

No sounds. Burgess didn't know whether it meant there was no one here or that whoever was here was asleep. It was a big structure. It might be a storage building for all the implements necessary to maintain such a big place. Or a garage that held Fenton's other cars or boats. Without turning on his flashlight, he couldn't be sure, but he thought it might have a second floor. Maybe a residence for Fenton's staff. Someone had to be keeping up that house and the grounds.

"You know whether Fenton has some staff?" he whispered. "House-keeper? Grounds keeper?"

"No one who lives in the house, but he must have people," Ryder said. "He didn't look like someone who could take care of all this by himself."

She took charge. "Terry, you go around to the right. I'll go around to the left. And Joe, you watch for anyone exiting because we've startled them."

"There's no car," he said, realizing he'd expected one.

"No *visible* car," she corrected. "This place is big. It could easily have storage on the ground floor and living space upstairs. Or it could be parked on the other side."

"Sherman says he saw Elyce Gabbro with a man in a boxy green car."

Ryder nodded.

She and Kyle disappeared into the night.

Burgess waited in a thicket of trees across the driveway from the door. There was a large, garage-type door, suggesting that the building was used to store vehicles or equipment and a smaller door beside it for people. Restless, he wandered around the area looking for any sign of habitation. Without a flashlight it was hard to tell but he thought there were tire tracks leading to the garage door.

Crouching down, and turning his back on the building so he could block the light with his body, he took out a tiny flashlight and studied the ground. Yes. Definitely tire tracks. And something else. Something small and pink. A hair elastic. As he reached for it, he heard footsteps coming his way. It was too soon for Kyle or Ryder. He shut off the light, tucked the elastic in his pocket, and backed slowly into the trees, Fideau still at his side, breathing quietly.

The person, a man he assumed from the size, stopped maybe five feet from him. So close Burgess could smell the man's aftershave. Probably people for miles around could smell it if they were paying attention. The powerful scent was good. It would keep the man from smelling the bug spray Burgess had doused himself with.

He wanted to warn Kyle and Ryder, but movement and the light from the phone would give him away.

The man lit a cigarette, drew deeply, and exhaled slowly. Not allowed to smoke inside, Burgess figured. The man smoked. Slapped at mosquitoes. Cursed. Ground out his cigarette and lit a second one. A light came on inside. The door opened and a woman called, "Tony? What are you doing out there? Aren't you ever coming to bed?"

Tony. Anthony Leblanc, Elyse Gabbro's fiancé?

"Smoking," the man said. Deep voiced. No discernable accent. "You didn't want me smoking inside, remember?"

"Because of Ari. You know. Her asthma."

"Is this how it's going to be?" he asked. "We get married, the kid lives with us full time, and I can't ever smoke in my own house?"

"My house," she said. "We're certainly not living in that hovel of yours."

"Elyse, I've been out here smoking every damned night since we got here. How come it's only tonight that it bothers you? That you noticed? Is your damned kid going to run our whole lives?"

"You knew I had a child when we met, Tony."

"Yeah. And that she was spending a whole lot of time with her dad. So if he's out of the picture, doesn't that mean no more time without her? Maybe you should hope he gets better, huh?"

"Right. And go to all this trouble for nothing? Bella will take her. She wants to anyway."

He laughed. "What about Danny?"

"I may not be the world's best mother, but even I wouldn't stoop to that. We can get Bridget to move in. She can take care of Ari."

He snorted. "There is no way I am having that battle ax living with us, Elyse. As for smoking in the house? This is not a house. It's a freakin' barn with some miserable living quarters upstairs. Place probably has a thousand things that bother the kid's asthma. Like grass and mouse turds and lawn chemicals. But oh no. I can't smoke in there."

"All right. All right, Tony. Come in. You can smoke inside. The bugs must be killing you out there."

Burgess's bum knee was killing him, crouching here like this. He tried to shift and his foot slipped on a rock. A small movement but Leblanc heard it.

"What's that?" he said.

Burgess held himself very still, breathing into his sleeve. Waiting. Fideau steadfastly silent beside him. The dog would make a great detective.

"Elyse," Leblanc called. "I just heard something in the bushes. Did that damned kid get out again?"

"She's asleep in bed," Elyse Gabbro replied. "I think." Silence. Then, "I'd better check."

The door shut, cutting off the spill of light. Burgess wondered if Kyle and Ryder were also listening to this. Not quite an admission of attacking Gabbro, but definitely showing an interest in doing away with him. Definitely confirming that Elyse Gabbro wasn't in Scotland and that they had Ari. The child wasn't missing. Hadn't been kidnapped. Although kidnapping could include taking a child from a custodial parent.

Parsing that was not his problem.

He wished they'd stayed there longer, arguing aloud. On the flip side, he wished Leblanc would go back inside so he could straighten up and take the stress off his knee. He was thinking about his knee, and about the glorious football days that had done it in, when she returned.

This time she flung the door wide open and rushed out. Pausing on the steps, backlit, he couldn't see her face but her figure was definitely worth noticing and her almost white hair glowed.

"That fucking little brat is gone again," she said.

"Let the bugs eat her," Leblanc said. "I am not traipsing through these woods looking for her. We'll find her in the morning."

"But Tony. What if someone finds her? Think about what she might say. She's not a little kid anymore. She sees everything. Hears everything. And talks like a little old lady. What if she says she ran away because her mother tried to kill her father? Or her uncle did, since he's the one who did the actual work. We've talked about it, Tony, and now I'm wondering if Ari was asleep or just pretending to be. She's been awfully strange lately."

"She's always been strange. You just didn't notice. Maybe we should take her for a swim, Elyse, like that boy scout Sherman."

"Yeah? Look how that turned out. Ted would go and rent a house right next door to a cop who just happens to come looking for Sherman. Anyway…" She took a few steps farther out. "We need her, Tony. If he survives, she's our leverage with Ted. Even if she doesn't inherit, we can trade custody for a bigger pay-off. That's what you wanted, isn't it? More of Ted's money?"

"Ha!" he said. "We all want more of Ted's money. You. Me. His sister. His brother. Who, by the way, turned out to be a total incompetent. He was supposed to replace all the insulin with water, not just tamper with one dose and throw the rest in the lake where someone could find it. Man's a fucking moron."

"I can't argue with that."

If he stayed here much longer, he'd get the whole story. And be limping for a month. Of course, no one had asked him to be out here in the night, hiding in the bushes, putting too much weight on his bad knee. He'd volunteered.

"I'll get dressed and we'll look for her. How did she get out, anyway? You were awake. You didn't see her go?"

"Stuff it, Elyse. She's not my kid."

"You stuff it, Tony. I've got a kid. That's just the way it is."

"She old enough to send to boarding school?"

Bridget O'Toole hadn't been kidding when she said Elyse Gabbro's fiancé wouldn't be a good stepfather for the girl. And any woman who stays with a man who'd suggest drowning her child wasn't fit to be a mother.

"I'm getting dressed." Elyse Gabbro went inside and shut the door.

Tony Leblanc stubbed out his cigarette and followed her in.

Burgess straightened, trying not to groan, and he and Fideau moved quietly back to the vehicles, where Kyle and Ryder joined him.

"Holy shit!" Ryder said. "Did you guys hear all that?"

"Hear it? I recorded it," Kyle said. "Probably not good quality and I may not have gotten it all, but I probably got enough. That poor little girl. No wonder she ran away."

Noticing Burgess was rubbing his knee, Kyle said, "You okay, Joe?"

"I don't know. You got a spare knee I could borrow?"

"Saving mine for my old age," Kyle said.

"So what now?" Ryder said. "If they come out to look for Ari, they'll see our vehicles."

"We'd better get moving then."

"Back to the main road or on to Fenton's?" Burgess asked.

"Fenton's," Ryder said. "I could just arrest them, but I think it would be jumping the gun, plus I'm concerned for that child. I wonder where she thinks she's going. If she even knows where she is."

"She'll head for the hospital," Burgess said. "She's been there before. And as they said, she's observant. She'll know which way to go."

"That's a good ten miles, Joe. And I hate to think of that little girl out in the night alone."

"She's a pretty determined girl. And staying here isn't safe either."

"Then let's head out to the road instead. She can't have been gone too long."

"I don't know. They don't seem to have been paying attention," Kyle said. "She could have been gone for hours."

Starting their cars would be noisy, but that couldn't be helped. Maybe the building was well insulated or Elyse Gabbro and her beloved were busy arguing. They started up and headed back toward the main road.

Burgess went last and in his rearview mirror he saw Leblanc come out and stare after them. Their lights were off, so all he'd see were dark blurs, but those dark blurs were moving and even in the dark, movement can catch the eye. He watched Leblanc run back inside and saw a burst of light as the garage door rolled up.

He called the others. "Leblanc saw us. He'll be coming after us."

"Not a problem for me," Ryder said. "I'm a cop just checking things out."

"Kyle and I are just out joyriding," Burgess said. "Recapturing our lost youth."

"I'm still young," Kyle protested.

They reached the main road and turned in the direction of the hospital. If Ari was walking, she'd be somewhere along the road. They wanted to find her before her mother and Leblanc did.

THIRTY-NINE

A few miles down the road, headlights loomed up in his rearview mirror. High. Piercing. Expensive. It had been quite a while since he was out on the road and knew every car by its lights, so Burgess wasn't sure, but he'd bet on a Hummer. Unless it was a fancy truck. It was coming fast.

He wondered if a man who was comfortable suggesting that a child be drowned was the kind who would run right into another vehicle. Rather than test the possibility, he put on his blinker and pulled over. If the driver suspected Burgess had been checking out his hiding place, he'd stop, too. Instead he roared past. Intent on what? If he was looking for Ari, that speed was ridiculous. He wouldn't see anything. Nor did it seem to have registered that even though Burgess's vehicle was unmarked, it was a Ford Explorer with extra antennas and lights in the window. Anyone who wasn't an idiot would know it was a police vehicle and that police were most likely to have been the ones checking out that building.

But Burgess wasn't going to chase. He was going to putter along, as he'd been doing, checking the roadsides for Ari. She was a clever girl, and likely to hide whenever she saw a vehicle coming, but that amazing hair was hard to hide. It would stand out in an otherwise black night.

He drove like he would any time he was searching for someone. Slowly, his head swiveling from side to side, looking for movement or for that flash of hair. Less than a mile later, he saw something. It was only a flash before it disappeared behind a tree. Could have been an animal. But he was going to check it out. He pulled over and stopped. Looked at his canine companion. The dog had found Ari once. Was that a fluke or might he do it again?

They got out and stood in the quiet night, Burgess listening. Fideau probably scenting, waiting to see what his human would do. Burgess patted his warm head and said, "You want to go to work, boy?"

He could swear the dog nodded. He walked the dog across the road, then used his hand to indicate the place he'd seen that flash of white. "Find Ari," he whispered. He released the collar and the dog took off. Quiet. Nose down, nose up. Moving steadily toward the woods. Burgess followed at a distance, giving the dog space to work. After a minute he heard a bark, short and sharp, as if the dog was saying, "Here, Boss, but let's not scare the kid."

He didn't want to scare her. He wanted to keep her safe from people who obviously didn't have her best interests in mind.

He snapped on his light, calling, "Fideau? Ari?"

Another bark. A small voice. "Mr. Burgess?"

He followed those sounds to Ari, who was crouched at the base of a big pine, Fideau beside her, her arms around the dog's neck. Burgess shifted his light so it wasn't shining in her face. Said, "You ran away again," and waited.

"Going to the hospital to see my dad," she said. "Or running away, I guess. My mother and…that man. Tony. They don't want me, you know, Mr. Burgess. They just took me because they want money. My father's money. They think if they have me, he'll have to give them more money to get me back."

So much depended on whether Gabbro recovered. And if he did, on whether the courts would hear about the mother's shenanigans and believe them. Burgess wondered if the people plotting against Gabbro had really thought this through. "Stupid" was a pretty common modifier for "criminal," even for criminals who tried to be smart.

"Let's go over to my truck and talk there, so the mosquitoes won't eat us alive. And tell Fideau he did a good job. He likes that."

She snuggled her face into the dog's neck. "You're a good dog, Fideau. I wish you were my dog."

She stood up, winced, and immediately sat down again. "I can't," she said. "I hurt my foot." She raised a tragic face. "I'm so stupid! Now there's no way I can get away."

"Then I'd better help." He picked her up and headed back to his truck, looking in both directions before emerging from the woods. It wouldn't do much good to rescue the girl if her mother and Leblanc came along and found them.

Burgess got her in the back seat with her seatbelt on, then called Kyle and Ryder. "I have the girl," he said.

"Great. We have Leblanc and Gabbro. And a damaged police car," Ryder said. "I have a broken nose, I think. And Kyle is holding them at gunpoint, trembling like a whippet, so you'd better get here pronto, before he shoots someone."

"If I show up with the kid, that's really going to complicate things," he said. "And she's injured her foot and needs to get it checked out."

Ryder sighed. "And I've injured my nose and *really* need to get it checked out. But I understand. I'll call some of my people and send Kyle home when they get here."

"Sorry about your nose." She did sound funny when she talked and Burgess knew too well how painful a broken nose could be. "What happened? Someone went past me like a bat out of hell. Looked like one of those stupid Hummers."

"And it *was* a stupid Hummer. Which, despite all the bells and whistles, didn't do an awful lot better than my vehicle. I've called a couple of tow trucks."

"You call the staties yet?"

"Not sure what to tell 'em. Not until I've had a chance to interview these two idiots."

"Tell 'em you had a hunch and found these two staying in a building on Fenton's property. You overheard them discussing the child who was supposedly abducted, saying that she had run away. That's your case anyway. Say you left to look for the child and they followed you and deliberately damaged your vehicle. Let them take it from there."

"Oh. God. My nose! I think my face is going to explode." A pause. She said, "Would you do that? Just hand them over without asking any questions? And what about Terry?"

They both knew the answer. This was complicated in every possible way. Kyle should leave. Ryder should go to the ER. And someone had to take charge of Elyse Gabbro and Leblanc. He knew exactly how she felt about handing it over to someone else. Been there himself. Shot. Knocked on the head. Shut out by his vindictive boss. He'd been lucky. He had Kyle and Perry. But there had to be other competent detectives in her agency that she could call on.

In the background, he heard Kyle growl, "I said stay still. Which means don't …fucking…move."

He remembered that she'd used her handcuffs on the three idiots back at his cottage. Hers and Kyles. So she needed patrol to show up to secure the two prisoners.

What a night. It looked so benign, as nights so often did while all sorts of violence and wrong-doing writhed under the surface.

He should be there to help. He'd gotten Kyle into this. Kyle had only volunteered to watch the cottage with him. Now he was up to his ears in a matter that wasn't his and might not even be Ryder's. All they needed at this point was for Burgess to show up to help and then Oh Really to show up to turn the whole thing into a giant clusterfuck.

"Mr. Burgess," Ari asked from the back seat, "am I causing trouble again?"

"I think trouble swirls around you, Ari," he said. "But the only way you cause it is by being the object of a lot of people's greed and desires."

"Is my mom going to go to jail?"

He decided to treat her like the mature child she seemed, and tell her the truth. At least, the truth as he understood it. "I don't know, Ari. It all depends on what we learn about her intentions. Their intentions, hers and Mr. Leblanc's. On whether she and others were somehow involved in causing your father's condition. In taking deliberate steps, I mean."

"Of course they were. It's a..." Ari hummed while she searched for the word she wanted. "A conspiracy, Mr. Burgess. A conspiracy to get rid of my father so they could get their hands on his money."

"How do you know this?"

"Oh. People talk." She tried to toss it off airily, but he heard tears lurking. "They think because I'm a child that I don't hear things or see things. Or that I'm asleep. How can I sleep when I know they're plotting? When I still don't know if my father will be okay—no one will tell me anything—and when they talk so openly about how they—my mother and Tony—don't want me? I feel..." More humming. Another search for words. "I'm scared, Mr. Burgess...uh, I mean, Detective Burgess. I mean, if they will try to hurt him, why wouldn't they hurt me?"

Burgess couldn't do much to comfort her while he was driving, but Fideau the wonder dog slipped between the seats and curled up beside her.

"Do you know anything about your father's plans...uh...in case something were to happen to him?"

A question he wouldn't normally ask a child. But Ari was no ordinary child, and her close relationship with her father might mean he had confided in her, appropriate or not.

"You mean like his will and stuff?"

Big mistake. Now she was really crying.

"I'm sorry, Ari. I shouldn't have asked you that. We'll be at the hospital soon. Maybe they'll let you see your father this time."

It had struck him as odd that they'd refused to let anyone see Ted Gabbro, not even Ryder.

"He's been refusing visitors to protect me, I think." She sighed like a weary old lady. "I hope it will be different this time."

How did refusing visitors, including the police, protect him? Could he even have truly blocked the police? Wouldn't it have been better to tell investigators what he knew and share his suspicions about what had caused his condition? Was he too afraid that someone would try to get at him in the hospital? So afraid he'd refused to see anyone? Perhaps he'd still been too unwell to talk, though that was surprising.

Since he was treating her like an adult informant, Burgess figured he'd go on. In the real world, where he was the investigating detective and she was a witness and a secondary victim, he would have to have an adult with her if he wanted to ask questions. The events surrounding his summer vacation were turning him into a serious rule breaker. Eventually someone, Oh Really most likely, would take his head off for all his breaches of protocol.

Unless no one found out he'd been involved. Hard to hide showing up at the hospital with an injured child in tow. "I found her by the side of the road" only worked until someone recognized him, remembered he'd been at the hospital before, or until someone—county or state—started asking hard questions. Like what the hell he'd been doing out on that road at that time of night anyway. And he still had three goobers duct taped to his porch. They would have to be dealt with, too.

Because they were dumb and self-righteous, the lead goober was likely to say, "Another cop shot me and then three of them duct taped us to the porch and left us there."

Of course, those same goobers would have to explain what they were doing at the cottage, and the presence of the boat, lighters and matches, and gasoline. Their prior history with a family just trying to have a quiet vacation at the lake would go far to eclipse their complaints.

What was anyone going to do to him? Fire him? He didn't work for any of them. Of course Captain Cote, his perpetual nemesis, would have things to say about how he was sullying the reputation of the department, but Burgess had gotten good at letting Cote's complaints drift past like puffs of smoke.

"Are we almost there?" Ari asked, reminding him that he had more questions for her. Also reminding him that he shouldn't be questioning a small child. Maybe he was asking too much, but he thought she was accustomed to being treated like an semi-adult.

"Bridget O'Toole," he said. "Is she somehow involved in this? Ari. Wait. I'm sorry if I'm asking too much of you when you're just a kid. You don't have to talk about any of this if you don't want to."

"It's okay, Mr. Burgess. I kind of like it that you don't treat me like I'm just some dumb kid."

"You're definitely not a dumb kid. You're a smart kid," he said. "How's your foot feeling? You holding up okay? We'll be there soon."

"It hurts a lot. But my father says that I am unusually brave. Do you think I'm brave?"

"Yes, Ari. I do."

"Thank you."

She returned to his question. "Do I think Bridget is involved with them? My mother and those others? No. She's just...I don't want to say anything bad about her, Mr.... uh, Detective Burgess. She tries to be good to me. It's just...I don't know . . . she's not very maternal, I guess. And she's disappointed about things, you know, like the fact that my father doesn't want to marry her and make her my new mother, and so she sometimes takes it out on me. She's not...well, she's not a terrible mother. She doesn't actually dislike me, like my real mother. But she's..."

Again that humming while the girl searched for a word. "She's not warm. I think she doesn't know how to be. It's kind of odd, since part of her job is looking after me, but she's not the huggy, kissy type. She's more the 'make sure the child is clean and properly dressed and given healthy food' type, if you know what I mean."

He did know. He also knew, from all he'd seen, how a family's attention or lack of it could shape the adult a child became. It was just plain sad. On the surface, this child had all the comforts and privileges the world could ask. She just had a mean and disinterested mother and a largely absent father, a reserved caretaker with an agenda of her own, and maybe a scheming aunt and uncle. She seemed to be doing all right, but she deserved more. Needed more. Like it or not, her father was going to have to step up.

Detective Joe Burgess, family counselor. Of course, social service work was one of the things cops did a lot.

The lights of the hospital loomed out of the darkness.

"We're here," he said.

Where he wanted to be was with Ryder and Kyle, getting the story. Catching bad guys. But as the Rolling Stones told us, you can't always get what you want.

As he parked the car, he asked, "Did your mother and Tony take you...abduct you...or did you go with them willingly?"

"They grabbed me," she said. "I was happy...well, sorta happy at the cottage, waiting for my father to come back. Except for...you know...not getting to come to your party."

One more question before he took her inside. Set of questions. "Did they take you to that place at Mr. Fenton's right away?"

"Yes."

"Did you meet Mr. Fenton?"

"I did. He let us stay in that place over where he stores his equipment. He didn't like me much because I wanted to swim in his pool and he said I was too noisy.

Ari? Noisy? Sure she talked a lot, but she was a lonely kid in a bad situation. Fenton must have been a horrible prig.

But Ari wasn't done. She said, "Do you want to know why they killed Mr. Fenton?"

FORTY

Now Burgess had stepped right in it. He needed an interview room. A recording of this. Not a chat with an injured child in a dark car in a hospital parking lot. Actually, this information was for the state police detectives investigating Fenton's death. Did he let her tell him now and later share it with the state police? Not let her talk and keep the story fresh for them? He wasn't even sure how much of what Ari said was the truth. He liked her and admired what his mother would call her "pluck" but he also knew her difficult family situation had made her a good actress and an accomplished manipulator.

He considered waiting until she'd been treated, then getting out his phone and recording her story. But it was too likely that by the time they were done checking out her ankle, some person with actual authority would appear and snap the girl up. One thing he knew for certain was that he was not going to take her home with him again. Not if he wanted any chance of an amicable reunion with Chris.

He gave her the choice. "You want to tell me about that now? Or wait until they've taken care of your foot?"

"We'll talk now," she said.

He set his phone to record. Identified her. Said, "Okay, Ari, if you know, who killed Orville Fenton? And also, if you know, why was he killed?"

"I do know."

"Go ahead."

When he glanced back, he saw that Fideau had his head in her lap and Ari was patting the dog.

"Maybe I need to explain some things," she said.

"Okay."

"I think you know that Mr. Fenton hired my father to look for gold on some property he wanted to buy."

"I did know that. From Peter Sherman. And from you."

This conversation was *so* weird, even for a man who'd had plenty of weird conversations.

"Well...the person who was really going to buy the property...I mean...who was pretending to want to buy the property...was my mother. Or her and Tony."

Ari burst into tears. "It's so awful, Mr. Burgess, what their plan was. I don't know if I can even say it. I'm so scared that no one will believe me. Because their plan is so awful. And I'm scared that my father won't get better and I'll have to live with them, with my mother and Tony, even though if I tell the truth about what happened I won't be safe."

True. If her mother had been in a plot to kill her father and Ari told what she knew—knew or surmised—she *wouldn't* be safe. After what he'd heard Leblanc say, he didn't think she was safe anyway.

Ari wasn't done. "Or if I'm not with them, then I'll be with my Aunt Bella and..." She lowered her voice, like someone besides Burgess was listening. "And *she's* in it with them. Maybe even my Uncle Daniel is part of it, though I don't know about that."

Burgess passed her a clean cloth handkerchief. He always carried them. Had given out so many over the years that he was half surprised his reputation wasn't as the meanest cop in Portland but as "handkerchief man."

She said, "Thank you," and buried her face in it. Her voice continued, slightly muffled. "I'm going to tell you anyway. I have to tell someone and I trust you."

He decided to lead her a little. "Tell me about who is pretending to buy the property? And why?"

He got a muffled "yes."

"Do you mean they asked Fenton to act for them and asked him to hire your father and Peter Sherman to look for gold?"

"Yes. Well. Hire my father. And Peter goes where my father goes. They're a team."

"Do you know why?"

"Why they wanted Fenton to hire my father or why he and Peter are a team?"

A precise little thing. Kid would make a hell of a good interviewer some day. "Why they wanted Fenton to hire him," he said.

Another muffled answer. "Yes. It's all about money."

He waited.

"I feel like some of it—giving them the chance to do this—is my fault, Mr. Burgess, because I wanted us...my father and me...to have a real vacation at a real Maine cottage. I'd seen pictures in a magazine and it looked so...I don't know, Mr. Burgess, summery. You know? Swimming and floating around in a tube and buying food at a farm stand instead of a grocery store. Maybe go out a boat and see puffins? Eat a lobster with my fingers. If I hadn't wanted it, if he hadn't done this to please me, they couldn't have gotten him alone and you know, vulnerable like this..."

She dissolved in tears and couldn't go on.

"Let's get you inside and get your foot taken care of, Ari," he said. "This is making you too upset."

Not what he wanted to happen. If she'd been an adult, he would have taken as long as it took. But it was very late and she was a tired, injured child. Just because she acted so adult didn't mean he should be fooled into treating her like one.

"Okay," she said. "But I promise I'll finish telling you about ...about things...after. If we're going inside, what happens to Fideau? Will they let him come in?"

"No. Not in a hospital. But he's a big boy. He can take care of himself. We'll leave the windows partly open so he can stay comfortable. It's cool enough tonight. And I'll give him some water."

"Will you give me some water?"

"Are you thirsty?"

"I am."

He cracked the windows. Gave Ari a bottle of water and poured another one for Fideau. Then he reached in to pick her up. "No. Wait," she said. "What if this is my only chance? What if they come here? What if they find me? I have to finish this."

He backed up and hit record and Ari told the rest of her story.

"My mother was all flirty with Mr. Fenton. It's something she does when she wants to get her way, see. Though it had stopped working with my father. Anyway, Mr. Fenton was getting impatient about the land she'd told him she wanted to buy, and she got impatient right back and told him that the land didn't matter and anyway, things hadn't worked out with Gabbro like they'd planned."

Ari paused. "I guess I should explain that since no one ever tells me anything, I do a lot of listening when people don't know I'm there. And this time, they were out by the swimming pool. My mother. Tony. Mr. Fenton. I'd put on my suit and was going to take a swim. By myself. I know, Mr. Burgess, that I'm not supposed to do that, but no one was paying any attention to me when I asked to go swimming. This was going to be my vacation and I didn't want to spend it in that hot, smelly old building with nothing to do."

She grabbed a breath before going on.

Burgess realized he was so focused on listening to her story he'd forgotten this was a young child who might be about to tell him she'd witnessed a murder. Before he could speak, though, she rushed on.

"Mr. Fenton said 'What's this really about? Are you saying you got me involved in something illegal? This isn't about buying the land?' and Tony said, 'What does it matter? You'll still make money' and he started explaining how Mr. Fenton should get Gabbro...he said Gabbro, not Mr. Gabbro...back out into the field to do some more tests. And then my mother kind of giggled and said they'd take care of the rest."

"Did you see them attack Mr. Fenton?" he asked, interrupting. He didn't like to rush her but couldn't shake the uncomfortable feeling that any moment someone official, someone who had a right to care for Ari, would appear and bring this conversation to a halt.

"I did," she said, eerily calm for someone who'd witnessed a crime. "They argued about what Fenton owed them and what they owed him and he said he was finished. Just for them to pay him what he was owed and leave. Tony said something like 'sorry, we can't leave.' And then they pushed him in the swimming pool and Tony jumped in and he held Mr. Fenton's head under the water and my mother jumped in to help and—"

A voice behind him, male, angry, impolite, said, "What the fuck do you think you're doing, Burgess?"

Oh fuck! Oh Really. He must be losing his edge. He'd been so engaged with Ari he hadn't heard the man coming.

"Is this Arielle Gabbro?" Oh Really asked. Well, shouted, because this was O'Really, who couldn't read a situation with a magnifying glass and extra large print.

"Calm down, O'Reilly. This is a child and you're scaring her."

"I hope I'm scaring you."

"I don't scare easily, Tim. But this is a frightened, injured child. You can bluster at me all you want, but you be considerate of her."

He shut off the recorder, picking Ari up and settling her comfortably in his arms, and locked his vehicle. "If you can."

Timothy O'Reilly was a big man. Not a broad-shouldered ex-football player like Burgess, though he might once have been. He was still tall, but it was as though whatever impressive chest and shoulders he'd once possessed had melted and run down to his waist. The belly thus produced made him look like he was ten-months pregnant, and he'd long ago started bending slightly backward to balance the weight. It was far from an intimidating sight unless someone was afraid of getting crushed.

He was also what a novel from an earlier age might have called "choleric." A red-faced, angry bully who manipulated people with fear and threats. It might get him cooperation but it didn't get him respect, nor draw the best from his people.

"You're done here, Burgess," Oh Really said, holding out his arms for Ari. "Give me the girl."

No "It's okay, dear, I'm a police officer, like Burgess." And no "Don't be scared." He never even looked at the girl as he held out his arms. Like Ari was a package, not a person.

Ari, part scared and part an excellent actress and reader of situations, gave a terrified scream and buried her face in Burgess's chest.

"I don't think so," Burgess said. He started walking toward the door, forcing the other man to come after him, arms still foolishly outstretched.

"Not your case," Oh Really bellowed.

As they reached the door, Burgess swung on him and glared. "Will you please tone it down, Tim? She's scared enough already."

"Look, I need to talk with this little lady, Burgess. We've got some things to clear up."

"You got a parent or guardian handy, Tim? Can't talk to her without one."

Reminding him that it wasn't proper procedure to try and interview a child without an adult present made him redder than he already was. Burgess couldn't help himself. He was willing to cooperate with another agency when the goal was catching bad guys and getting justice. Cooperating with a bully so the man could claim the glory of rescuing a kidnapping victim when he hadn't done a damned thing to make it happen? Not so much.

Observing correct procedures was not something Oh Really was good at. "Fuck you, Burgess," he said.

"You watch your language, Tim. There is a child present, in case you've forgotten." Speaking slowly. Calmly. "An injured, frightened child. We don't talk like that in front of children."

Burgess had an idea. "I think her father is still here in the hospital. Maybe he's well enough to sit with her, see her through the procedure and then maybe you can interview her."

———

He wondered how Oh Really knew to be here. Was it just because he couldn't stand letting Burgess have any credit? If there was a scene he needed to attend to, it was the one where a man and woman in a

Hummer—a woman who had told everyone she was out of the country and unreachable—had deliberately run into one of his detectives and injured her. The man couldn't not know about that. Ryder had had to call for back up and tow trucks.

Had he already been to that scene? Pressured Ryder into telling him about Burgess and the girl instead of showing concern for an injured officer? It didn't seem like there had been enough time for that. Had his spy gone to the scene? Somehow gotten the information and Oh Really had chosen to come here instead of checking on his injured officer while Ryder was tied up without a vehicle, with a broken nose and who knew what other injuries?

If it was possible for the man to slip lower in his estimation, the likelihood that he knew about an injury to one of his officers but had chosen to come to the hospital without her did it.

The two attempted murders on Oh Really's watch had involved people connected to Elyse Gabbro, as had the apparent abduction of her daughter, all while the information the sheriff's office had was that the woman was hiking in Scotland and unreachable. For her to suddenly turn up like this should have focused Oh Really's attention on her like a heat-seeking missile. Given the damned fool a chance to solve a case and hand it over to the state police for the glory. Wasn't coming here a strategic blunder?

Burgess kept walking into the hospital, Oh Really still trailing him like a bit of toilet paper stuck to his shoe. He carried Ari up to the reception window. "Detective Burgess, Portland police," he said, "Got a little girl here with an injured foot."

The woman pulled up a computer screen and started asking questions like every bureaucrat in every hospital except his own, where they practically had a Joe Burgess room permanently on reserve, and Dr. Cohen, one of the ER physicians, went out of her way to make sure he was cared for.

The woman asked. Ari answered. The woman wrote things down. Finally, she looked at Burgess and asked, "Do you have her insurance information?"

Right. He finds an injured runaway child by the side of the road in the middle of the night and has the necessary insurance information. But this was Arielle Gabbro, a nine-year-old little old lady who was forced to fend for herself because she was surrounded by indifferent or distracted adults.

She said, "Right here," and pulled a card from the pocket of her shorts.

The woman typed in the information without a blink and handed back the card.

"Just wait in those chairs," she said, "and someone will call you."

"Will it be long, do you think?" Burgess asked, knowing that hospital ERs could make you feel like your whole life was slipping away.

"Pretty quiet tonight, so maybe not."

Burgess settled Ari in a chair and sat down beside her. Oh Really sat on the other side. He hadn't left them for a moment, so Burgess figured he hadn't yet checked on the Ted Gabbro.

"You find out if Ari's father is well enough to join her?" Burgess asked.

"I've been busy," Oh Really said.

Burgess could have gone on baiting him, starting with "Doing what?" but he was tired and didn't want to play the game anymore. He wanted to save his energy for the child. He told Ari, "I'll be right back. If that man tries to ask you questions, just tell him he can't."

He walked over to the window, not looking back to see if there was steam coming out of Oh Really's ears. Scarlet face. Enormous belly. Steaming ears. It would have been a sight.

He asked the receptionist if she could check on whether Theodore Gabbro was still in the hospital. She checked and shook her head. "I'm sorry, Detective. Dr. Gabbro left us about three hours ago."

What the heck. Left? Without being in touch with Ryder? How, Burgess wondered? He didn't have a car. And where had he gone? Back to the cottage or back to Cambridge? Why, if he was well enough now to be discharged, had neither Burgess nor Ryder been able to see him? Had the mysteriously missing Bridget O'Toole come to pick him up? Wouldn't he have raised hell if he learned Ari was missing? Been in touch with someone about his daughter? Unless he had some plan neither Ryder nor Burgess knew about? Or maybe Ryder did. She didn't—couldn't—tell him everything.

Burgess pictured the man storming Fenton's house. Or back in Cambridge, storming his ex-wife's house. Not too productive if he didn't know the details of Ari's abduction or where the players were. Imagining was hard to do anyway since he had no physical sense of Gabbro. He'd only seen the man unconscious in bed.

He stepped away from the desk, his back still to Oh Really and Ari, and called Ryder.

"It's Burgess," he said. "Where are you? Why aren't you at the hospital?"

"Can't talk right now," she whispered. "Is Oh Really there?"

"He is. We need to talk. I've just been told that Gabbro left the hospital tonight."

"I know. Gotta go, Joe."

She ended the call before he could object, leaving him puzzled and frustrated. He understood, though, that her circumstances might prevent her from talking. She must be surrounded by other officers, including her partner/spy. Managing a scene. In pain.

He went back to Ari and Oh Really. Oh Really was leaning over the girl, using his size to intimidate her. Ari had squirmed back in her chair as far as she could to get away from him. Before Burgess reached them, she yelled, "You leave me alone!" and ducked under the arm planted to trap her in place, sliding into Burgess's seat.

"Please, Mr. Burgess," she said. "Help me. This man is scary and he won't stop asking questions even though you said he couldn't."

At that moment, a nurse came through a door and called, "Arielle Gabbro."

Burgess scooped Ari up. Oh Really rose to follow.

"Stay here, Tim," Burgess said.

"No way. I'm the law around here, not you, Burgess. If anyone should be bringing an unattended child in for treatment, it should be me."

"Back off, Tim. Now. Or you'll be needing treatment, too."

"You and whose army?" Oh Really blustered. Surrounding himself with yes men and women had spoiled him. He really did think he was a big, important policeman. He was big, Burgess would give him that, but if the man wanted respect, he'd need to earn it with competence. And competence was something he didn't have. Too many years behind a desk, getting told what he wanted to hear.

Ignoring him, Burgess headed toward the nurse. "This is Ari," he said.

"Oh, honey," the nurse said, taking in Ari's scraped and dirty legs, bug bites and muddy clothes. "What happened to you?"

"I was running away after my mother and the man who will be my stepfather were talking about drowning me in the lake and I twisted my foot."

This kid was such a natural manipulator. Burgess hoped when she grew up she'd use her talents for good. "We should call the police," the nurse said. She looked at Burgess. "Then who are you?"

"Detective Sergeant Joe Burgess, Portland police. My family is renting the cottage next door to Ari and her father. I found her by the side of the road. It's a long story," he said. "I hope you can take care of her. It's late and she's very tired."

A lot of information left out. He hoped it was enough to let them treat her.

"Well, I don't know..." the nurse began.

"Please," Ari said. "It really hurts."

She led them to a treatment room where soon a doctor who looked far too young came in, examined Ari's foot, asked some questions, and declared it a bad sprain. He wrapped her ankle up, told Burgess to keep it elevated and give her children's Tylenol, and was ready to rush away when Burgess asked, "Is there another way out of here besides back through the waiting room? There's a man out there who's been paying too much attention to the child. I'd rather not take a chance that he might follow us."

The doctor studied Ari, then Burgess, then asked, "Ari, is Detective Burgess right?"

Right. Ask the kid, not the cops. A smart move that was fine with Burgess. He figured Ari could handle this.

"Yes, Doctor. He's big and fat and creepy...and he doesn't observe personal boundaries." She burst into tears.

Half real—it was late and she was exhausted—and half, again, a fine acting job.

"This way," the doctor said.

As Burgess followed, he hoped Oh Really didn't anticipate this move. He wasn't a good cop. He was careless about rules and procedure and a bully to his people, but he was a wily one, and a wily cop might expect another cop to try and outwit him. Especially a wily cop who always wanted to win.

Burgess liked to win, too. Just not, he hoped, at the expense of others. Except bad guys.

They went out the back door and around the side to the entrance, staying as best they could out of the light. Dammit! There was a figure leaning against his car.

Burgess hesitated, studying the size and shape. Tall, lean, dark-haired. Definitely not Oh Really. It was Kyle.

"Where's your car?" he asked Kyle when he was close.

Kyle pointed toward the dark end of the parking lot.

"You have any idea what's going on?"

"In the universe? The world? The country? Or just in this cluster-fuck of a night?"

"The night."

Kyle looked at Ari. "Sorry for the language."

"Oh, it's not a problem. My father swears sometimes when he's trying to figure something out. Or when he's talking to my mother."

Burgess said, "This is Detective Kyle. He's my partner."

The girl he was holding gave Kyle a sweet smile. "Pleased to meet you," she said. To Burgess she said, "What are you going to do with me?"

Burgess didn't know, but Kyle said, "Take you back to your cottage. Your father is there, waiting for you."

"I hope he's got some food," Ari said, as though this news was not at all surprising. As though her absent-minded father had just stepped out for a bit instead of nearly dying. Maybe his distracted parenting was enough to make the irregularity of their lives seem normal.

"Is Bridget there, too?" Burgess asked.

Kyle shrugged. "Yes. Ryder said Gabbro was there and so you could bring Ari back to him. She was a bit cryptic. Hard to talk with a lot of people around. And a broken nose."

Burgess thought next year he'd look for a cottage that was totally isolated. This set of neighbors and their catastrophes was too much trouble. He looked at Kyle. "How and when did that happen? Gabbro getting sprung, I mean."

Kyle shrugged. "Dunno. Ryder told me on the down low that that O'Toole woman had picked Gabbro up earlier and taken him to the cottage. I guess she got a call about it. Just now, I mean. The doofus Oh Really has spying on her showed up at the accident scene, so she couldn't talk freely. "

Burgess felt almost dizzy trying to keep up with the endless permutations of this case. Ryder hadn't mentioned that Gabbro was getting released, nor that she'd spoken with O'Toole. Last he'd heard, they'd had a meeting scheduled and O'Toole had disappeared. He reminded himself Ryder must have gotten the call recently. That they'd all been rather busy.

"Yeah. I know," Kyle said. "She says she's sorry she couldn't talk when you called."

"She coming here? To the hospital to get her nose fixed?"

Kyle shook his head. "Think she hitched a ride back to Portland with one of the deputies. She was not eager to show up here with Oh Really in the waiting room.

"Why do you call that man Oh Really?" Ari asked.

Kid didn't miss much.

"Because his name in Timothy O'Reilly. Sheriff Timothy O'Reilly," Kyle explained. "He's the county sheriff but he doesn't seem to know much about real police work, and when people explain things to him, he always says 'Oh, Really?' so it's become his nickname."

Ari giggled.

"We'd better get out of here before he comes looking for us," Burgess said. "Want to stop at the cottage for a beer?"

"How about stopping at Gabbro's cottage for some answers."

"Maybe a bit of both?"

"Sounds like a plan."

Kyle headed for his vehicle. Burgess settled Ari in the back of his car with Fideau, and drove slowly out of the lot.

As he was turning onto the entrance road, he saw Oh Really come rushing out the door.

"I win," he said. He headed for the cottage. And Gabbro.

FORTY-ONE

Ari was asleep by the time they reached the cottage. Burgess left her sleeping in the truck, with Fideau standing guard, while he and Kyle knocked on the cottage door. Bridget O'Toole answered, her quick indrawn breath signaling her intention to launch into an objection to their presence.

"Here to see Dr. Gabbro," Burgess said, pushing past her. "And please don't give me any excuses or bullshit. His problems have pretty much ruined my vacation. I'm owed some answers."

From behind her, a man's voice, sounding weak and hesitant, said, "Let them in, Bridget. It's time I thanked Detective Burgess for saving my life."

Burgess and Kyle went into the living room, where Gabbro, looking pale and fragile, was lying on the couch, covered with a plaid blanket. He smiled pleasantly but Burgess thought there was something off about his affect. Maybe it was just being in a strange place after a recent hospitalization or because it was late.

Burgess introduced himself and Kyle, and they took chairs across from the couch. Bridget O'Toole retreated to the kitchen where she parked herself on a stool, watchful, poised to interfere.

Gabbro looked after her apologetically. "I'm sorry," he said quietly.

"Bridget's social graces are sometimes lacking, and of course, she's been very worried about me."

"But not about Arielle?" Burgess said.

Gabbro looked down. "Perhaps another area where her skills are sometimes lacking, as, I fear, are mine."

Not that Burgess needed to be told that. Suppressing the question, "Is there anyone in her life capable of looking after her?" Burgess asked, "Did Bridget tell you about the abduction?"

"Abduction?" Gabbro said. "What abduction?"

"Ari's abduction."

"Arielle is staying with my sister."

Burgess glanced toward the kitchen and lowered his voice. "Did Bridget tell you that?"

Gabbro, looking confused, shook his head. "I don't know about that, but..." He trailed off.

Burgess decided to revisit that and moved on. "Let's start with what you've been up to. Both the county police and I have tried to see you at the hospital and always been told that you were unconscious or too ill to have visitors. And while that's been going on, someone tried to kill Peter Sherman, whom I would have supposed meant something to you, and abducted your daughter. You're obviously well enough to have left the hospital. Have you been in touch with the police to inquire about Ari or Sherman?"

"I spoke earlier with Detective Ryder. Earlier tonight, I mean. I think."

Kyle cleared his throat, a reminder to Burgess to slow down, take it easy, notice what was going on. His usual check on Burgess's "bull in a china shop" approach when Burgess was wound up.

Burgess caught his eye and nodded. Definitely something off. More gently, he asked, "Did your doctors say that it was all right for you to leave the hospital?"

"I don't...didn't...uh, Bridget said it was fine. She said she'd come to get me. We'd go back to the cottage and then Annabella would bring Ari and we could finish our...uh..." He seemed to search for a word. "Vacation." Forming that simple answer seemed to wear him out.

Burgess decided to keep questioning. There was something wrong with Gabbro but maybe he could get some answers before the man faded completely.

"So Bridget told you that Ari is staying with your sister?" He checked that Kyle had his eye on O'Toole and got a faint nod.

Gabbro said "Yes."

"She didn't tell you that Ari had been abducted by your ex-wife and her fiancé, Tony Leblanc? Snatched off the dock and taken away in a boat?"

Gabbro shook his head, puzzled. "Not possible. Elyse and Leblanc are in Scotland."

"No. They're here, making no end of trouble. They're the ones who abducted your daughter, the ones who hired Fenton and got him to involve you in looking for gold on that property, and the ones who killed Fenton."

Too much at once, he knew, but he was wound up and sick of playing nice with the people who'd ruined his vacation.

Gabbro looked stunned. "I know nothing about any of this," he said. "Nothing." He looked at Burgess. "Fenton is dead?"

Perhaps he should have been gentler with someone just recovering from having nearly died, but Burgess found Gabbro's naiveté and lack of curiosity or concern about his daughter infuriating, even as he wondered whether O'Toole had sprung the man too soon and what her agenda was. Was she trying to get control of the man while he was befuddled and helpless? Or was she working with someone else, if not the ex-wife and Leblanc, maybe the sister, Annabella, or the brother, Daniel?"

"You didn't know your ex-wife was here? That they had taken Ari?"

Gabbro shook his head. "Bridget told me…"

Burgess cut him off. Wanting to gauge Gabbro's reaction, he said, "Ari isn't safe with them, you know. She overheard them discussing whether they should drown her in the lake."

"Oh, you know, Detective, Arielle is quite the fabricator." Gabbro spoke slowly, like someone only half emerging from a fog. "She can spin some quite impressive yarns."

Burgess tried not to raise his voice. The man was obviously unwell. But he was the best that Ari had. "Well, Detective Kyle and I are not fabricators, and we both heard the same discussion between your ex and her intended. They've been staying in an outbuilding at Orville Fenton's place."

Burgess considered, then took a conversational step backward. "So you are not aware that your daughter was physically abducted from off the dock of this cottage?"

Gabbro rubbed his forehead absently. "Uh. I did know...um...I think I knew. Bridget thought it was my sister. She has something of the same flair for the dramatic as Ari."

"And you were all right with that?"

Gabbro didn't reply.

"Did you check with your sister to be sure your daughter was with her?"

Gabbro didn't reply. Then he said, "I've been sick."

"Yes. Because someone tried to kill you by tampering with your medicine," Burgess said, "then throwing the rest of it, and your cell phone into the lake, leaving you in a coma and your daughter without any way to get help."

There were rules about how to treat crime victims. Burgess was ignoring them.

Gabbro stared at him.

Maybe this was new information. Burgess had no way of knowing what Gabbro had been told by the hospital. Or by Bridget O'Toole. And as far as he knew, neither Nikki nor any other investigator had had a chance to speak with Gabbro.

When he got no response, Burgess switched subjects. "Were you aware that Orville Fenton was acting for someone else? That he wasn't actually the potential buyer of the property you were hired to assess?"

Gabbro scratched his head, looking perplexed. "I was not. He seemed very interested in the property and under a lot of pressure to ascertain the presence or absence of gold in a short time frame."

"He never told you any specifics about rivals for the property?"

Gabbro shook his head.

"But he did tell you there were rivals?"

Gabbro nodded vaguely. "I got that impression."

"Were you in touch with Mr. Fenton after the medical event that landed you in the hospital?"

"We spoke on the phone. I directed him to Peter, who had our results and could answer his questions."

"Did you speak with Peter Sherman during the time you were hospitalized? When I, at least, was told you were too ill to answer questions."

"I'm afraid I have no idea what you were told." Snippy. Or annoyingly precise. Maybe professorial?

"Did you speak with Peter Sherman while you were in the hospital?"

Burgess was beginning to wonder why he bothered. At this point, he could simply deliver Ari, go next door, have a beer with Kyle, and put this whole mess behind him.

Except, of course, that he still had the three goobers to deal with. And he wasn't comfortable leaving Ari with Gabbro when he was so impaired and Bridget's role in everything so uncertain.

Gabbro said, "Yes," and nothing more.

"Before or after someone tried to kill him?"

"I spoke with Peter," Gabbro said. "He's fine."

"An attack on your assistant meant to leave him dead is fine?"

Gabbro waved a shaky hand. "Peter's tough."

"So you're not concerned about the attack? About someone knocking him on the head and leaving him to drown. About what it meant?"

"Oh. Uh…someone he rubbed the wrong way, maybe?"

"Out here? In the middle of nowhere? And that someone would know to look for him at your rented cottage?" Burgess grabbed a breath and tried to slow down. "When, if I'd been a minute or two later, he would be dead?"

Gabbro gave the airy hand wave again. He seemed to struggle with an answer, then gave up. "I don't know. You know, I'm awfully tired. I need to rest. Maybe you could come back tomorrow?"

"Dr. Gabbro, do you know where your daughter is?"

"She's with my sister."

Burgess was tired and annoyed. He did not want to bring Ari back into this, where her father seemed out of it and Bridget O'Toole had evidently been telling him lies. Where he probably shouldn't be out of the hospital and might possibly have been given drugs to make him more malleable. Trying to keep his doubt and frustration from showing, he asked, "Do you have any reasonable basis for that belief, Dr. Gabbro? Have you spoken with your sister?"

"Bridget said she thought the person who took Ari looked like my sister."

As though it would be okay for anyone to abduct Ari. Burgess felt deeply sorry for the child. He was sick of trying to sort out a mess that had dragged him in and occupied too much of his time but wasn't his to sort but he couldn't leave Ari in a situation like this.

He looked at Kyle, perched on the edge of his chair, his cold eyes fixed on Gabbro. Kyle hated to have kids mistreated even more than Burgess did. He obviously had a few questions of his own.

Burgess signaled that Kyle should ask his questions. Kyle immediately returned to the issue of Elyse Gabbro and Tony Leblanc.

"Would you be surprised to learn that your ex-wife never went to Scotland? That it was Elyse and Tony who took Ari, planning to use her as a financial bargaining chip?" Kyle said.

Like a parrot, Gabbro said, "Ari is with my sister Annabella."

"You don't know that," Kyle said.

Burgess and Kyle exchanged looks, then gave up. Talking to Gabbro was like arguing with a marshmallow. Nothing left an impression. This was Ryder's problem anyway. Ryder, who, they hoped, was at the hospital getting her broken nose treated. They would update her and she could sort this out.

Outside, Kyle said, "Still recovering or has he been drugged?"

"I'd say drugged. I'd say O'Toole got him sprung from the hospital as part of some bigger plot. I'd say that we have done our best and it's time to move on to those three morons at my place. Though I would really like a beer before we do that."

Burgess wasn't a big beer drinker. Except on rare occasions, he wasn't a big drinker, always cautious about following in his father's miserable footsteps. But he wanted to put a breather between Ari and Gabbro and the three goobers. Except he still had Ari in his truck.

He said, "Fuck!"

"The kid?" Kyle said.

"Yeah. I don't see how I can turn her over to those two."

"Arielle has always been a great fabricator," Kyle said. "What bull-crap. Like he could really think she—and we—were making this up."

"He couldn't think," Burgess said.

"So how can you leave her with him?"

"With Chris and the kids coming back in the morning, I can't keep her."

"This is really Ryder's problem. Let's call her, see if repairs have been made and she's ready to tackle the goobers. We need her for that anyway."

When she answered, Ryder was repaired and in remarkably good spirits. She was Burgess's kind of cop. Make things hard, throw barriers in her path, and she jumped over the barriers and kept on going.

"I've taken care of your arsonists," she said. She sounded funny because of the broken nose. "They've been whisked away to jail. I knew you'd want me to take care of it and I do like things tidy."

"You are so right. Sure we can't convince you to transfer to Portland PD?"

"Got my own career track, thank you very much. And your food chain has its own issues."

"True. Planning to replace Oh Really at some point, are you?"

"Truth?" she said.

"Whenever possible."

"I am. Now can we all go home and go to bed? My face is killing me."

"They didn't give you any good drugs?"

"Don't want to be impaired until I finish my work."

Yup. His kind of cop.

"Go to bed, Joe."

"Can't. We've still got Ari," Burgess said. "Things don't feel safe at Gabbro's."

They didn't have Ari. As they spoke, the girl hobbled past him. She had woken up and gotten out of the truck. He watched her hobble inside.

"Long as you don't want me to take care of your dog," Ryder said.

Fideau, who had gotten out of the truck and was leaning against Burgess's leg, gave him a look. Burgess read it as, "Who, me?"

"No. I'm happy to take care of my dog."

Burgess sighed. He should do something about Ari. He understood she had been navigating her impossible family for many years, but this level of neglect—and threat—couldn't be ignored. He went back into the cottage. Found Ari and her father on the couch. "Right next door if you need me, Ari," he said.

"Thank you, Mr. Burgess," she said. "I'll be fine."

Burgess looked at O'Toole, still perched like some oversized bird— Vulture? —on her stool. "Tylenol if she needs it."

Expressionless, the woman nodded. Neither she nor Gabbro had asked any questions about Ari's injury or her condition.

"Do you have children's Tylenol?"

No one answered.

"What the fuck is wrong with you?" he exploded. "Ari is a child. A child who has been abducted. Who has overheard her mother and the man her mother plans to marry calmly discussing drowning her because she's inconvenient. A conversation three police officers also overheard. Not something she said because, what were your words, Dr. Gabbro? Arielle is a great fabricator?"

He stepped back so his gaze took in Gabbro as well as the useless woman on the stool. "Ari is a child who witnessed her mother and that same man kill Orville Fenton. She's been injured while she was fleeing for her life. She has been terrified and needs responsible adults in her life. And you—" He pointed at O'Toole, "Sit there like a toad after telling Dr. Gabbro lies about the child."

He wanted to knock her off her stool and kick her when she was down. He wanted to shake Gabbro until his brain rattled.

Kyle waited and watched, in case Burgess went too far. Burgess wasn't sure anyone could go too far in rattling this complacent pair. At this point, he didn't even care if his words took effect. He had to say them.

Burgess moved until he stood in front of Gabbro, commanding the man's attention. He said, "You need to step up and take better care of your daughter. Protect your daughter. Act like a parent and stop indulging yourself in your love of rocks and your absent-minded professor shtick." He glared down at the man. "If you don't, I will get social services involved. Here or in Massachusetts, and trust me, I can do it. Do you understand?"

Gabbro looked surprised, as though no one had ever called him on his negligence before. Financially comfortable and indulged in his love of field work, he'd skated on his absent-minded professor act and neglected to step up when his child needed him. Everyone had let him get away with it except the people who tried to take advantage of it.

Burgess switched his gaze to Ari. "I need to know you're safe," he said.

The girl snuggled up closer to her father. "We'll be okay, Mr. Burgess."

As though Burgess wasn't there, Gabbro said, "I'm sorry, Ari. I promise I'll do better."

Burgess was hopeful but not convinced. He had one more thing to say. "You must get rid of that woman. Bridget O'Toole. Who lies to you about your daughter being kidnapped and really doesn't care."

He looked over at O'Toole, still perched on her stool. A normal person, a caring person, the person who claimed to have raised Ari since she was a baby, would have been fussing over the girl. Offering blankets and snacks. Washing her dirty face and offering clean pajamas. But she was doing nothing.

It was Ari who answered, certain again. "Mr. Burgess. Thank you for everything. But really, we're going to be okay."

He was glad she thought so. He continued to glare down at Gabbro. "Dr. Gabbro? Will you be okay? Will you get rid of that useless woman? Will you ask questions? Learn the story? Actually step up for your daughter? Because things cannot go on like this."

As though someone had finally found a way to plug in his cord and energize him, Gabbro said, "Bridget. Go back to Cambridge. We can discuss your future later." He got to his feet, a little shaky but more focused, and held out a hand to Ari. "Let's go find your pjs and get you ready for bed."

Ari gave Burgess a smile that he thought was somewhere between hopeful and reassured. "We'll be okay," she said, and led her father away.

He'd done all he could. He'd check back in the morning, though. Because it was a lot for a child to handle, even a little old lady like Ari.

He and Kyle went back to the cottage. The goobers were gone. The boat and gas cans were gone.

Burgess felt a large weight lifted off his shoulders.

They went inside. It seemed, then, like beer wouldn't be enough after the night they'd had. Burgess poured them each some bourbon and they went outside to sit in the quiet darkness. A nice breeze had come up to keep the bugs at bay.

FORTY-TWO

I t was companionable. No need to talk or assess what they'd just seen and done. Just the night breeze, the call of loons, the occasional tinkle of ice against glass.

After a while, Burgess said, "Getting married, huh?"

"It's time."

"I thought I'd be next but we don't seem to be getting any closer. I'm trying to accept that being together is enough."

Ice. Loons. Sometimes a rush of wind in the trees.

"Maybe it *is* enough. No reason for a lovely woman like Chris to tie herself down to an old dinosaur like me."

Ice. Loons. The slap of waves against the shore. The distinctive smell of lake water. Overhead stars, brilliant in a sky without city lights. A shooting star in a surprising flash of green flew through the sky.

"Maybe it is for the best, if her condition for getting married is she wants you to stop doing what you do, Joe," Kyle said.

Ice. Companionable silence. "I'll get the bottle," Burgess said.

Door opened. Slammed. Opened. Liquor gurgled.

"I've tried to imagine what it would be like. Retirement. Or taking a nice safe desk job. It feels like putting on someone else's clothes. Clothes that don't really fit. That are choking and tight. I can't imagine how I'd learn to let things go. Like with Ari. And Gabbro."

"He would have died. She would have gone to live with those two monsters full time. Or maybe, money being the underlying reason for this whole mess, she'd be sold to the aunt who wants her. Made weird and warped and prematurely adult. Or become a runaway. Or drowned in the lake," Kyle said. "People don't know, you know, when they say they want to do away with the police, when they come at us full of hate and anger, all the things we do."

"Mission creep," Burgess said. "We're cops. Social workers. Mental health professionals. EMTs. Child protective services. Babysitters. What's that word for advice columnists? Agony Aunts? We're agony uncles. Foster parents."

"Garbage collectors," Kyle said. "Animal control. Mind readers. We're blotting paper, soaking up all the horror to protect the public from seeing it."

"Blotting paper. I like that one," Burgess said. "Also punching bags. Shock absorbers. Guardians and gladiators."

"I can't imagine wanting to do anything else," Kyle said, "though sometimes, when I look at the girls…especially before Michelle…I'd think about what would happen to them if they had to go and live with their mother. And I remind myself that she wasn't able to ruin them before, with all that hate and anger. They're good people and they'll keep on being good people. Better than I was when I was a kid. I was so full of anger and frustration I just wanted to break things. Funny how I ended up a cop."

Quiet. A long period of quiet. Neither of them felt any need to fill the space with chatter.

Kyle said, "Yeah. Married. Feels odd, saying it, when getting unmarried was so important. When getting divorced saved my life and then nearly killed me. Getting divorced and then getting custody of the girls. For a while there…" He trailed off.

"I know. I'm always amazed at how you do it. Coming to parenting so late…I'm never sure…"

"No one who's honest is ever sure, Joe. You do your best and then hope. But the stuff we've seen…we have to believe we're doing better than that. So, you gonna be my best man?"

"I'm flattered."

"It's a big job. Bigger maybe even than with young Stanley. I know what I'm getting into."

"Still flattered. Unlike Stan, you aren't leaving a city full of mournful women behind and you're doing the right thing by a good one. And I won't have to drag you off to the Emergency Room because you screwed up your meds."

"I don't know," Kyle said. "There may still need to be some dragging."

"I'll be there."

There was the sound of a car engine and tires crunching on the gravel. The car stopping. Footsteps coming around the cottage. From the dark, Ryder said, "Is there room for one more?"

"Bourbon?" Burgess offered.

"Gratefully accepted. My face feels so broken."

Burgess got another glass. Put in some ice. Got an ice pack from the freezer. Chris would never come on vacation without one. He came back outside, gave her the ice pack, and poured her a drink.

"Wow. Thanks. Long day," she said.

"That was yesterday."

She joined them in their silence. In just being in the quiet night. After a while, she said, "I guess that means tomorrow is today, huh? And so today is going to be a busy day as well."

"Oh Really gonna give you a hard time?"

She laughed. "Maybe not. Much as he likes to piss on me, getting a chance to piss on the staties pleases him more. I solved their crime. They didn't even think to look in that building. Probably never even saw it. Of course, I might not have noticed it, either, except for the intrepid Detective Sergeant Joe Burgess, who knows all, sees all, and manages to be in the center of more crime than anyone I know."

"The three goobers?" Kyle said.

"If it doesn't stick this time, I'll shoot them myself. What about Ari? What's happening with that?"

"Kyle and I were dubious," Burgess said, "but she opted to go home. I read her father the riot act. Told him to fire that useless woman. Told him if he didn't step up I'd involve social services. I hope he rallies and gives her the support and attention she needs. There didn't seem to be a better option. I am hoping they all leave soon and stop being my problem."

"And if they don't, you'll be there. Here. While I'll be up to my... uh..." She debated, then said it, "Up to my tits in bad guys. And paperwork. Though I don't know. Tony, Elyse and the three goobers sounds like a children's book."

"Too scary," Kyle said.

More silence. Burgess went inside and got more ice. The bottle poured. They wouldn't run out. Like Chris with her ice pack, Burgess believed in being prepared.

"I think I'm done with the good neighbor shit," he said.

Ryder laughed but she didn't say anything. They all knew how Burgess was. How Kyle was. How she was. Serve and protect tattooed on their hearts. The insides of their heads. They could no more turn their backs than they could fly.

But, as Scarlett O'Hara once said, "Tomorrow is another day." Except in their case, tomorrow was already today.

The End

SUCH A GOOD MAN

A JOE BURGESS MYSTERY, BOOK 8

For once, the call hadn't come in the middle of the night nor in foul weather. It had come in on a sunny, mild September morning, at a civilized hour when Burgess had already had his coffee. A homicide detective learned to be grateful for small things. As he stepped through the door into the neat and airy condo, he had something else to be grateful for: the place didn't reek of decomp and the air wasn't buzzing with flies.

The sun's reflections off the busy waves danced on the high ceiling. Tall, open windows allowed in fresh sea air which mingled with the faint smell of cleaning products. Unsurprising, since the body had been found by the cleaner when she went up to clean the second floor. The woman, who had called the police and immediately left the premises, was now sitting outside on a bench, weeping, while his teammate, Terry Kyle, tried to get her story. Before Burgess left the conversation, he'd gotten basic background on the victim. As he rose to head inside, the weeping woman had gasped, "But he was such a good man. How could anyone do that to him?"

Soon, Burgess knew, he would understand what "that" was. Her reaction suggested something shocking and horrible.

According to the cleaner, a middle-aged woman named Lena

Nowak, the front door had been locked when she arrived and the windows were open. Open windows were unusual. The owner was scrupulous about keeping things locked. Living in the city had made him paranoid about being robbed.

Burgess thought it was crazy to buy a place on the ocean in Portland, Maine and then not open windows to let the sea air in, but if he know anything at all, it was that people often made strange choices, or choices he would never make. He wouldn't have to worry about this one—he'd never be able to afford a place on the water on a cop's salary.

The third member of their team, Stan Perry, was back at 109, researching their victim's background, and the ME was on his way, while Burgess was about to climb the wide blond wood stairs to the second floor and meet the victim, Dr. Eliot Spence.

Burgess was grateful for the absence of frightened animals, feces, bags of trash and other clutter, and air that was breathable. The fact that a cleaner had been through the downstairs before discovering the body and calling 911 was troubling, though. A nicer situation for cops to work in but any evidence of the killer, if in fact this was a homicide, had probably been dusted and vacuumed away. He might hope she was a careless cleaner, but the pristine rooms around him suggested she was not. At least the upstairs, where the body was, hadn't been touched, except by Lena Nowak's footsteps as she approached to change the bed.

There's always a moment at or enroute to a crime scene, before seeing the body, when a detective catches his breath in anticipation. When the imagination, running on the meager facts supplied by dispatch, in this case a name, address, and the fact of a body, begins to throw up possibilities about what is waiting. The deceased person was a doctor. Did that mean a possible overdose? A suicide resulting from a medical failure? A homicide perpetrated by an aggrieved patient or the patient's family? A natural death incomprehensible because of his age? The doctor was only in his forties.

Over three decades, Burgess had seen plenty, but every case was new. Assuming he'd seen it all was dangerous. It could make any investigator careless. Now he moved slowly, taking in his surroundings as he climbed the stairs, focusing on what they might tell. It was a two-story condo on the waterfront. Huge windows. Gorgeous views. Modern furniture and large, dramatic art. The décor was expensive and carefully designed either by the occupant or a decorator. There was a sparseness to it. Burgess thought there was also darkness.

The staircase was lined with framed black and white photos of glamorous women. All taken from the rear with the women looking over their shoulders. Seductive, smiling, and in a few, looking nervous. All of the woman had long hair. All appeared to be undressed. At least no clothes were shown but that might just be the way the women were dressed and the photos cropped. Spence's work or someone else's?

Burgess wondered how a woman ascending the staircase might feel. Would she compare herself? Feel inadequate? Would she wonder whether a man who decorated like this viewed women as objects?

The upstairs was one large open room. A sitting area, black leather furniture on a tufted black and white rug facing a fireplace with a large flat-screen TV mounted on the wall above it. A pair of ornate screens, dark carved wood, separated the seating area from from the bedroom. He stepped around the screens, stepped around a pile of dropped bedding, and there was Dr. Spence. He was sprawled face down on a fluffy white duvet, his face buried in the fabric, glossy dark curls set off by the pristine white. His feet were bare and hung off the side of the bed. He wore a white tee shirt and jeans. The jeans had pulled down below his hips. He had been sodomized with a liquor bottle.

There was no blood. No sign of a struggle. Nothing in the immaculate room was out of place. Except that he'd been violated with that bottle, the doctor might just be sleeping. Although he assumed the housekeeper had done it before she called them, Burgess checked for signs of life. The body was cool. There was no pulse. Here, as downstairs, the windows were open, letting the fresh morning breeze, the sound of moving water, and the crying of gulls into the silent room.

Burgess wondered if Dr. Spence had enjoyed the good life while he had it. The decor told him that the doctor had been precise, particular, with an eye for detail, and that no expense had been spared to make the house very personally his. The headboard was black leather that matched the furniture in the seating area. The bedside tables were shiny dark wood. Current fiction and nonfiction books were neatly stacked on the bedside tables. On one side of the king-sized bed, a cell phone rested on a charger. On the other, tissues in a shiny black holder. Bedside lamps were mounted on the wall.

He stepped past the bed and opened the door that led into the bathroom. It was bright and modern. A rainfall shower with pebbled walls and floor. Black granite surrounding the sink had raw edges and matching granite had been used on the floor. One wall was entirely mirror, the other black geometric wallpaper. The sconces were deco.

Like the bedroom, the bathroom was unnaturally neat. Sink and shower were dry. The towels were dry, except for a damp one in the hamper. The toothbrush and soap were dry and the soap dish also clean and dry. The air was neutral, not scented with deodorant, shampoo or aftershave. Nothing was out of place except one of the medicine cabinet doors, which was partially open. When he finished opening it with a gloved finger, he found everything neatly aligned except a single bottle of prescription medicine for erectile dysfunction. He photographed its placement and the label.

Depending on what the ME learned about the cause of Dr. Spence's death, he might need to speak with the prescribing physician. In a man this young, ED drugs were often used to enhance sexual performance rather than from any medical need.

Leaving the bathroom, he opened a second door, which led to a large walk-in closet tricked out with racks and shelves and a blond wood bench where someone could sit to put on shoes. Everything neat and orderly. A single pair of new-looking athletic shoes were neatly aligned under the bench. A blue shirt and boxers in the hamper. Nothing disturbed except a rack of ties where one seemed to be missing and others slightly rumpled like they'd been hastily shoved aside. Clinging to one of the ties was a long blonde hair.

It was all a little too much like walking into a store display before opening time.

Nothing else to learn here. He'd need to learn about Dr. Spence from his colleagues and friends, as well as the distraught woman downstairs. Perhaps from his neighbors.

He returned to the bedroom and checked the drawers beside the bed. On the side where the phone rested, he found an interesting collection of lubricants, a variety of condoms, and several different dildos. He checked the drawer on the other side. More of the same. There were no signs of a woman in the apartment, but evidently the doctor enjoyed an active sex life with a partner. Or multiple partners. Nothing except that long blonde hair and the photos on the stairs to suggest the sex of the partners.

Even that was far from conclusive.

He went back down the stairs to wait for the medical examiner, going slowly as he took a second look at the row of ladies. *No,* he thought, if her were a woman, *he would not enjoy walking past them.*

As he reached the bottom of the stairs, a woman pushed past the officer who was guarding the door and ran into the room. Tall and slender. Beautiful. Totally disheveled. She stopped when she saw Burgess. "Who are you?" she demanded. "And what are you doing in Eliot's house?"

Right on her heels was the medical examiner.

————

Available in Paperback and eBook from Your Favorite Bookstore or Online Retailer

ABOUT THE AUTHOR

Kate Flora's fascination with people's criminal tendencies began in the Maine attorney general's office. Deadbeat dads, people who hurt their kids, and employers' discrimination aroused her curiosity about human behavior. The author of twenty-one books and many short stories, Flora's been a finalist for the Edgar, Agatha, Anthony, and Derringer awards. She won the Public Safety Writers Association award for nonfiction and twice won the Maine Literary Award for  crime fiction. Her most recent Thea Kozak mystery is **Death Comes Knocking**; her most recent Joe Burgess is **A World of Deceit**.

When she's not writing, Flora gardens in the writerly town of Concord, Massachusetts and on the coast of Maine, and bakes when she gets stuck in story. She's been married to a delightful man for more than forty years.

facebook.com/katecflora

twitter.com/kateflora